Margaret Dickinson

The Tulip Girl

PAN BOOKS

First published 2000 by Pan Books
and simultaneously in hardback by Macmillan

This edition published 2012 by Pan Books
an imprint of Pan Macmillan
20 New Wharf Road, London N1 9RR
Associated companies throughout the world
www.panmacmillan.com

ISBN 978-1-4472-2682-6

3 5 7 9 8 6 4

A CIP catalogue record for this book is available from
the British Library.

Typeset by SetSystems Ltd, Saffron Walden, Essex
Printed and bound in Great Britain by
CPI Group (UK) Ltd, Croydon, CR0 4YY

Visit **www.panmacmillan.com** to read more about all our books and to buy
them. You will also find features, author interviews and news of any author
events, and you can sign up for e-newsletters so that you're always first to hear
about our new releases.

The Tulip Girl

Born in Gainsborough, Lincolnshire, Margaret Dickinson moved to the coast at the age of seven and so began her love for the sea and the Lincolnshire landscape.

Her ambition to be a writer began early and she had her first novel published at the age of twenty-five. This was followed by twelve further titles, including *Plough the Furrow*, *Sow the Seed* and *Reap the Harvest*, which make up her Lincolnshire Fleethaven trilogy, and her most recent novels, *The Miller's Daughter*, *Chaff Upon the Wind* and *The Fisher Lass*. Married with two grown-up daughters, Margaret Dickinson combines a busy working life with her writing career.

For all my family and friends, with love

Acknowledgements

The glorious tulip fields of Spalding and district were the inspiration for this novel, although the story is entirely fictitious. I am very grateful to Mr Reg Dobbs, OBE, author of *Bulbs in Britain – A Century of Growing*, for his kind interest and help and the loan of photographs to help with the cover design.

Aspects of Spalding – 1790–1930 and *Aspects of Spalding – People and Places* by Norman Leveritt and Michael J. Elsden were a wonderful source of general information.

My very special thanks to Mr Robert Molson, who generously gave his time to introduce me to the area and to share his memories with me.

My love and thanks as always to my family and friends, especially those who read and helped edit the script in the early stages; my sister and brother-in-law, Robena and Fred Hill; my brother and sister-in-law, David and Una Dickinson; my friends, Pauline Griggs and Linda and Terry Allaway.

Prologue

'No, please. Don't shoot.'

Trembling, Maddie stretched out her hand towards the man holding the gun. Beyond him, through the barn's open door, she could see the tulips, row upon row like a multicoloured rainbow, dazzling in the warm sunlight. She had planted those fields with her own bare hands. Was everything she loved, everything she had worked for, striven for, now to be blown away in a moment's madness?

Here in the barn it was cool and dim. They stood facing each other, the four of them. Maddie, the two men and the boy.

'Please,' she whispered, begging as she had never begged in her life. 'Please, let the boy go?'

'Why should I?' His tone was harsh and cruel, so different from the voice she knew so well. Or thought she had known. 'If it weren't for him and . . .' The barrel of the shotgun wavered slightly and then swung sharply away from pointing at Maddie and the boy towards the other man, standing so still and silent in the shadows. 'You!'

There was such venom in his voice, a bitter hatred that had been festering for eleven long years.

A shadow appeared in the barn doorway. A woman's shadow. Maddie's eyes widened and she gave a little gasp of fear. Then she touched the boy standing near her on his shoulder, giving him a tiny push. 'Go,' she breathed. 'Go to her.'

1

She saw him glance at the two men, who seemed, now, only aware of each other.

'Go on,' she urged.

The boy took a step, his gaze still on the men. Then he ran. The barrel swung again, following the small figure hurtling towards the door.

As she saw the man's finger move towards the trigger, Maddie lunged forward, her hand outstretched to push the barrel aside and spoil his aim.

'No!' Maddie cried but the deafening blast drowned her scream. Lead shot splattered against the wall of the barn and in the doorway a figure fell, sprawling in the dirt.

Before Maddie's eyes, the rainbow field of tulips beyond seemed to turn blood red . . .

One

'What's her name?'

'Madeleine March.'

'Far too fancy . . .' Harriet Trowbridge sniffed her disapproval.

'We call her Maddie,' the matron said hastily.

'Plain little scrap of a thing, isn't she? I imagined she'd be . . . Are you sure she's the one?'

'Oh yes. Abandoned outside the gate in 1932. No one's ever come to see her so there's no family that we know of and I don't think anyone's going to come looking her for now after fourteen years, do you? That's what you were looking for, isn't it?'

'It is, yes. But she doesn't look old enough.' Harriet shot a disbelieving look at the matron. 'She only looks about twelve. And a small twelve, at that.'

Mrs Potter began to bridle. 'I hope you're not doubting my word, Mrs Trowbridge?'

'No,' the woman murmured, her thoughtful gaze still on the girl standing before them. 'But now I see her, I don't know if she'll manage the work.'

'She's strong.' The matron now cast an anxious look at her visitor. 'And – and biddable.' There was only the merest hint of hesitation in Mrs Potter's voice. She wasn't above lying through her teeth if it meant seeing this particular child gone from her orphanage. Mrs Trowbridge seemed Heaven-sent, though anyone less angel-like would have been hard to find.

She was tall and bony-thin and dressed from head to foot in black. A felt hat was pulled down low over her forehead and the well-worn coat fell almost to her ankles, covering thick lisle stockings and stout, good-quality lace-up shoes. Her features were sharp. Her nose was straight and thin and her mouth seemed permanently pursed. Her grey eyes were bright and missed nothing, but there was no warmth in them, no humour, no kindliness.

'I should need to see her birth certificate. I presume she has one?'

Mrs Potter sighed. 'Well, yes. But it won't tell you much. Even the actual date of her birth is a guess. She was brought here on the twenty-fifth of March 1932 and we reckoned her to be no more than a week or two old – a month at the most – so that's the date we used.'

The surname was now obvious, but Harriet asked, 'Whatever possessed you to give her the name of Madeleine?'

'We didn't,' Mrs Potter snapped, trying valiantly to hold on to her patience. 'It was scribbled on a bit of paper and pinned to the blanket she was wrapped in.' The matron shook her head sadly, expressing a sudden pity for the child, whom, though she had been the bane of the woman's life for the past fourteen years, Mrs Potter could still not wholly dislike. 'Poor little mite hadn't any clothes. She was completely naked, 'cept for the blanket.'

Years earlier when Alice Potter had come to work at the Mayfield Home as a young widow, she had lavished upon the poor, motherless mites all the affection she would have given to her own children had she been so blessed. It was only the passing years and the responsibility of the post she now held that had made her often brusque and

4

insensitive. Still, at times, her maternal instinct surfaced and she would promise herself that she would be kinder, more affectionate towards the unfortunate waifs and strays in her charge.

But her resolution faltered when dealing with the likes of Maddie March.

The girl stood facing them now in mutinous silence, scowling so fiercely that her eyebrows almost met above the bridge of her tiny nose. Her teeth were clenched so tightly that they squeaked against each other and her mouth pouted ominously. The girl was thin and pale, but her blue eyes glittered with a rebellion that Matron and all the staff could not quite quell whatever dire punishment they inflicted upon her. Her short, straight hair was fair and could have been pretty but it was badly cut, hacked at by a harassed Mrs Potter with no time to spare for pandering to vanity. Washed only once a week by being plunged beneath the bathwater and soaped with carbolic, it was dull and lifeless. The girl wore a shapeless grey gymslip, tied around the waist with a girdle, a white blouse, knee-length grey socks and lace-up shoes.

Arriving back at the orphanage from the village school that took all the local children from five to fourteen, except those who transferred to the High School in the nearby town, Maddie had been told to report to Mrs Potter's room at once. She had not even been given time to change into her navy dress, her 'Sunday Best' that was only worn to Church or on very special occasions; Christmas Day, New Year's Day or when Sir Peter Mayfield, the Chairman of the Board of Governors, visited.

Maddie eyed today's visitor who was taking in every aspect of her appearance. Boldly, the girl returned the woman's critical stare, but resisted the urge to stick out her tongue.

The two women continued talking as if Maddie were not present.

'March 'thirty-two, you say?' For a moment, Harriet Trowbridge seemed almost as if she were thinking back and remembering what life had been like then. 'So,' she added slowly, 'she is old enough to leave school.'

The matron nodded vigorously. 'Oh yes, she's only kept going to school because . . .' Mrs Potter cleared her throat and altered what she had been going to say. 'I mean, until a position could be found for her.' It wouldn't do for this woman to know that already Maddie had been turned down for two jobs during the three weeks since her fourteenth birthday let alone the four prospective foster homes who had, over the years, sent her back to the orphanage, the last one after only two days.

Harriet sniffed. 'Right, I'll take her, then. When can you have her ready?'

'Oh, right away . . .' Then, lest she should appear too eager to rid herself of the girl, Mrs Potter added hastily, 'To save you the trouble of coming back for her, ma'am.'

The woman nodded and seated herself in a chair. 'Very well, but be quick about it. I don't like being away from the farm for long.'

Maddie felt Matron's hand gripping her shoulder and propelling her from the room. 'This is your lucky day, Maddie March.' And mine, Mrs Potter was thinking. 'Get your things together. You're leaving. And this time, m'girl, there's no coming back here if you don't suit, so just you mind you . . .'

'Leaving?' Maddie tried to stand still but the stout woman was no match for her and she was pulled across the hall and up the stairs towards the long dormitory. 'Where'm I going?'

'You're going to work on a farm. Be a milkmaid or summat. You'll like that.'

Maddie tried to imagine what it would be like, but failed. She had seen little beyond the high walls of the Mayfield Home for Orphan Girls except on the walk through the village in crocodile fashion with the other fourteen girls to school or to the church. There was the occasional trip on the bus to the nearest town of Wellandon, but even then there was no freedom to wander the streets and gaze in shop windows.

Apart from one or two, who at the age of eleven went on the bus to the Girls' High School in the town, all the girls from the Home attended the local village school until they reached the lawful leaving age. But no one else there wore uniform – only the Mayfield girls. Immediately, they were different, set apart.

So, for nine years, Maddie had marched to and from the school in Eastmere's village centre. Through rain and snow or beneath boiling sun. In winter, her hands were blue with cold for she had no gloves. In summer, she sweated in the gymslip and blouse they wore all the year round. Only the High School girls were provided with their school's regulation gingham summer dress.

But on Sunday, everything changed. Sunday was Maddie's favourite day of the week. No school and hardly any chores about the Home that all the girls had to take turns to do. No weeding in the vegetable garden or peeling potatoes. No helping to wash up twenty sets of plates, cups, saucers, knives, forks and spoons for the girls and the live-in staff after tea when the day workers had gone home. No washing in the laundry that was Maddie's Saturday morning chore with her hands becoming red and wrinkled in the hot water or her fingers trapped by the mangle if she wasn't quick enough feeding in the sheets. On a Sunday, there was only helping the younger girls to make their beds and clean their shoes for Church.

It was all thanks to the local vicar who served on the Board of Governors. He had insisted that the girls should strictly observe the Lord's Day. True, they had to attend Matins and Evensong and go to Sunday School, winter and summer, and the only book they were allowed to read on the Sabbath was the Bible, but for Maddie it was a day of blissful idleness.

Only on a Sunday could she dawdle to look over the hedges at the fields of waving corn or cows grazing in the meadows or pause to gaze into the window of Mrs Grange's village shop. And only on a Sunday had she seen whole families together, mothers and fathers with their daughters dressed in pretty frocks and sons in white shirts and ties and short, neatly-creased trousers. Or older, spotty-faced youths in their first pair of long trousers sporting, like a badge declaring their entry into manhood, an occasional tiny tuft of cotton wool on their chins where they'd tried their first attempts at shaving. Boys who, unseen by their parents and Mrs Potter, gave a cheeky wink to the girls from the Home.

Maddie had lost count of the times she had been reprimanded for smiling saucily back at them.

Oh yes, thought Maddie, only on a Sunday had she ever really seen the outside world. Suddenly, she quickened her pace and ran up the stairs ahead of Mrs Potter, who was puffing already.

Maddie March was leaving the orphanage. She was going out into the great, big world. Her heart beat faster and her eyes sparkled with excitement.

Wherever it was she was going, it couldn't possibly be worse than this place.

Two

'You don't mean we're going in that thing?'

Maddie would not have admitted it in a month of precious Sundays, but the huge black and white horse, standing patiently on the drive and harnessed to a farm cart, frightened her.

'Huh! Not good enough for you, eh, Miss Hoity-Toity?' Harriet sniffed. 'If it's good enough to deliver milk around the village every morning, it's good enough for the likes of you to ride in, girl. We can't afford a fancy pony and trap.'

Maddie glanced behind her at the faces pressed against every window on the three floors of the towering Victorian building.

Word had gone round. 'Maddie March is leaving. Come and see her go?'

'Whatever for? She'll be back in a day or so. No one can put up with her.'

'She won't be coming back this time. I heard Mrs Potter say so. She's too old now.'

'Not – not coming back?' Tears filled a small girl's eyes. 'Not never?'

Jenny Wren, so foolishly named by the over-sentimental Deputy Matron on duty when the child had been found abandoned outside the gates, ran in search of Maddie.

'Don't go, Maddie. Don't leave me. What'll I do without you?'

'You'll be all right. The others'll look after you.'

The child hiccupped miserably. 'They won't. They tease me. Only you ever stick up for me, Maddie.'

It was true. The scrawny child, who always managed to look unkempt no matter how ever much they scrubbed her, brushed her hair or tidied her clothes, was the butt of cruel bullying. Only Maddie, feisty and spirited, was ever on her side.

Jenny and Maddie had a lot in common. They were both thin and small for their age. Both had blonde hair and blue eyes and both had been abandoned outside the orphanage, Jenny as a newborn baby. But there the similarity ended, for Jenny was timid and weak, a born victim. Yet Maddie had loved her like a younger sister and had tried to protect her.

'I'm sorry, honest I am,' Maddie said, reaching out and touching the other girl's pale cheek. And she was, for she knew what Jenny's life would be like once she, Maddie, was gone. 'Mebbe in September when you're fourteen, they'll find you a job an' all.'

The younger girl sniffled hopelessly. 'Who'd want me?'

To that, Maddie had no answer.

Now, as she glanced back at the other girls, she grinned and stepped boldly towards the horse. As she stood beneath him, he lowered his massive head and nuzzled her shoulder leaving a wet patch on her grey coat.

'What's his name?'

'Rajah.'

Maddie reached up and patted his white nose and, without consciously thinking about it, she made a soft crooning noise in her throat. Then, her fear of the animal overcome, she looked up again at the windows and gave a royal wave to the watchers. But only to Jenny, standing at the top of the steps, did she blow a kiss. 'Chin up, Jen. I'll write to you.'

'Promise?' came the quavering voice.

'Cross me heart.' Maddie made the sign over where she presumed her heart to be.

'Come along. We're wasting time.' Harriet was climbing up on to the front of the cart. 'Put your box in the back and sit up here beside me.'

Mrs Potter herself helped Maddie lift the wooden box containing all her worldly possessions into the back of the cart. 'Now you be a good girl this time,' she hissed. 'I don't want you turning up on my doorstep again. You hear?'

'Not a chance, Mrs Potter,' Maddie grinned impishly. 'You won't see me again.'

'Let's hope not,' the matron answered tartly. 'You've put more grey hairs in my head, Maddie March, than all the other girls put together over the twenty years I've been here.'

If she was expecting the girl to feel contrition then Mrs Potter was wasting her time, for Maddie's grin only widened as she climbed up to sit beside Harriet. As the woman slapped the reins, the horse plodded forward and the cart scrunched down the gravel driveway away from the imposing square building that had been the only home Maddie had ever known. But the young girl did not even glance back once.

Nothing could dim her excitement at leaving, not Jenny's tears nor the silent, ramrod-stiff Mrs Trowbridge driving the farm cart with surprising expertise. Not even the rain that began to fall steadily as they drove away could dampen Maddie's spirits.

The village of Eastmere lay amidst the flat, fertile land of south Lincolnshire, three miles east of Wellandon, a thriving market town clustered along the banks of the River Welland. But it was not towards the town that

11

Harriet Trowbridge drove the horse and cart but along a lane leading out of the village southwards into the open countryside.

On the outskirts, they passed the gateway leading into Mayfield Park, the home of Sir Peter. Reminded of that tall, severe gentleman, whose every edict had ruled her life so far, Maddie asked inquisitively, 'Haven't you got a motor car?'

Sir Peter had a motor car with huge bulbous wings and when he drew up outside the Home, the girls would line the windows to watch, wishing they could have a ride in it. But not one of them – not even Maddie March – had ever dared to ask.

The woman beside her sniffed. 'Aye, sheeted down in the barn where it's been for the last six years or more. No petrol, y'see. Because of the War.'

'But the War's over now.'

Confined to the orphanage she might have been, yet even Maddie knew that much about the outside world. But only, she had to admit, because the evacuees with their strange speech no longer lined the lane to school, jeering at the crocodile of orphan girls and even throwing clods of earth at them.

'Barstards! They're a lot of little barstards, who ain't got no muvvers and farvers.'

And then had come the day they would never forget, the day that Mrs Potter had been obliged, by Sir Peter himself no less, to allow the girls to join in the VE Day party on the Village Green.

Oh, Maddie would never forget that day. A boy had kissed her on VE Day. She could almost still taste the sticky jam he had left on her upper lip.

'Aye, the War might be over for some, girl, but we're still feeling the pinch. Mind you . . .' the woman's tone mollified a little, 'we've been luckier than most, living on a farm.'

'What's it like, living on a farm?'

'A lot of hard work for everyone. As you will soon find out.'

Harriet flicked the reins and the horse clopped smartly along the lane, its silky cream mane and fetlocks rippling in the breeze. It didn't seem to mind the wet, Maddie mused, so I won't either. But she screwed up her eyes and pressed her lips together as the rain stung her face. She could see nothing of the surrounding countryside, shrouded in grey mist, and she had no idea where they were going or how long it would take to get there.

But they had travelled less than a mile when Maddie found herself clinging to the side of the cart as the horse, sensing home, turned sharply into a farmyard.

'Are we here? Is this it?'

The woman made no reply but climbed down. Maddie followed suit and then looked about her. In front of her was a square farmhouse surrounded by sheds and barns and wall-enclosed yards. As Maddie tried to take in her new surroundings, a black and white dog came rushing towards them, jumping up and barking furiously.

'Down!' Harriet thundered. The dog dropped to its belly, ceased its racket and gave a whine of surrender.

Maddie glanced admiringly at the woman. 'Isn't he good?'

'He's a working dog. Been trained to be obedient. Let's hope you have too, girl.'

She led the way into the house by the back door and, following, Maddie found herself in a wash-house. Along the wall near the door hung coats and capes and beneath them a line of boots and shoes.

'Come along, look sharp.' Harriet had paused in the

13

doorway leading further into the house to beckon her. Maddie's curious glance darted about her, still trying to take in the clutter; a brick built copper with wash tubs and dolly pegs and a mangle close by, a heap of coal boarded off in the far corner, two bicycles and a step ladder leaning drunkenly against the wall.

She followed the woman into the kitchen that smelled, not of stale cabbage water like the huge kitchen at the Home, but of freshly baked bread. Then stepping into the living room, Maddie saw that a fire burned brightly in the gleaming black-leaded range, to one side of which was an alcove lined with shelves of books. Directly opposite her, the window looked out on to a square of garden.

'Come along, I'll show you your bedroom. Bring your things.'

Carefully, Maddie skirted the table, covered with a green velvet cloth, and went towards the door Harriet was opening in the far corner of the room.

At the top of the steep, dark staircase they turned to the left into a narrow landing that ran the width of the house. Doors led off on either side and the woman pointed to the first door to the left and said, 'This is my room and you, girl, will be in this one opposite. So I can keep my eye on you.' She waved her hand further down the landing. 'There's a bathroom of sorts next to your room, but it's open to the landing. Further on, down that step there, is the master's room and the boys' bedroom opposite.'

The 'master' and – and 'boys'! Maddie blinked.

Harriet opened the door to the right into a small bedroom and jabbed Maddie on the shoulder. 'Just put your things in there for now. You can put them away later.'

Maddie stepped onto the peg rug at the side of the bed and looked around the room. The single bed, tight against the wall, was covered with a bright patchwork quilt and in the corner beside the tiny window was a marble wash-stand with a pink flowered ewer and bowl on it. Beneath the window was a chest of drawers.

'You'll wash in here of a morning. You can bring the water up each night. I don't want you running into the boys in your nightgown. They use the bathroom, but you'll only have use of it once a week to bath and wash your hair. I'll mind the menfolk stay out of the way then. There's no inside lavvy. Turn left outside the back door and it's on the corner of the house, opposite the water tank. Now, come along, there's work to do.'

By the time the men came into the house at six o'clock for their tea, Maddie felt like a little ragamuffin. She had swept the floor and shaken the peg rug from the hearth in the living room, dusted the furniture and cleaned the windows and now her face was smudged with grime and her apron looked as if she'd been crawling all over the coal heap.

'Hey, what have we here?' a cheerful voice spoke behind her. 'You had her up the chimney to sweep it, Mrs T?'

Still on her knees sweeping the hearth, Maddie turned around to find that the tall young man who had spoken had squatted down on his haunches to bring his face level with her own. She found herself gazing into the softest brown eyes she had ever seen. Kind, they were, and yet at the same time they sparkled with mischief. His face was tanned and his jaw square and when he smiled, she saw that his white teeth were even and perfect. Unruly curls, so black that they shone and glistened, fell onto his forehead.

Maddie swept the back of her hand across her brow and, unwittingly, left another streak of dust.

The young man chuckled. He leant towards her and

15

said softly, 'Go into the kitchen and wash your face and hands, else Mrs T won't let you to the table.'

'But I – I haven't finished yet,' Maddie said, flustered and blushing beneath the dirt on her face.

'It'll still be there in the morning, young'un.' He touched her shoulder, giving her a gentle push. 'Go on. She's setting the table now. You'd best hurry.' He nodded towards the kitchen where Maddie could hear the clatter of pots.

Giving one last swift polish to the fender with her duster, Maddie picked up all the cleaning materials and scuttled out of the living room into the kitchen. Stowing the polish and dusters in the cupboard under the sink as she had been told, she removed her hessian apron and bundled it under there too. Then she turned on the tap over the deep sink that was not, close to, so white as she had imagined. Tiny cracks, brown stained, gave its surface a mottled, dirty look. The ice-cold water spluttered into her hands. Maddie took the soap and nail brush from the dish on the draining board and scrubbed and scrubbed until her hands were red and raw, but clean. Then she sluiced her face with the cold water and smoothed back her short hair behind her ears.

She was moving hesitantly away from the sink when the door leading into the kitchen flew open, almost knocking her over.

'Sorry, lass. I didn't hurt you, did I?'

'No, no, mester. Just made me jump, that's all.' Maddie looked up into the man's face and found that it was an older version of the young man's she had met a few minutes earlier. Though his dark hair was liberally streaked with grey and his handsome face was weather-beaten and deeply lined, the brown eyes still twinkled and the smile was as gentle.

'You must be the little lass from the orphanage?'

Maddie nodded. 'Yes, sir.' She smoothed her hands down her gymslip and smiled at him.

He looked her up and down, assessing but not unkindly. 'The work's hard, lass,' he said, doubtfully.

'I'm stronger than I look, mester.'

'Aye well,' he smiled. 'Mebbe you'll grow. We'll have to feed you up a bit, won't we?'

He gestured towards the living room. 'In you go. Tea'll be ready. I've to change me boots and wash me hands and then I'll be in. Go and sit down, lass. I won't be a minute.'

A joint of boiled bacon sat in front of where the master would sit at the head of the table, a carving knife and fork set on either side. In the centre of the table was a selection of pickled onions and home-made chutney and a large freshly baked crusty loaf with yellow butter in a dish.

'You sit here, girl,' Harriet pointed to a chair beside her, setting down a plate of buttered slices of plum bread for afters. 'And speak when you're spoken to and not afore. You've a mite too much to say for yourself, to my mind.' She frowned down at Maddie. 'You're only on trial here, you know. I can still send you back if you don't suit.'

Across the table the young man winked broadly at her. Maddie smiled back but managed to keep her mouth firmly closed.

Three

There was a fifth person sitting at the table. A boy not much older than she was, Maddie guessed. He was very thin, so thin that his wrist bone protruded and his long fingers looked as bony as a skeleton's. Although his face and hands were lightly tanned from working out of doors, under the open-necked shirt Maddie could see a 'V' of pale skin. His mousey-coloured straight hair fell forward almost covering one eye. Every so often he flicked it back with a toss of his head. His grey eyes were large behind round, steel-framed spectacles. Maddie noticed that he kept looking at her from beneath the flop of hair, glancing up swiftly and then away again. She smiled at him but her attention was drawn back again and again to the taller, good-looking young man who came to sit beside him and directly opposite her and whose broad shoulders seemed twice as wide as the younger boy's.

The master came and sat down at the head of the table and they all bowed their heads while he murmured a short prayer in a soft, deep voice. Then he took up the carving knife and fork and began to carve the meat.

'Don't give the girl too much. I don't want her leaving any,' Harriet said.

The man glanced at Maddie, smiling. 'You can always come back for more if you can manage it.'

'Thank you, Mr Trowbridge,' Maddie said politely and was surprised when the young man opposite her threw

18

back his head with a gust of laughter whilst the younger
boy sniggered behind his hand. The master was amused,
but beside her Maddie heard the woman's sniff of
annoyance.

'I think we'd better introduce ourselves properly,' the
man said. 'My name's Frank Brackenbury and the young
rascal sitting opposite you is my son, Michael. Mrs Trowbridge you know already and this . . .' he indicated the
young man sitting on his immediate left, 'is her son,
Nicholas, but more usually called Nick.' He chuckled as
he leant forward to say in a loud whisper, 'Much to his
mother's disgust.'

So where, Maddie wondered at once, was Mrs Brackenbury? What had happened to her? And what about
Nick's father?

'We don't know your name, young'un,' Michael said,
interrupting her thoughts.

'Madeleine March.'

'She's called Maddie,' Harriet said at once. 'We don't
want her getting fancy ideas about herself. If I had my
way, she'd be plain Jane.'

Maddie felt the eyes of all three men upon her and a
flush of embarrassment crept up her cheeks. No one spoke
and the girl knew that, despite their kindness to her
already, Mrs Trowbridge's veiled reference to her plainness
could not be refuted.

Maddie lay on the soft feather bed watching the clouds
scudding across the bright face of the moon. She was
tired, yet sleep would not claim her. So much had happened in just a few hours. This morning she had woken
up at the Home to the familiar sounds in the long dormitory: girls chattering, jostling each other to get to the

washroom and then Jenny appearing like a wraith at the side of the bed.

'Walk to school with me, Maddie?' It was the same every morning.

''Course I will,' Maddie responded, patient as always, swinging her feet out of bed to touch the cold linoleum. Then the younger girl was smiling, skipping away happily to get washed and dressed, safe in the knowledge that her protector would be with her.

But tomorrow morning, Maddie thought now as her heavy eyelids began to close and the moon became a blurred, distorted shape, poor Jenny Wren would be on her own at school.

Maddie slept fitfully, waking every so often bathed in sweat to fling off the covers, only to wake again feeling cold. It's this bed, she thought. It's lovely and soft, but it's too hot. When she could stand it no longer, she got out and pulled the soft feather bed away leaving only the lumpy, hard flock mattress beneath it. She was about to climb back in when the door to her room flew open and the light was switched on, flooding the room and causing Maddie to screw up her eyes against it. Harriet, in a long white nightdress, her grey hair straggling down to her shoulders, stood in the doorway.

'What on earth is all the noise, girl? And what is this doing on the floor?' The woman pointed at the feather mattress heaped beside the bed.

'It was too hot,' Maddie declared. 'So I took it off.'

'Well!' Harriet was flabbergasted. 'Well, I never did. You ungrateful little chit.' The woman bent and, picking it up, said, 'We take the feather beds off in May and put them back in November, but if that's how you feel, you can do without it. Just one thing, me girl, don't come running to me in the middle of winter when you're cold in bed of a night.'

Suddenly remembering the nights of shivering in the cold dormitory, when ice formed even on the inside of the windows, Maddie realized that such a bed would be a luxury. She lunged forward and grasped the feather mattress, trying to tug it from the woman's hands.

'Leave it here in my room, if it's mine.'

Their faces only inches apart, the girl and the older woman glared at each other. 'It isn't yours,' Harriet insisted. 'At least, it won't be if you carry on like this. You'll be back in that orphanage where you belong.'

'Is something wrong? Is she all right?' The deep voice spoke from the doorway, making them both jump.

'Oh, Mr Frank. I'm sorry you was disturbed.'

'Is she all right?' the man repeated, his glance going beyond Harriet to the girl.

'She complaining she's too hot,' the woman's tone expressed anger at the girl's daring, but the man was smiling.

'I'm not surprised. It's a warm night. I was too.' He nodded towards the offending bag of feathers. 'But I shouldn't take it right away, Harriet. This time of year the nights can turn just as cold again. Let her keep it in her room and she can do what she likes.'

The woman thrust the mattress away from her, pushing it towards Maddie and almost knocking her backwards onto the bed. 'Whatever you say, Mr Frank. Now . . .' She turned back to the girl. 'If you'd be so kind as to get into bed, then maybe the rest of us could get some sleep.'

The light was switched off and the door closed firmly, leaving Maddie in darkness.

The mester had been kind, Maddie thought as she

climbed back into bed, but in sticking up for her he had shown Mrs Trowbridge up. The woman would not forgive her for that.

Tonight, Maddie knew, she had made an enemy of Harriet Trowbridge.

Four

The banging on her bedroom door woke Maddie with a start before it was even light.

'Jenny . . .?' she said aloud and then remembered where she was.

'Come along, girl. Get up,' the woman's voice came from the other side of the door. 'There's work to do.'

Maddie groaned. 'It's the middle of the night.' But she pushed back the covers and scrambled out of bed.

Washing in cold water in the ewer was no hardship for the girl raised in an orphanage where the use of hot, or even warm, water was thought to be pampering the children.

'A little hardship is character building,' had been Sir Peter's edict, though Maddie doubted he, in his mansion, had ever washed in cold water in his life.

Maddie had only ever seen Sir Peter's house once. In the spring of 1943 there had been a garden party in the grounds to raise funds for the War effort. The girls from the Mayfield Home, which Sir Peter's own father had founded during the 1890s, had been marched, two by two, through the village to the home of their benefactor. Arriving at the entrance where once massive wrought-iron gates had hung, the children had found they still had a long walk through parkland before they came in sight of the house. Maddie remembered how weary Jenny had been. Then they had been required to stand in the sun on their

23

best behaviour and smile politely whilst the smartly dressed ladies told them how lucky they were to have someone like Sir Peter with their best interests at heart.

That had been the day, she thought with a shudder, that they had seen the Hanging Tree.

There were several of the village children at Mayfield Park that day with their parents. Steven Smith, whom Maddie was obliged to sit near in school, had soon sought her out.

'It's the Mad March Hare.' He tweaked her hair and then stepped back sharply before she had time to lash out at him. 'What you doing here? Didn't think they'd let you out of the madhouse to come.'

Jenny shrank behind Maddie, clinging to the back of her skirt and peeping round the older girl to watch him. But Maddie grinned at him. 'Hello, Stinky. Didn't think they'd let a smelly little beggar like you come here, either.'

He drew himself up to his full height – an inch taller than Maddie. 'My dad shoes all Sir Peter's horses, so there.' Steven's father was the village blacksmith and the boy's clothes always reeked of the forge and the smell of singeing hoof. It was not an unpleasant smell, but Maddie used it to go one better on the nickname he had given her.

'Bet you've never seen the Hanging Tree,' he said.

From behind her came a little squeak of terror from Jenny. But Maddie said, 'The what?'

The boy moved closer dropping his voice to a scary whisper. 'There's a tree in the woods here where a feller hanged himself a few years back. Want to see it?'

Maddie felt Jenny's fingers on her skirt clutching tighter.

''Course we do,' Maddie said boldly, ignoring the whimper behind her. 'Oh no, Maddie, no.'

'Come on then.' The boy turned and began to walk,

hands thrust into the pockets of his short trousers and with a swagger in his step, towards the woods.

With a quick glance around her to make sure that Mrs Potter was not watching, Maddie prised Jenny's clinging fingers from her skirt and whispered. 'You stay here, if you don't want to come.'

'No, no. Don't leave me.' The small child seemed uncertain as to which would be the worse fate. Being left alone amongst all these strangers or following Stinky Smith into the dark unknown of the woods.

Taking her hand, Maddie said, 'Come on, then.'

Entering the cool dimness, their feet squelched on the mulch of several autumns' leaves. The breeze rustled through the trees overhead and birds rose from the topmost boughs at the arrival of the three intruders.

'Come on,' shouted their guide, his voice echoing eerily. 'It's this way.'

They came to a small clearing and at the edge Maddie stopped and gasped aloud. 'Oh how pretty it is. Just look, Jen, at all these flowers.'

The whole clearing was a carpet of wild bluebells, yet in the centre was a heart-shaped bed of yellow tulips edged with a border of forget-me-nots.

Steven pointed to the golden flowers. 'Them's been planted.'

'Who did it?'

The boy shrugged. 'Dunno. Someone belonging to the feller who hanged himself, I s'pect.' He moved towards a tree at the side of the clearing and put his hand flat against the trunk, tilting his head back to look up into the branches. 'This is where he did it.'

Maddie moved closer, but Jenny hovered on the edge of the clearing hopping from foot to foot. 'Maddie, I want the lav.'

Maddie stood beneath the tree as Steven pointed upwards. 'See them marks on that branch. That's where he tied the rope.'

'Maddie . . .' came Jenny's wail. 'I gotta go. Now!'

'Bob down behind those bushes then,' Maddie murmured, her gaze still on the tree.

'I daresunt. There might be – be . . .'

Steven turned, grinning wickedly. 'Think a bird'll peck ya bum?'

Maddie gave the boy a shove on his shoulder. 'Don't tease her. She's only little and we haven't ever been in a wood before.'

His eyes widened. 'Never been in a wood. Blimey. They don't let you out of that place much, do they?' But now there was a note of sympathy in his tone instead of mockery. For the village lad who had been allowed to roam the fields and lanes at will, never to have been able to walk in a wood before reaching the age of eleven seemed like being locked away in prison.

'Wait there,' Maddie instructed as she turned and went back to Jenny to lead her behind the nearby bushes. Moments later the two girls emerged, the younger one pulling up her knickers as, this time, she walked alongside Maddie right up to the tree.

'Who was he, then?' Maddie asked, once more squinting up into the branches. 'And why did he do it?'

Now he had more of an audience the boy ran his tongue around his lips and grinned. With a sly glance at Jenny he said, 'John Cuppleditch, they called him. He was a groom for Sir Peter and there was a – a scandal, yes, that's what me mam called it – a scandal . . .' He savoured the word. '. . . About him and Sir Peter's daughter, Miss Amelia.'

'What about them?' Maddie demanded.

26

'Me mam ses it was all round the village at the time. He was already married, see, and him and his wife had a little babby, an' all. Everyone reckoned him and Amelia Mayfield was going to run away together, but Sir Peter locked her up in the house and wouldn't let her see him no more. But . . .' The boy, young though he was and maybe not even understanding fully the meaning behind the words, was relishing repeating the village gossip. 'He came back at night to try to see her and Sir Peter chased him off the estate with his twelve bore.'

'You're making it all up.'

'No, I'm not. He did hang himself from that tree because Sir Peter threw his whole family, even his mam and dad and his little brothers and sisters as well, out of their cottage.'

'How could he do that?'

''Cos he owned the cottage where they lived. His dad was head groom, see. So he got the sack an' all. They was all living rough for a while in the woods, me mam said.'

'What happened to them?'

Steven shrugged. 'Dunno, but him . . .' The boy was warming to his gruesome tale. 'He comes back here one night, throws a rope over that branch, ties a loop round his neck and then climbed up and jumped off.'

The two girls shuddered and instinctively moved closer to each other.

'It was two days before they found him.' Steven leaned closer, whispering, 'His face was all bloated and black and he was just swinging here, the branch creaking in the wind . . .' He made a rasping noise in his throat, trying to imitate the sound.

Jenny squeaked and buried her face against Maddie, who put her arm about the girl. 'Come on, we're going.

27

Mrs Potter'll miss us.' As she began to lead Jenny from the clearing, she glanced at the boy and grinned. 'I tell you what, Stinky. You tell a good story.'

The boy swaggered as he followed them, saying, 'T'aint no story. It's all true.'

'Yeah,' Maddie said sarcastically, but she was smiling as she said it. All the same, as they left the clearing and plunged back into the gloom beneath the trees, she glanced back to take a last look at the heart-shaped bed of tulips, shining golden in a ray of sunlight that streamed in through the trees.

Maybe, she thought, his sweetheart, Amelia Mayfield, had planted the flowers near where her love had died.

Maddie was still thinking of her little friend, Jenny, as she went down the stairs and presented herself to Harriet in the kitchen.

'There you are at last, girl,' was the housekeeper's greeting. Maddie felt her glance assessing her.

'Why are you dressed in your gymslip and blouse? You aren't going to school any more, y'know.'

Maddie felt an angry flush creep up her face. Her eyes glittered and her mouth tightened. 'I haven't any more clothes. Only me Sunday best and I'm not wearing that to work in.'

The 'out of school' skirt and jumper that she had worn at the Home had been far too small for her and almost worn out.

'You can't possibly take these with you,' Mrs Potter had declared, holding up the jumper, shrunken and matted from constant washing in water that was far too hot. 'What'll they think?' she had muttered, shoving the offending garments into the rag-bag. So all Maddie had been able to bring with her was her school uniform and the navy dress.

Neither of them had heard Frank Brackenbury approach until, from the doorway between the kitchen and the living room, he said, 'Then we'll have to get you some suitable work clothes, lass, won't we?'

Maddie spun round and gave him a beaming smile. Politely, she said, 'That would be very kind of you, Mr Brackenbury.'

'Mrs Trowbridge can take you into the town tomorrow. It's market day.' He lifted his head slightly and looked beyond Maddie. 'You wouldn't mind going for once, Harriet, would you? You needn't stay long.' Without waiting for an answer he looked down again at Maddie. He chuckled and his dark eyes twinkled. 'And Mr Brackenbury is such a mouthful. Call me "Mr Frank" like everyone else does.'

Behind her, the woman said nothing, but Maddie heard her sniff of disapproval. The girl stood waiting, unsure what she was supposed to do. Without even glancing at Maddie again, Harriet, her mouth tight, moved between the pantry and the cooker where a huge black frying pan of bacon, fried bread and eggs sizzled.

As if sensing her uncertainty, Frank said, 'Do you want her to help you, Harriet?'

'No, she'll only get under me feet. She'd best start learning what she's come for. The milking.'

'Right you are, then.' Again he looked down at Maddie and frowned thoughtfully. 'We'll have to find you summat to wear for today, lass. Them clothes aren't suitable for the cowshed. Come on, let's have a look-see what we can find.'

He led the way into the wash-house and searched amongst the clothes hanging from the line of pegs.

'Ah,' he said with sudden satisfaction. 'Here we are. I thought I remembered seeing these still here . . .' From the peg the man pulled a pair of khaki dungarees and held them out towards Maddie. 'The Land Army girls we had in the War used to wear these. They'll be a bit big for you, but you can tuck them into your boots. There's a pair of rubber boots here that should fit you. An old pair of Nick's. Oh, and there's a pair of socks here too. They'll keep you warm and help to fill the boots a bit.' He smiled at her as he held out the trousers and set the boots on the floor in front of her.

Maddie took the pair of trousers with the bib and cross-over braces and pulled them on, tucking her gymslip inside them.

'Now, roll the legs up to your ankles and then put the socks on over them . . .' the man suggested, holding out his hand to steady her as she thrust her feet into the boots.

'There now,' he said, surveying her. 'Not bad. Not bad at all. A bit big on you, but you'll do. You'll need a jacket, though.' Again he searched. 'This'll do. It'll swamp you, but it'll be warm.' He held it out for her and she slipped her arms into it. 'Right. Now we'd best be on our way or my poor beast'll be bursting their udders.'

As they stepped into the yard, Frank gave a piercing whistle and the black and white dog came racing round a corner to hurl itself against him. Then the excited animal bounded towards Maddie, jumping up at her.

'He won't hurt you,' Frank said swiftly. 'He's only young and a bit boisterous, that's all.'

Maddie laughed as the dog leapt even higher and she felt his tongue against her cheek. 'He's lovely. What's his name?'

'Ben.'

At the sound of his master's voice, Ben paused to look

round enquiringly, but hearing no further command, he carried on leaping and bounding around the young stranger.

Maddie summoned up her sternest voice, pointed to the ground and said firmly, 'Down, Ben.'

The dog gave a bark but then dropped to the ground, looking up at her with soulful brown eyes.

'Well, I never did,' Frank Brackenbury laughed. 'You've certainly got a way with him, young'un. Are you any good with cows?'

Maddie smiled up at him. 'I don't know, mester. I've never tried.'

'Well, lass, now's your chance.'

They walked down the lane, side by side, Frank with easy strides, Maddie clumping along in her oversized boots, trying desperately to keep pace with him. Ben ran ahead, pausing every so often to investigate an intriguing smell in the hedgerow.

It was a bright April morning, sharp, but promising warmth later in the day.

'Where are we going?' Maddie asked.

'To fetch the cows in for milking.'

Ahead of them she saw a meadow where six or seven cows stood herded together near the gate. Two stood close to the gate, their great heads over the top of it looking up the lane.

'They're bigger than I thought,' Maddie murmured, 'close to.' But still she went forward, undaunted, to try to pat the nose of the nearest beast, but it stepped backwards.

She felt the man watching her and turned to meet his gaze. He smiled and gave a little nod. 'I'm glad to see you're not frightened of them, lass.' He chuckled, a low sound seeming to come from deep inside him. 'But they're a bit wary of you, 'til they get used to you. One of the Land Army girls was frightened to death of them. I never did get to teach her how to milk all the time she was here.'

He opened the gate and the cows meandered into the lane, turning towards the farm.

Maddie laughed, her voice clear and ringing in the early morning air. 'They know the way.'

''Course they do. They travel the same bit of road night and morning. They should do by now.'

Maddie glanced back into the field and saw, at the far end near a hedge, two cows still grazing contentedly.

'What about those two?'

Frank's smile broadened. 'Lazy pair. We'll have to fetch them.'

Maddie looked back towards the lane where the small herd were wandering towards the farmyard with Ben, now wholly committed to his task, barking at their heels.

'Do they go into the cowshed all by themselves then?'

'More or less,' he answered, as they began to walk across the grass towards the two dawdlers. 'But Michael and Nick are there finishing off the first lot.'

'The first lot?' The girl was surprised. 'You mean you've more than just these?'

'Oh yes. We've fifteen milkers and then some beast for beef.'

'Goodness.'

'We supply all the village with milk and even Mayfield Park.'

'Sir Peter?'

The man glanced at her. 'Aye, his household and all the folks who live on his estate.' He waved his arm to encompass all the land around them. 'This is all his. We only rent it to farm, y'see.'

'Oh.' Maddie was silent. Then she blurted out suddenly, 'He owned the orphanage, too.' She looked at the man walking beside her and, with a maturity far exceeding her years, added quietly, 'It seems Sir Peter Mayfield rules a lot of people's lives.'

'Aye,' Frank nodded. 'Aye, you could say that lass. He's a local magistrate an' all. He certainly rules the lives of anyone who dares to be brought up in front of him.' He gave a wry laugh and the young girl wondered fleetingly if he had ever had cause to stand in the dock in front of Sir Peter. She glanced at him again, doubting her own thoughts. Mr Frank seemed a kindly, God-fearing man. She couldn't imagine him ever doing anything against the law.

They reached the cows who raised their heads, chewing sorrowfully.

'I don't think they want to be milked,' Maddie laughed.

'They're not so bothered as some of the others.' He pointed to their udders. 'Their milk yield's declining now. See?'

Maddie looked and saw that their udders were not so swollen as some of those already on their way to the farmyard.

'We only milk them once a day now. Just in a morning.' He slapped the nearest one on the rump and slowly it began to move reluctantly towards the gate, still chewing as it went.

Maddie was about to follow when she suddenly caught sight of a flash of colour from beyond the hedge. Standing on tiptoes, she peered over into the next field and what she saw made her gasp with amazement and delight.

'Oh! Oh look. Just look,' she exclaimed, quite forgetting that the man with her must have seen the sight many times and be quite used to it.

Beyond the hedge stretched a field of tulips. They were planted in blocks of six rows and each block was a different colour, from pastel pink through red and yellow to dark purple, rippling and swaying in the early morning breeze.

'Isn't that the most beautiful sight you've ever seen?' the young girl murmured, enraptured and enthralled. 'It's like a rainbow. Except,' she added, 'that it's straight.'

He came and stood beside her. 'Well, you'd best enjoy it, lass, 'cos they don't last long. They'll be cutting the heads off soon.'

Maddie turned wide eyes to look up at him. 'Why?'

'They grow them for the bulbs, you see, and part of making the bulbs mature is to remove just the heads so that a lot of the goodness from the plant goes back into the bulb and makes it grow bigger.'

'It's a shame, though,' Maddie said, understanding the need but bemoaning the destruction of the pretty flowers.

Reluctantly, she turned to follow him back down the field, dragging her gaze away from the multicoloured carpet of flowers that stretched into the distance as far as she could see.

Then she skipped after the farmer, filled with a sudden happiness such as she had never felt before.

Five

'Now, you'll have to sit close up, 'cos you're only little.' Michael was laughing down at her but his teasing was not cruel. 'We'll start you on Betsy. She's a soft old thing and she'll stand good as gold whilst you milk her, won't you, old girl?'

The cow, tethered to the wall, flicked her tail but munched contentedly on the hay in the heck level with her nose.

'Sit on this little stool, put your head against her belly and reach underneath. Then, very gently, squeeze her teats. Like this, see.' The young man squatted down and Maddie watched as he squeezed and pulled and the milk squirted into the bucket beneath.

He stood up again. 'Right, now you have a go.'

A shadow appeared in the doorway and Maddie looked up to see Nick carrying two empty buckets and moving towards the next stall. 'She'll never manage it,' he said. 'She'll have to kneel underneath Betsy to reach her udders.'

'Tek no notice of him,' Michael grinned good-naturedly. 'He's only jealous 'cos he'd like to be the one teaching you, 'stead of me.'

Nick gave a wry snort and then nodded towards Maddie. 'You want to watch him. He's a bugger with the girls.'

Now Michael frowned. 'Less of that sort of language in front of her.'

35

Nick smirked and tugged his forelock in mock obedience. 'Right you are, sir. Sorry, I'm sure, sir.'

Maddie sat down on the low, three-legged stool and rested her forehead against the cow.

'I think you'd do better if you rest your cheek against her with your shoulder sort of almost underneath,' Michael advised. 'You might be able to reach a bit further that way.'

'But I can't see what I'm doing then.'

Michael chuckled and winked. 'You'll have to feel your way, love.'

As Maddie giggled at his cheeky remark, she heard Nick clash the buckets together and Betsy moved restlessly at the sudden noise, jerking her back leg sideways and pushing Maddie off the stool so that she fell backwards onto the cobbled floor of the cowshed.

'Now look what you've done,' Michael shouted at Nick as he stooped to offer a helping hand to her.

'What's going on?' Frank stood in the doorway and then, as he glanced from his son towards the figure of Nick making his way along the line of tethered cows to the far end of the cowshed, he gave a quick, irritated shake of his head. 'Oh, you two at it again, are you? Give it a rest, Michael, and show this lass what to do.'

'I was doing,' Michael muttered. 'If others'd leave us alone.'

But Maddie noticed that he kept his voice so low that his father could not hear his words. Only she, close to him, heard.

'Now the milking's done, Nick,' Frank said, 'we'll show Maddie around. Where we're standing, lass, is the crewyard and besides the cowshed . . .' Frank gestured towards the buildings on two sides of the yard, 'there's Rajah's stable in the corner and then pigsties down that side. We've only two pigs just now. Then, in that far corner, is the boiler house. We use it in winter to heat the hen-house. That's that long building over yonder.' He pointed beyond the yard. 'Come on, I'll show you my battery house, but you must never . . .' for a moment his expression was stern, 'go inside it. I'm only just teaching Michael how it all works.' His expression lightened a little. 'I've promised Nick that I'll show him too, when he's older.' Now Frank smiled. 'But even he's banned at the moment.'

Frank led the way towards the lean-to barn at the side of the house. From his trouser pocket he pulled out a bunch of keys on the end of a long chain attached to his braces and inserted a key into the Yale lock.

'You stand there,' he said firmly. 'Both of you.'

As he stepped into the dark interior and switched on a light, Maddie and Nick leant against the door jambs, peering inside.

'This is a Lister engine,' Frank explained. 'It drives this generator that's linked to these batteries.'

The engine and the generator were set on a concrete plinth in the centre of the barn, but close by, set against one wall, was a wooden rack holding three rows of glass containers with lead plates suspended in each one and with cables running between them.

'These are full of sulphuric acid,' Frank warned. 'And the current is what they call direct current. Very dangerous.' His face was serious. 'It might kill a person if they touched the bare wires and the acid would burn if you got any on you. So promise me, lass, you won't ever come in here on your own. You'll hear us start up the generator about once a week to charge up the batteries, but as long as you do as I say, there's nothing to worry about. And

37

this . . .' He was pointing to one side of the rack of batteries now. 'Is the control panel.'

It seemed to Maddie to be a confusing array of dials and switches. 'What's it all do, Mr Frank?' she asked, mystified, yet intrigued.

'It generates the electricity that feeds the house and all the lighting.'

He switched off the light and stepped out of the barn, closing the door carefully behind him and checking that it was locked. 'See these?' He pointed to cables running above them from the corner of the barn across the yard to the hen-house and the buildings around the crewyard. 'They're connected to lights in all the buildings.'

'It's very clever,' Maddie said with genuine admiration.

'Well, we're too far out for mains electricity. A lot of farms out in the countryside have their own system. It's not so unusual.' Frank smiled down at her, touched by her ingenuous praise. 'Now, let's show you the front garden and then, except for the rest of the fields, you've about seen it all. I'm sure Mrs Trowbridge will have our breakfast waiting. I bet you're hungry, lass, aren't you?'

It took a week for Maddie to learn how to milk properly and, even then, she was much slower than the experienced Michael and even the younger Nick. Between milking, she was expected to help in the dairy, churning the butter, and in the house helping Harriet, who was, Maddie had now learned, the housekeeper. She and her son were treated like members of Frank's own family and Maddie's mistake had been a natural one to make. To outsiders, Harriet had all the appearance of being the farmer's wife. Only those within the walls of the farmhouse knew that Frank Brackenbury and Harriet Trowbridge went to their own bedrooms each night and, as far as the young girl was aware, stayed there.

Michael, Maddie learned, was in charge of the milk round. After milking each morning he would set off with the horse and cart and with three or four milk churns on the back.

'You'll have to come with me one day, young'un,' he told Maddie. 'I could do with some help some mornings. All this traipsing up and down folks' paths to fetch their milkcans and then all the way back to the door to deliver it.' He sniffed. 'Time was when they'd come out to the cart and fetch it themselves. Folks is getting lazier I reckon.' He winked at her. 'I blame the War.'

Maddie laughed. 'I've heard that before. Mrs Potter was always saying it.'

'Who's Mrs Potter?'

'The matron at the Home.'

The young man's face sobered and there was pity in his dark brown eyes. 'Were you happy there?'

Maddie shrugged her thin shoulders. 'Dunno,' and added wisely, 'it was all I'd ever known really . . .' She paused, omitting to tell him of her brief times of trial in foster homes. 'I've never known anything different.'

'Are you happy here?'

Her smile broadened in genuine pleasure so that he smiled too. 'Oh yes.'

'So you don't miss your old home, then?'

Now a tiny cloud shadowed her face. 'There's only one person I miss. My friend, Jenny.'

'Who's Jenny?'

Maddie told him. 'I promised to write, but – but I haven't had the chance.' She hesitated, not wanting to sound ungrateful.

He grinned. 'We've kept you too busy, you mean?'

'It's not that. It's . . .' She stopped.

'Go on,' he prompted.

'I – I haven't any writing paper and envelopes or – or a stamp,' she blurted out.

'Ah,' was all he said as he turned away, but the following day, when Michael returned from his milk round he handed her a brown paper bag.

'There,' he said, smiling down at her, his brown eyes teasing, 'now you've no excuse not to write to your little friend.'

Opening the bag, Maddie found a pad of writing paper, a packet of matching envelopes, six postage stamps and even a fountain pen and a bottle of blue ink.

'Oh thank you, thank you,' she said gazing up at him, her eyes filling with tears.

Maddie March had never known such kindness.

As the young man nodded, winked and then turned to stride away across the yard, Maddie watched him go, adoration in her blue eyes.

Six

'I meant you to buy new clothes for the girl, Harriet. Not someone else's cast-offs from Mother Topham's market stall. She'll look like a ragamuffin.'

'That's just what she is.' Harriet's voice was shrill. 'A wilful little ragamuffin bastard that nobody wants.'

'Harriet!' Frank was shocked. 'I never thought to hear such words pass your lips.' Now there was sarcasm in his tone. 'And you, a good Christian woman. Besides, how can you say that about her? She's only been here five minutes and I certainly haven't seen any sign of wilfulness. Have you?'

'You didn't see that matron at the orphanage, Frank Brackenbury. Couldn't wait to get rid of Miss Madeleine March. Why, she even helped load the girl's box on to the cart herself. Oh, I could tell all right. I dare bet you – and as you've just pointed out I'm a good Christian woman who doesn't believe in gambling and the like – but I dare bet you a week of my wages that girl has been in and out of that orphanage to different folks and been sent back a dozen times. Well, I'll tell you summat, Frank. She'd better mind her P's and Q's with me, else I'll be sending her back an' all.'

Maddie hadn't meant to overhear the quarrel. She had come into the wash-house by the back door and was removing her boots when she heard the raised voices from beyond the kitchen door. Now she stood immobile, not

41

knowing what to do. She certainly didn't want to go into the kitchen and if she went outside again, they might hear the door open and close this time and know that she had been eavesdropping.

'I never liked the idea of having a girl here, anyway. It's not right with two young lads in the household. Who knows what might happen. I can't keep me eye on the little madam all day.'

Maddie frowned. Why, then, if she didn't want her here, had Mrs Trowbridge been the one to come to the Home to pick her?

'I just thought a girl would be more use to you, Harriet,' Frank was saying, 'in the Dairy and helping with the housework. You seemed quite keen on the idea when I first suggested it and it was you proposed approaching the Orphanage, if I remember. I thought you wanted to give some poor lass a proper home.'

'Huh! That wasn't me reason.'

'Then what was?'

'Oh I – er – well . . .' For a moment, even to Maddie listening beyond the door, the woman seemed flustered. 'I thought she'd be less trouble if there are no parents to come banging on the door making sure we're not working her too many hours or making her do work that's too heavy for a girl.'

Maddie heard Frank's gasp. 'I'd never do that anyway, Harriet. You know that.'

'Mebbe so,' the woman said tartly as if she did not agree. 'But we'll have no trouble from Mrs Potter, I can tell you that. Pleased to be rid of the little baggage, she was.'

'I don't know what you've got against the little lass. She's a bit slow with the milking, I'll grant you, but she's careful and gentle with the cows.'

42

'She's a wilful little tyke. Mebbe you don't see it, Mr Frank, but I tell you she'll likely bring trouble on this house 'afore she's done.' She paused and then added ominously, 'There's bad blood in her veins, you mark my words.'

'I'm sure Maddie is quite safe in my household.' There was a slight emphasis on the word 'my', but Harriet did not agree.

'Well, I can vouch for my Nicholas, but I can't say the same about your lad. He's a one for the girls if the village gossip is to be believed. And if she leads him on . . .'

'He's just a normal seventeen-year-old.'

'Are you implying that my son isn't?'

Frank's voice was heavy now, tired of the argument. 'No, no, of course I'm not. He's only fifteen. Plenty of time for him to . . .'

'I wouldn't mind him meeting a nice girl. Of course I wouldn't.' Her tone implied the opposite. 'But he'll not be mixing with the village girls, I can tell you that. Oh no. If I let him even think of getting married some day, she'd have to be from a decent family. A girl who knows just who her parents are.'

'I think you might find, Harriet, that you have no say in the matter.'

'Oho, won't I, indeed?'

'The Victorian age has gone, my dear. And young men not much older than our sons have just been through another dreadful war. Do you really think they are going to allow their parents to dictate to them how they should run their lives? We haven't made a very good job of this century so far, now have we? We're not even halfway through it and yet we have allowed the flower of our youth to be decimated by two disastrous World Wars. No, Harriet, we owe it to those that are left to allow them to

43

forge their own future out of the ruins we have left them. I don't envy them their task.'

'I don't know what you're talking about, Mr Frank,' Harriet said impatiently. 'You talk as if the War were our fault.'

'Well, wasn't it?'

'Of course it wasn't. It was the Government's. Besides, what did you expect them to do? Let that Hitler walk all over us?'

'It was our generation's fault, Harriet. That's what I meant.'

'Oh, you're getting too deep for me and changing the subject. We were talking about that little madam and the trouble she could cause living here. I still don't know why you wanted a girl here in the first place. But, that said, she's not worth spending a lot on. She might not be here long.'

The argument had come full circle and when there was no reply from Frank now, Maddie was terrified that the door would open and she would be discovered.

Suddenly, she had an idea.

She crept forward and opened the back door. Then she slammed it as if she had just come in. Then, humming the tune of her favourite hymn, 'Rock of Ages', she stamped her feet on the mat and clomped across the floor towards the coat pegs. She heard the kitchen door open behind her and plastered a smile on her face in readiness.

The smile became genuine when she saw who it was.

'We've finished the milking, Mr Frank. I reckon I'm getting the hang of it now.' She giggled at her own pun. 'Michael's gone on the milk round and Nick and Ben are taking the cows back to the meadow.'

'Good lass,' the man said kindly though Maddie, knowing what had just taken place, could still see the anger in his eyes even though he was trying to hide it behind a smile. 'Come and get your breakfast and then I'll show you what I want you to do in the Dairy. It's time you started learning that side of things now.'

Divested of her outdoor clothing, Maddie stepped into the kitchen to see the housekeeper standing at the stove vigorously stirring a pan of porridge, her back rigid with righteous indignation.

Maddie had never witnessed a row like that before. Not between two adults, who, though employer and house-keeper, seemed to be on almost an equal footing. She had seen the staff at the orphanage in trouble with Mrs Potter, but they, like the children in her charge, had been obliged to just stand there and take it. She had even, once or twice, heard the younger members of staff threatened with the dreaded cupboard under the stairs, the 'prison' as the children called it, where Matron locked them in the spider-ridden dark for the slightest wrong-doing.

But Harriet Trowbridge, it seemed, did not have to stand there and take it, not even from her employer, and whilst the quarrel had ceased now, Maddie knew instinctively that the animosity between the farmer and his housekeeper was far from over.

And she was the cause of it.

'I've got another little present for you, young 'un.'

'For me?' Maddie's blue eyes widened in genuine surprise and delight.

'Er – yes.' Michael seemed doubtful now and strangely unwilling to hand over the small package. 'I hope you won't take this the wrong way?'

'Why should I?'

'Well . . .' He paused and she saw that he was glancing at her hair. Self-consciously, she touched it.

'I thought . . .' he went on haltingly. 'I mean, you don't seem to have any proper shampoo. You use soap to wash your hair, don't you?'

Maddie nodded.

'Well, see – proper shampoo would make your hair shine. You've got pretty hair. At least . . .' He faltered again and his voice fell away.

Maddie smiled at him warmly. 'Thanks,' she said, reaching out for the brown paper package. 'I'll try it on Friday night when I'm allowed to use the bathroom.'

He grinned back. 'And you're not offended?'

''Course not.'

The first time Maddie used the shampoo, she used far too much and lather spilled out over the washbasin and onto the linoleum. But after she had rinsed and rinsed the soapiness away her hair squeaked with cleanliness.

As she stood up and towelled her hair vigorously, she jumped as Harriet spoke from the opening on to the landing. 'You're running far too much water, girl. And just look at that mess on the floor.'

Maddie was incensed as she felt the woman's glance lingering on her nakedness.

'Go away,' Maddie said. 'You're not allowed up here either. Leave me alone.'

Harriet's face twisted into a sneer. 'And what do you think you've to hide, miss? Just get on with your bath and don't use much water now. There's others need hot water after you and there'll be none left.'

If she hadn't known that it would be Michael who

wanted to take a bath later, Maddie would have run and run the hot water all away to spite the woman. But knowing the two boys followed after her, she did as she was bade and only used six inches, the regulation depth that had so been instilled in them all in the orphanage.

Later, as she towelled her hair dry, she could tell the difference even after using the shampoo only the once. It felt clean and silky. In the privacy of her bedroom she picked up the pair of scissors she had found in the kitchen drawer and had earlier smuggled up to her room. Combing the hair forwards onto her face, she carefully snipped and combed and snipped again until she had a fringe and wisps of hair drawn forward onto her cheek. In her thin face her blue eyes looked enormous and now, with the blonde hair framing her face, she looked like a little elf.

'Why,' Maddie whispered to herself, marvelling at her own reflection though without a trace of conceit. 'I look almost pretty.'

She got into bed and turned out the light to lay in the semi-darkness listening to the sounds from the bathroom beyond her bedroom wall.

She could hear Michael warbling and splashing.

Smiling, Maddie fell asleep.

Seven

'You know that field of tulips just beyond where your cows are, Mr Frank?'

Seated at the breakfast table Maddie spoke about the sight that had intrigued her ever since the morning she had first seen the field. Each time she fetched the cows, she would stand for a few moments just drinking in the beautiful sight.

'Stop your chatter and get on with your breakfast,' came Harriet's harsh voice.

Maddie saw Frank glance towards the housekeeper. He said nothing but brought his gaze round to Maddie and said quietly, 'Aye, lass, what about it?'

Early that morning she had seen a line of women moving amongst the blooms. 'They were cutting them this morning. Not leaving any long stalks on the flowers like you do to put in a vase, but cutting just the heads off.'

'Aye well, lass, they have to. Like I told you, they're running a business.'

'They use some as cut flowers, though,' Michael put in.

'That's true. They pack and send a lot away, but there's a market stall in town that's loaded with flowers this time of the year.'

'Oh, I'd love to see it.'

The man's smile broadened. 'Well, it's market day tomorrow and I was going to go myself to look at some beast. You can come with me, if you like.'

'It's the Spring Fair as well, isn't it, Dad?' Michael said. 'There'll be roundabouts and swings, won't there?'

'You're right, Michael. I expect it'll be in the Black Swan Yard and the field behind it.' Frank glanced round the table, now including everyone. 'I tell you what, we'll all go. Make an outing of it and have lunch at the White Hart.'

'Great,' was Michael's reply but Maddie saw Nick look towards his mother.

'Not me, Mr Frank,' she said sharply and then added, 'but thank you for the invitation.'

'Oh come along, Harriet,' Frank coaxed. 'You can't avoid going into the town for ever. Besides, you went not long ago when you got those clothes for Maddie.'

A glance passed between them and Maddie, anxious not to give away the fact that she had overheard their quarrel about the clothes, stared down at her plate.

Harriet too averted her eyes from Frank's gaze now, hesitating before admitting, 'No, I didn't. I got Mrs Grange from the corner shop in the village to get them for me.'

Frank was nodding slowly. 'Ah yes, Mrs Grange.' He picked up a forkful of bacon and chewed it slowly, his thoughtful gaze still on his housekeeper.

'Besides,' she was saying, 'who's to see to things here if we all go off gallivanting?' Her mouth was tight with disapproval. 'And what about your milk round, Michael?'

'I'll tell everyone on my round this morning that their milk will be a little late tomorrow. I'll come back from town once we've had this posh lunch and do the round in the afternoon.'

'Folks won't like that.'

'We'll see to everything before we go,' Frank said. 'And I'd really like you to come with us, Harriet.' His grin was boyish and he looked, for a moment, nearer the age of his own son. 'I'll even try to get the car going. If I can scrounge a drop of petrol, we'll travel in style. I'll have a look at it after breakfast.'

'We'll help you, Dad. Won't we, Nick? I'll only have time for a quick look with you now before I have to get off on my round, but I'll help this afternoon.'

Now the younger boy smiled but avoided looking at his mother. Maddie had no such qualms and watched the housekeeper's face. It was obvious that the woman was struggling to overcome some kind of fear that only Frank seemed to understand. To Maddie's amazement, she saw the tightness around Harriet's mouth slacken as she put her head on one side with an almost coy expression. 'Well, in that case, Mr Frank, yes, Nicholas and I would be delighted to go.' Turning to her son, she added, 'Now, you help Mr Frank by doing some of his jobs if he's going to be busy with the motor car. You can start by cleaning out the hen-house. And you can feed the pigs.'

Nick's mouth was suddenly sulky as he muttered, 'Yes, Mam.'

They rose from the table, Frank and Michael chatting animatedly about the motor. Outside, Maddie touched Nick's arm. 'I'll do the hen-house, if you want to go with Mr Frank and Michael.'

The pale grey eyes behind the spectacles blinked. 'Would you really?'

''Course I will. What do I know about cars and engines and things?' She grinned. 'But I have learnt how to muck out.'

A flush crept up the boy's face as he said, so quietly she hardly heard the words, 'I never thought you'd do something like that for me. If you're really sure, I would like to go an' watch. I like engines. Anything mechanical.'

'What about the pigs?'

'I'll do them later.'

It was the longest conversation she had had with Nick. She smiled at him. 'Go on, then. Go and stick your head under the car bonnet with Mr Frank.'

The hardened layers of chicken dirt were more difficult to scrape up than she had imagined, but once she had dug down to the concrete floor of the building and could get the sharp edge of the spade beneath the layers, it was easier. She was actually singing to herself when she heard Harriet's voice behind her.

'What are you doing? I told Nicholas to do this job. You should be in the Dairy.'

Maddie felt herself trapped. She knew if she told the housekeeper where Nick was, he would be in trouble.

Cheerfully, she said, 'There's nothing much to do in the Dairy, Mrs T, so I thought I'd help Nick.'

'Don't answer me back. There's always work in the Dairy, girl. And my name's Mrs Trowbridge to you.'

She moved into the dimness of the building treading carefully across the slippery floor and came close to Maddie. Gripping the girl's arm, she leant towards her. 'I know your little game, miss. Flirting with young Michael and even fluttering your eyelashes at Mr Frank. Don't think I don't know. Well, if I had my way, you'd be back at that Home quicker than you came.'

'You picked me,' Maddie shot back. Harriet blinked, shocked by the girl's effrontery.

'You cheeky little madam. I wish I'd left you where you were.' She thrust her face even closer. 'If you really want to know, girl, I didn't so much "pick" you as you was the only one available. The matron said that the other two who were school-leaving age had already got fixed up with

51

jobs.' Her grip on Maddie's arm tightened. 'That should have warned me, shouldn't it? Nobody else wanted you.'

'No, you didn't. You picked me purposely,' Maddie flashed back, now so angry that she forgot caution. ' "Are you sure she's the one," you said.'

For a moment, Harriet looked perplexed, almost guilty, as if she had been caught out. 'How . . .?' she began, but Maddie interrupted, unable to stop the words bursting form her mouth. 'I know exactly why you picked me. You thought I'd got no family. I heard you ask Mrs Potter if I'd got anyone belonging me and when she said "no", you thought no one would ever come looking for me. You thought you could work me to death and no one would know – or – or care.' Her voice threatened to quaver, but she carried on defiantly. 'Well, I have got family, so there. And one day they'll come looking for me . . .'

'Oh no they won't . . .' Harriet began, her eyes sparkling with malice, but whatever she had been about to say ended in a cry of alarm, as, hurt and humiliated, Maddie twisted herself free of the woman's grip so suddenly that Harriet was thrown off-balance. She tottered backwards, dropping the basket, half-filled with eggs. Her arms flailed helplessly as she sat down heavily in the dirt that Maddie had just scraped into a pile. For a moment, Maddie had the overwhelming urge to laugh, but as the woman groaned and screwed up her face in pain, the girl's mirth died.

She held out her hand to help. 'I'm sorry, Mrs T – Mrs Trowbridge. I didn't mean . . .'

'You – you little hussy. Wait 'til I tell Mr Frank about this.' Ignoring Maddie's hand, the woman struggled to regain her feet. 'Just look at all that waste.' She pointed to the eggs smashed on the floor, their yellow yolks oozing across the wet dirt. Already hens were running to peck at the raw egg. 'Get it cleaned up quickly. You'll have the hens breaking their own eggs to eat them next, once they get a taste.'

'What do you mean . . .?' Maddie began, but the woman's voice rose.

'Get it cleaned up, I tell you. Get this finished and then get the rest of the eggs collected.'

She turned and limped away, holding her right buttock.

Maddie no longer felt the desire to laugh. Now she was in real trouble.

'Send her back. She's useless. Good for nothing. She's trouble with a capital T.'

'Harriet, she's only a little lass. How can she be expected to do everything right just yet? Besides, what actually happened in there?'

Maddie waited, holding her breath. This time she was not eavesdropping on the quarrel between Frank and his housekeeper. This time she was right in the middle of it.

'She pushed me over.'

'No, I didn't. You'd got hold of my arm and I pulled myself free and you fell over.'

The woman glared at her. 'You pushed me. Said I was walking on your clean floor.' Harriet's mouth twisted into a sneer. 'Clean floor. I ask you, Mr Frank. Clean floor in a hen-house?'

Maddie gasped and felt her face flush with anger. 'That's a lie. I never said that.'

'Oh, calling me a liar now, are you? It's you that's the little liar.' Harriet turned to Frank. 'See how red her face is. Are you going to take her word against mine?'

Helplessly, Frank glanced from one to the other.

Maddie had always hated deceit of any kind. She'd

53

hated it in the Home when girls had taken one another's belongings and then lied their way out of trouble. She'd once sat on a girl until she'd confessed to taking Jenny's hairslide.

Through gritted teeth Maddie said now, 'I never tell lies.'

'Send her back, Mr Frank. Back where she belongs.'

For a moment he closed his eyes, sighed heavily and shook his head, irritated by the whole incident. Then he looked down at Maddie. 'I really don't want to have to do that, so try to be a good lass, eh?' His tone was gentle, almost sad, and then he reached out and touched her hair in a gesture of tender affection.

And that was Maddie's undoing.

She gave a little sob, turned and fled from the kitchen, through the wash-house and out of the back door.

Then she ran and ran. Out of the yard, down the lane to the meadow where the cows grazed, not stopping until she had run the full length of it and come to a halt at the hedge overlooking the field of flowers.

Now breathless, her crying was coming in huge, wracking sobs. The pretty blooms were all gone, only the headless stalks and the green leaves were left.

Gone too, was Maddie's feeling of security.

If Harriet Trowbridge could lie about a silly thing like that today, then there was no telling to what lengths she would go to get rid of Maddie. But what hurt the girl the most was that Frank had believed his housekeeper.

He had not believed Maddie.

Eight

'Are you getting ready then? We'll be going in half an hour.'

Maddie, watching Michael standing before the mirror over the mantelpiece to tie his tie, said, 'I didn't think I'd be going. Not now.'

It was almost eight o'clock the following morning. Everyone had risen early to finish the milking and have breakfast so that they could arrive at the market as early as possible, but nothing more had been said about Maddie going.

Michael came and leant on his hands on the table. 'That's all forgotten, young'un. Go and get ready. Look sharp.'

Still Maddie did not move. 'Hadn't you better ask Mr Frank?' Her voice was husky with the tears she was trying to hold back.

Since the previous morning, Maddie had been awaiting her punishment. For the first time since coming to Few Farm, Maddie felt as if she was back at the Home. It was just the same as Mrs Potter had done when Maddie had, to the matron's mind, misbehaved. Hour after hour had been allowed to tick by whilst Maddie pondered upon the inevitable punishment. What would it be this time? Extra chores, like scrubbing the tiles of the kitchen floor until her hands were red raw and her knees ached. Or would it be the cane? Maddie would imagine the thin cane whistling through the air behind her before it struck her bare bottom.

She shifted uncomfortably in the chair now under Michael's gaze, already feeling the anticipated pain. She guessed it would be Mrs Trowbridge who would administer the strokes and she knew that the housekeeper would relish each and every weal that appeared on Maddie's skin.

Or maybe she would be shut in a cupboard somewhere, though offhand she couldn't think of one here that resembled the one under the stairs at the Home . . .

She would have stood any one of these punishments without a murmur, Maddie thought, if only they would let her go with them to the market today. But she knew that Harriet Trowbridge would guess that the very worst punishment she could inflict upon Maddie would be to leave her at home.

Maddie bit her lip as she looked up at Michael. 'Mrs T won't want me to come.'

Michael straightened up. 'Well then, I'll take you. We'll go on our own, just you and me. But hurry up, 'cos if we've got to walk all the way to town, we'd best be off now.'

Maddie swallowed and her heart began to thump with excitement. 'D'you mean it? Really?'

He was grinning at her now. ''Course I do. Go on.'

Ten minutes later she was back downstairs, face scrubbed, hair brushed and dress changed, though the latter still caused her anguish. The yellow cotton dress, one of the second-hand garments from the market stall, hung shapelessly on her thin frame, the hem too long and uneven. And her stout, lace-up brown shoes were too heavy for a fine early summer day. But Michael smiled down at her and winked.

'Pretty as a tulip,' he said kindly, but she knew he couldn't mean it. 'Come on, then.'

As they were leaving by the back door, they collided with Frank coming in.

'Hello, you two. All ready?'

'We thought we'd go on our own, Dad,' Michael said quietly. 'Leave more room in the car.'

Frank glanced shrewdly from one to the other. 'Well, that's all right, but I was looking forward to us all going together. Won't you come with us?' He glanced from one to the other and then Maddie felt Michael's gaze upon her. He was trying to shield her, but it was up to her to tell the truth. Hadn't she said, so vehemently, that she never told lies. Well, neither would she let someone else even bend the truth to help her.

Squarely she faced Frank. 'I didn't think I'd be allowed to go. Not after what happened yesterday. So Michael said he – he'd . . .' She shot a glance at the older boy, hoping she wasn't about to get him into trouble with his father. 'He'd take me.'

'Oh Maddie.' To her surprise, Frank's voice was sorrowful rather than angry. His expression told her that maybe he guessed what had been in her mind, perhaps even imagined the harsh discipline she had endured already in her young life. 'You're not at the Home now, love. We're not going to punish you like that. If you do something wrong, well, we'll tell you about it at the time.' He moved closer to her and put his arm about her shoulders, looking down into her upturned face. 'We might get a bit cross now and again, but once it's over, that's it. See?'

Wordlessly, Maddie nodded. She couldn't speak for the lump in her throat, not caused by misery now, but by this man's kindness. She was even prepared to forgive him for seeming not to believe her the previous day.

'So,' he was saying, 'shall we all go together?'

Maddie looked at Michael, who smiled and nodded.

'Yes, please,' Maddie said in a small voice.

He gave her shoulder a quick squeeze and said, 'Good. Now, I'd better go and make myself look respectable.'

Harriet made a great play of limping across the yard to the motor car and easing herself into the front passenger seat beside Frank. Maddie, squashed between Michael and Nick in the back seat, said nothing.

'All set?' Frank asked as all the doors were slammed shut. 'Here we go. Come on, Bertha, old girl. I hope you haven't forgotten how to do it after all this time.'

With a grating of gears and a couple of kangaroo hops, they were out of the gate and gaining speed down the lane.

'I don't think it's Bertha that's forgotten, Dad,' Michael shouted. 'I reckon it's you that's forgotten how to drive her.'

'You could be right, son. Hang on to your hat, Harriet, I'm about to take you round this next corner on two wheels.'

Harriet gave a little shriek of alarm and clutched at her black hat whilst in the back seat the three youngsters held onto each other and thrust their hands across their mouths to stifle their laughter.

The cattle market was held in a wide street. There were no pens for the animals, like in the sheep market, and the beast just stood, quite patiently, in the open, cobbled street in clusters of four, five or six with only a drover to tend them.

Brought up in an all-female establishment, Maddie had never seen so many men together in one place in her life.

'Where have they all come from?' she asked, gazing around her in wide-eyed amazement.

'All over Lincolnshire,' Michael said. 'They even come from Nottingham, Leicester and Cambridgeshire.'

'Really?' She couldn't take her eyes off them. Some were dressed in farmers' workaday clothes, jackets, caps and stout boots, but some were smartly dressed in checked jackets and plus-fours. There were even one or two elderly gentlemen who wore black suits and bowler hats.

Maddie was fascinated by the sounds, the sights and even the smells. She breathed in the whole atmosphere, revelling in being a part of it, relishing the feeling of belonging. She watched the beast being paraded around before interested buyers and listened, open-mouthed, to the auctioneer rattling off the bids so quickly that she could scarcely follow him.

'Mind you don't nod your head, young'un, else you might find yourself the proud owner of half a dozen cows,' Michael teased.

Maddie laughed, but the next time the auctioneer's glance went around the crowd, she stood rigidly still, even holding her breath.

'Maddie! Maddie!'

She knew the voice even before she saw the small figure darting amongst the crowd, pushing her way through to reach her.

'Jen. Oh Jen.' The two girls flew into each other's arms.

'I've missed you so much,' the young girl was crying now, tears running down her face as she hugged her friend. 'It's awful there without you.'

'Did you get my letter?'

'Yes, yes.' She pulled back and looked up into Maddie's face, smiling now through her tears. 'It's the first letter I've ever had in me whole life.'

Maddie giggled. 'It's the first time I've ever been able to write one. But what are you doing here? In town?'

'Mrs Potter brought me. She's over there. I had an interview with someone who grows flowers, but I don't think I'll get the job. I'm too little to stand at the bench to pack them into the boxes, the man said.' She pulled a face. 'I don't think she's very pleased with me.'

'So, what's new?' Maddie grinned and they hugged each other again until Frank cleared his throat and said, 'Aren't you going to introduce us to your friend, Maddie?'

The girls pulled apart and Maddie, with the habit of years, pulled Jenny's coat straight and smoothed back her wayward hair. Then she bent and pulled up the girl's socks that were wrinkled about her ankles, as she said, 'I'm sorry, Mr Frank. This is my friend, Jenny, from the Home.'

Jenny smiled shyly as each member of the household from Few Farm acknowledged her in their different ways. Frank stepped forward and shook her hand, Michael flashed her his engaging grin whilst Nick smiled shyly from behind his spectacles. Only Harriet gave a curt, unsmiling nod, though her glance took in the child's appearance from head to toe. Maddie heard her sniff of disapproval when Frank said, 'Would you like to join us, Jenny? We were just going to have lunch at the White Hart.'

Jenny glanced over her shoulder. 'I'd love to, Mr Brackenbury. But I daren't. Mrs Potter . . .'

'Well now . . .' Frank held out his hand, 'let's you and me go and find this Mrs Potter and ask her if the Brackenbury family might have the pleasure of your company for lunch. How would that be, eh?'

'Ooh yes, please.'

It was the earnest 'please' that touched Frank's heart. He cleared his throat quickly and said firmly, 'Come on, then.'

They set off through the crowd together, the broad-shouldered farmer and the little girl who, though almost fourteen looked only eleven or twelve years old. Behind them, Maddie followed, intrigued to see Mrs Potter's face when confronted by a request that one of her charges, not to mention the infamous Maddie March too, should be asked out to lunch with a gentleman and his family. She turned briefly to tell Michael that she'd be back in a minute or two, but found, to her surprise, that not only he but Harriet and Nick were following in her wake.

This'll be good, the girl thought and smiled.

'Good morning, Mrs Potter.' Moments later Frank was raising his hat to the startled matron.

There was suspicion in her eyes as she eyed the man before her, then, ignoring his greeting, she hissed at the child, 'Get back where you belong, girl, and don't let me catch you darting off again. Ain't I told you about talking to strange men?'

Maddie stifled her laughter at the indignant look on Frank's face. 'My name,' he said stiffly, 'is Frank Brackenbury and I believe you know this young lady?'

He moved aside to reveal Maddie, and the others, standing behind him.

Mrs Potter's eyes narrowed. 'Indeed I do.' She sniffed and, seeing Harriet too, she nodded. 'I suppose you want to bring her back to me, eh? Well, there's no place for her now. She's too old to come back to the Home. You'll have to fend for yourself, Maddie March.' She turned back to face Frank. 'I'm sorry, sir, if she's caused you bother, but I can't say I'm surprised.'

'On the contrary, Mrs Potter, we are delighted to have

Maddie live with us.' He paused and then added quietly, as if unable to resist doing so, 'I wouldn't send her back to your orphanage if I was to go bankrupt tomorrow.'

Mrs Potter had the grace to flush in embarrassment and, flustered, to say, 'Oh well, sir, I am pleased to hear it. Perhaps all my efforts were worthwhile in the end.'

With a hint of sarcasm, Frank said, 'Maybe so, Mrs Potter, maybe so.' He cleared his throat and said, 'What I came to ask you was would you allow young Jenny here to have lunch with us? I will bring her back to the Home later, if that would be convenient. In fact,' he added, as if he had just thought about it, 'she could go home with us and I would bring her back to you at whatever time you say later this evening.'

'Oh well, now, sir, I don't know about that.' Mrs Potter's mouth pursed primly. 'We don't normally let any of our girls go out with strangers.' But then she appeared to be calculating swiftly in her mind, the girl was coming up to school-leaving age. That very morning she had been turned down for one job. Maybe if Mr Brackenbury was pleased with one of her orphans then . . .? Mrs Potter smiled. 'But, of course, in your case, sir, since I know Mrs Trowbridge and you have already taken Maddie March, then I don't see any problem.'

She turned now and prodded the young girl on the shoulder. 'You just mind you behave yourself, miss.'

'Yes, Matron,' Jenny said in her meek voice and slipped her hand into Maddie's.

As they moved away from Mrs Potter, Jenny began to skip and chatter. Her excited, piping voice rose above the hubbub around them. 'Guess what happened last week? Mr Theo Mayfield came to the Home to visit. You know, Sir Peter's son. We was all called together and he told us that he's been appointed to the Board of – of – what is it they call them, Maddie?'

'Governors.'

'That's it. To the Board of Governors. He's ever so nice, Maddie. Ever so friendly and handsome. Fair curly hair, he's got. I always used to be a bit frightened of Sir Peter, but I don't think I will be of Mr Theo. I wish you could see him, Maddie.'

After they had walked all round the market again and Frank and Michael had stood before two cows for sale, pondering whether to make a bid and then deciding against it, Frank turned and said, 'It's too early for dinner yet, but I could murder a cuppa. How about the rest of you?'

'I could do with a sit down, Mr Frank. I can't stand on me feet any longer.'

Frank's eyes twinkled. 'You should have worn your comfortable shoes, Harriet, not your "Sunday-go-to-meeting" pair that pinch your toes.' He turned to the younger members of the party. 'You coming, or do you want to go off by yourselves?'

'We'll go and have a look at the fair, Dad.'

'Don't leave these two young lassies on their own, will you now?'

' 'Course not,' Michael said, almost indignantly.

'Right then. We'll come and find you there.'

As Frank and Harriet moved away, Michael said, 'Come on, I'll buy us all an ice cream each.'

Now that his mother was out of earshot, Nick was not to be outdone. 'Fancy a ride on the roundabout?' he said to Maddie. 'I'll treat you.'

Maddie grinned. 'You're on. What about you, Jen?' But the younger girl hung back. 'I daresunt. You go, Maddie. I'll just stand and watch.'

'We'll watch 'em and laugh at 'em when they fall off, shall we, young'un?' Michael said to Jenny and put his arm casually about her shoulders.

Maddie was startled by a sudden strange feeling that stabbed at her. She had never felt this way before, but when she looked at Michael with his arm around Jenny and saw him smiling down at her, she felt such resentment towards Jenny that it frightened her. And he'd called her 'young'un' too, the nickname that Maddie had thought was only for her.

Nine

The fair had come to Wellandon, as Frank had said, to the field behind the Black Swan a short distance from the cattle market. Fairground organ music greeted them as they drew near and they could hear the merry laughter and the shrieks from young girls as the handsome, dark-haired young man in charge of the roundabout sent it faster and faster. There were swing boats, dodgem cars, a waltzer, a helter-skelter and even a big wheel, as well as all manner of stalls; hoopla, a coconut shy and a shooting gallery. There was even a gypsy fortune teller in a small striped tent with an elaborate sign that said 'Madam Pallengro, Palmist and Clairvoyant'.

'Come on, Nick,' Maddie said deliberately, 'we'll show 'em.'

'Let's go on the Galloping Horses,' Nick said and held out his hand for her to climb up onto one of the white-painted horses whilst he climbed onto the one next to her. The ride, when it began, not only went round but also up and down and Maddie had not expected the peculiar feeling in her stomach. 'When it goes down,' she shouted to Nick above the hubbub, 'my tummy feels as if I've left it up there and then I meet it coming down as I'm going back up.'

Nick laughed and pretended to be galloping his charger. Faster and faster the music played and faster and faster the world spun around, so that soon the faces of those watching became a whirling blur to Maddie. She began to feel slightly sick and was thankful when the ride slowed and the earth began to regain its rightful shape.

'You all right?' Nick said as he held up his hand to help her slide down from the horse. 'You look a bit green.'

'Don't you dare tell them,' she muttered.

'They're round the other side. Let's go over there,' Nick suggested, 'make out we haven't seen them. Just till you've recovered.'

'Thanks,' Maddie said gratefully and followed Nick towards a shooting gallery, willing her legs to stop feeling quite so wobbly.

'There you are,' came Michael's voice.

Nick turned. 'Couldn't see you,' he lied glibly. 'We thought you and Jen had gone off together.'

'Not 'til I've challenged you to a shooting match. I might just stand a chance of beating you while you're still dizzy from that roundabout.' He turned to the two girls. 'Nick's a crack shot. Much better than I am.'

'Only 'cos I always get the job of going out to shoot rabbits in the fields or rats when the outside buildings get overrun with them,' Nick muttered, but Maddie could see that he flushed at Michael's compliment.

As they approached the shooting gallery, Nick's grin widened. 'It's a tube shooter. Ah well, you've no chance now, Michael Brackenbury.'

'What's a tube shooter?' Maddie asked.

'The guns are fired through a tube at the target,' Michael pointed. 'Look.'

On the side of a gaily painted wagon she saw that there were two guns mounted on stands, each pointing down a long metal tube which passed right through the wagon and out the other side.

'It looks like a gypsy caravan,' Maddie said and

Michael laughed. 'It is – in a way. The chap who owns the gallery lives in the wagon. I saw inside it last year and those tubes run right under his bed.'

'However do they move it all?'

'Like everything else on the fairground, it all comes to pieces and then he packs it all on the top of his wagon and off he goes. I like to come and watch them taking everything down. Talk about "a fine art". Everyone knows exactly what he's got to do. It's a sight to see, I can tell you.'

Maddie glanced at Nick, who was already moving towards the man collecting the money. She didn't think she had ever seen him looking so animated, so clearly enjoying himself. When he was smiling happily, he looked a different person to the sullen boy going about his work on the farm under his mother's watchful eye.

'Go on, Nick,' she called above the organ music coming from the roundabout, so loud that it dominated the whole fairground and even echoed into the surrounding streets. 'Win me a prize.'

He glanced back over his shoulder at her, a look of incredulous delight on his face. 'Right. I will.'

'Don't worry, Jen,' Michael said. 'I'll win one for you.'

Jenny, with a daub of vanilla ice cream on the end of her nose, smiled shyly up at him.

The girls stood side by side and watched the two boys take up their positions, covering their ears a moment later at the resounding bang, bang, bang from each one.

'They sound like real guns,' Maddie said when they came back.

'They are,' Michael said. 'With real live ammunition.' He smiled. 'So don't go standing near the end of those tubes – just in case!'

The man was coming towards them with the two

cardboard targets in his hand. 'The one on the left . . .' He
glanced from Michael to Nick, who said, 'That's mine.'

'Well, young feller. Bull's eyes every time.' He grinned,
showing worn, brown-stained teeth. 'I'll have to give you
a prize.'

'What about me?' Michael asked.

The man slapped the target playfully against Michael's
chest. 'You, son, will have to go away and practise harder.
Way off the bull, you were. Every time.'

'Let the lady choose what she wants,' Nick said and
Maddie followed the man to his wagon.

Sitting on top of a box, resplendent in a blue silk gown
edged with lace, was the prettiest doll Maddie had ever
seen. Her eyes widened when she saw it and she didn't
even need to speak for the man to reach up for it and then
place it in her arms.

'Oh, isn't it beautiful?' Jenny breathed when Maddie
returned to them.

'Sorry, Jen, I'll . . .' Michael began, but at that moment
they heard Frank's voice behind them.

'There you are. We've been looking all over for you.
Come along now, we'd better go and get that lunch else
there'll be none left.'

In the dim interior of the White Hart, Frank said, 'Now,
you young ones sit at that table together and we'll sit over
here in this quiet corner. All right, Harriet?'

As Maddie slid into the bench seat, she noticed the look
of concern on Frank's face as he held out a spindle-backed
chair for his housekeeper. Harriet looked pale and her eyes
darted nervously about her. She kept the brim of her felt
hat pulled low over her forehead and sat with her back to
the other diners.

Maddie shrugged and turned her attention to Jenny, who slid onto the seat beside her, her wide eyes drinking in all the sights around her.

Jenny reached out and squeezed her friend's hand. 'This is fun, isn't it?'

Maddie nodded as she sat the doll between them and watched as Jenny touched the frilled skirt gently, almost reverently, with her small fingers. 'Isn't she lovely?' Maddie heard her murmur, more to herself than to anyone else.

Then she looked up and smiled around her, nodding across to where Frank and Harriet sat. 'Isn't Mr Brackenbury kind?'

Michael squeezed himself into the seat opposite Maddie and Nick perched beside him. He seemed almost as ill-at-ease as his mother and kept glancing furtively over his shoulder towards her.

'What about me?' Michael teased, hearing Jenny's remark. 'Aren't I kind too?'

Jenny blushed. 'Oh yes, you're all very kind. But I mean, him offering for me to join you for dinner. He doesn't even know me.'

'If you're a friend of our Maddie's, then that's good enough for us,' Michael said and winked at Maddie. She felt a warm glow suffuse her and felt sure now that Michael was only being friendly towards Jenny for her sake. He was not pushing her out in favour of a new and prettier little face.

She glanced at her friend. In the short time since Maddie had left the Home, Jenny seemed to have grown and filled out a little. Today, no doubt in honour of the interview with a prospective employer, she had on her Sunday best navy dress and a short blue jacket. Her hair, though clean, lacked the shine that Maddie's now had. How Maddie longed to give her friend some of the precious shampoo that Michael had bought for her. Then Jenny's, too, would be a shining golden halo. And hers would be curly, whereas Maddie's was straight.

As if reading her thoughts, Jenny turned to her and said, 'Your hair's ever so pretty, Maddie. I like it cut short around your face. And it shines so now.'

Maddie glanced across the table at Michael. 'That's because I can now wash it in some lovely shampoo instead of that awful carbolic, Jen.'

The younger girl's eyes were envious as her glance roamed over Maddie's hair. 'I wonder if mine would shine like that?' she murmured.

The young waitress was standing at the end of their table, notepad in hand. Michael ordered for them all and as the waitress left them again, Jenny stared at Michael and Nick, glancing from one to the other. 'Are you brothers? You don't look much alike.'

'No, we're not related but Nick and his mother have lived with us since we were both babies. We're like brothers, though, aren't we, mate?'

Suddenly, Nick grinned and Maddie marvelled once more at how different he looked. Gone in an instant was the sulky mouth, the resentful look in his eyes. 'Yeah,' he agreed, 'we even fall out like brothers.'

Michael laughed. 'That's very true.'

Maddie opened her mouth to ask what had happened to Michael's mother and to Nick's father but before she could speak, Jenny leant against Maddie's shoulder and said, 'Me and Maddie always say we're sisters. Don't we?'

Feeling guilty now about her earlier feelings of jealousy, Maddie nodded.

'Of course, we're not,' Jenny went on. 'We know we're

not, but we like to think we are. Maddie always stuck up for me. The others tease me, you know. Me being small.'

'I know what that's like,' Nick said suddenly, but Maddie noticed that he glanced swiftly towards his mother before he spoke and he kept his voice low. 'The kids at the village school used to tease me and Mam sent me to another school. I had to travel miles on a bus all on my own to get there.' He paused as the remembered pain flitted across his eyes. 'I didn't like it there much either.'

'So that's why you never came to our school,' Maddie said. 'I wondered why I couldn't remember either of you. Did you go to the same school as Nick, Michael?'

'Part of the time.'

'He went to the Grammar School here in town. He's clever, is our Michael.' Once more, there was a tiny hint of resentment in Nick's tone, but Michael laughed it off easily. 'Oh, an absolute genius, that's me. I must say I use a lot of French on my milk round.'

'Did you learn French?' Jenny was round-eyed with admiration.

'Well, they tried to teach me it,' Michael said, 'but I don't think I learnt a lot.'

'He could have gone to university if he'd worked harder and stayed on,' Nick contradicted.

Michael pulled a face as if in embarrassment but, at that moment, their meals arrived and the subject was dropped as the hungry foursome picked up their knives and forks.

'Oh I couldn't eat another thing.' Jenny leant back in her seat and placed her hand over her stomach. 'I'm full right up to busting.'

'Me too,' Maddie said.

'Yes, not bad. Not bad at all,' Michael remarked and, raising his voice, he called across to his father and Harriet. 'Not up to your mark, Mrs T, but not bad at all.'

'Oh, go on with you, Mr Michael,' but Maddie could see that the housekeeper, flushed with the drink that Frank had bought for her, was flattered by Michael's remark.

As they stood up to leave, Maddie noticed that as Frank went to pay the bill, Harriet, with head lowered, scuttled towards the door and out into the street. As they followed her, Maddie whispered to Nick, 'Doesn't your mother like crowds?'

'Eh?' His grey eyes were owlish behind the lenses of his spectacles. 'Oh – er – no. She doesn't really like coming into town. Likes to keep herself to herself. Says the towns-folk are a lot of nosey parkers.'

'And do you?'

'Do I what?'

'Like to keep yourself to yourself?'

He shrugged and for the first time she heard the bitter-ness in his tone that this time was most definitely directed at his mother. 'I ain't had much choice one way or the other.' There was a significant pause before he added, 'Yet.'

Maddie grinned at him, confident that, given another year or so, he would stand up to his mother and be as rebellious as she would be in his shoes.

As Frank and Harriet joined them and they were about to cross the street towards the cattle market once more, a large black motor car drove slowly towards them, the market day shoppers parting, like the Red Sea, to let it pass.

'That's Sir Peter's car,' Maddie said, immediately recog-nising the vehicle she had seen parked outside the Home on many occasions.

They stood on the pavement for the car to pass by but as it drew alongside them, Harriet suddenly stepped off the kerb and stared in at the windscreen.

'Harriet!' Frank cried in alarm. He grasped her arm and pulled her away from the moving vehicle, steadying her as she tripped against the kerb. 'Whatever are you doing? You could have been knocked over.'

But her gaze was still on the black car moving on beyond them now. Maddie, too, stared after the car and saw, through the rear window, the pale face of a young woman. Long blonde hair curled onto her shoulders, though her eyes were shaded by the brim of her hat. The car moved on and the image became blurred.

'Good Lord!' Frank exclaimed. 'That must be Miss Amelia. You don't often see her out. I . . .' Frank stopped whatever he had been going to say and looked anxiously towards Harriet.

But Harriet Trowbridge did not appear to have heard a word he said. She was staring after the car, transfixed as if she had seen a ghost.

Ten

'Are you sure you're all right, Harriet?'

'Yes, yes, I'm fine, Mr Frank. I – wasn't thinking, I'm sorry. My mind was on other things.'

'Well, you must be more careful, my dear. There's getting to be more traffic about now than we've been used to.'

'I don't like the town. You know I don't. I didn't even see the car.'

Maddie glanced at Harriet. Why, the woman had been staring straight at it. She looked at Frank and saw the puzzled expression on his face. Maddie could see that even he, this time, did not quite believe Harriet.

'In that case,' he said slowly, 'you'd better take my arm, Harriet.'

Maddie watched as he held out his crooked arm towards his housekeeper and she, with a sudden smile of satisfaction, put her hand through it.

'Now, are you sure you're all right?'

'Oh yes, Mr Frank. I'm fine. It – just shook me up a little.'

'I want to have another look at those beast in the cattle market and then I think it's time we went home.'

'I'm just popping into that shop over there,' Michael said. 'I shan't be a minute. I'll catch you up.' Whistling, he sauntered across the street, his hands in his pockets, his cap set at a jaunty angle.

Maddie's gaze followed him until she felt Jenny suddenly clutch her arm. 'Look, there's that gypsy from the fair talking to that woman. She's holding her hand and looking at her palm. I bet she's telling her fortune. Oh Maddie, let's have our fortune told.'

'I haven't any money,' Maddie whispered.

'Oh.' The girl's face was crestfallen. 'Neither have I but I thought you would have. Now you're working.'

'Ssh,' Maddie said, 'I don't want . . .'

'What is it, love? What is it you want? Here . . .' Frank was pulling coins from the depths of his pockets.

'No, no, mester. I'm sorry. I didn't mean . . .' Jenny was flustered with embarrassment now.

'I know you didn't, love. I should have thought to give Maddie some spending money before we set out.' He caught hold of Maddie's hand, held it palm upwards and tipped the coins into it.

'Don't you go frittering good money away on such things.' Harriet had overheard the younger girl's suggestion. 'A lot of nonsense. Fortune telling.'

Frank glanced towards the darked-haired woman dressed in colourful gypsy costume.

Michael, rejoining them, asked, 'What's going on?'

Frank turned to his son. 'The girls would like to have their fortune told. Harriet doesn't approve, but I should like to know whether I'm going to become a millionaire.'

Michael laughed and slapped his father on the back. 'No chance, Dad, you'll still be fetching the cows in for milking when you're a hundred.'

But they all moved towards the Romany woman, who smiled a welcome. Only Harriet Trowbridge seemed reluctant, though she still stood with her arm through Frank's, close enough to listen to what was being said but not close enough to be involved. She doesn't want to miss anything, Maddie thought shrewdly.

'You stand by me, Nicholas. I won't have you taking part in such nonsense.'

Scowling, Nick obeyed his mother. So much for rebellion, Maddie thought wryly.

The Romany was much younger than she expected. In Maddie's imagination all gypsies were old and wrinkled, but this one's face was unlined, her black hair as shiny as a raven's feathers and her dark violet eyes were bright and knowing. Her flowing skirt and shawl were patterned with vivid, colourful scrolls and gold bracelets jangled on her wrists.

'Isn't she lovely?' Jenny whispered.

'Yes, yes, she is,' Maddie agreed, admiring the vibrance that was not just in the young woman's clothes but in her eyes too.

'How much for all of us?' Frank asked.

The woman smiled, showing even teeth, brilliantly white against her olive skin. She named a sum and Frank dug deep into his pocket. She took his hand into her own and studied his palm. With long fingers she traced the lines.

'You work hard. On the land?'

Frank nodded and Maddie heard Harriet sniff. 'Should've thought that was obvious to anyone.'

Maddie saw the Romany woman flash a quick, hooded glance at Harriet. 'You have a son . . .'

Harriet's muttering came again. 'That's obvious too, considering he's standing right beside him and looks the spitting image of him.'

'One son,' the gypsy said firmly. 'And she . . .' Now she looked fully at Harriet. 'Is not your wife.' She turned her brilliant smile upon Frank, 'Your housekeeper, maybe?'

'Why, yes. Yes, she is.'

'And that . . .' the gypsy pointed to Nick, 'is her son, but not yours.'

'Yes, yes. That's right.'

'That doesn't take a lot of guess work,' Harriet was scathing now, as if she feared Frank was getting drawn into believing the woman's powers.

Frank ignored his housekeeper. 'Go on, love,' he urged the fortune teller.

'You are a kind man, but that generosity of spirit is going to lead you to make a great sacrifice to save a loved one. Yet that sacrifice will bring you both happiness and sadness, too. A mixed blessing.'

Gently she closed Frank's fingers over his palm and looked deeply into his face. 'You will not see it as a sacrifice,' she said gently.

'Huh,' came Harriet's mutter again. 'Such nonsense.'

The woman turned to Michael. She studied his palm for several moments, until Michael grinned and said casually, 'Go on, tell me I'm going to die young and all the girls for miles around will weep at my grave.'

The gypsy did not smile but looked up to meet his gaze. 'No, you are not going to die the hero. But you are going far away, and though your heart will remain here, you will not return home. Not for many years. Maybe never.'

''Course he's going away,' Harriet said. 'His National Service is coming up next year when he's eighteen.'

Next the Romany turned to Maddie and Jenny and stood looking at them both, from one to the other and back again, before she picked up Maddie's hand.

'You are going to be very successful. Everything you touch will turn to gold. You will have a child . . .' She paused and frowned. 'You will know great love but also deep heartache. Joy and sorrow in equal measure.'

She turned away abruptly, as if not wanting to say more. She took Jenny's hand then and studied it but let it drop and, turning away without even looking into the young girl's face, she said, with almost a sharpness in her tone, 'You are too young. I do not read the palms of children.'

'But I'm only a few months younger than Maddie.' Jenny was disappointed. 'You read hers.'

The gypsy turned once more and regarded them thoughtfully. Quietly, she said, 'There are sometimes things it is better not to say. I'm sorry.'

Now she looked towards Harriet and Nick. She made no attempt to take their hands, to do a proper reading. Instead, she pointed towards them. 'You have great bitterness in your hearts. Both of you – mother and son. It will cause destruction.'

With that, she turned quickly away and walked back towards the fairground.

'Well!' Harriet was indignant. 'If ever there was a waste of good money, Mr Frank, then that was it. I'm surprised at you.'

But Frank was staring after the gypsy, lost in thought.

Back home, Michael insisted on showing Jenny all round the farm. As Maddie began to follow them out of the back door she heard the housekeeper's voice. 'You can help me set the tea, girl. And then you'd better get set into the milking.'

Harriet put her white apron around her waist, twisting the ties to form a bow behind her back with an angry movement. 'All this gallivanting. I don't know,' she muttered. 'And work here not getting done.'

Maddie cast a disappointed look across the yard to see

Michael waving his arms, gesturing towards the barn, the crewyard and the hen-house, whilst Jenny trotted beside him. Sighing, she went into the kitchen to help set the table for tea.

Later, as they were finishing the meal, Jenny said, 'Can I stay and watch you milk the cows?'

Frank glanced at the clock above the mantelpiece. 'Well, I did promise to have you back home before dark, but you've time enough to see the start and then Michael can run you home in the car.'

Jenny's eyes widened. 'Can you drive?'

Michael nodded and his father went on, 'Everyone on a farm ought to be able to drive. Nick can too, but he's not old enough yet to drive on the road.' He glanced towards Harriet and smiled, 'The only person I haven't been able to persuade to get behind the wheel is Mrs Trowbridge.'

'Shall you teach Maddie when she's old enough?'

'Oh yes,' Frank said, and Maddie felt a warm glow, but her growing confidence in belonging somewhere at last was cut short as she heard Harriet's familiar sniff followed by the words, 'That's if she's here that long.'

Eleven

'You go with Michael to take Jenny home,' Frank said, as dusk crept across the fields. 'Nick and I can manage the rest and Ben can take the cows back to the field.'

Maddie straightened up and carefully moved the bucket of milk. 'If you're sure, Mr Frank?' Then she turned towards the boy. 'Thanks, Nick.'

For a moment he looked a little sullen at being left out of the car ride, but then he smiled, perhaps remembering, Maddie thought, her offer to clean out the hen-house so that he could tinker with the car's engine – a kind gesture that had almost resulted in her missing the day out all together. His next words confirmed it.

'We're quits now, then.'

Maddie grinned and nodded and then hurried to change out of her Wellingtons.

In the yard, Jenny was playing with Ben, throwing a stick for the excited young dog to fetch and carry back to her. 'Isn't he lovely, Maddie? I wish there was a dog at the Home.'

'Maybe there'll be a dog where you go to live when you leave there.'

The girl's face sobered. 'I reckon the only job I'll get is at the Home. Peggy, one of the kitchen maids, is leaving to get married. Mrs Potter did say that if she can't fix me up, she'll give me a try.'

'Oh no,' Maddie cried. 'Don't stay there all your life,

Jen. Get out. Do anything rather than stay locked up in that place.'

'I would, but nobody else seems to want me.'

'You'll find something.' Maddie put her arm around the younger girl's thin shoulders and hoped she sounded more convincing than she actually felt. 'I'm sure you will. Why, look at me. Mrs Potter thought nobody would ever take me off her hands.'

Jenny smiled. 'Yes, you've been lucky. They're so kind to you. That Mrs Trowbridge is a bit sharp, but I expect that's just her way.'

Not for the first time in their young lives, Maddie marvelled at Jenny's placid nature, at her acceptance of what life handed her. Despite being abandoned by her mother and not even knowing who she was, despite living under the strict regime of the Home, despite being small, being picked on and teased by the majority of the other girls, little Jenny Wren rarely said an unkind word about anyone. It was as if she thought it was she who was at fault and deserved the treatment she received.

'Don't make excuses for her, Jen. She's a bad tempered old beezum . . .' Jenny giggled as Maddie grinned herself and added, 'But meeting Michael has made up for anything she can throw at me. I can handle her. What was it Brer Rabbit used to say?'

The two girls, who had often sat huddled together to read their favourite stories, now repeated the words together. ' "Born and bred in a briar patch, Brer Fox. Born and bred in a briar patch." '

Jenny was thoughtful. 'I know what you mean, but Mrs Potter does have a nice side to her. I'm not sure that Mrs Trowbridge has. She seems – well – spiteful, somehow.'

Maddie stared at her friend. To most people Jenny

Wren appeared to be childish for her age and weak, but every now and again she surprised even Maddie with her shrewd observations.

'You've hit the nail on the head, Jen. That's just what she is. Spiteful.'

Jen sighed. 'Like some of the girls at the Home. And I've got to go back to them.'

Maddie hugged her. 'Not for much longer. You'll get a job and get out of there. You'll see.'

'Come on then, you two,' Michael was calling. 'It'll be dark soon and I don't want someone waving a big stick at me when I pull up outside the Home.'

The two girls sat in the back of the car, laughing and chattering, the doll between them, but as the car drew nearer and nearer to the Mayfield Home, Jenny fell silent, her face pale, the joy dying in her eyes.

'Oh Maddie,' she said flinging herself against her. 'I've had such a lovely day. I don't want to go back.'

Maddie hugged her. 'Come on, Jen, chin up. It'll not be for long. Look . . .' She picked up the doll and put it into Jenny's arms. 'You take her.'

'Oh no, no, the others'll take her off me.'

'No they won't. Stand up to 'em, if they do.'

'I – I can't. You know I can't.' The whimper was back in the girl's voice.

Maddie grinned. 'Then let me know and I'll come back and sort them out. I won't let anyone take her off you. You keep her to remember the day.'

'Oh I don't need anything to remind me of today,' Jenny breathed and she was smiling again, if a little tremulously. But she hugged the doll to her. 'Thank you, Maddie. I'm going to call her Miss Amelia after that pretty lady we saw in the back of Sir Peter's car today.'

When Michael drew the car to a halt outside the front

door, there was no one in sight. He got out of the car and held open the door for Jenny to clamber out.

'I hope you don't get into trouble. We're a bit later than we should have been.'

'It'll have been worth it even if I do,' Jenny smiled up at him.

As Maddie watched, Michael drew a small parcel from his jacket pocket. 'Here, I'm sorry I couldn't win a doll for you, but I got you this to make up for it a bit.'

Jenny pulled in a breath of surprise. 'For me? Oh thank you, thank you.'

'You don't even know what it is yet. You might not like it.'

'Oh I will. I will like it – whatever it is,' the girl said fervently, clutching the brown paper bag to her chest along with the doll. Then she turned and bent her head to look into the car once more. ''Bye, Maddie.'

''Bye, Jen.' Now, Maddie had to force a smile on to her mouth. 'See you soon.'

As she ran up the steps and reached the top, Jenny turned to wave before disappearing behind the heavy front door.

'Come and sit in the front with me, now,' Michael said as he climbed in behind the wheel.

She did as he suggested but she did not look at him or speak to him. They had travelled about half the distance between the Home and Few Farm when he said, 'What's the matter?'

'Nothing.'

'Yes, there is. Are you sad to see her go back to – that place?'

'Yes.' She was, but it was not the reason she was sitting so silently beside him.

'She'll soon be able to leave, won't she?'

'September.'

'Well then?'

Maddie said nothing.

'It's more than that, isn't it?'

Still she did not reply.

'Ah. I know. You didn't like me giving her a present.'

'Of course I didn't mind that,' she answered quickly. Too quickly.

He took one hand from the steering wheel and reached out to touch her hand, squeezing it for a brief moment. His touch was warm and sent a shiver through her whole being. 'I only gave the poor kid a bottle of shampoo. Like I got for you.'

That was just it, Maddie thought. Like you got for me. She swallowed the lump in her throat and felt angry with herself. How can you be so selfish? she told herself sternly. And over poor little Jen too.

'That was kind of you,' she said and hoped he didn't notice the tremble in her voice. 'She'll love it – as long as the other girls don't take it off her.'

'Oh. I never thought of that. Will they really do that? Does that sort of thing happen a lot when you live in – in a Home?'

'Yes, but mostly only to someone like Jen. It never happened to me.'

Now Michael threw back his head and laughed aloud. 'I bet it didn't.'

As they pulled into the yard at Few Farm, even Maddie was smiling again.

Just before supper, Maddie thanked Frank for the day.

'You're very welcome, love.' He smiled gently. 'I don't think your little friend wanted to go home.'

'She didn't. She – she . . .' Maddie hesitated, for once in her life not wanting to appear pushy. 'She said she wished she could stay here for ever.'

Frank's eyes clouded. 'She was a nice little thing,' he murmured, 'but we haven't the work for another lass. And she's even smaller than you.' Now his eyes twinkled with merriment. 'I must admit, Maddie, that when you first came, I didn't think you'd be up to the work. But you have proved me wrong, lass. And, for once,' he added comically, 'I am pleased to have been wrong.' He shook his head. 'But yon little lass, well . . .' He paused leaving the unspoken words hanging between them.

Now Maddie had to be honest, but there was a note of disappointment in her voice that the man could not miss. 'No, she wouldn't be strong enough, Mr Frank.'

'Well, you invite her to come here to visit whenever you've time off, love. She'll always be welcome.'

Maddie's eyes shone. 'Oh thank you, Mr Frank. Thank you.'

At that moment Harriet's shrill tones came from the kitchen. 'Where are you, girl? I need a hand.'

Maddie grinned at her employer and turned away to help lay the table for supper.

'Reckon you two smell it,' Maddie said when Michael and Nick appeared as the last dish was placed on the table.

''Course we do.' Michael leant over the table and sniffed appreciatively. 'Rabbit pie. My favourite. And that pastry looks a treat, Mrs T. There's nobody can make pastry like Mrs T.' Michael nodded towards Maddie. 'You'll have to get her to teach you how to make it.'

Maddie watched as Frank at the head of the table served the pie, cutting through the flaky pastry with a sharp knife. Then with a spoon he lifted out the portions of pinkish-brown meat and the rich, tasty gravy.

'Leg all right for you, Maddie?'

She blinked. 'I – er – I've never eaten rabbit before, Mr Frank.'

'Ah. Then I'll give you a tiny piece to try and if you like it, you can have another helping.'

The plates were passed down the table for Harriet to put the potatoes on. Trying to blot out the vision of the cute fluffy little animal that the meat on her plate had once been, Maddie put a piece in her mouth. To her surprise it was sweet-tasting and different from anything she had tried before.

'Do you like it?' Michael asked and when Maddie nodded he reached across, lifted her plate and held it out towards his father. 'Give her a bit more now, Dad.'

For a while, there was a silence around the table whilst they all ate. Then, thinking she might learn more by feigning ignorance, Maddie said, 'Who was the lady in the back of Sir Peter's car? Miss Amelia, did you say her name was?'

Four pairs of eyes regarded her, but no one spoke.

Frank glanced away, down at his plate again and said nothing.

'Mr Theo was sitting in the front with Sir Peter,' Michael said. 'I did see that, but I didn't notice anyone else.' He turned to Maddie. 'Mr Theo's his son, but I expect you know that.'

Maddie nodded. 'There was a lady sitting in the back. A pretty lady,' she went on. 'With long blonde hair and . . .'

'It was her, wasn't it?' Harriet's voice was harsh and she was staring down the table at Frank.

'Aye. It was,' Frank, though reluctant, was obliged to agree. 'It's many a long year since she was seen in the town.'

'But who is she?' Maddie persisted.

Down the table, Frank and Harriet looked at each other for what seemed to Maddie, waiting impatiently for an answer to her question, an age.

'The lady was Sir Peter's daughter,' Frank murmured, but his gaze was still on Harriet's face. 'Miss Amelia May-field.'

Harriet sniffed. 'I'm surprised at him. Bringing her out in public.'

Frank sighed. 'Oh Harriet. It was all a long time ago now. The poor girl can't be locked away for ever.'

'I thought she'd gone a bit . . .' Harriet tapped her temple with her forefinger.

'Who could blame her if she had?' Frank murmured.

'Well, she brought it on herself, didn't she?'

'I suppose so, but . . .'

'Is she the one who planted the flowers in the woods?' Maddie began. 'Is she the one whose sweetheart . . .?'

Harriet reached out across the corner of the table and gripped Maddie's wrist so tightly that the girl cried out in pain. 'Get on with your supper, girl, and speak when you're spoken to and not afore.'

Maddie couldn't sleep. The events of the day were buzzing around her brain. She was reliving the excitement of it all. The bustle of the market place, the strange and yet exciting atmosphere in the pub and then, the touch of Michael's hand on hers in the darkness of the car.

Her heart thumped loudly at the memory and every nerve twitched and jumped so that sleep seemed impossible. But as tiredness eventually overcame her and she drifted into sleep, Maddie's dreams were disturbed by the memory of that sweet, sorrowful face looking back at her from the window of the car. Then the image became distorted and Miss Amelia's face became Jenny standing at the top of the steps at the Home, clutching the doll and Michael's gift, tears running down her face as she waved goodbye.

Twelve

'If you're going to be late up just because you've had a day out, then I'll mind you don't have another.'

'I'm sorry, Mrs Trowbridge. I couldn't get off to sleep.'

'Too much excitement. Well, get on then, girl, now you are up.'

Maddie raced to the field and up the slope to round up the cows. This morning the bulb field, bereft of all its magnificent colour, did not distress her so since she had seen for herself the previous day that people were able to buy at least some of the pretty flowers to take home. She had stood in front of the colourful stall in the market marvelling at the vibrant colours, red, yellow, pink and purple, and although she could understand now the necessity for their removal – it was a matter of business – she still thought it a shame that some way could not be found to make use of the discarded flower heads that she could see heaped in the corner of the field.

This morning she watched the workers in the tulip field, wishing, for a moment, that she was one of them instead of having to milk smelly cows twice a day.

'There you are,' was Frank's greeting as she herded the cows into the yard. 'Overslept a bit, did we?'

'Sorry,' she began, but he held up his hand. 'No matter, love, we're only just ready for these anyway. You take the ones we've milked back to the other field and we'll see to these few.'

Prompted by his words, Maddie said, 'Why's it called Few Farm?'

'Eh? Oh that.' Frank chuckled. 'Someone with a sense of humour, I suppose. Way back. Afore we ever came here.'

Michael, shooing the beast from the cowshed and into the yard joined in. 'A few acres, Maddie. A few cows, a few pigs and a few hens. And . . .' he added pointedly, glancing at his father with a cheeky look. 'Far too few workers to cope with all the work.'

Maddie laughed aloud, the sound ringing through the sharp morning air. 'Come on then, Daisy,' she slapped the rump of the nearest cow. 'I'll take you a few yards down the lane back to your field.'

Maddie felt a surge of happiness run through her. She loved it here. Already she loved Mr Frank and Michael. Her heart beat a little faster. Well, every time she even thought about Michael she got a strange trembly feeling in her legs and when she saw him, there was a funny sort of fluttering just below her ribs.

If only, she thought, Mrs Trowbridge and Nick were a little more friendly, life would be just perfect. Although, she had to admit, that once away from his mother, Nick was so much nicer.

The following Saturday morning, Michael said, 'Would you like to ask your little friend to come to tea this afternoon?'

'Oh yes, please,' Maddie said, but then her face clouded. 'Would Mrs Trowbridge mind?'

'Not if I ask her,' he said, grinning, and Maddie giggled. Michael had even the strait-laced Mrs T wrapped around his little finger.

'But how can I let Jenny know? It's too late to post a letter to her.'

'Ring her up.'

'Ring her. On a telephone you mean?'

'Well, we haven't got bush-telegraph, young'un. There's a phone box in the village. Come with me on the round this morning and we can ring her from there.'

Perched up on the front of the milk cart beside him, Maddie smiled up at him.

'I can't believe Mrs Trowbridge has let me come with you. Whatever did you say to her and how did you get Nick to do the dairy work?'

Michael winked at her and tapped the side of his nose. 'I have my methods, young'un.'

He paused and as she was still looking up at him expectantly, he said, 'I just reminded him about the day of the hen-house and how you had taken all the blame upon yourself.'

'Oh.'

'Oh, indeed.' His voice was grim now, though still gentle towards her. 'Are you used to taking the blame for what others do?'

Before she answered, Maddie thought back. It was not so very long ago and yet it seemed an age away. Slowly, she said, 'Yes, I suppose I did sometimes.' She smiled, remembering. 'Usually for Jen. Always for Jen. But I would never tell tales, see. Not about anyone. So I sometimes took the blame for others too.'

'I thought as much,' Michael muttered and then added firmly, 'Well, in our house, you need never take the blame if it isn't your fault. You hear me?'

A warm glow spread through her and there was a catch in her voice as she said, 'Yes, Michael. I hear you.'

They drove for a while without speaking but the silence

between them was comfortable, although Maddie was acutely aware of his arm brushing hers every now and again.

At last Michael said, 'First call is Mayfield Hall.'

Maddie glanced sideways at him. 'Shall we see her?'

'Who?'

'The pretty lady we saw in the back of the car yesterday. In Wellandown.'

'Oh. Miss Amelia. Shouldn't think so. I've been coming here for three years now – more if you count all the times I helped me Dad out even when I was still at school – and that's the first time I've ever set eyes on her.'

'Really?'

Michael nodded and his face was solemn as he added, 'Kept hidden away, she is, poor thing. She's . . .' he hesitated and stumbled over the words. 'Well, I don't quite know how to put it without sounding unkind.'

Maddie remembered Mrs Trowbridge's action the previous night when talking about Miss Amelia. She had no intention of repeating the housekeeper's unfeeling gesture, so she murmured, 'I know what you mean.' There was a pause before Maddie said, 'Perhaps she's getting better. Perhaps that's why she had a ride out in the car yesterday.'

'Maybe. I rather think,' Michael said slowly, 'that Mr Theo might have had something to do with that. He's a nice chap, Mr Theo. Now, I do meet him sometimes when I come to the Hall. He goes riding early most mornings and because we have to go round to the back door, I often see him going to the stables. Mind you, he's away a lot. At university, I think. Doing a law degree, somebody said.' Michael grinned down at her, his eyes twinkling. 'He's a very handsome chap. I shall have to keep my eye on you, else he might be running off with you, young'un.'

He was teasing her, she knew he was teasing her, but it

was a nice kind of affectionate teasing. What she couldn't say to him was that however handsome Mr Theo Mayfield might be, he didn't stand a chance with her. Not whilst Michael Brackenbury was around.

But as they drove up the long driveway and round to the back of the imposing house with its arched windows that always reminded Maddie of the windows in a church, they saw no one except the kitchen maid who answered the door to take in the milk.

Leaving Mayfield Park, they reached the outskirts of the village and Michael pulled the cart to a halt outside the first house and said, 'You run to the door and get Grannie Barnes's can.'

Not sure exactly what he meant, Maddie skipped up the uneven flagged path. As she raised her hand to knock at the door, it opened and a wizened old woman appeared. Her toothless mouth sank in and her white hair was drawn back from her face, but the brown eyes were sharp and knowing.

'So you're the little lass young Michael's been telling us about, are you?' She thrust a white enamel milk can towards Maddie. 'Well, let's see if you can fetch me milk without spillin' it, eh?'

Dutifully, Maddie trotted back to the cart, waited whilst Michael filled the can and then carried it carefully back to the old woman.

Taking it from her, she put the coins into the girl's hand, nodded and taking a step back, said, 'Ta, see you again.'

Maddie smiled. 'Thank you, Mrs Barnes. Good morning.'

After half a dozen such stops, Michael said, 'D'you know, I could do with you coming on the round every day. We're getting done in half the time.'

Maddie beamed, feeling again the fluttering beneath her ribs.

At the phone box, Michael showed her how to make the call.

'I think you'd better do it. Mrs Potter won't believe me.' She pulled a wry face, remembering the hen-house again and Harriet. 'Nobody ever seems to believe me.'

For a moment, squashed together in the red phone box, Michael looked down into her face. Softly, he said, 'I'll always believe you, Maddie.' It was the first time she could remember him using her name instead of his nickname for her. 'I don't reckon you could tell a lie if you tried.'

She felt hot all over and suddenly tongue-tied. He was so close that she could feel his breath warm upon her face, smell the earthiness of him, see that the dark eyelashes fringing his brown eyes curled slightly. His skin was smooth and weather-beaten and there was a faint growth of dark stubble on his jaw. His black hair was covered with a checked cap, but tendrils escaped from beneath it and curled into his neck.

'Right,' he said, breaking the spell that had enveloped them both for a moment. He picked up the receiver and whispered, 'D'you reckon I can sound like me Dad?'

The tension broken, Maddie giggled. 'You look like him, so maybe you can.'

Moments later after dialling, feeding coins into the slot and pressing button A, Michael said, 'May I speak to the matron please?'

'Mrs Potter,' Maddie hissed.

There was a long wait and Maddie heard the pips and watched Michael frantically feed in another coin.

'Ah, yes. Hello, Mrs Potter. This is Mr Brackenbury of Few Farm . . .' Maddie stuffed her hand into her mouth to stifle her laughter. How neatly Michael was avoiding telling a deliberate lie.

'We so enjoyed having Jenny Wren with us last week, we would like to invite her to tea this afternoon.'

There was a pause, then Michael said, 'Right . . . Yes . . . Yes . . . That will be fine. Three o'clock, then. Thank you. Goodbye.'

He replaced the receiver in its cradle and Maddie clutched at his arm. 'What did she say? Is it all right? Can she come?'

''Course she can. We're to fetch her at three o'clock.'

'Oh.' Maddie's face fell. 'But have you asked your dad? I mean, will he let you drive the car again?'

'Probably not. We haven't a lot of petrol to spare, but we'll fetch her, Maddie. You and me. In the cart.'

Excitement surged, yet she dare not be too hopeful even yet. 'And – and what about taking her back?' Michael usually went out with his mates on a Saturday night.

Michael shrugged. 'Either Dad or I'll take her.'

And now Maddie's pleasure knew no bounds. Michael was going to stay at home all afternoon and maybe the evening too. He couldn't be planning to go out or else he wouldn't be offering to take Jenny back to the Home later.

Would he?

Thirteen

The four young people stood in the yard at Few Farm.

'So,' Michael began. 'What are we going to do?'

Nick scuffed the ground with the toe of his boot, hands thrust deep into his trouser pockets. 'What is there to do?'

'Well, we can go into the village to the pub later . . .'

'They're too young,' Nick countered and, glancing at Jenny, added, 'and they look it.'

'We could go into town.'

'I've no money. Have you?'

'A bit,' Michael said, but then looked around at the other three as if to say, but not for all of us.

'Looks like a walk then,' Maddie said cheerfully. 'Let's show Jen all the animals and . . .'

'Huh, I spend all day with them. I aren't spending me time off with them,' Nick muttered.

'What do you want to do then?'

He shrugged. 'I don't know.'

'We'll go for a walk in the woods. How about that?' Michael suggested.

Maddie brightened. 'Oh yes.'

There was a sly, devious look on Nick's face as he said, 'We'll show you the Hanging Tree.'

Jenny gasped in alarm. 'Oh no, Maddie, I don't want to go there. I don't like it. It's – it's creepy.'

Maddie tucked her arm through her friend's. 'It's all right. There's nothing can hurt you.' She was intrigued.

Now she had glimpsed Amelia Mayfield, the girl over whom a young man had killed himself, she wanted to visit the tree again. To think that he had died for love touched Maddie's heart. Maybe Amelia had been the one to plant all the golden tulips and forget-me-nots in his memory. 'We'll see if those pretty flowers are still there.'

'Maybe Jenny's right to be frightened,' Nick's voice dropped a tone, like a storyteller telling ghostly tales around the fire at night. 'It's an evil place. It's a crime to take your own life, y'know. Maybe he still haunts the clearing . . .'

'Stop trying to frighten them, Nick,' Michael said. 'And you should feel sorry for the poor chap who was desperate enough to do that. And poor Miss Amelia. She's never been right since. Her father keeps her a virtual prisoner in that great house of his. How would you like that, eh?'

Nick glared at him resentfully. 'I know how she feels,' he muttered.

'Don't talk daft. It's up to you to cut loose from your mother's apron strings. Come on, Maddie. You and me'll go. These two can do what they like.'

They walked through the village and out towards the woods on the edge of Mayfield Park, Michael and Maddie forging eagerly ahead, Nick following slouching along, hands thrust deep into his pockets and scuffing stones on the road with the toe of his boot. Some distance behind them all, Jenny hung back reluctantly.

Beneath the shadowy trees, Michael and Maddie walked close together.

'I love it here,' he said softly. 'It's so quiet and peaceful.'

Maddie lifted her face up, closed her eyes for a second and breathed in deeply, savouring the musty smells of dead and rotting leaves mingling with the scent of the new growth of blooms. 'So do I.'

She felt Michael take her hand and they walked on, Maddie's heart beating faster, until they came to the clearing.

'Oh, they're still here. No one's picked them,' Maddie said, delighted to see the heart-shaped bed of yellow tulips. But the pretty blooms were dying now, drooping forlornly, lonely and neglected.

'I suppose only Miss Amelia would pick them.'

'Did she plant them?' Maddie asked.

Michael shrugged. 'No one knows for certain, but that's what everybody thinks.'

Nick came to stand beside them.

'Where's Jen? You haven't left her alone? She'll be frightened,' Maddie asked.

Nick glanced over his shoulder. 'She's coming.' His smile was sly. 'She dun't like it here, does she? I wonder why?'

'She's sensitive,' Maddie stuck up for her friend. 'She feels things. She's easily frightened.'

'I'll go and look for her then,' Nick said and turned back to disappear amongst the trees the way they had come.

'Thanks,' Maddie called after him, grateful for his offer so that she could stay with Michael.

He released her hand and put his arm about her shoulders, pulling her closer, holding her against him. 'I'm glad you've come to live with us, Maddie,' he murmured against her hair and she felt the familiar churning just below her ribs.

'Oh Michael . . .' She turned towards him and lifted her face to look up at him. In the dimness of the wood, she could hardly see his features but she could feel his breath warm on her face. He was bending towards her, his mouth coming towards her own.

98

Suddenly, there was a shriek of terror and Jenny thrust her way through the bushes, her hair awry, her dress torn, tears running down her face.

'He's here. The man who 'anged hissen.' She flung herself forward against Maddie, wrapping her arms around the older girl and clinging to her.

'It's all right. It's all right,' Maddie soothed her at once and then more firmly said, 'Now, don't be silly. There's no such things as ghosts . . .'

At that moment the breeze rustled through the leaves overhead and an eerie wailing sound seemed to come from the tree.

Jenny screamed again and buried her face against Maddie.

Angrily, Michael said, 'That's no ghost. That's human and I know who it is.'

He ran across the clearing, skirting the bed of tulips and disappeared behind the tree.

'Michael . . .' Maddie called, suddenly afraid herself. What had seemed such a peaceful, even if poignant, place had now become fearful and threatening.

They heard a scuffling in the undergrowth, saw a bush shake and then from behind the Hanging Tree itself, Michael appeared dragging a wriggling Nick by the scruff of his neck.

'This is your ghost, Jen. Just Nick playing cruel tricks. Now, say you're sorry for frightening her.' He gave the younger boy a little shake. 'Go on.'

'I'm sorry, Jenny. I was only having a bit of fun.'

Jenny lifted her face from Maddie's shoulder to look at him. 'It's all right.' She scrubbed away her tears. 'I shouldn't be such a scaredy cat.'

'Come on,' Maddie said. 'We'll go back now.'

To her surprise as they all turned to leave the clearing

and make their way back through the woods, she saw Jenny fall into step beside Nick, glancing up at him with a shy smile.

'Just look at that,' she said to Michael. 'Would you believe it after what he's just done?'

Michael laughed. 'There's no accounting for taste.'

Fourteen

'I've told you never to go near that place,' Harriet Trowbridge raged at her son.

'Don't tell of him, Maddie,' Jenny had pleaded as they entered the farmyard. 'He didn't mean it. He was only playing. It was my fault for being so silly.'

But there was no way they could hide Jenny's torn dress nor the steak of tears on her face and Harriet missed nothing. 'Whatever is Mrs Potter going to say if you go back to the Home in that state?' She sniffed. 'I don't think you'd better come here again if you can't behave yourself, child.'

Jenny's chin quivered with disappointment.

'We were just playing, Mrs Trowbridge,' Maddie was anxious as ever not to tell lies, but not wanting to tell tales on Nick either. She doubted the housekeeper would believe anything said against her precious son anyway. 'And Jenny caught her dress on a prickly bush.'

'You shouldn't be going into the woods anyway. Don't you know better than to go into places like that and with two young lads? No better than you should be.' Her glance went between the two girls. 'But then I suppose it's to be expected. Bad blood in the pair of you.'

'Aw, come on Mrs T,' Michael smiled engagingly and put his arm about the woman's shoulders. 'Don't be so hard on them. They'll come to no harm with us. You trust us, don't you?'

Harriet glanced sideways at him. 'Now, none of your smooth talk with me, young Michael. You might charm all the young lassies, but not me. As for trusting you, well, my Nicholas, certainly. But as for you . . .'

To Maddie's amazement the woman actually smiled as she tapped Michael playfully on the end of his nose. 'I wouldn't trust you no further than I could throw you.'

'Aw, Mrs T, I'm wounded. How can you say such a thing about me?'

'Go on with you. You'd better get this child tidied up and take her home.'

Mrs Potter was even more direct. 'That's the last time I let you out on a visit, miss. Just look at you.' She thrust her face close to Jenny's whilst both Maddie and Michael looked on helplessly. 'I hope you haven't been doing anything you shouldn't have.' Then she glanced up at Maddie. 'I might have known you'd have been behind all this. Well, Maddie March, you've seen the last of your little friend while she's in my care, let me tell you.'

'Mrs Potter . . .' Michael began, but the Matron held up her hand. 'Don't you start, neither. I've had enough of this pair to last me a lifetime. I thought I'd got shot of you . . .' she jabbed her finger towards Maddie. 'But you're still bringing trouble to me door. And as for you, young feller, you want to watch her. She's a bad'un.'

As the heavy door closed behind them and they climbed back into the cart, Michael let out a sigh of relief. 'What a dragon! How on earth did you stick living there?'

Settling herself beside him, Maddie said in a small voice, 'We've no choice, have we?'

On the drive home they were both silent. Maddie was saddened to think she would not see Jenny again for several months, probably not until she was fourteen and Mrs Potter had found someone to take her. She doubted Mrs Potter would even deliver letters to Jenny if Maddie wrote to her.

Once or twice she glanced sideways at Michael who seemed lost in his own thoughts, his mouth pursed in a hard line.

As he manoeuvred the cart in through the yard gate, he put his arm briefly around her shoulders and gave her a quick squeeze. 'Don't worry, young'un, this is your home now. We'll look after you. But I am sorry about poor little Jenny.'

Tears prickled Maddie's eyes and she felt a lump in her throat at his kindness. Trying to smile she said, 'We'll just have to wait until September. That's all.'

'Oh well,' Michael said cheerfully. 'That's not long.'

Maddie said nothing but she was thinking it's an awful long time if you're living in the Mayfield Orphanage under Mrs Potter's rule.

'Why did you give Jenny that doll? She told me you'd given it to her. I got it for you. You'd no right.' Nick's expression was a mixture of hurt and anger.

Swiftly Maddie said, 'I'm sorry, Nick. But that night when we took her back to the Home, she looked so lost and lonely and I felt so lucky being able to live here with all of you. I just – well, I . . .'

She fell silent but Nick was making no effort to understand her generous gesture. Instead, he said again morosely, 'It was for you. I wanted you to have it. I thought you liked it.'

'I did. I do, but Jen's like my little sister and I – I thought you'd understand and not mind. I am sorry, Nick.'

He was unforgiving. As he turned away, he flung the words back at her over his shoulder. 'I bet you wouldn't have parted with the doll if Michael had given it to you.'

Maddie opened her mouth to say, Of course I would, but the words were not spoken for even as they came automatically to her lips, she knew them to be untrue. And even to save Nick's feelings, Maddie could not lie.

He was right. Had Michael won the lovely doll for her she would not have given it away to anyone. Not even to little Jenny Wren.

Towards the end of August, Michael asked her, 'Would you like to come to the village hop with me on Saturday night?'

Over the past few weeks Maddie had felt that she and Michael were getting closer and closer. He would touch her hand, wink at her as he passed her in the yard and touch her foot with his own toe beneath the table at mealtimes.

And now he was asking her out. Properly.

Thinking of the pretty summer dress hanging in her wardrobe that Harriet had grudgingly bought for her on Frank's instructions, Maddie beamed and, a little breathlessly, said, 'I'd love to. Thanks.' Then her face sobered. 'But I can't dance.'

'No problem.' Nothing ever seemed a problem to Michael. 'Place gets so crowded, you can't dance the proper steps anyway. I tell you what, though,' he added as a sudden thought struck him. 'We'll get the gramophone going in the front room. I've got some Glen Miller records and I'll show you a few dance steps before we go. Besides,' he added with a mock leer and moved closer to her, 'it'll be a good excuse to hold you close.'

He put his arm about her waist and began to hum softly.

Nick's shadow appeared in the cow-house doorway. 'Your dad's waiting for you by the tractor to help him cut Five Acre Field.'

Michael pulled a comical face and whispered, 'Trust him to spoil our fun.' Louder he said, 'Right then. I'll see you later, young'un, for your first dancing lesson.'

As he left the crewyard, whistling, Nick sidled closer. 'You don't want to take any notice of him, y'know. He's got a string of girls in the village.'

Maddie faced him. She didn't want to fall out with Nick. It was bad enough having his mother forever sniping at her and finding every little fault with her whenever she could. She didn't need another enemy, but nor was she going to let him get away with trying to spoil everything.

'Michael's asked me to the village dance on Saturday night.'

'Huh!' Nick's voice was scathing. 'Well, he might take you, but once you're there you'll find yourself trampled in the rush. The girls are potty over him.'

'You jealous?' The question was out of her mouth before she could stop it.

Nick's mouth curled. 'Of him? Nah, not likely. He's heading for a fall, that one. Me Mam says he'll bring trouble to us all. She doesn't believe in all that nonsense, you know, that fortune telling at the fair a while back, but she did say she thought the gypsy had got it right about Michael.'

Maddie stared at him. 'Maybe,' she said thoughtfully, remembering what the dark-eyed Romany woman had said about them all and about Nick and his mother in particular. 'Maybe she got a lot more things right than we know.'

'Oh aye. You reckon you're going to end up a millionaire then, do you? Everything you touch will turn to gold. Is that it?'

Maddie turned away. 'I've work to do in the Dairy. I'd better get on with it. The only thing I'm going to turn into gold is the cream into butter.'

Suddenly, Nick smiled and Maddie noticed how swiftly he swung from one mood to another. He was so much nicer when he smiled and his pale grey eyes, huge behind his glasses, wrinkled with laughter. 'Well, if you look at it that way, I suppose she could have been right.'

Now Maddie laughed. 'It's the only way to look at it. I can't imagine me, a waif and stray with no real family and no proper name, ever coming into a fortune of real gold, now can you?'

The promised dancing lesson did not happen that night.

The tractor, old and temperamental, took twice as long to cut the corn in Five Acre Field.

'I reckon that tractor's about had its day. I'll have to think about getting another before harvest next year,' Frank said when he and Michael returned home after ten in the evening, looking exhausted.

When Harriet decreed, 'Supper and bed for the pair of you,' neither of them had the strength left to argue.

As he passed Maddie's chair on his way upstairs, Michael put his hand on her shoulder. 'I'm sorry, young'un. Maybe tomorrow night, eh?'

But the next night was the same; too late and too tired.

'I told you so,' Nick said. 'Makes all sorts of promises he's no intention of keeping.'

Maddie shot Nick a vitriolic glance, but said nothing.

On Friday night, Michael came into the kitchen where

Maddie was standing at the sink washing up the supper dishes.

'Come into the front room when you've finished. We'd better have that dancing lesson.'

Maddie hurried through the rest of her work and was soon scurrying through to the front room.

'Are we allowed in here?' she asked peering round the door. 'Mrs Trowbridge is looking daggers already.'

Michael had pushed back the huge leather settee and the armchairs from the centre of the room.

'Never mind Mrs T.' He wound up the gramophone and placed a record on the turntable. 'What are you standing there for? Come on in.' He paused whilst he bent over the gramophone, lifted up the head and gently placed the needle on the edge of the record. As the strains of 'In the Mood' filled the room, Michael straightened up and held out his arms to her. Maddie moved towards him and felt his arm go around her waist and his left hand take hold of her right. Her legs felt weak with love for him.

Though holding her, he stood a little apart from her, teaching her the steps. Their heads were close together as they both looked down at their feet.

'Don't worry too much,' he told her. 'Just get the feel of the music. The rhythm. Like this, see?' He swayed in time to the beat of the music and, watching his feet, Maddie copied him.

'That's great!' he said. 'I reckon you're a natural.'

They heard the door open and glanced up to see Nick watching them, hands thrust deep into his pockets as usual.

'Want to join the dancing class?' Michael shouted above the music.

For a moment there was a look of longing on the younger boy's face, rather like a child outside a sweet-shop

107

window with his nose pressed to the pane but with no money in his pocket to buy anything. 'Mam ses it's time Maddie was in bed.'

The music slowed to a growl as the gramophone wound down and Michael let go of Maddie and hurried across to turn the handle vigorously.

'Go on.' Looking at Nick, Michael nodded his head towards Maddie. 'You two have a dance. You can come with us tomorrow night, Nick, if you like.'

Maddie opened her mouth to say, Oh no, I just want it to be the two of us, Michael, when she saw the pleasure leap into Nick's eyes. Suddenly, she felt an affinity with the boy. She knew what it was to be the odd one out. The one outside always looking in. Mistakenly, she had thought he couldn't possibly be lonely, not living here. He was part of a family; he had a proper home. But now she saw that with a joyless mother, living in a house that was not theirs and with the handsome, ever-cheerful Michael who was like a brother, but not a brother, Nick was perhaps even more lost and lonely than she had been. At least she had always known exactly what she was. He was like a piece of a jigsaw puzzle that belonged to the picture, but somehow just didn't quite fit.

So Maddie smiled and beckoned him towards the middle of the room. 'Come on, then. If we dance, Michael can watch and tell us what we're doing wrong.'

Half an hour later, the three of them were helpless with laughter, dancing round in a circle, their arms entwined across each other's shoulders like Russian dancers. They didn't hear the door open again until Harriet's strident voice made them all jump and spring guiltily apart.

'Nicholas! What on earth do you think you are doing? Get to bed at once. And as for you, girl, you can pack your bags and leave. Right now.'

Maddie blanched at the threat, but stood her ground. 'You can't sack me. Only Mr Frank can do that.'

The woman stepped closer to her. 'I hired you. I can fire you.'

Maddie bit her lip. The first bit was true, so maybe she could.

'Now, now, Mrs T,' Michael began, moving towards her and attempting to put his arm around the house-keeper's shoulders. But she shrugged him off.

'Don't you "Mrs T" me. You and your flannel. You might think you can charm all the village girls and this one here too. But it dun't work on me.'

'But I take the blame, Mrs T. It was all my fault. I'm taking Maddie to the dance tomorrow night and she can't . . .'

'Oh no, you're not. You're most certainly not.'

Michael sighed and glanced towards Maddie. 'You'd better go to bed, young'un. We'll talk about it in the morning.'

'In the morning,' Harriet declared as she turned and marched out of the room, 'she'll be gone.'

Fifteen

Maddie hardly slept. She was torn between memories of being in Michael's arms and the final threat from Mrs Trowbridge hanging over her.

Could Michael really like her? she asked the darkness. She knew she had changed since she had first come to Few Farm. Good food and fresh air had made her grow and fill out in all the right places. Lying in her narrow bed, she ran her hands down her body, feeling the soft mound of her breasts, the tautness of her stomach and the growing pubic hair. She wished it were Michael's hands caressing her and at the mere thought a thrill of excitement gripped her, tingled in her groin.

She gave a groan as she turned on her side and squeezed her eyes tightly shut. By the morning, she might well be gone from the farm. Maybe she would never see Michael again.

'She's going nowhere, Harriet. And if you'll take my advice, you'll let the three of them go to the village dance tonight. What harm can it do, for Heaven's sake? They're young. They all work hard. These two lads – aye, your Nick as well – do men's work. At the end of the week, they deserve a bit of fun. And the lass does too. Heaven knows, she must have had precious little of it in her life so far.'

The quarrel was going on right in front of her as Maddie stood waiting for her fate to be decided. There was no escape. She couldn't turn and leave the room. She was forced to stand there, listening to it all. And yet they seemed to have forgotten her presence.

'Fun? Fun, you say? Life's not meant to be fun. When have I ever had any fun?'

'Harriet,' Frank's tone was softer, 'you must have been in love once. When you married . . .'

Harriet's face was purple and to Maddie's horror, she actually shook her fist in Frank's face. 'Don't you even speak his name in my hearing. Not after what he did to me.'

'My dear, you're letting the bitterness eat you up. And it's destroying Nick's life too. You can't keep him locked up here with you for ever.'

'He's got *his* blood in his veins. Bad blood. I've got to save him from himself.'

'He's a boy. Just a boy. Let him go with them tonight, eh?'

Harriet turned away. 'You do what you like with your own son, Mr Frank, and with the girl. I wash my hands of her. If she brings trouble to your door, don't look to me for help. As for Nicholas, he's my son and he'll do as I say.'

She marched from the room and they heard her banging pans onto the stove in the kitchen. Frank turned to Maddie. 'Run along, lass, and help with the milking. I'll be out in a minute.'

'Yes, Mr Frank.' She turned and scuttled through the kitchen and the wash-house and out of the back door. She was not to be sent away. She could stay here – with Michael. But her relationship with Mrs Trowbridge was getting worse by the minute.

She was subdued the rest of the day, concentrating on

111

not doing anything silly, working hard and anxious not to make any mistakes.

It was strange now, she thought, trying to understand her own feelings. She had never cared before about trying to please anyone. At the Home, she had invariably been in bother and had, quite justly her honest nature reminded her, deserved the title of troublemaker. Whatever dire punishment had been threatened and usually inflicted upon her had never deterred her. Madeleine March had gone her own way to the despair of Mrs Potter and the admiration of her peers.

But now she felt vulnerable. Now she didn't want to be sent away from Few Farm in disgrace. She wanted to stay here, close to Michael, and it was her feelings for him, she realized, that made her defenceless. Loving someone made you weak, she thought. Perhaps that was what it was like to be part of a family. You behaved yourself because you didn't want to hurt or upset those you loved. You didn't want to give them cause to be angry with you because you would then be hurt in turn by their anger.

Maddie sighed. It was all very complicated. Having feelings made life complicated. It had been much easier at the Home where no one had cared for her and she hadn't cared for anyone, she thought. Except little Jenny, of course.

Less complicated it might have been, she thought, as she caught sight of Michael drawing the milk cart into the yard, but she wouldn't go back to the Home in a million years. And as he saw her, waved, jumped down from the cart and came towards her with long, loping strides, her heart gave a lurch.

Not even for a million pounds, would she go back.

*

112

'If I had my way, girl, you'd be back to that orphanage before your feet could touch the ground.'

For one unguarded moment, Maddie was rash enough to answer back. 'Well, it ain't up to you, is it? Mr Frank's the boss around here. Not you.'

'Why you . . .'

They were standing in the bathroom, open to the landing, where Maddie had been washing her hair in the washbasin there in readiness for her night out with Michael. Now she stood, rubbing it dry with a towel. Soon, the soft shining blonde hair framed her face and her blue eyes met Harriet's resentful expression squarely.

The woman was staring at her and now it was not with rage, but something else. Some sort of emotion that Maddie could not put a name to.

'What's the matter?' Maddie asked.

The woman jumped, startled out of her own reverie. 'Eh? What? Oh – er . . .' Then she seemed to recover herself and she stepped closer and thrust her face close to Maddie's. 'Bad blood. You've bad blood in you, girl, that's what. I can see it in you by just looking at you.'

She turned away and Maddie heard the door of the housekeeper's bedroom slam.

Maddie blinked and shook her head. 'Funny woman,' she muttered. 'Seems obsessed with "bad blood" in everybody.' She had even said it of her own son.

Suddenly, for all his moody ways, Maddie felt acutely sorry for young Nick Trowbridge.

They heard the music and laughter from the village hall even before they reached it. Maddie clung to Michael's arm, suddenly unaccountably nervous.

'I don't know if I dare go in.'

113

Michael strained to see her through the darkness. 'Not scared, young'un, are you? Not you, surely?'

'Well, I am a bit. You won't leave me and go off with other girls, will you? I expect there'll be some here who knew me at school.' She pulled a wry face. 'The village girls never liked us. Some of their parents didn't like them mixing with the likes of us from the Home.'

Michael's face was a study. 'You're kidding me.'

Maddie pursed her mouth. 'I only wish I was.'

'Well then,' he tucked her hand firmly into his arm, 'tonight, we'll show 'em. You just stick with me.'

To Maddie's surprise, he was as good as his word, he did not leave her for a moment the whole evening. In the lull between the dancing he paraded her around the room as if showing her off to everyone and Maddie was secretly thrilled when more than one local girl cast furious glances in her direction. Only one dared to approach and, winding her arms about Michael's neck, said, 'I hope you're saving the last waltz for me, Michael Brackenbury, and seeing me safely home *as usual*.' The emphasis on the final two words was not lost on Maddie.

Gently Michael unfastened the girl's hold around his neck. 'Not tonight, Susan. I've to look after Maddie.'

Susan turned huge, innocent eyes upon Maddie. But in their depths the look was not so guileless. 'She'll be fine, won't you? All the boys are panting to dance with her. Let her have a bit of fun.'

'I don't want to dance with anyone else, thanks,' Maddie said quickly, returning the girl's stare, which was rapidly turning frosty. Now there was not even the pretence of friendliness. 'I'm with Michael.'

With the merest hint of emphasis on the word 'I', Maddie staked her claim.

The girl glanced back at Michael, who made no effort to contradict Maddie, so Susan shrugged. 'Have it your own way then.' And she flounced away, heels tapping angrily on the floor, her full skirt bouncing as she walked.

'Oops, I think I've upset her,' Maddie said, not in the least contrite.

Michael laughed. 'Don't worry about it. Susan was getting far too possessive for my liking, anyway. Do her good.'

For a fleeting moment, Maddie wondered if he was using her to rid himself of Susan, but as he drew her into his arms for the lilting last waltz, she forgot all about the other girl and even about poor Nick left sulking at home, too afraid to rebel against his mother.

It was a beautiful evening, but already the sharpness of autumn was in the air. Leaving the village, they walked into the pitch blackness of the lane leading to the farm.

'I love the dark nights, don't you?' Michael said, pulling her closer.

Maddie thought about her life in the Home. Bedtime was an hour earlier in winter in a freezing dormitory where the whole night was punctuated by the sound of one or other of the girls coughing and sneezing with colds or flu. On winter mornings, the girls woke to find ice on the inside of the windows and had to run, shivering, to the washroom to wash in cold water.

No, she thought, she didn't like winter and doubted she ever would.

When she didn't answer, Michael said, 'It'll be Christmas before we know it. What do you want Father Christmas to bring you, eh?'

In the darkness, Maddie grinned. 'Just you.'

'Eh?' Close beside her, she felt him give a start. 'What do you mean – just me?'

'I'd like you for Christmas.'

'What?' Now he was laughing, joining in her fun. 'All done up in pretty paper and tied up with tinsel?'

'If you like. Then you'd be all mine and I could play with you all day.'

His arm tightened around her waist. 'Oh Maddie,' he whispered close to her ear. 'You're a little darling. Do you know that?'

She didn't answer, didn't know how to. Michael stopped and in the middle of the lane, beneath the bright stars and the fitful moon, he put his arms around her and held her close. She lifted her face and felt his mouth warm upon hers.

'Don't be frightened,' he murmured. 'I won't hurt you. I won't ever hurt you. You're my girl now and I'll always look after you. I promise. I love you, Maddie.'

As he said the magical words, words that had never before in the whole of her young life been said to her, Maddie let the love that was in her heart for him overflow.

'And I love you, Michael. I've loved you from that very first day when I was sweeping the hearth.'

He laughed softly, his breath warming her cold cheeks. 'You had a smut on your nose, did you know?'

They laughed softly together, even though there was no one out here in the darkness to hear them.

He kissed her again and then they walked on slowly, their arms entwined around each other. 'What about your dad? Will he mind?'

''Course not. He's very fond of you, you know. I can tell. Specially when he sticks up for you against Mrs T.'

'Is she – I mean – are they . . .?'

116

'Sharing the same bed?' he said bluntly.

'Well, yes.'

'Lord, no. Who'd want to make love to that sourpuss?'

There was silence between them. Maddie longed to ask what had happened to his own mother, but their newfound closeness was so new, so fragile, that she dared not risk breaking the beauty of the moment.

He must have read her mind, for he said, 'Me mam died when I was born and for a while me dad coped with the help of his sister, who came here for a few months, and then later with help from the village. That's one of the good things about village life, you know. They do rally round when someone's in trouble. Mind you, the down side is that everybody knows everybody else's business. But there you are, I suppose you can't have one without the other.'

She was silent as he went on. 'Anyway, when I was about two, dad heard that Mrs T's husband had died in tragic circumstances and she'd been left with a tiny baby. So he did his own bit of rallying and asked her if she'd like to come and be his housekeeper and look after me.'

'How did her husband die?'

'Dunno. I've never been told and if you even so much as mention the subject she goes off the deep end.'

'Does Nick know?'

'Shouldn't think so. Even he's not allowed to ask questions.'

'Not about his own father?' She was astounded. 'That seems unfair.'

'Mm.' Michael was thoughtful. 'I have wondered if there's some dark secret about it all. I mean, I wonder if he went off with some other woman or something. Maybe he's not even dead at all. There's no grave in the church-yard. I know, because I've looked.'

Maddie laughed. 'You nosy parker, you.'

'Well, you'd think if he'd just died, or even been killed, that she would talk to Nick about him. I mean me dad doesn't talk a lot about me mam, because it upsets him. But if ever I ask about her, he will tell me.'

They had arrived at the farmyard now and the house was in darkness.

'Let's go into the hay shed,' Michael whispered. 'We'll be lovely and warm in there.'

As Michael opened the rickety door, the squeaking noise it made sounded loud in the stillness.

'There – there aren't any rats in here, are there?' Maddie asked nervously. 'I don't like rats.'

'I didn't think you were scared of anything, young'un,' he teased and then, sensing that she really was afraid, he added swiftly, 'Don't worry. We do get them in here sometimes. Wherever there's animal feed, you'll always get Mr Rat and his family. But we keep a supply of poison and put some down regularly. Besides . . .' he paused as he laid his jacket on the hay for her and then put his arms around her. 'I'm here to look after you.'

They snuggled down together, side by side. He kissed her and held her close and whilst her knowledge of kissing and petting was non-existent, Maddie found herself responding with a naturalness that surprised her. Even shocked her a little. Perhaps, after all, a little corner of her mind whispered, you have got bad blood in you, just like Mrs Potter and Mrs Trowbridge said.

But then Michael was kissing her with such ardour that every other thought was swept from her mind.

Sixteen

'I know where you were last night.' Nick's tone was sly.

Maddie glanced at him, puzzled. Of course he knew where they had been. At the dance. What was he on about?

'So?'

'There was bits of hay all over our bedroom floor this morning. Just you wait till me mam goes up there. You'll be for it. She's not daft neither.'

Now Maddie hid her face against the cow's side, her fingers trembling as she gently squeezed the milk from the beast's udder. Oh no, she thought. How could Michael have been so thoughtless? She had been so careful to remove every trace of hay from her clothing when she had got to her room. She'd pushed it all into an old paper bag and had thrust it into the stove in the kitchen this morning.

'And you were very late in. I don't think Mr Frank was best pleased either.'

Maddie quailed inwardly. This was worse than ever. Even Michael could not stand up to his father. If he was angry with her then . . .

'Did he kiss you?'

Angry now, Maddie shot back, 'That's none of your business.'

Nick smirked. 'So he did. I thought so. Well, you're not the first. And you won't be the last.'

Maddie opened her mouth to retort, but then she

thought about the girl at the dance, remembering the intimate way she had spoken to Michael, the way she had looked at him.

Maddie swallowed. 'Are you trying to get me into trouble?' she said. 'Go away and let me get on with me work.'

Nick gave a wry, humourless laugh. 'I don't have to make trouble for you. You're doing a good job of that yourself. And as for "getting you into trouble", if you know what I mean . . .?' Again the smirk was back. 'Well, Michael'll do that for you, all right.'

'You're just jealous,' she snapped.

Nick laughed. 'I aren't jealous of a little trollop like you.' The name-calling sounded strange coming from the young boy's mouth and Maddie knew instinctively that the words were not his own, but his mother's. 'A little bastard that nobody wants.'

Maddie stood up and faced him. 'So why did she come to the Orphanage and pick a little bastard to come and work here, eh?'

'You know why,' Nick said nastily. 'Because you ain't no family to make trouble.'

'The old beezum!'

'Don't you call my mother names.'

'I'll call her what I like and I don't care if you do tell her, because one of these days, I'll tell her mesen.'

Maddie picked up the buckets and marched past him on her way to the Dairy, the stirrings of pity she had begun to feel for this boy gone in an instant.

She was still dreading coming face to face with Frank, but when they all sat down together at the dinner table, he was smiling and, to her astonishment, he actually winked at her and said, 'Enjoy yourself last night, little lady?'

Under the table she felt Michael's foot gently touch

hers, but she dared not risk a glance at him as she said, 'Yes, thank you, Mr Frank.'

Close beside her she heard Harriet's irritating sniff.

Towards the end of October as they were sitting down to supper one evening, Frank said, 'I'll be going to market this week, Michael. I've heard that old man Weatherall is giving up his farm and selling his stock.'

'You're not thinking of buying his cows, Dad, surely? He's a mucky farmer.'

'He used to be a very good farmer, son. But the last few years he's got too old and ill to manage his farm properly. He's no son to carry it on.' There was a note of pride in his voice and yet his tone was tinged with pity for the man who had not been so fortunate as Frank believed himself to be. 'I've heard tell he's giving up all together. His beast are up for sale this week.'

Michael shrugged. 'Never mind what he used to be, Dad. It's what his herd's like now that matters.'

'Well, it's worth a look anyway and they'll be going cheap.'

'Maybe so. But are they a good buy, Dad, or a bad buy?'

'We'll take a look, son. Just a look.'

At the beginning of November, three scrawny looking beast arrived at Few Farm.

'I tried to tell him,' Michael spread his hands as Maddie and Nick stood surveying Frank's purchase. 'But would he listen?'

'Think you know more about cattle than your dad?' Nick said.

Michael shot him a look. 'Well, if he's going to buy beast like these three, then yes, I reckon I do.'

'They'll be all right.' Frank was coming towards them. 'Once we've fattened them up a bit. Take them to the meadow, Maddie.'

'Don't you think we ought to keep them separate from our stock? Just for a few days at least?'

'No, Michael, I don't.' It was the first time Maddie could remember hearing Frank speak sharply to his son. Then he asked a similar question to the one Nick had asked a few moments earlier. 'Don't you trust my judgement?'

'Dad, it's not that, it's just . . .' Michael's voice petered away. 'Oh all right, then. Have it your way.'

'I will. They were a damned good price.'

'They would be,' Michael muttered, but he kept his voice so low now that only Maddie, standing close to him, heard.

'Which field do you want them in, Mr Frank?' Maddie asked quietly. Even with her limited knowledge, she, too, was worried by the sight of the cows. They looked neglected, as if they had not been fed properly for weeks.

Frank jerked his thumb in the direction of the field adjacent to the tulip field. 'South End Meadow, lass.'

'Right. Come on, Ben,' Maddie called and the dog bounded towards her, his pink tongue lolling, his eyes bright and eager. But the cows ignored his excited barking and just continued to stand in the centre of the yard, their heads lowered, not moving an inch.

'Come on, cush, cush,' Maddie said and slapped the nearest one on its rump. She recoiled in horror as she felt the animal's bones through its skin.

Frank was right about one thing, she thought, they certainly needed fattening up.

122

Slowly, almost painfully, the three cows lumbered out of the gate and, with Ben barking at their heels, turned to the left towards the meadow. Maddie looked up as a dark shadow passed over their heads, a flock of starlings wheeled and dived above her head. As she opened the gate and Ben cleverly guided the newcomers into the field to join the other beast, the birds swooped down into the field, some landing on the hind quarters of the cattle, others on the hedges and on the ground. Ben ran about, barking excitedly, so that some of the birds, startled, rose into the air once more. But those perching on the cows' backs, were more daring and cocked their heads to one side to look down upon the dog with cheeky conceit.

Maddie laughed. 'Come on, Ben. Leave them alone. They can't do any harm.' She closed the gate and whistled to the dog, who obeyed her reluctantly. All the way down the lane towards the farm, Ben kept stopping, his tongue hanging out, and glancing back towards the impudent starlings.

It was a week later when, in the mist of early morning, Maddie went to South End Meadow to fetch the cows for milking and she found one of Mr Weatherall's cows lying dead in the middle of the field.

Seventeen

'I told you not to buy old man Weatherall's bloody rubbish.' Michael was blazing as they stood over the dead beast.

'Watch your tongue, boy. I won't have that sort of language.'

'Oh, you won't, won't you? Well, it's enough to make a saint swear and I'm no saint. Who knows what it's died of. It could have brought anything on to our farm that'll infect our whole herd.'

'Do you think I haven't the sense to examine beast thoroughly before I buy? Give me some credit. They were undernourished, I grant you, but that was all.' Even Frank's voice rose to a roar now. 'There was nothing wrong with them.'

Michael thrust his head forward and shouted, 'Well, there is now.'

For a moment they glared at each other and Maddie noticed that Michael clenched and unclenched his hands, but he kept them firmly by his side. Suddenly, the anger seemed to drain out of Frank and his shoulders sagged. He took off his cap, ran his hand through his hair and then replaced his cap.

'What's done's done,' he muttered. 'Let's have a look at it before . . .' His voice petered away as they both squatted down, one on either side of the beast, whilst Maddie stood near the animal's head and watched.

The Tulip Girl

'Mr Frank,' she began tentatively. 'Its tongue's hanging out of its mouth and it looks all sore, sort of blistered.'

'What?'

She pointed and Frank moved to look at the animal's mouth. Michael was looking at the feet.

'There's sores and blisters here too, Dad.' His voice was flat now, sorrowful.

Maddie felt sudden fear as she watched father and son stare at each other, horror on their faces.

'Oh no, lad, not that. Oh please, not that,' Frank whispered hoarsely.

Soberly, Michael said, 'I'm sorry, Dad, but I think it is. It's foot and mouth.'

Frank stood up but his gaze was still on the cow lying at his feet. He drew the back of his hand across his forehead. 'Let's look at the rest of them.'

Rising too, Michael pointed across the field and said, 'Look at that one over there. It's got a trail of saliva hanging from its mouth. That's another sign, isn't it?'

Grimly, Frank agreed.

The three of them moved around the field inspecting the cattle.

'Mr Frank,' Maddie called. 'This one's lame. And – and it's not one of Mr Weatherall's. It's one of yours.'

Frank shook his head and stood in the middle of the field looking for all the world as if he were lost.

Michael and Maddie walked back to him.

'We've got it right enough,' Frank said as they drew near to him.

'What do we do, Dad?'

'We'll have to inform the local vet or the police – or both. Come on, let's go back to the house.'

As they walked down the lane, Maddie slipped her hand into Michael's and gave it a comforting squeeze, not

125

caring, for once, if his father saw them. Michael gripped her hand in return and, even though no words were spoken, she could feel his despair.

When they reached the farmyard, Michael put his head round the cowshed door and called, 'Nick, come into the house a minute.'

The boy appeared. 'Why? Where's the cows? Everything's ready.'

Michael, already walking towards the back door of the house, merely beckoned him. Shrugging, Nick followed.

Inside, Frank sat down at the table, resting his arms on it. 'Get us a cup of tea, lass, would you?' and Maddie, glad to have something to do, picked up the teapot.

Michael, too, sat down at the table, opposite his father. Once more the two exchanged sober glances.

'What is it? What's the matter?' Nick began as his mother came into the room from upstairs. She blinked as she saw everyone sitting there at the time when the milking should be in full swing. Her startled glance came to rest on Frank and she stood very still, waiting to hear the answer to Nick's question.

'One of Weatherall's cows is dead,' Frank began and glanced again at his son as he added heavily, 'and it's got blisters in its mouth and on its feet.'

Harriet gave a cry and her hand fluttered to her mouth. 'Oh no, Frank.' In her agitation she quite forgot the 'Mr' but no one other than Maddie seemed to notice.

Quietly, Maddie placed a cup of tea in front of Frank and then pushed one towards Michael.

Frank spooned sugar into the liquid and stirred it, intent on his action. 'That's it, then. We're finished.'

'No, we're not.' Harriet's voice was shrill. She sat down at the end of the table and leaned towards Frank. 'Why don't you bury it and say nowt? You keep an eye on all the rest and if any of them get it, you can isolate them in the barn and treat them.'

Slowly Frank lifted his head as everyone turned to look at her.

'It's a notifiable disease, Mrs T,' Michael said. 'We can't do that.'

'Who's to know?' Harriet snapped at him, her gaze leaving Frank for a moment. 'We can isolate ourselves too. No one need leave the farm for a while. We've plenty of food . . .'

'We can't do that,' Michael repeated. 'And supposing we did, what about the milk round? People will soon know something was wrong when I don't turn up with their milk every morning and I can hardly supply the locals with milk from a herd that's got foot and mouth.'

'But it's treatable. I've heard of it being done. Way back in '23 there was a case where a big estate got it and they got permission to be isolated. They only lost two or three. If you tell the authorities, Mr Frank, they'll slaughter all your cattle, every last one, and the pigs too, and where's your living to come from then, eh? And they'll probably kill everyone's for several miles around. They'll close the market. You know they will. Think what hardship that'll cause.'

'There's not that many farmers with cattle around here, Mrs T, you know there aren't. It's not a cattle area, so . . .'

'So all the more reason to keep quiet about it. We can keep it contained.'

'That wasn't what I had been going to say,' Michael said.

'Do you want to see your father ruined?'

'Of course not, but . . .'

127

'So who's to know,' Harriet said again, and this time there was a veiled threat in her words, 'unless someone tells 'em?'

Frank stood up and leaned on his knuckles on the table. Looking at Harriet he said, 'I am not going to do anything against the law. We'll notify whoever we have to.' Then he looked towards his son. 'Michael's right. I've only myself to blame. I should have known better than to buy those beast of Weatherall's.'

'We can't be sure how they got it,' Michael said. His anger had died now and already he was prepared to be more understanding. 'I mean, they say it can be carried on the wind or brought by birds . . .'

'Oh!' Maddie could not stop the cry escaping her lips even though she clapped her hand to her mouth. Wide-eyed she stared from one to the other. Now everyone turned to look at her.

'What is it, love?' Frank asked.

Slowly she let her hand fall away from her mouth. 'Oh Mr Frank. The – the day Mr Weatherall's cows arrived and I took them to the field . . .'

'Yes, lass, what about it?'

'There – there was a huge flock of starlings landed in the field. Some even sat on the cows' backs. Ben was barking, trying to frighten them away, but – but . . .' She bit her lip. 'But I brought him away. I – I said they couldn't do any harm. Oh Mr Frank, I didn't know. Ben knew, but I didn't.'

There was a moment's silence and then Frank, even amidst the drama of the moment, actually laughed. He moved and put his arm around her shoulders.

'It's not your fault, love. How many times a day do you think birds land in the field or take a ride on a cow's back when we're not there to shoo them off?'

'I – don't know.'

'Exactly. We can't be there every minute of the day watching over them. If it has been carried by the birds, there's not a thing we could have done about it.'

'Really?' Maddie felt comforted but she still felt very guilty because she had not followed Ben's example and frightened the flock of starlings away.

Frank gave her a quick squeeze, then he sighed. 'Well, I'd better go and get it over with.'

'If you're going down to the phone box in the village, Dad, don't forget to disinfect your boots before you go. There's some in the barn, I'll get it for you.'

As the three menfolk left the house, Harriet stepped towards Maddie and gripped her arm. 'You! I might have known you'd have had a hand in all this. You've brought nothing but trouble to this house from the moment you stepped into it.'

Eighteen

All Frank's cattle and his two pigs had been slaughtered and their carcasses burnt. That day had been heartbreaking for everyone on Few Farm. Even the slaughterman who came to carry out the operation did so in silence, the sympathy on his face plain to see. Then the dead cattle were piled in the middle of South End Meadow. Michael stacked bales of straw, wood and old tyres around them and in amongst them and doused the whole lot in diesel. The fire burned for two days and at the end of it Michael and Nick had to dig a hole as deep as they could to bury the ashes and then fill it in again.

Since then, the family had been confined to the farm and hollows had been dug in the lane on the approaches to the farm and filled with disinfectant.

'It's like having the plague,' Michael muttered, leaning against the five-barred gate leading into the farmyard, which had been closed and padlocked. For several days after they had made the awful discovery, Nick had sat on top of the gate, Frank's shotgun across his knees as a warning to inquisitive sightseers. From time to time they had heard a bang as he took a pot-shot at birds flying over the farm.

'I don't know what good he thinks he's doing,' Michael had muttered.

Maddie had sighed. 'I think he's just taking his anger and frustration out on them.'

'Well, I think he's venting his anger in the wrong direction. He should shoot old man Weatherall!'

Maddie had said no more. She knew Michael didn't really mean what he said but the fact that the thought even came into his mind, never mind the words actually passing his lips, told her the depth of his bitterness.

Now Maddie climbed up and sat on the topmost bar of the gate. 'I bet you miss your milk round, don't you?'

'Yeah, I do. Funny, I always used to moan about having to get up so early seven days a week but now I can't go, I'd love to be out there on the cart meeting all the old dears bringing out their milk cans.'

'You will again,' Maddie said, touching his shoulder. 'Soon.'

'We could restock but Dad doesn't seem to have the heart now.'

'Well then, when the authorities give permission, you'll have to be the one to do it,' Maddie said determinedly.

Michael smiled up at her. It was the first time she had seen him smile since their dreadful discovery, but even now it was only fleeting as he added worriedly, 'I really don't know what to do. The infection thrives in the cold, you know, and I don't reckon even the regulations allow long enough to let the land get really clear of it.'

'But no one else round here has got it, have they?'

'Not that I've heard. The chap from the Ministry or the Council or wherever he was from, congratulated us on our prompt action and said we'd probably saved the whole area from an epidemic.'

They glanced at each other, remembering Harriet's suggestion.

They heard the splashing of water and Maddie narrowed her eyes to look down the lane. 'There's somebody coming.'

'Really? Can you see who it is?'

'It's Jenny!' Maddie cried in delight and was about to jump down into the lane when Michael caught hold of her.

'No. You mustn't. We mustn't go out of the yard. She can come to the gate, but she can't come in.'

'I'm sorry. I forgot,' Maddie said at once.

Michael remained standing with one arm around Maddie's waist, making no move to remove his hold on her.

'Maddie!' Jenny called and waved as she clumped along the lane in oversize Wellington boots. 'Are you all right? All of you?'

Panting a little, she stood a few feet from them and read the large notice saying 'FOOT AND MOUTH PRECAUTION – KEEP OUT'. Jen pulled a face but then gave a little nod, understanding at once that she must stay in the lane.

'Where's Nick? Is he all right?' Jenny's glance went beyond them to search the yard.

'He's about somewhere.' He raised his voice and bellowed, 'Nick? You there, Nick? Young lady to see you.'

But the yard was empty and silent and Michael made no effort to move away to find him.

'Never mind. I'll see him another time, maybe?' Jenny said. 'Do you want anything bringing from the village if you can't go out?'

'We're fine, Jenny,' Michael said, 'but it's lovely to see you.'

'I got permission to come,' Jenny said, proud of her own initiative. 'I asked at the police station and the man there said as long as I got some boots and was sure to wash them well in the disinfectant.' She gestured back towards the hollow through which she had just splashed. 'Mrs Grange lent me these boots.'

'Mrs Grange? Her at the corner shop in the village?' Michael said.

'That's right.' Jenny was beaming now. 'That's what I've come to tell you, Maddie. I've got a job there and – best of all – I live in.'

'Oh Jen. I'm so glad. Oh I want to hug you, but I mustn't.'

The younger girl's face clouded. 'Is it that bad? I mean, I can't catch it, can I?'

'Well, there is a human form of it, but it's usually harmless,' Michael said. 'It's more to prevent you carrying it on your clothes to other places, see?'

The girl nodded.

'Tell me more about Mrs Grange and how you got the job. Did Mrs Potter arrange it?'

Jenny looked happier than Maddie could ever remember having seen her. 'No, I got it for myself. She'd taken me to a few places. You remember about the flower packing?'

Maddie nodded.

'Well, there were one or two other places, but always I was too small, not old enough or not strong enough.' Jenny frowned. 'D'you know, Maddie, it was almost as if she was taking me for jobs where she really knew I hadn't a chance of getting them.'

'She probably did, Jen. I wouldn't put anything past Mrs Potter.'

'But why? I mean, she always wants to be rid of us all as soon as we're old enough.'

'Not everybody. She keeps her chosen few on as staff. She kept Peggy on, didn't she? And Winifred. And it looks to me as if she'd her eye on you for the vacancy as kitchen maid.'

'But I wasn't one of her chosen ones.'

Maddie grinned. 'Not when you were with me, you weren't. But maybe since I left . . .' She left the words unspoken but they both knew that it had always been Maddie who had been the ringleader, the troublemaker. Jenny, on her own, was biddable and docile. Just the sort that Mrs Potter liked for her skivvies.

'Well,' Jenny puffed out her chest. 'I thought about what you said and decided there was no way I was going to stay there, so after school instead of going straight home, I started asking round a bit in the village to see if there were any jobs going and, guess what?' She clapped her hands together. 'When I went into the corner shop and asked Mrs Grange if she knew of anyone who might be looking for someone she said, "Well, now, in't that funny,"' Jenny mimicked Mrs Grange's broad Lincolnshire dialect perfectly. '"I were just thinking I'd like to get mesen a lass to help in the shop, like."'

Maddie and Michael clutched at each other, laughing at Jenny's clowning. 'Anyway,' the girl went on in her normal voice. 'I went several times to chat to her and last week I told Mrs Potter and moved my things out of the Home and into a lovely little room all of my own in Mrs Grange's place above the shop. There's pretty curtains at the window and even a bit of carpet on the floor. A comfy bed and a chest of drawers for my things. Not that I've got many, but I've got Miss Amelia sitting on the top of the chest.'

Michael laughed. 'Miss Amelia?'

Jenny nodded. 'The doll that Nick won at the fair. Maddie gave it to me and I called it Miss Amelia because we'd seen her that day in the car. You remember?'

'Oh, yes. So we did.'

'What did Mrs Potter say?' Maddie asked.

Jenny pulled a comical face. 'She wasn't very pleased. Said why did I want to leave when she had a nice little job all sorted out for me in the kitchen?'

'And?'

'And what?'

'What did you tell her?'

'Oh, well, I daren't tell her the truth. I mean, I couldn't tell her that I didn't want to stay there all my life, could I?'

'I would have done.'

'Well, yes,' Jenny glanced down, 'but I didn't like to.'

'I expect you're too nice to hurt the old girl's feelings. Is that it, Jenny?' Michael said and Maddie glared down at him.

'I suppose you mean, I'm not "too nice" then?'

Michael looked up at her but before he could answer, Jenny blurted out, 'No, it's not that. I'm just too scared, that's all.'

'But you weren't too scared to get out and find yourself a job. Well done, little Jenny, I say,' Michael smiled at her.

Maddie pushed Michael's arm away and jumped down from the gate. 'We'd better go in. It's nearly tea-time. 'Bye, Jen. You'd better not come again, though. I'll see you when we're let out.'

Then she turned and marched across the yard without a backward glance.

She heard Jenny's plaintive voice. 'But Maddie, it'll soon be Christmas. I'll see you at Christmas, won't I?'

She did not turn nor answer her even though she could feel their eyes on her. Jenny's puzzled and hurt, and Michael ... Well she dare not think about the way Michael might be looking at her.

135

Nineteen

Christmas was a miserable affair. Although they were no longer confined to the farm, they were still asked to take meticulous precautions and none of them seemed inclined to leave it. Not even Michael wanted to go into the village to the pub or to a dance.

'They'll only start asking questions,' he told Maddie. 'And I don't want to talk about it. We've got to look forward now and plan what we're going to do.'

'Yes, but what are we going to do? Your dad won't even talk about it.'

'Well, he'll have to soon because we can't survive on a couple of acres of wheat and a few hens' eggs.'

On Boxing Day morning, Maddie asked, 'Mr Frank, could I ask Jenny to tea today, please?'

'Of course you can, love.'

'Oh aye,' Harriet put in at once. 'Another mouth to feed when we've scarcely enough for ourselves.'

'I'll go and see her this afternoon,' Maddie said, as usual ignoring the housekeeper. She was anxious to make amends for the way she had treated Jenny the last time she saw her. Since the day she had stood outside the gate, Jenny – just as Maddie had told her – had not visited the farm again.

She loved Jenny dearly, she always had done, so why

was it, she asked herself, that the moment Michael was even just nice to the younger girl, did she feel this awful jealousy, so acutely that made her act unkindly towards Jenny? It wasn't Jenny's fault. She didn't play up to Michael or flirt with him. In fact, she always seemed a little in awe of him. So how could she, Maddie, be so horrible? Jenny was like a sister. Hadn't they always said so? So how . . .? Maddie sighed. Not ever having lived in a proper family, she did not know how real sisters carried on. Perhaps, sometimes, even real sisters were jealous of each other. Especially if one was pretty and vulnerable; the sort that men liked to protect. And she didn't blame Michael, not at all. He was just being kind to the young girl, she knew, probably for her sake too. He knew that Jenny was the closest Maddie had to real family and he wanted to make her welcome, so why . . .?

Maddie sighed and shook her head, angry with herself. 'Just don't do it any more,' she told herself sharply as she put on her coat and left the house to walk to the village.

It seemed a long time since she had been into Mrs Grange's corner shop. The bell clanged as she opened the door and she stepped into the fascinating world of the shop that sold everything from sweets in glass jars that lined one shelf, fruit drops and aniseed balls, through jars of Bovril, packets of Quaker Oats with the picture of a man in Quaker dress on the packet, tinned tongue and salmon and Heinz beans to packets of Lux soap flakes. In the centre of the counter in pride of place stood an ornate cash register showing that the last customer's purchases had cost one pound four shillings and eleven pence ha'penny. Sacks of potatoes stood on the floor and along one counter was a line of second-hand books. Mrs Grange ran a lending library at one penny a loan.

There was a movement in the room at the back of the

shop and Jenny appeared from behind the brown curtain across the doorway.

'Maddie, oh Maddie.' She rushed round the counter and flung herself against Maddie, who hugged her tightly.

'Now then, you're the little lass from Few Farm, aren't you?'

Maddie looked up to see a woman had now appeared from the back room, dressed in a navy-blue skirt, a floral striped blouse with a brooch at the neck and a cardigan. She was small and dumpy but she smiled in welcome, her eyes bright behind round spectacles. Strangely, it seemed to Maddie, she wore a navy-blue felt hat, even indoors.

'This is my friend Maddie, Mrs Grange.'

The woman shook her head sadly. 'Aw lass, I'm real sorry to hear the trouble poor Mr Brackenbury's had. And him such a good man, too.' She shook her head. 'It dun't seem fair.'

'Well, we've been "let out" now so he can start to get back to normal.'

The woman shook her head. 'Not so easy, lass, is it? We're lucky it didn't spread, though. No one else has got it as I've heard.' She chuckled. 'And I'd be the first to know.'

Maddie smiled as Mrs Grange chattered on. 'Everyone's very thankful that Mr Brackenbury was so honest. You know, telling the authorities straight away, like. Some farmers . . .', she tapped the side of her nose, 'might have been tempted to keep it quiet and treat them theirsens.' She nodded knowingly. 'It's been done 'afore.'

Maddie swallowed.

'But Frank Brackenbury's a good man. He's proved that and it's not the first time, let me tell you.' Mrs Grange wagged her finger at Maddie. 'Oh, there's a lot I could tell you about Frank Brackenbury, if I'd a mind.'

'You mean, he's had foot and mouth before?'

'No, no, lass, not that. I didn't mean that. I meant some of the things he's done in his time has shown what a good man he is. Oh yes, I could tell you a thing or two.'

Maddie almost bit off the end of her tongue to stop her demanding at once, What things? But she managed to curb her curiosity. No doubt, she told herself, Jenny would soon hear everything, living with the local mine of information and she would always tell her best friend.

The shop bell clanged again as a customer stepped in and as Mrs Grange moved to serve her, Jenny whispered, 'How are you all? How's Nick and Michael?'

'They're all right, but everyone's very fed up. Poor Mr Frank doesn't seem to have the heart to get going again. And nobody else, not even Michael, can do anything without his approval.'

'Oh dear. So you've not had a very good Christmas?'

Maddie pulled a face. 'Not really. What about you? What did you do yesterday?'

'Mrs Grange went to her sister's the other side of the village and took me with her. Wasn't that kind?'

'Is the shop open all day today?'

'No. Only for the morning. Just to let people get their milk. Now Michael can't deliver they're coming here for it.'

'So, are you doing anything this afternoon, then?'

Jenny shook her head.

'Would you like to come to the farm for tea?'

Jenny's eyes lit up. 'Ooh yes, please, Maddie. Will Nick be there too?'

Maddie laughed. 'What's all these questions about Nick? You sweet on him?'

The girl was blushing. ''Course not. He's just – well – shy, isn't he? Like me. I mean . . .' The colour in her face deepened. 'I mean, Michael's lovely. So good-looking and – and confident. But he'd never look at someone like me. Besides . . .' Now she smiled coyly at Maddie. 'You like him, don't you?'

'Ssh.' Maddie glanced around. 'Not so loud.'

Jenny's voice dropped to a whisper. 'Does he like you?'

Maddie shrugged. 'Well . . .'

'Yes, he does.' The young girl nudged her. 'I could see last time I came. He'd got his arm round you. And the way he looked at you. I wish Nick would look at me like that.'

Maddie grinned and returned the playful nudge. She felt better now. At least Jenny had not set her sights on Michael. As far as she was concerned, Jenny could have the moody Nick and welcome to him.

'I'll see what I can do for you.'

When Jenny arrived at the farm later that afternoon, she shyly handed out a quarter of Butter Drops to everyone.

'You shouldn't have done that, love,' Frank said. 'It's very kind of you.'

'It's kind of you to have me here.'

'You'd have done better to have brought us a quarter of tea or a bag of sugar,' Harriet said tartly.

'Oh I'm sorry. I could have done, Mrs Trowbridge. I'll bring some next time.'

'No need, love,' Frank put in swiftly. 'Mrs Trowbridge is only teasing, aren't you, Harriet?'

Maddie knew that the housekeeper never teased or joked but the look that Frank now gave her forced the woman to stretch a smile on her mouth and say, 'Of course, Mr Frank.'

140

But as she turned away, Maddie heard the familiar sniff.

Michael had already popped one of the round brown sweets into his mouth. 'Mmm, thank you, Jen.' He winked at her but Maddie saw that Jenny's eyes were on Nick. He flicked the hair out of his eyes and muttered, 'Thanks.' Then he smiled at her and seeing it, Maddie marvelled once again at the change in the boy's appearance.

'What shall we do 'til tea time? It's too cold to go out.'

'I'll beat you all at Ludo,' Michael offered.

Nick's smile widened to a grin. 'No, you won't. I beat you last time.'

He hurried to the sideboard to get out the coloured board and the tiddlywinks that acted as each person's marker.

'Where's the dice?'

'Should be in the box.'

'Oh yes, here it is.'

For the next hour, the four sat round the table playing Ludo, Nick becoming more and more animated as he began to win whilst Maddie and Michael, sitting close to each other, held hands beneath the table between their turns.

And then, when Jenny began to catch up to Nick who could not throw the final number he needed to win, the game became noisier and noisier until Harriet appeared in the doorway. 'That's enough. I can hear you out in the kitchen. You must be giving Mr Frank a headache.'

'They're all right, Harriet,' came Frank's voice from his deep armchair near the fire. 'Let them have a bit of fun. There's not been much in this house this Christmas.'

'Well, I want the table now, if we're to have any tea today.'

'Three more goes each, then,' Michael said, 'and the one who's got the most counters home has won.'

Ten minutes later Jenny was shouting gleefully, 'That's my last counter home. I've won, I've won.'

Harriet came to stand at the end of the table, waiting with the white cloth in her hands to spread it. 'I could do with some help in the kitchen now, girl,' she said to Maddie.

'Can I help?' Jenny offered.

'No, no. You're a guest,' Michael said before the housekeeper could answer. 'Come on, I'll show you the piano in the front room. We usually light the fire in there at Christmas and play games, but this year, well . . .'

He said no more. There was no need to say that this year the family had had to cut expenses wherever they could.

As Maddie moved between kitchen and living room laying the table, she heard the murmur of voices from the best room. Then she heard the tinkle of the piano as Michael demonstrated the sound of the instrument to their guest.

He's never once shown me the piano, Maddie thought. Was there, after all, some truth in what Nick said about Michael?

Swiftly, she tried to quell the rising resentment. Remember, she chided herself, Jen's your sister – or as good as. No more jealousy. Besides, it isn't Michael she likes, it's Nick.

But who, the little voice inside her would not be silenced, liked Jenny? Nick – or Michael?

Twenty

The first snowfall came on the sixth of January, but Jenny still plodded from the village out to the farm to tell them, 'Mrs Grange says her next allocation of Jaffa oranges will be coming soon. It'll be one pound per ration book.' Shyly, she slid a blue bag of sugar onto the table and glanced sideways at the housekeeper.

'That's very kind of you,' Harriet said as she picked it up. 'A lot more use than sweets.'

Frank shook his head as if despairing of Harriet ever giving gracious and heartfelt thanks. From his chair he held out his hand, inviting Jenny towards him. He seemed to do little nowadays except sit by the fire.

'Will you be getting some more cows soon, Mr Frank?' the girl asked as she sat on the hearthrug at his feet and held her cold hands out towards the glowing coals in the range.

'I don't know, lass. We haven't had clearance from the authorities yet. Three months, they reckon, before we can restock.' He sighed heavily. 'But I don't know even then.'

'What we need is a good hot spell,' Michael remarked. 'But by the look of it,' he nodded towards the window and the heavy grey clouds beyond, laden with the threat of more snow, 'we won't get that for a long time yet.'

At the beginning of February, the blizzards began in earnest. It began like fine white dust, floating through the air, outlining the trees and coating the ground in a

143

fluffy white blanket. Then the flakes became bigger and came thick and fast until it was impossible to see more than a few feet ahead. Soon, hedges, lanes and roadways were lost and only the tallest trees stuck up out of the snow.

'We've no water,' Harriet announced. 'The pipes must be frozen.'

'Maybe it's frozen in the tank in the roof. And I doubt we'll be able to pump any more up out of the well,' Michael said whose job it was to keep the household supplied with water.

'And the snow's banked to the top of the back door,' Harriet complained. 'I can't even get out this morning.'

'We'll come dig you out, Mrs T, if you get stuck in a drift.'

'I don't know what you're so cheerful about, Master Michael. You'd do better to get a shovel and start clearing some of it.'

'Aye, aye, Cap'n.' Michael saluted her smartly and then seeing that the housekeeper was really frightened by the atrocious weather, he put his arm about her shoulders. 'Come on, Mrs T, we'll sort it out. Nick and I will clear the snow in the yard and . . .'

'Have you seen it out there?' her voice rose shrilly. 'We're going to be cut off. Trapped out here. With no water and no heat and soon, no food.'

'We'll have plenty of heat. There's still some coal in the shed and plenty of wood in the barn. And I'll start the generator up today. We'll be all right.'

It seemed strange to Maddie that it should be the young man comforting the older woman, but her heart warmed to Michael for his gentle understanding.

'We've no milk or butter. No bread.' Harriet was determined to be pessimistic.

144

'We've potatoes in the barn and eggs.'

'I found three of the hens dead yesterday morning. From the cold, I expect.'

'I'll check the boiler.' Again it was Michael taking the lead. 'But,' he was saying, a cheeky smile twitching at the corners of his mouth, 'we could always rig up a pen in the wash-house and bring them where it's warmer.'

'Bring them into the house?'

'Better that than they all die of the cold, Mrs T.'

'Oh Michael,' Frank sank down wearily into his chair in front of the fire, 'it's a good job you're here. I don't know what we'd do without you.'

Michael turned and winked at Maddie. 'Come on, young'un. You can help too, but don't fall into a snowdrift or we'll never find you.'

The hardest part was digging their way out of the back door, but once they had cleared the snow that had drifted and piled up against the door and they could close it behind them, they stood a moment to rest, their breath like steam in the cold air.

'We'll make a pathway to the barn and then the generator shed and the hen-house,' Michael decided.

'It's like pictures you see of the North Pole,' Maddie murmured, her glance scanning the countryside.

Nick leaned on his shovel. 'It looks completely different, doesn't it? It's changed the landscape. I mean, if you didn't know where the road was and the fields and dykes, you couldn't find them.'

'That's the dangerous bit,' Michael said. 'Going through the ice into a dyke or a drain. But at least I reckon we could dig our way as far as the village, if need be, without too much trouble.'

'I wonder,' Maddie murmured as she picked up her own shovel once more, 'how Jenny is?'

'She'll be all right,' Nick said. 'She's about the only one who is, surrounded by all that food in the shop.'

But Michael thought otherwise. 'Not for long, she won't be. It's the only place the villagers will be able to get to for a while. The roads to Wellandon will be blocked. Mrs Grange's shop will soon be sold out.'

'Do you think so?'

'I know so, so if we want to get stocked up with a few supplies, we'd better get digging!'

'Dad, if you don't come out and see to the batteries, we're going to be without electricity an' all. You ought to check the voltage and the specific gravity.'

Frank waved him away. 'You see to it, Michael. You know what to do now.'

'No, I don't. Not really. Come on, Dad. Please. And we could use a little help with the digging. Maddie's about dead on her feet.'

It was the third day since they had started trying to dig their way to the village shop and already it was looking like a hopeless task. Fresh falls of snow filled in the pathway they had made and the lane resembled a glacial ravine.

Frank raised his head and looked towards her.

'I'm all right,' Maddie tried to smile, but the weariness was swamping her in waves.

Frank levered himself out of his chair. 'What am I thinking of? Sitting here, feeling sorry for myself when this lass is almost passing out. Why did you let me sit here, Michael?' He went towards the kitchen, still muttering to himself.

Maddie almost laughed out loud at the comical look on

Michael's face. He said nothing but grinned at her and pointed to the chair his father had just vacated. 'Now it's your turn, young'un, to have a rest.' As she opened her mouth to protest, he added, 'Go on. Do as you're told, for once. And I'll ask Mrs T to bring you a hot drink with a drop of whisky in it. You're not to do another thing all day. You hear?'

Maddie nodded. She had not even the strength left to argue.

'Oh, it's so cold. I don't think I'll ever feel warm again,' Harriet was still grumbling. These days she wore a thick cardigan over her blouse, skirt and the ever-present paisley apron. She continually pushed her hands up the opposite sleeve, not caring if she stretched the garment out of shape in her efforts to beat the cold.

Even Maddie, hardened throughout her childhood to the Spartan conditions at the Home, huddled near the fire in the range and stayed up as late as she could, putting off for as long as possible going to her ice-cold bedroom.

'That's the last of the coal, Mrs T,' Michael said, setting the brass coal scuttle at the side of the range. 'We're down to whatever wood we can find now. There's not as much in the barn as I thought.'

'There's always the wood pile behind the barn,' Nick suggested.

'Oh aye,' Michael countered. 'Under six foot of snow. You volunteering to dig it out? No, I thought not. Besides, it'll be too wet to burn decently. It'd smoke us out.'

'Maybe we could bring some in and dry it out a bit,' Nick said, but his suggestion lacked enthusiasm. It was as if the cold had seeped into their bones and sapped them of all strength and vigour. With long faces they all gazed at the fire, wondering just how much longer they would be able to enjoy its heat.

'I'd have a good bake-up tomorrow, if I could,' Harriet murmured, 'but I've already run out of flour.'

'At least we've still got electricity. I bet a lot of folks have got power cuts,' Michael said.

Frank cleared his throat. 'Er, I've been meaning to tell you. We're running very low on diesel. I won't be able to run the engine many more times.'

Now there was silence in the room as they all faced the prospect of being marooned amidst the frozen, wind-swept white landscape, totally isolated from the rest of civilization.

The following morning Michael said, 'I'm going to try to get to the village today. At least I'll get some news, even if there's no supplies to be had.'

'You'll never get there,' Nick said scathingly. 'It's impossible.'

Calmly, Michael said, 'I'm not going to try to *dig* my way there. I'm going to make myself a pair of skis.'

'Skis?'

Michael grinned. 'That's what I said. I know it's no good trying to wade through it, either. It's too deep, but if I get some long, narrow boards, the lightest I can find and strap them to my feet . . .'

'That won't work,' Nick said.

'Why not?' At once Maddie defended Michael's idea.

'Skis have to curve up a bit at the front, don't they? Otherwise they'll just dig into the snow. You'd be better with some flat boards on your feet, like snowshoes.'

Michael shook his head. 'Take too long. I'd have to plod along so slowly with those. I want something where I can glide over the surface of the snow.' He gestured with the flat of his hand.

'A strip of metal would be better,' Nick suggested, 'because you could bend the end up then.'

'You're right, Nick.'

There was silence whilst the three of them thought hard.

'Isn't there a sheet of metal in the hay shed?' Despite the gravity of their present situation, Maddie smiled at Michael. 'I've heard it rattling in the wind.'

'You can't use that,' Nick began, 'it's blocking up a hole . . .'

'Oh yes, I can. One more hole in that shed won't matter.'

For the rest of the day there was a lot of banging and not a little swearing whilst Michael cut and shaped a rough pair of skis.

'You'll need some poles,' Maddie joined in excitedly, now seeing Michael's idea really taking shape. 'I don't know what they call them, but you know . . .' She clenched her hands and held out her arms as if holding a skier's pole in each hand. 'And you need a round circle near the bottom, but leaving a spike at the end to drive into the snow. I've seen pictures.'

Michael was nodding. 'See what you can find for me, young'un.'

By the time they'd finished, it was too late for Michael to go but the following morning Maddie was standing near the gate, the snow piled up on either side of her, watching as Michael set off on his homemade skis towards the village.

'You will be careful?' she called after him anxiously. 'Mind the dykes.'

'Don't worry, young'un. I'll be back.'

But when dusk fell in the late afternoon and Michael had not returned, the whole household became anxious.

Twenty-One

'You two go to bed. Mr Frank and I will wait up for him.'

'I'm not going until Michael's safely home,' Maddie said, her steady gaze never leaving Harriet's face. She had to admit that even the housekeeper was agitated and her order to Maddie and Nick had lacked its usual vigour. Whatever Harriet felt about her, Maddie, there could be no doubt in anyone's mind that she was fond of Michael. Very fond. It showed in the way she kept glancing at the clock above the mantelpiece and going to the kitchen window every few minutes to press her face close to the cold glass and stare out into the black night, the only light from the moon shining on the snow.

'Maybe he's stopped in the village. With Mrs Grange and Jenny at the shop,' Frank put in, with a sound faith in Michael's common sense. 'Surely, wherever he is, he wouldn't be trying to get home again at this time of night?'

'Maybe he's stayed at Susan's.' Nick's remark sounded casual and Maddie might have accepted it as such if she hadn't noticed his quick, sly glance at her as he spoke.

But it was Harriet who voiced the sharp question. 'Susan? Who's Susan?'

'Oh . . .' Nick shrugged and said airily, 'Just one of his girlfriends in the village. Maybe that's why he went in the first place. All that talk about going for supplies was just that. Talk. I reckon he was missing his girlfriend.' He paused a moment and then added, with even more pointed emphasis on the plural, 'Or girlfriends.'

Maddie could not stop the words from bursting out. 'Michael wouldn't do that.' As three pairs of eyes turned to stare at her, she felt herself blushing but muttered again defiantly, 'Well, he wouldn't.'

'Of course he wouldn't, love,' Frank said. 'You're right. He wouldn't worry us this way. Not deliberately.'

Maddie saw Nick open his mouth to speak, but then he closed it again thinking better of whatever he had been going to say.

'I still think you young ones would be better in bed,' Harriet murmured again, as she moved once more to look out of the window.

'Let them stay if they want to.' Frank sighed heavily. 'Besides, there's nothing they have to get up early for in the morning, is there? Not now.'

'We should go out and look for him,' Maddie said.

Frank shook his head firmly. 'No. Not in the dark. It would be too dangerous. There's no point in all of us getting . . .' He stopped suddenly, biting back the words and looked at Maddie. Each saw the dread in the other's eyes.

Maddie took a deep breath. 'Mrs Trowbridge,' she called. 'Come and sit down by the fire. I'll make us all some cocoa . . .'

The woman came back into the room, her hands pushed up the sleeves of her cardigan, her shoulders hunched against the cold.

'We've no milk.'

'Then I'll heat some water and make us some Horlicks. At least Michael managed to get the tap running again yesterday.'

A few minutes later, as she was handing round the

hot drinks, Maddie thought she heard a noise. She froze, her hand holding the mug outstretched towards Harriet suspended in mid-air. 'Listen. Did you hear anything? I thought I heard a noise . . .'

Then they all heard Ben barking. She thrust the mug at Harriet and now ran herself to peer out of the window. With a joyous shout, she cried, 'He's here. He's back,' and pulled open the kitchen door. Ben, allowed to sleep in the wash-house since the blizzards had begun, was scratching at the back door. As Maddie opened it, a flurry of snow swirled into the wash-house and Michael, looking more like a snowman come to life, was standing on the threshold stamping his feet and trying to shake off the snow.

'Oh come in, come in, do!' Maddie tried to grasp hold of him and pull him inside. 'We've been worried sick. Where have you been? Are you all right?'

The others were crowding behind her now, all firing questions at him.

'We thought you'd got lost.'

'How could you worry us so?'

'Wait a minute, wait a minute . . .' Michael was still not stepping inside but tugging at something behind him.

'Get down, you silly dog,' he said, but it was said with affection as Ben leapt up at him, barking excitedly. 'Nick, give us a hand, will you? I'm dead beat.'

Then they saw that Michael was pulling a sledge behind him loaded with sacks covered with a tarpaulin.

They pulled it into the wash-house and finally closed the door against the cold night. Michael leant against it, panting heavily. 'I'm – sorry,' he gasped. 'I didn't think it would take me so long . . .'

Suddenly his legs buckled beneath him and he slid down into an ungainly sitting position, still with all his outdoor clothes on and covered with snow.

'Here, son, let us help you. You must be exhausted.' Frank, Harriet and Maddie were all reaching towards him now, pulling him up, helping him out of his heavy coat and boots and half-carrying, half-pushing him towards the fire in the living room.

Harriet, her own discomfort forgotten, bustled about her kitchen, heating soup and setting the kettle to boil.

Only Nick stood aloof, just watching.

Michael sat in his father's chair, leant back and closed his eyes. 'I'm sorry, Dad. I didn't mean to worry you. I got to the village and there's hardly anything left in the way of provisions. You should see poor Mrs Grange's shop. I've never seen it looking so bare. So, I pressed on to the town.'

'To Wellandon? You went all the way to Wellandon? In this lot?'

Michael nodded. 'I know. It was stupid of me, I suppose. But at least . . .' He raised his head now and grinned, even though there were dark shadows of exhaustion beneath his eyes. 'I got us a bag of coal, some flour, milk and butter for Mrs T and even – a gallon tin of diesel for the engine.'

Frank put his hand on his son's shoulder. 'Oh Michael . . .' But he could say no more, for his throat was choked with emotion.

'Here, out of the way, Mr Frank, let the boy have this soup . . .' Harriet was her old self once more. 'And you two . . .' She turned towards Maddie and Nick. 'Bed.'

For once Maddie said meekly, 'Yes, Mrs Trowbridge,' and turned away to do as she was told, so thankful to have Michael safely home again that at this moment she would have done anything at all that the housekeeper asked her.

As they went upstairs to their rooms, Nick muttered, 'I

still reckon he's been with that Susan in Eastmere. It wouldn't take him the whole day and half the night to get to Wellandon and back.'

As she opened her bedroom door, Maddie turned and glared at him before she slammed the door in his face.

The following morning over breakfast – later than usual now there was no milking to be done – Michael told them about his treacherous journey.

'I was fine going from here to Eastmere because I know the road so well, but it wasn't quite so easy from there to Wellandon.'

'Haven't they cleared the road at all?' Frank asked.

'They've tried, but as fast as they've cleared it another snowfall has blocked it again.' He grinned at Nick and Maddie. 'Just like when we tried to dig a way along our lane.'

'You did well to get all you did,' Harriet was smiling at him, her hero of the hour. She placed a plate of bacon, eggs, fried bread and sausage before him. 'That's the last of the eggs. The hens have stopped laying, but you've earned it.'

'How are things in the town? Are they running short of supplies?'

Michael, his mouth full, shook his head. 'Not really. There's talk of supplies being dropped by plane to outlying farms that are cut off if they put something out in the snow that will show up. We could try that if it goes on much longer.'

'Oh surely we'll have a thaw soon.'

Michael's face sobered. 'There's going to be even more trouble when we do. When this lot melts, the river's never going to cope with the volume of water.'

There was silence around the table until Frank said, 'There's going to be floods, you mean?'

As Michael nodded, Frank let out a low groan of final defeat.

When the thaw started, Michael's foreboding came true.

'What are we going to do? First, foot and mouth and now this. We're ruined.' Frank had taken to his chair by the range once more. He sat with his elbows on the chair arms and dropped his head into his hands.

Michael stood on the peg rug in front of him. 'Come on, Dad, don't give up. At least the water hasn't come into the house, nor even the outbuildings. We've not got it as bad as some poor folks, 'specially in the town. They've been sandbagging the banks of the river, but they're fighting a losing battle because some of the streets are lower than the river level. Their homes are in danger of being flooded, Dad. And south of the town, they say it's much worse.'

The area Michael referred to was low, flat fenland that regularly flooded when the swollen Welland overflowed its banks.

'I know. I know there's a lot worse off than us, but . . . Oh it's just – everything. I don't even think it'll be worth trying to plant crops, the land will be so water-logged.'

'We can get a new herd. Start again.'

Frank shook his head helplessly. 'What's the use?'

Michael glanced at Maddie and then back to his father. He tried again. 'Come on, Dad, surely you've received clearance from the authorities, haven't you?'

Frank's only reply was a disconsolate shrug.

'But there must be something in all that paperwork you've been getting to say we can restock by now?'

'I don't know, lad. I haven't had the heart to read it. Just – just the instructions for what we had to do to deal with the outbreak . . .' His husky voice petered out.

Frank Brackenbury was a broken man. His years of struggle to make a meagre living had ended in defeat. All because of a disease and now the worst winter he could remember. Something he couldn't have foreseen, couldn't deal with and didn't know how to fight.

'We'll have lost the milk round anyway after all this time. Once folks find they can get their milk elsewhere, they're not going to come back to us, are they? Not just out of loyalty.'

Michael forced a laugh. 'I'm sure all my old dears would be delighted to have their handsome milkman back again.'

But Frank could not even raise a smile.

'Well, if you don't want to restock with beast,' Michael was trying his best to be enthusiastic, 'how about we use all the land for crops of some sort? Plough up the meadows. What about extending our acreage of potatoes or caulis?'

The man shook his head. 'I don't know. I think we'd have to get Sir Peter's approval to do that. To change the use of his land. And I don't even know if there are any sort of regulations about growing foodstuff on land that has been infected with the foot and mouth.'

'We can find that out one way or the other.' Michael was refusing to be defeated.

Maddie closed her eyes for a moment against the distress on Frank's face, against the worry creasing Michael's handsome features. The picture that came suddenly into her mind's eye made her reel with the excitement of it. The sheer, blinding beauty and the simplicity of it made her heart miss a beat and then thud loudly in her chest. She swayed and reached out for the edge of the table to steady herself.

'Maddie. What is it? What's the matter?' Michael's voice was full of concern as he caught hold of her arm to steady her.

Her eyes flew open. 'Nothing. At least . . .' She moved to Frank's side and touched his shoulder. 'Mr Frank, I've got an idea.'

The man looked up slowly, but before he could speak Harriet's shrill voice sounded as she came into the room from the kitchen. It was obvious she had been listening to every word that had been said. 'You? Got an idea? And how do you think a chit of a girl like you is going to come up with an idea if a man like Mr Frank can't . . .?'

Maddie felt Frank watching her closely. She knew he could see the fire in her eyes, her lips parted as if bursting to tell her thoughts. His quiet voice stilled the house-keeper's tongue. 'Let's at least hear what the lass has to say, Harriet.'

Maddie took a deep breath. 'Why don't you grow tulips, Mr Frank? The land must be right, because Mr Randall's fields are right next to your meadow.' Again in her mind's eye was the rainbow field that she had so often stood to admire.

'Flowers!' Mrs Trowbridge spat dismissively. 'What would a man like Mr Frank, a farmer born and bred, want with flowers, girl?'

'No, wait a minute. She might have got something, Dad.' There was excitement in Michael's voice too now. 'There would be nothing to stop us using the ground for bulbs, surely?'

Maddie's smile widened. 'You don't eat tulips, Mr Frank. Surely, they wouldn't come under any restrictions, would they?'

Frank stared at her for so long, trance-like, until Maddie, feeling suddenly awkward, prompted, 'Mr Frank?'

He blinked and seemed startled from his reverie. 'No, no, I don't suppose so. I don't really see how there could be? And, yes, the soil would be suitable, I'm sure.'

'Mr Frank,' came Harriet's aggrieved voice. 'Surely you're not going along with this foolish idea? You're a farmer not a – a flower-grower.'

Michael turned his charm on the woman. 'Oh Mrs T, it's a marvellous idea. We'd be horticulturalists.'

'Oh very grand, I'm sure.' Harriet was not to be mollified, not even by Michael. 'And what do any of you know about growing flowers, might I ask?'

'Nothing – yet.' Michael's grin widened. 'But give us a couple of weeks and Maddie and I will know all about it.'

Even Frank was smiling gently now and some of the hopelessness had gone from his eyes. 'Oh the confidence of youth, Harriet. Isn't it wonderful?'

Harriet sniffed. 'Very misplaced, if you ask me. But since I don't seem to have any say in the matter, I'll say no more about it.' With that, she turned away back to the kitchen where they could hear her banging saucepans onto the cooker.

Father and son exchanged a smile and Michael said softly, 'Well, I don't believe that we'll hear "no more about it" for a minute, but . . .' Now he turned to Nick who had stood silently throughout. 'What do you reckon?'

The young boy pushed his fingers through his flop of hair and blinked behind his glasses. He glanced, just once, towards the kitchen door and then looked back at Michael. Softly, he said, 'I think it's the only thing we can do. Even if we do wait the time they tell us before we restock, who's to say the same thing won't happen again.

And to change it all to crops would take an awful lot of work.'

'It'll still take a lot of work to plough it up for bulbs.'

'Yes, but it won't matter if there's a few wild oats and other weeds amongst tulips, will it?' Nick argued. 'Whereas, if you've got a lot of rubbish growing amongst wheat and such, it can ruin your crops if you want to sell it for grain.'

'You're right, Nick. Yes.' Frank leant back in his chair and rested his head, seeming to really relax for the first time in weeks. 'Growing flowers won't be plain sailing. I've no doubt there'll be some sort of blight they can get, or greenfly, or something. But . . .' He turned his smile on Maddie. 'I think it's a wonderful idea and, if it works, we'll all have you to thank, lass.'

Maddie swallowed. 'And if it doesn't?'

'It will work. We'll make it work,' Michael said, putting his arm about her shoulders. 'Won't we?'

Maddie looked up into his deep brown eyes. 'Oh yes,' she whispered and, meaning far more than growing a few fields of flowers, she repeated, 'We'll make it work.'

Twenty-Two

The discussion continued whilst Harriet set the table for supper.

'Of course, I'll have to go and see Sir Peter and ask his permission,' Frank took his place and picked up the carving knife and fork. 'It is his land, after all.'

'What's in the tenancy agreement?' Michael asked.

Frank shrugged. 'Can't say I've ever read it.'

'You're not very good with paperwork, are you, Dad?'

Frank smiled, more life in his eyes than they had seen for weeks. 'The farm just passed from me Dad to me. Same terms, same rent, same everything. Of course, the rent goes up every so often, but that's to be expected. Other than that, Sir Peter's never interfered.'

'What I mean is, Dad, does it actually say that you have to inform the landlord of change of use of the land?'

'Dunno, but I think it's courteous anyway. Don't you?'

Michael sighed. 'I suppose so, yes. But I just don't want anything – or anyone – to stand in the way.' He paused and then grinned as he glanced across at Maddie. 'I know. We'll send Maddie. She can charm Sir Peter into agreeing.'

Maddie's fork was suspended halfway between her plate and her mouth as she gaped, horrified, at Michael. 'You're not serious?'

'Of course, he's not, love,' Frank said quickly. 'Besides, it's my place to go. I'm the legal tenant.'

'I am perfectly serious. It's Maddie's idea. Why shouldn't she take the credit?'

Frank smiled at her. 'Well, you could come with me, lass. Your enthusiasm is certainly infectious and if Sir Peter hears for himself all your ideas, then perhaps it would be useful for you to be there.'

Maddie laid down her fork. Suddenly, she could eat no more for the nervous fluttering in her stomach as Frank added, 'We'll go as soon as the weather improves.' She was being asked to face the man who for so long had ruled every aspect of her life. What she ate, how she was dressed, what school she attended. And yet she had never even spoken to him. Not one word. He probably didn't even know she existed. At least, not by name. To Sir Peter Mayfield she was just another orphan in the Home his family had benevolently set up for orphaned or unwanted children.

But by the time they were able to visit Mayfield Hall, when Maddie had washed her hair and put on the new red dress that the family had bought her for Christmas, she no longer felt nervous. She felt ready to do battle.

'There you are,' Michael greeted her, his brown eyes appraising her approvingly. 'You look like a flower yourself. Sir Peter won't be able to resist you. My little tulip girl.'

Maddie giggled and felt her cheeks glow.

'I wish I was coming with you.' He stepped a little closer and gently touched her chin with the tip of his finger.

'Why – why don't you?'

He shrugged. 'Oh, I think it's best if just Dad and you go. We don't want it to look like a mass attack.'

'You ready, lass?' Frank's voice came from the kitchen and Maddie said a swift goodbye to Michael and hurried outside.

Frank, too, was dressed in his best suit and it was he

who was looking very nervous now. As she climbed into the car beside him, he said, 'I'm glad you're coming with me lass. I don't mind admitting, I get all tongue tied.'

'Do you mean you want me to do some of the talking?'

'Well, only if I get sort of lost or – or dry up, like. You know what I mean?'

Maddie nodded and sat back in her seat to run over in her mind all the arguments to support what they wanted to do.

They did not speak again until they drew up outside the front door of Mayfield Hall.

'Should we go round the back, do you think? To the servants' entrance?' Frank murmured.

'Have you never been here before to see Sir Peter about anything?'

Frank pushed back his cap and scratched his head. 'No. I've never had the cause. Sir Peter's been to the farm now and again. On horseback. Even though he's got two cars, he still likes to ride around his estate on horseback, you know. But no, I've never been here. At least, not like this. To seek an interview with him.'

'Well,' Maddie said firmly, with a great deal more confidence than she was feeling inside at this moment. 'You're a respected tenant. A gentleman farmer. I think you have a right to enter by the front door, don't you?'

Frank leant his arms on the steering wheel and looked up at the imposing mansion towering above them. 'I suppose so.'

'You sound doubtful.'

'Well, a few weeks back, I'd have agreed with you. But I'm a farmer no longer. Not now.'

'Mr Frank,' Maddie touched his arm, 'you've had some rotten bad luck. But it's not your fault. No one can say it's your fault. Not even Sir Peter.'

163

Frank's expression was still doubtful. 'I keep going over and over it in my mind. How did it happen? Was it my fault because I bought those beast of Weatherall's? Or was it birds that brought the disease because two of our own started at the same time, didn't they? I lay awake at night going over it all. '

'And do you have any answers?'

Frank shook his head and his voice was hoarse with sadness as he whispered, 'No. No, lass, I don't.'

Her hand still on his arm, she said gently, 'Then why not put it all behind you and look to the future? It's happened and we can't alter it. But we can do something different.'

Frank turned his head to look at her and, with eyes that were so like her beloved Michael's, he smiled down at her. 'You know, lass, I've heard the saying "an old head on young shoulders" but I've never before met anyone it fitted. Not until you came into our lives. For a lass of fourteen, you've a very sensible head – and a pretty one – on those slim shoulders of yours.'

Now was not the time to remind him that she had just passed the date of her official birthday. She was fifteen now. Instead, Maddie squeezed his arm, taking his words as the compliment she was sure he meant them to be. 'Come on. Let's go and face the lion in his den.'

Twenty-Three

They were both standing facing Sir Peter across the wide desk in his book-lined study, like two naughty school children summoned to the headmaster's office.

Maddie had never before been this close to Sir Peter. Of course, she would have recognized the tall figure dressed in check tweeds, the loud, bluff voice, so used to issuing orders and so used to being obeyed. But never before had she been close enough to see that his round face had a florid complexion with tiny red veins like a railway network on his skin; that his over-large nose was almost purple and that his moustache was now almost white. His hair, too, was white and so thin and sparse that the pink of his scalp shone through it. But his blue eyes were surprisingly bright and very sharp and knowing.

'Well, Brackenbury,' he barked. 'What is it?'

Frank twisted his cap round and round between nervous fingers as he began, haltingly, to explain. 'Well, sir, you know how I'm placed now. My livelihood's all but gone.'

Maddie could see the strain on Frank's face as if he carried the whole burden of guilt for the disease that had stricken his cattle.

'I have to admit, sir, that I was about ready to give up.'

Sir Peter said nothing. He leant back in the chair, his penetrating gaze never leaving his tenant's face.

'But then,' Frank went on, 'this lass here had what we

think is a very good idea. But, out of courtesy, I thought it only right to come and – well – discuss it with you first.'

Still Sir Peter did not speak, but his gaze came to rest now on Maddie as Frank looked to her and said, 'You carry on, lass. You tell Sir Peter about your idea.'

The landowner's scrutiny was disconcerting. He had been such a powerful force in her life, albeit from a distance. His name had always been the ultimate threat held over all the girls at the orphanage that carried his family's name and still enjoyed his patronage. He was staring at her now and there was a strange look on his face that had nothing to do with the reason for their visit to his home. It was as if he half recognized her and was searching his memory to place where he had seen her before.

Maddie almost laughed aloud. Oh he'd seen her before all right, but only dressed in the clothes of his own orphanage waifs. Now, with her hair washed and cut to a soft, crowning glory, her young body firm and yet showing the curves of womanhood, she could understand the man not recognizing her.

Maddie took a deep breath. 'Mr Frank isn't sure whether the restrictions extend to crops, you know, edible crops, as well as cattle when the land's been infected, so I said, why don't we plant tulips? Even if the disease is still on the land, it surely won't harm tulips.'

Sir Peter sat forward suddenly and leant his arms on the desk, staring at her. 'Flowers? You want to plant flowers on my land?'

Maddie's heart sank at his words and she was sure that, beside her, Frank's did too. There was the same scathing note in his voice that had been in Harriet's when Maddie had first made the suggestion.

'What else can we do?'

Sir Peter spread his hands, palms upwards, as if the matter were simple. 'Wait until you can restock.'

Frank and Maddie exchanged a glance and then both faced the landlord again. The girl, young though she was, guessed that Frank found the admission he was being forced to make, degrading. 'I haven't enough put by, sir, to buy ten or fifteen beast all at once. And despite waiting the regulation period, if the disease is still on the land, the same thing could happen again.'

'Ah,' Sir Peter said shortly and leant back in his chair again. 'I see.' There was a silence in the room before he said, 'If I waive a year's rent, would that help?'

'Well, it would, sir, but . . .' Frank said no more but the meaning in the unspoken words was plain enough.

'Mm, well, I'll give the matter some thought, Brackenbury,' was all Sir Peter would promise before they were shown out and found themselves walking down the front steps to the car.

'Oh well, it was a good try, lass, but it's obvious he's not keen.'

'But he did say he'd think about it.'

Frank cast her a wry glance. 'I wouldn't like my life to depend on him saying "yes", though.'

Maddie pulled a comical face in return. 'Neither would I,' she was forced to admit.

'I can't believe it. You and your father before you have been farming his land for years and never a bad word between you and the landlord. You told me so yourself. So why can't he trust your judgement now?'

Maddie gaped at the housekeeper in astonishment. Harriet was incensed, but it was Frank who voiced Maddie's own thoughts. 'I thought you didn't agree with us anyway. I'm surprised you don't say "I told you so".'

'That's as maybe,' Harriet bridled. 'What I say in this house is one thing, but when it comes to an outsider disagreeing, that's different.'

Frank smiled gently. Harriet Trowbridge, it seemed, regarded the household as her own family. She would strongly disagree with them in private, but was prepared to present a united front to the world at large.

'He's no right to stop you if it's what you really want, Mr Frank,' she railed. 'If you really think it's a good idea . . .' Maddie felt the woman's resentful glance rest on her for a brief moment before she added, 'and it's what you want us to do, Mr Frank. Then that's what we'll do.'

'Oh Harriet,' Frank ran his hand through his hair. 'I don't know now. I really don't. If I go against him, he could give me notice.'

Harriet's mouth dropped open. 'He wouldn't do that. He wouldn't dare.'

'There's no "dare" about it. He owns the land, when all's done and said.'

In a voice so low that Frank did not hear, although Maddie's sharp ears caught her words, Harriet said, 'We'll see about that.'

As the woman turned away and went back to her kitchen, Maddie saw a strange gleam in Harriet's eyes.

Now what, she thought as she gazed after her, was the housekeeper up to?

The following morning Maddie was even more astonished to see Harriet putting on her black coat and felt hat.

She rarely left the farm, Maddie knew. Either Michael or Nick did any shopping they needed. She never went into the nearby town nor even down to the village shop. She didn't even seem to have any family or friends who came to the farm to visit her. Her whole life was centred around Few Farm and Frank Brackenbury. Apart from her visit to the orphanage and that one trip into Wellandon at Frank's insistence, Maddie could not now recall ever seeing the housekeeper leave the farm.

So Maddie's mouth almost dropped open when the housekeeper came to stand close by her. 'Now, girl, just you keep quiet about me going out,' she said in a low voice, glancing furtively about her to be sure no one was either watching or listening. 'Not a word to Mr Frank, nor to Michael. You hear me?'

Maddie shrugged. 'Nothing to do with me, Mrs Trowbridge. Is there anything you want me to do for you while you're out?' And she added sadly, 'As I've no dairy work now.'

'You can start the bedrooms for me. But leave Mr Frank's. I'll see to that.'

Maddie hid her smile. Thursday was the day of the week when Harriet always 'did' the bedrooms. Not even an obviously necessary trip out could be allowed to interfere with her routine.

'Right you are, Mrs Trowbridge. Off you go and have a nice time.'

'Huh. I don't know about that,' was the housekeeper's sour reply as she opened the back door. Maddie, following her into the wash-house to collect cleaning materials, watched as Harriet paused on the threshold, glanced quickly around the yard making sure no one was about and then hurried towards the gate.

'What *is* she up to?' Maddie murmured.

*

The mystery was solved three days later when, on the Sunday morning, Theo Mayfield rode into the yard of Few Farm on horseback.

Dismounting, he tethered the horse to the gatepost. Maddie was in her bedroom changing her dress ready for Church in half an hour and saw him from the window as he walked towards the back door.

She hurried down the stairs calling, 'Mr Frank, Mr Frank. There's a gentleman coming across the yard. I think it's Mr Theo.'

'What?' Startled Frank leapt up from his chair by the fire, throwing down the Sunday newspaper he was reading and then hastily stopping to pick it up and fold it neatly. 'Go and let him in, Maddie. Bring him in here.' He stood before the mirror over the range to straighten his tie and smooth down his hair that had already been combed into neatness ready for Church. But the action betrayed his nervousness.

'Good day. Miss March, isn't it?' Theo Mayfield actually touched his riding hat with the end of his whip in a courteous gesture. 'Is Mr Brackenbury at home?'

'Yes, sir. Please come in.' She turned and led the way through the kitchen and into the living room where Frank was waiting anxiously.

'Won't you sit down, sir? Can I offer you a drink or . . .?'

'No, no, Mr Brackenbury.'

Maddie was swift to notice that, unlike Sir Peter, Theo gave Frank the courtesy title of 'Mister'. 'I can see that you and your household are about to leave for Church. I'll not delay you, but I felt I should ride across to tell you that my father is ill.'

Frank cleared his throat. 'I'm sorry to hear that, sir. Nothing serious, I hope.'

Theo's face was sober. 'I'm afraid it may be. He suffered a stroke the night before last and the next few days are critical.'

'Oh, I am sorry.'

'Thank you.' Theo nodded and was obviously touched by the older man's genuine concern. Maddie saw that the young man pulled in a deep breath as he went on. 'Fortunately, my father had mentioned to me your idea of turning your land into growing tulips.'

'Yes, sir,' Frank began doubtfully. 'But Sir Peter didn't seem very taken with the idea.'

'Well, I think it's a very good idea. I told him so and he did seem to be coming round to your way of thinking. So, as he's obviously going to be incapacitated for some time and I have come home to take up the reins of running the estate, I'm happy to tell you that I'm in full agreement with your proposal.'

'Are you sure, Mr Theo? I mean, I wouldn't want you to go against your father's wishes.'

'No, no. No more would I, but, as I said, we talked at length about it and I think he began to realize that there's very little else you can do in the circumstances. Although I think it was the visit from your housekeeper that clinched it for you.'

'My housekeeper? Harriet?' Frank's surprise was obvious.

'Why, yes. Didn't you know? She was closeted with my father in his study for almost an hour on Thursday morning.' The young man laughed and shrugged. 'I don't know what she said to him, but she was obviously very persuasive because afterwards he just said to me, "I think we'll let Brackenbury have his way." Besides,' Mr Theo added, and this was obviously his own belief, not that of his father, 'the land is perfect for it.'

'Well, I'm very grateful to you, sir, if you're really sure?'

'I am. I understand, also, that when he spoke to you my father offered to waive a year's rent?'

'He did, sir, but that was to give us time to restock.'

Theo smiled at the honesty of the man. 'Well, you'll still have to buy stock, only bulbs instead of beast. And it will be some time before you get your first harvest of blooms so we'll still stick to that offer.' His smile broadened. 'I'm sure my father would agree.'

Frank's weather-beaten complexion, was even more ruddy. 'That's very generous of you, sir.'

'There is just one more thing. You'll have to write to the authorities – the County War Agricultural Executive Committee.' He pulled a comical face. 'A mouthful, isn't it? They're called War Ag's for short. They came into being in the War to oversee food production, but I think they still have some powers as we've still got quite a lot of rationing. I think you'll have to get clearance from them, Mr Brackenbury.'

'Oh.' Frank scratched his head, clearly puzzled. 'Well, yes. Thank you, sir.'

Maddie could see that Theo had noticed Frank's dilemma. He didn't know how or where to start.

'Tell you what,' the younger man said. 'I'll make the initial contact for you. I know one of the chaps there. Philip Taylor. I'll have a word with him, if you like, and ask him to get in touch with you.'

Plainly relieved, Frank said, 'I'd be most grateful, sir. That would be very kind of you.'

Maddie found herself beaming at the young man, who had not only given them his approval but had made a practical and helpful offer too.

'And see Bill Randall,' Mr Theo went on. 'He's a good-hearted fellow and I'm sure he will give you all the advice

he can.' Theo held out his hand. 'Good luck, Mr Brackenbury, and please don't hesitate to let me know if there's
anything more I can do.'

'Thank you, sir. You've been most kind.'

Maddie felt the young man's glance linger on her for a
moment as he said softly, 'Good day to you, Miss March.'

She smiled and said, 'Goodbye, Mr Theo and – thank
you.'

Both Frank and Maddie followed the young man to the
door and watched him walk back across the yard to his
horse.

'Well, that's a surprise, isn't it?'

'It is, lass. But all I hope is that the lad won't get into
trouble when his father recovers and finds out what he's
agreed to.' He shook his head, mystified. 'And I still can't
understand why Harriet thought she could help.'

Maddie begrudged giving praise to the housekeeper, but
her innate honesty made her say, 'Well, she obviously did.'

'Yes, she must have done. But how?'

'I don't know, but it sounds,' Maddie said slowly, 'as if
you've no need to worry about Sir Peter being well enough
to object for some time.'

And though she was not, by nature, a vindictive person,
Maddie could not find it in her heart to be sorry for Sir
Peter Mayfield.

Twenty-Four

'So then what do we have to do, Mr Randall?'

The big man laughed, the sound seeming to come from deep within his rotund belly. 'By heck, mate, you're keen, I'll say that for you.'

Maddie chuckled. She had met Bill Randall only once before and his habit of calling everyone he met – male or female, young or old – 'mate' always amused her. But it was a friendly term and Maddie warmed to him.

His expression sobered now. 'And I'll give you all the help I can, because I was sorry to hear about what happened to Frank Brackenbury. Very sorry. He's a good man and dun't deserve to lose his livelihood in such a cruel way. So, mate, let's get down to brass tacks, shall us? Has Frank got approval from the War Ag's?'

Maddie nodded. 'Mr Taylor visited us the day before yesterday and told us what we can do. Mr Frank's got seventy-five acres altogether. We're to plough up the meadows and plant about ten acres of bulbs to start with, he said, and the rest to potatoes and vegetables for a while, or wheat if we want to. Then we should be able to increase our bulb production gradually as the regulations relax.'

Bill Randall raised his eyebrows. 'I don't know if you'll manage ten acres in your first year, mate. It's not a good time to be setting up, y'know.'

Maddie's heart plummeted as the man went on. 'Bulbs is very expensive still, since the War, see. We're still having to import a lot and not only are we restricted in how many acres we can grow, but we can't get hold of the bulbs easy.'

Maddie bit her lip and nodded, but the big man was still smiling at her. 'Tell you what, though, I'll have a word with a few of my mates and we'll see what we can do to help old Frank.'

'Oh thank you, Mr Randall.'

'And you could try the bulb auction. They hold one in the cattle market every Tuesday in Wellandon. But be careful, don't go paying too much. And another thing, you do know that bulbs become like another crop? You have to rotate them along with whatever else you grow?'

Maddie nodded. She wasn't quite sure what he meant but she would report faithfully back to Frank and Michael everything that Bill Randall said and they would understand.

'I was forced to cut my bulb production right back in the War, y'know,' he was saying, 'and they're still only letting me increase steadily. A lot of our production went to America.'

'Why?'

'Because of the War, their supplies from Holland were cut off.'

'Oh.' Maddie tried to show polite interest but she didn't really understand. She was far more interested in finding out how Few Farm could get started with its first few bulbs. Mr Randall's next words brought her further disappointment.

''Course, it's the wrong time of year for planting, but I'll tell you what could be a good idea for Frank. A greenhouse.' The man beamed as if he personally had solved all of Frank Brackenbury's problems.

'A greenhouse?'

'Yes. Forcing flowers to grow out of season, 'specially in time for Christmas. It got very popular in the Twenties, but, of course, even they had to turn their greenhouses over for food production in the War. Y'know, tomatoes and such. But that way, you can get better prices. It's like everything else, mate. If you get a glut of flowers all ready at the same time, the price drops. But if you,' he winked down at her and tapped the side of his nose, 'can be the one to have flowers ready when no one else has. Well, then, you can up the price.'

'I see,' Maddie said slowly. 'At least, I think I do.'

With a willing listener, Bill Randall launched into the practicalities of forcing bulbs to bloom earlier than nature intended. 'It's hard work, lass. You pick out the biggest bulbs for forcing. They need to be in a cold store for a while and then you plant them in boxes outside in autumn. Keep them well watered and bring them into the heated greenhouses in batches, so that when they flower they'll do so at different times.'

Maddie smiled and nodded. 'I understand, so that you'll have a few trays ready for Christmas then a few at the beginning of January and so on?'

'You've got it, mate. That's the idea.'

'But wouldn't it be very expensive to build a big greenhouse?'

'Well now, it just so happens that I know where's one going for a song. Weatherall's old place. It's a bit dilapidated. The woodwork would need painting up and some of the glass needs replacing. But it could be taken down and moved to Frank's yard without a deal of trouble.'

Maddie pulled a face. 'I'm not sure how Mr Frank would react to hearing that it's from Mr Weatherall's.'

Mr Randall looked puzzled for a moment before he said, 'Oh aye, I was forgetting.'

Maddie tried to make a joke of it. 'He might think it'd carry some sort of disease that tulips get.'

The big man laughed. 'Well, I don't think a bit of timber and glass could do that. You won't be using his soil, now will you? You'd need to make your own foundations first and then just buy the wooden frame and the glass.'

'I'll see what he says.'

'Don't forget to tell Frank that he's got one thing in his favour.'

'What's that, Mr Randall?'

'His own electricity supply. He'll be able to run pipes from that boiler house of his to heat a greenhouse and control it with a pump . . .' The man beamed, 'Run by his electricity.'

Maddie's smile widened. 'I'll tell him, Mr Randall. And thank you for all your help.'

'Think nowt on it, mate, think nowt on it. I'm looking forward to the day when I can look over yon hedge and see your field of tulips.'

Frank, Michael and Nick listened intently to all that Maddie had to relate. Even Harriet, though she tried hard not to look as if she was taking any interest in the project, hovered within earshot.

When she came to the point of telling Frank just who owned the greenhouse that was 'going for a song', Maddie hesitated. But she need not have worried. Frank laughed wryly and said, 'Well, I reckon old man Weatherall owes me one, don't you? So now, we've just got to let Mr Theo know what we're doing and then . . .' Frank stood up and look around. 'We can get started.'

Michael gave his father a slap on the shoulder and then

turned and slapped Nick on the back, too. But he put his arms about Maddie's waist and picked her up and swung her round.

'My little Tulip Girl,' he said. 'It's going to happen, Maddie. We're going to make it happen. And it's all thanks to you.'

Maddie wound her arms about his neck and hugged him hard, the lump in her throat too big to let her speak.

Then, over his shoulder she caught sight of the venomous look in Harriet's eyes and the joyous moment was spoilt.

They ended up with not one, but two greenhouses.

As Frank and his near neighbours, and even the village folk and the townsfolk too, counted up the cost of the winter's blizzards and began to try to restore some sort of normality to their lives, Mr Theo called again at Few Farm. He arrived one blustery late April day when the noise of Mr Randall's concrete mixer filled the yard.

Michael, stripped to his sleeveless vest, shovelled gravel, sand and cement and tipped water into the rotating drum whilst Nick barrowed each mix to where Maddie and Frank waited. For a week they had dug out an oblong shape approximately eight inches deep to the length and breadth of Mr Weatherall's greenhouse for the foundations. They had put wooden boards all around the inside of the oblong – shuttering, Frank told Maddie – and now Nick tipped barrow load after barrow load of concrete mix into the hole for Frank to spread with a spade.

'Right, lass, now we have to tamp it,' Frank said and then, one at each end, they picked up a long wooden board and smoothed out the concrete with the edge of it, level with the top of the shuttering. The lumpy gravel sank into the mixture and the top was skimmed with the wet cement and left to dry into a smooth surface.

It was as the last load was tipped in that Maddie jumped to hear Mr Theo's voice just behind her. She had not seen him arrive nor heard him above the noise of the mixer.

'I'm sorry,' he said at once as she turned around swiftly, her lips parted in a startled gasp.

'I didn't hear you,' she shouted above the clatter, but at that moment Michael turned the engine off and the noise died away. He came towards them and Maddie noticed that the two young men smiled at each other.

'Mr Theo. It's good to see you. Sorry I can't shake hands.' He spread his hands to show their dirty state. Theo laughed and stepped back a pace, but it was obvious that his action was only in jest.

'How are you, Michael?'

'We're fine, thank you.' He nodded down at the foundations. 'This is for a greenhouse.'

'A greenhouse?' Theo's glance appraised the size of the proposed structure. He watched as Frank and Maddie bent to their task to level out the last of the concrete.

Standing up and easing his aching back, Frank said, 'We've picked one up from old Weatherall's place, sir. We've already taken it down and brought it here in sections. We've even managed to salvage most of the glass too.'

'The woodwork needs painting, of course,' Michael put in, 'but it'll be a good start for us.'

Theo's eyes were still upon the wet cement and he tapped his lips with the tip of his riding crop, deep in thought. Then he glanced around him assessing where they had positioned the greenhouse alongside the hen-house, next to the crewyard.

'You didn't think of taking that old barn down, then, and building it there?'

'Well, sir,' Frank was hesitant. 'I didn't like to without your permission.'

'This is nearer the boiler house, sir,' Michael pointed to the corner building in the crewyard where the boiler house was situated. 'It'll be easy to run the pipes from there to the greenhouse to heat it. Like we do the hen-house.'

'Mm.' Theo's attention turned to the barn. He walked slowly towards it and stood looking up at it. Then he turned and wandered across towards the crewyard and the hen-house and even walked round the rear of the buildings. While he was gone from their sight for a few moments, Michael glanced at his father and asked in a low voice, 'What's he up to?'

Frank shrugged, 'I don't know,' and then they both turned to face Theo as he emerged from the nettles and thistles at the back of the hen-house. Still saying nothing, he walked past them once more and went towards the house, looking over the gate leading into the fenced garden at the front of the house.

'I just wondered,' he said, as he came back to them once more, 'if you wanted another greenhouse. We've got one that we're taking down, but it's a lean-to. It was on the outside of a walled garden. Never used. Allowed to fall into ruin and it's become an eyesore. I've instructed Talbot . . .' Theo referred to the Head Gardener at Mayfield Park, 'to take it down. If you can do anything with it, Mr Brackenbury, you're very welcome to it. But you'd need a suitable wall to put it against. There's no point in putting it behind there.' He gestured towards the hen-house. 'It wouldn't get enough sun. The best place . . .' he pointed with his crop, 'appears to be the house wall overlooking your garden. It would catch all the sun there. The greenhouse isn't worth very much, so I wouldn't charge you anything. Talbot was just going to scrap it. And whilst we're on the subject,' again he pointed with his riding crop, 'if you should want to, for any reason, you have my permission to take down the barn. And another thing . . .' Even yet, Theo wasn't finished, 'How about covering in the whole of the crewyard?'

'What?' Frank's mouth almost dropped open.

Theo smiled. 'Yes, I know it would be a huge building. But that's exactly what you're going to need. I suggest you leave the outbuildings just as they are . . .' He pointed with his whip. 'You'll need all sorts of places – a cold store, ordinary storage, cool and airy, for bulbs for replanting in the fields . . .'

Maddie was listening intently, soaking up the knowledge.

'. . . And,' Theo went on. 'Plenty of space for packing cut flowers, cleaning and grading bulbs and so on . . .' His keen eye was running over the whole area. 'Yes, the more I think about it, the better I like it.'

'I'm sorry, but I couldn't . . .' Frank began but Michael cut in. 'Oh Dad, it's a marvellous idea.'

'I know. I know it is, but . . .'

Theo held up his hand. 'Of course all the costs would be met by the estate, Mr Brackenbury. I would never expect a tenant to undertake such an expense. After all, to my mind, it'll improve the value of the property.' He gave them all a broad wink. 'Well, at least that'll be my argument when I have to justify the expense to my father.'

'Well . . .' Frank seemed almost overcome with emotion. 'That's very kind of you, sir. We'd certainly be able to make very good use of a big barn like that, and yes, we'd like to come and take a look at the greenhouse, if we may?'

'Of course. Any time.' Maddie felt his glance come to rest on her as he said again, softly, 'Any time.'

'We'll come over tomorrow afternoon, Mr Theo,' Michael said as he moved to stand beside Maddie.

She noticed Theo's glance move from her to Michael and then back again and she knew that he had sensed that there was something between her and Michael.

Theo gave a nod and touched his riding hat. 'See you tomorrow, then.' He turned away and walked back to his horse tethered at the gate.

'He's a nice young man,' Frank said. 'And generous too. A mite more generous than his father.'

Maddie turned in surprise. For one who had had it drilled into her the whole of her life that she owed everything to the kind benevolence of Sir Peter, it came as a shock to hear that he was not universally regarded as being so. It was only now that she was outside the walls of the Home and she could see how other people lived and conducted their lives that she could begin to make any sort of comparison.

Her thoughts were interrupted as Ben came bounding across the yard and paddled straight across the newly smoothed concrete.

'Oh Ben!'

'You bad dog!'

'Get away, animal.'

Poor Ben, thoroughly chastened though not understanding what he had done that was so dreadful, ran away into the lane whilst, laughing now, Frank and Maddie once more picked up the tamping board to smooth out his paw marks.

*

Later that night, when supper was over and everyone was about to go to bed, Michael said, 'Come on, Maddie, we'd better go and look if anyone else has decided to leave their mark on our handiwork.'

They stepped out into the clear night and walked across the yard. Michael slipped his arm around her shoulders. 'I've being trying to think of a way to get you to myself for a few minutes. And now I have the perfect excuse.'

Maddie giggled and put her arm about his waist. As they stood looking down at the concrete foundations, Michael moved to one corner and touched it with his finger. 'As I hoped, it's not quite dry yet. Still soft enough to leave a mark.'

'As you hoped? Oh you mean, we've got to stand guard all night?'

'No, I didn't mean that, although that's a very good idea, my little Tulip.' His lowered his voice to teasing wickedness. 'Are you game?'

Maddie stifled her laughter that sounded so loud in the night air.

'Come here,' Michael whispered. She stepped towards him and squatted down beside him.

He shone his torch on to the wet cement. 'Press your hand into it. Right here, in the corner.'

'But your Dad . . .?'

'He won't mind. He was annoyed at Ben, of course, because he went prancing about all over it. But just here, no one will notice when the building's finished because it'll be under all the trays of bulbs, won't it? Let's leave our mark, Tulip. Yours and mine.'

The idea appealed to her. The imprint of their hands set in concrete, side by side for ever.

'All right then.' She rolled up her sleeve and placed her right hand flat on the soft cement, pressing until it squelched through her fingers. 'It's setting already, isn't it?'

Carefully she lifted her hand away to see that she had left a perfect impression.

'Now you,' she whispered.

Michael's hand hovered over her mark as he turned his left hand to the position he wanted and pressed it down. When he lifted his hand away, she saw that his imprint had overlapped hers a little so that it looked as if their two smallest fingers were entwined.

'Hold the torch for me,' he said as he pulled a screwdriver from his pocket. With the sharp end he drew in the cement the shape of a long-stemmed tulip curving around their two hand imprints. Underneath he wrote the year – 1947.

'There. Now that's there for our children and our grandchildren and even for their children to see.'

'Oh Michael.'

He leant towards her and in the cold night air, his lips were warm upon hers. 'Come on,' he murmured, 'we'd better go in, else I'll want to take you into the hay shed again.'

'Well,' she said boldly, 'why don't we?'

He stood up. 'Little hussy!' But he was laughing softly as he said it. 'My father warned me about girls like you.'

Maddie rose too and faced him in the darkness. But she was not laughing. She was very serious as she said, 'Did he? Did he really?'

He put his arm about her shoulder and began to lead her back towards the house. 'Yes, he did. He said, "One day, a lovely girl will come along and steal your heart and you'll have eyes for no one else after that." And do you know something, my darling little Tulip Girl?'

'No,' she whispered, hardly daring to breathe in case she woke and found she was dreaming. 'What?'

'He's right. I haven't. I haven't eyes for anyone else in the world now except you.'

Twenty-Five

'Do you know,' Michael said one evening at supper, 'I've just realized something.'

The summer had passed in a blur of hard work. They all still rose as early as they always had done and worked until the light faded in the evening. Some nights, Maddie almost fell asleep at the supper table. Then she would climb the stairs to fall into bed and wake the next morning feeling as if she hadn't been there five minutes. But once out in the yard or the fields, the thought of field after field of glorious tulips the following April spurred her on and her weariness would disappear. They harnessed Rajah to plough up the meadows. There were so many stones and roots that had to be picked out by hand that Maddie felt she would never stand upright again.

But all of them were working happily together. Frank seemed to have taken on a new lease of life and Nick looked healthier than Maddie had ever known him. His skin became tanned in the hot summer of that year and his rather mousey-coloured hair was streaked blond by the sun. Even his mother lost some of her sourness and brought their dinners out to the field where they sat under the shade of a tree to eat cheese and pickle with soft, crusty bread followed by her freshly-baked apple pasties.

'Why does food always taste so much nicer out of

186

doors?' Michael would say, and then gallantly add, 'not that yours doesn't taste wonderful wherever we eat it, Mrs T.'

'Oh, you and your flattery, Michael Brackenbury.'

And in the warm, soft nights Michael and Maddie would sometimes sneak out to the fields again, their arms about each other to stand together and dream of their golden future.

And now it was September and the greenhouses were both ready for the very first bulbs and the ground in the field too, was prepared.

'What's that, son?' Frank wanted to know in response to Michael's statement. Even though the anxiety was sometimes still in his eyes as to whether this venture would work, most of the time he worked so hard now that he had neither time nor energy left to worry. Whatever happened, it wouldn't be for the want of trying. Everyone in the household was doing their bit towards making it work.

'Maddie's been here almost eighteen months and she's never had a birthday.' Michael's own birthday was on the seventh of September in a few days' time.

'I haven't really got one,' she said glancing at Harriet and remembering vividly standing beneath her scrutiny whilst she and Mrs Potter discussed her. 'Only the date the Home gave me.'

'I don't understand,' Michael said.

'I was abandoned outside the door of the Home in March so they just gave me that date as my birthday. They thought I was about a month old.'

She heard Harriet's familiar sniff. 'That's why she's got such a fancy name,' the housekeeper put in, talking again about her as if she was not present, 'Madeleine indeed.'

There was a silence around the table, then Maddie said, 'Jen was left outside the door too. In the September and they thought she was newborn, so her birthday's the tenth of this month.'

Michael's smile widened. 'We'll have a party then, on the tenth. For Jenny, me and a rather late one for you, Maddie. What about it, Dad?'

Maddie saw Frank glance at Harriet, but before he could speak, Maddie cut in, 'No, it'd be too much work and we're all far too busy.' Then she added hastily as she smiled her thanks across the table, 'But it's very kind of you to think of it.'

'I don't see why we couldn't do something,' Frank said. 'What do you say, Harriet?'

Maddie almost laughed aloud as she saw the housekeeper's dilemma. Her glance went from Michael to Maddie and back again. How she would love to throw a party for her favourite's birthday, but if Maddie and the other little waif and stray were to be linked, then enthusiasm for the idea stuck in Harriet's throat.

Tight-lipped, Harriet said at last, 'Whatever you say, Mr Frank. But might I suggest it would be better on your birthday, Michael, as it's a Sunday.'

'All right, then. I was only thinking of having it on little Jen's birthday. Make it special for her, you know.'

Maddie, powerless to stop it, felt the sudden thrust of jealousy once more, despite her vow to quell it. She swallowed and forced herself to say, 'Can I help you, Mrs Trowbridge?'

Rising from her chair and beginning to gather the dishes together, Harriet said, 'I'm sure I can manage a few jellies and blancmanges without your interference, thank you.'

As fragile as a gossamer dandelion in seed, the house-keeper's good humour was blown away in a few seconds.

Beside her, Maddie heard Frank's sigh.

It was like the Christmas they should have enjoyed and birthday celebrations all rolled into one. Jenny arrived mid-afternoon on the following Sunday, her face pink with excitement. Shyly, she handed out the gifts she had brought, not only a tie for Michael and soaps for Maddie, but a small box of chocolates as a 'thank you' to Harriet and three white men's handkerchiefs for Frank, but also – and Maddie shrewdly guessed most important of all – she had brought a present for Nick, too.

'It's not my birthday 'til next month,' he said as he took it, but Maddie could see the pleasure in his eyes, his cheeks creasing in a wide smile. 'What is it?'

'Open it and see.'

Nick pulled off the wrapping paper. 'Oh! Oh!' His face was pink with delighted surprise. 'Thank you, Jen. It's great.'

'I'm sorry it's not new, but it is in good condition.'

'Yes, yes, it's hardly been used. It's great,' he said as he opened the book on engines and lovingly turned the pages.

'Maddie told me once how you like car engines and things.'

'Fancy you remembering that,' he murmured. Already the giver of the gift was rapidly losing his attention. But Jenny was quite content to sit and watch him poring over the book she had brought him. It was thanks enough for her.

*

They had a wonderful party. Even Harriet seemed to unbend a little when Frank kept refilling her glass with elderflower wine.

'You'll have me tipsy, Mr Frank,' she actually giggled protestingly, but Maddie noticed that she still held out her glass for more.

As yet another game of blind man's buff ended, Frank glanced at the clock. 'Nine o'clock already. I hate to break up the jollifications, but I think we'd better see Jenny back home.'

Maddie saw her glance hopefully at Nick. A walk in the moonlight with him would be the perfect end of a perfect day for Jenny. But Nick had already picked up his book and settled himself in the depths of an armchair.

'We'll walk you home,' Michael said. 'Me and Maddie.'

Maddie held her breath, waiting for Harriet's disapproval, but the housekeeper was lying back in her armchair, her gaze intent on the swirling pale liquid in her glass, a small smile on her mouth.

'Off you go then, else Mrs Grange will be locking you out.'

Goodbyes and thank yous were said all round and then they were out in the night air that already had the hint of autumn in it.

Maddie positioned herself between the other two and linked arms.

'It was nice to have a bit of fun,' Michael said, 'because from now on, it's going to be work, work and more work.'

Maddie laughed. 'It's been like that for months.'

'I know, but it'll get worse.'

'Or better,' Maddie said, 'depending on how you look

190

at it. We'll be even busier when the flowers and bulbs are ready for picking.'

'I could come and help when Mrs Grange doesn't need me,' Jenny offered.

'You're on,' Michael said, 'come next spring, we'll need all the help we can get.'

They saw Jenny safely to the back door of the shop and then Michael and Maddie retraced their steps down the lane. They walked side by side, not touching, until they left the outskirts of the village and Maddie felt Michael reach for her hand. They walked along, not speaking, just content to be together, hand in hand, until they came almost to the farm gateway. Behind the shelter of the hedge and hidden from the farmhouse, Michael stopped in the middle of the lane and took her in his arms.

'Oh Maddie, how long I've had to wait for you to grow up and there I was not even realizing you'd had another birthday.'

Maddie buried her face against his neck, winding her arms about him. She could feel the beat of his heart even through his clothes. It matched the beat of her own. He was kissing her face, her forehead, the tip of her nose and then his lips sought her mouth. 'Oh Maddie,' he murmured against her lips. 'I want you so.'

'Come on,' he said at last, taking her hand. They crept into the yard and without protest she allowed him to lead her to the hay shed. He began to kiss her in earnest, pressing her down into the soft hay. Then his fingers were searching beneath her clothing and she quivered as his cold hand found the warmth of her breast.

'Maddie, oh Maddie,' he breathed and then they were lost in the wonder of discovery of each other. Lost to time and place. Lost to sense and reason.

As Michael lay on top of her and gently, lovingly, made her his own, the whole world exploded into golden light. It was like a summer's day and they were lying amidst a rainbow field of tulips, the sun bright and warm and shining down benignly upon their love.

Twenty-Six

The work was even harder than any of them had imagined and what they would have done without Bill Randall's practical help and advice, Maddie could not think. Not only had he already lent them his concrete mixer and his wooden-framed plough to prepare the ground, but he obtained their very first supply of bulbs.

The day after the party, Bill's old truck rattled into the yard at Few Farm. Climbing down from the driver's seat he called out cheerfully to Maddie. 'I thought you might be able to make use of this little lot, mate.'

When she went to the back of the truck and saw pallet after pallet stacked high and every one filled with bulbs, her mouth dropped open.

'It's not easy for someone just starting,' Bill said, 'but I've spoken to one or two mates and we're all chipping in with some stock for you.'

Maddie felt a lump in her throat. Funny, she thought, I only want to cry when someone does something so unexpected and so kind for me.

'It's very good of you,' Maddie said, her eyes sparkling.

'There's different varieties but I've put labels on them, mate, to show you which is which. There's Clara Butt, that's a pretty pink, Inglescombe Yellow and Bartigon Red. Then there's Rose Copland, another pink, and William Copland, that's purple. Now,' he pointed to three trays, each marked with a black cross. 'These have been in my cold store since the beginning of August. They're the ones for forcing in your greenhouse and they ought to be planted now in boxes, like I told you, ready to bring into your glasshouse at the right time. They're different colours, an' all.'

'Our very own rainbow,' Maddie murmured.

'Eh? What did you say, mate?'

She smiled at him. 'Oh nothing, Mr Randall. Thank you so much for all these. What do we owe you?'

'Don't worry your pretty head about that just now, mate. We'll wait for our money. We know Frank of old. He'll pay us when he can. We all know that. Oh, and I've brought you these.' He picked up a small cardboard box. 'A few very special bulbs just for you. They're called Keizerskroon and they're red with yellow edges. Very pretty, they are.'

Now the tears spilled over and Maddie wiped them away hastily and smiled up at the big man. 'I don't know how to begin to thank you, Mr Randall.'

He put his hand on her shoulder. 'Think nowt on it, mate. Think nowt on it.'

But Maddie thought a great deal of it.

'By heck, we're going to be busy planting this lot,' Frank said, scratching his head when he saw the bulbs, but Maddie only grinned. Already in her mind's eye she could see the waving tulips in full bloom.

'Then we'd best get cracking.'

'Well, yes, I agree. But what do we actually have to do?'

'Mr Randall said there's only enough here to plant a few acres for our first year, but because we've already got Mr Taylor's say-so, we can increase the acreage as soon as we can.'

'Maybe Mr Theo could help us,' Michael put in.

'Oh, I don't like to ask him,' Frank shook his head. 'He's been so good already.'

'We'll send Maddie,' Michael laughed, winking at her. 'I think he's a bit sweet on our Maddie.'

'We've enough to be going on with here, at the moment,' Maddie said, though she was laughing along with Michael, not even thinking that his suggestion might be serious. 'And the rest of the land we can use for potatoes or caulis.'

'Ah well, now I do know about growing them, but I have to admit, lass, I'm a bit lost with these flowers.'

'We need to start planting now,' Maddie told him. 'Mr Randall says the usual way is to plant them in rows, leaving every seventh row empty.'

'Why?' Nick asked suddenly. He had been standing listening to the conversation but until this moment had not joined in.

'To walk along for hoeing the weeds out and later for the picking.'

Frank and Michael nodded.

'What about the greenhouses? Do we plant some in there?'

Maddie shook her head. 'No. You only bring them into the greenhouse roughly a month before you want them to flower, though the time depends a bit on the different varieties. Take the Rose Copland, say you want that to flower say for Christmas, then you'd bring it into the greenhouse a month before.'

'What about the temperature?' Frank asked. 'We'll have to mind to get that right, won't we?'

'For the first week you keep it very moderate and then increase it to about sixty-five degrees.'

'Sounds easy,' Michael said, 'but I wonder if it's going to be.'

'We'll make it work,' Maddie said and she saw Frank and Michael exchange a smile.

'But what do we do with them 'til then?' Nick asked. 'Just leave them like this?'

'No. We plant them out first . . .'

'In the field? You mean we have to plant them out and then dig them all up again to bring in? That sounds like a lot of unnecessary work . . .'

'No, no. We put them in boxes. Look, like this one. Mr Randall brought a couple to start us off. He couldn't spare any more so we'll have to get some more from somewhere.' Maddie pointed to a wooden box approximately twenty-four inches by fifteen. 'You put them in these, well spaced, and then cover them thinly with soil and bring them into the glasshouse at the right time.'

There was a silence as the menfolk took it all in.

'Where do we put them until then?'

'In the field but I should think as near to the yard as possible. After all, we've got to carry them to the glass-houses, haven't we? How about in a row along the hedge side?'

'Sounds sensible,' Michael murmured.

Frank glanced at Nick. 'How's the trench coming along for the pipes from the boiler house to the first glasshouse?'

'All right. I should get it finished today.'

'I'll go into Wellandon to see a chap I know about the heating pipes,' Frank said. 'And I'll see about some more boxes, love.'

'And we'll get started with the planting, shall we, Maddie?' Michael said. 'I'll go and harness Rajah.'

*

The following morning when they were all seated at the breakfast table, Frank said, 'You know, it's not going to be an easy task to monitor the temperature in the glasshouses. I've been thinking about it and, Nick, since you like dealing with engines and mechanical things, how about I teach you all about the battery house and the boiler house and between us we'll look after the heating system for the greenhouses. Maybe we can think about a pump, like Bill Randall suggested.'

'And a thermostat,' Nick joined in and Maddie noticed the sudden spark in his eyes. Frank nodded and jerked his thumb over his shoulder towards the greenhouse that Mr Theo had given them. It had been built on to the side of the house and now covered the window of the living room. 'In fact, I'd like to know what you think about this greenhouse. How do you think we should heat it? I was wondering about running pipes from the boiler in the kitchen.'

'What? Dig up my floors?' Harriet said indignantly.

'No. We'd come through the wall from the kitchen there,' Frank pointed to the corner near the ceiling. 'And run them along just under the ceiling and out there . . .' Now he pointed to the corner near the outer wall. '. . . and into the greenhouse. What do you think, Nick? Of course, you'd still have to help with the field work, but what do you say to learning how to handle that side of things?'

Maddie didn't think she had ever seen such pleasure light the young boy's face. But before he could answer, his mother cut in, 'I don't want Nicholas meddling with anything dangerous, Mr Frank. You've always kept the boys out of your battery house.'

Frank sighed but this time he looked at Harriet down the length of the table. 'They're hardly boys now, Harriet, either of them. And I've already shown Michael quite a lot about how things work. Nick's sixteen in a week or so and if his interest lies in the direction of things mechanical, then it's up to us to help him learn all he can. After all, maybe he won't want to stay at Few Farm all his life . . .'

'He'll do as I tell him,' she snapped and Maddie glanced at Nick in sympathy. No wonder he always seemed to have a sulky twist to this mouth. To Maddie's surprise there was a sudden flash in the boy's eyes as he turned to his mother.

'Mr Frank won't let me get into any danger and I'll always do exactly as he tells me.' Without waiting for her answer, Nick turned towards Frank. 'I'd like that very much, Mr Frank. Thank you.'

Harriet said no more but her face turned red with a rage she could hardly suppress.

'Good old Nick,' Michael said later as they snatched a few brief precious moments. 'I never thought I'd see him stand up to her like that.'

'Where's he gone now? I saw him going out of the gate after breakfast.'

'He's taken Dad's gun on a walk around the fields.'

'Why?'

'Rabbits. They'll nibble anything and everything if we don't keep them down.'

'I'm surprised his mother lets him have hold of a dangerous thing like a gun.'

Michael winked at her and put his finger to his lips. 'She doesn't know, so not a word. All right?'

Maddie nodded.

Michael sighed and kissed her forehead briefly, 'Well, we'd better get on with the work. Come on, Tulip.'

The Tulip Girl

The autumn passed in a haze of hard work and loving Michael. Their times together were brief and snatched but all the more precious and exciting. Then came the day they were all waiting for – the first of the trays to bloom in the glasshouse. It was Nick, out early in the morning two days before Christmas Eve to check the temperature, who came rushing into the house.

'Come and look. Quick!'

'What is it? What's the matter?' Maddie cried, but he had raced off again without further explanation.

'Oh, don't say . . .' Michael was already out of the door, following him, whilst Maddie, still struggling to pull on her Wellingtons, shouted, 'Wait for me. Michael, wait.'

When she arrived at the door of the first greenhouse it was to see Michael and Nick just standing drinking in the sight of a tray of pink tulips that had burst into flower. Silently, Michael held out his hand to her and she moved slowly towards him, taking his hand but her gaze was on the beautiful flowers.

'We've done it,' he whispered and his voice was hoarse. 'We've really done it. Isn't that the loveliest sight?'

Maddie nodded, unable to speak. Since she had first seen the heart-shaped bed of golden tulips deep in the woods and then Mr Randall's rainbow field, as she always called it, she had dreamt of such a moment. True, it was only one tray of the flowers, but Maddie could not have felt prouder if it had been fifty acres.

And one day, she vowed, it would be.

Whilst Nick had been put in charge of the heating and Maddie had undertaken the day-to-day care of the bulbs, Michael had been the one to organize the selling of the blooms once they were ready. Already he had a buyer

199

waiting in London and transport would be by train from Wellandon Station.

'Right,' he said now, breaking their trance. 'I'll get the boxes and we'll get these packed now. Then I'll take them to the station for the night train.'

'If they're not going until tonight, Michael,' Maddie said, thoughtfully, 'I think we should leave picking them until as late as possible. Mr Randall said we should pick early in the morning or late at night. I know that's right for the fields, but I suppose the same applies to the blooms in here.' She glanced at him. 'Doesn't it?'

Michael wrinkled his forehead. 'Well, I would have thought that now they're just coming out they don't want to be left much longer in the heat. We don't want them too far out, do we?'

Maddie bit her lip worriedly. 'No, I suppose not.'

'I don't think just the rest of today will hurt.' Nick shrugged his shoulders. 'Let's face it, we're going to have to learn by our own mistakes a bit at first, aren't we? I mean Bill Randall can't tell us everything. We've got to stand on our own feet.'

Maddie and Michael exchanged an amused glance. Nick was right, they had to agree, but such a statement coming from the boy whose mother ruled his every waking moment made them want to laugh.

'You've got a point there,' Michael put his hand on Nick's shoulder. 'So what do we do? Pick 'em and pack 'em now or wait 'til tonight?'

'Pick half of them now and the other half tonight and let's see for ourselves if it makes any difference,' Nick suggested.

Michael laughed. 'You're full of bright ideas this morning. That's exactly what we'll do, but we must get them to the station by six o'clock at the latest. At tulip time, you know, Wellandon handles hundreds of boxes every night. Before the War it was thousands and the number is building up again as more and more flower growers are turning away from food production as soon as they're allowed. Of course, there won't be that many this time of the year, but I don't want ours to get left aside in favour of the regular growers.' He bit his lip. 'I think I'll drive into town this morning, just to make sure that everything's all right for this first consignment. After that, it should be plain sailing.'

Through the day, Maddie picked all the flowers that were ready, laying them carefully in the wooden boxes in neat bunches. 'I'm coming with you,' she informed Michael as she helped him load the boxes into the boot of Frank's car. 'I want to see this first lot on their way for myself.'

'Don't you trust me with your precious tulips?'

She grinned at him, 'Of course I don't. You might decide to give them away to all your girlfriends in the village.'

Michael's dark eyes sparkled with fun. 'And when have I had time to see any girlfriends the last few weeks? Besides . . .' Now the look in his eyes was serious. 'The only girl I want is right here with me all the time.'

He reached out and grasped her hand, squeezing it tightly. 'Come on, let's go and sell your flowers.'

'Our flowers,' she corrected him as she climbed into the passenger's seat beside him. 'Everyone deserves the credit. Even . . .' she smiled impishly at him, 'even Mrs Trowbridge.'

'Oho,' Michael laughed. 'Now it really hurt you to say that, didn't it?'

Maddie said no more; she didn't need to.

*

It was dusk when they returned to the farm.

'Well, Tulip, that's the first safely away and we're still living up to our name,' Michael said as he got out of the car and stood in the yard.

'Eh?'

'Few Farm. Only now it's a few 'taties, a few caulis and a few tulips.'

'Oh you!' Laughing Maddie pushed Michael on the shoulder and, playfully, he caught hold of her hands, pulling her close to him, his dark brown eyes looking down into hers. The longing flared between them and suddenly the smile faded from Michael's eyes. She felt as if the breath had been knocked from her body as she looked up at him, her lips slightly apart. For a brief moment they were lost in a world of their own until Harriet's voice from the back doorway made them both jump and spring apart.

'Your supper's ready.'

When Maddie turned to walk towards the housekeeper, it was to see the look of pure hatred on the woman's face. For some time Harriet must have suspected that there was something between her favourite and the orphan girl she had brought into the house.

Now she had seen it for herself and knew for certain.

Twenty-Seven

It was in the January, when the blooms in the glasshouse were at their most delicate stage, that Maddie began to feel unwell.

Carrying another heavy tray in from the field to the second glasshouse, she felt suddenly dizzy and before she realized what was happening she had dropped the box and was pitching forward, the ground coming up to meet her.

'Maddie! Maddie, what is it?'

She heard Frank's anxious shout from behind her. She was trying to rise as he reached her.

'Have you hurt yourself, love? I shouldn't be letting you carry these heavy boxes. I ought to have got Michael or Nick to do it.'

'I – I'm all right, Mr Frank. Please. I must have tripped . . .' She bit her lip, not wanting to tell him a deliberate lie yet determined not to admit that she had been feeling queasy for the past week now. She couldn't be ill. Not now when there was so much work to do.

'You look a bit pale, love. You've been overdoing it. We shouldn't let you work so hard.'

Slowly Maddie got to her knees and then, carefully, she stood up. Frank held her arm, supporting her. 'We've all been working hard, Mr Frank.' She made herself smile at him, even though the waves of dizziness were still washing over her.

Frank nodded and looked down at her. 'We have. But

you, harder than any of us.' Gently, he added, 'You didn't need to prove yourself to us, you know. We wouldn't have blamed you even if your idea hadn't worked.' Then he smiled broadly. 'But it is doing, lass, I know it is. You should be feeling very proud of yourself.'

Maddie swallowed the bile that threatened to rise into her throat. 'We all should, Mr Frank,' she insisted, but nevertheless she was very touched by his words.

She took a few deep breaths and began to feel a little better. Together they knelt down and gathered the spilt bulbs back into the box.

'I just hope I haven't harmed these. They damage very easily, don't they?'

'Mm,' Frank agreed. 'I sometimes wonder if we shouldn't have daffs as well. They're a bit hardier. But I don't know.'

'Maybe we could. In time.'

He chuckled. 'You had thought about it, then?'

'Oh yes, I'd thought about it.'

Now Frank laughed louder. 'I thought you might have.'

They stood up together as he lifted the tray from the ground. 'Now, young lady, I'm carrying this into the greenhouse for you and you're not to carry any more heavy boxes today. And you get an early night. You hear me?'

Maddie managed to smile and say, 'Yes, Mr Frank.'

'You little slut!' The bedroom door was flung open so violently, it struck the bed behind it and ricocheted, shuddering.

Maddie, spittle running from her mouth where she had been retching into the bowl, raised bleary eyes to see Harriet towering over her.

The Tulip Girl

'You're in the family way, aren't you?'

Horrified, Maddie straightened up and reached for the towel to wipe her mouth. 'What – what do you mean?'

'I've heard you. Every morning this week you've had your head over that bowl there. You've got morning sickness, girl. And last night when Mr Frank said you'd fallen in the field and looked as if you were going to pass out, then I was sure.'

Maddie gasped, her eyes widening. 'No. Oh, no.'

'Oh yes,' the housekeeper said grimly. 'Well, we'll see what Mr Frank has to say about this little lot, shall we?'

Maddie reached out and grasped the woman's arm. 'Please don't tell him, Mrs Trowbridge.'

Maddie didn't think she had ever seen such malice in anyone's eyes. Such venom, such glee. 'I can't *wait* to tell him.'

'Look, I know you want me gone from here. So, all right, you win. I'll go away but not until we've got all the cropping done at the end of April, and maybe the lifting in June. Then I'll go. But please don't tell Mr Frank. I mean – I mean you don't want to cause him any more worry, do you?' She was babbling now in her anxiety. 'He's just getting back on his feet. The flowers from the glasshouses made good money in London at Christmas and New Year and they're still selling well. But there's a lot of work. I can't possibly go yet.'

Harriet's face was a sneer. 'How do you think you're going to hide it, eh? You'll start to show before then. Don't you know anything about having babies?'

Maddie didn't answer. No, she knew nothing or she would have already guessed. Instead, she said, 'Then I'll go before I start to – to show. Mr Frank needn't know. No one need know.' Casting about frantically for another reason, she added, 'And you don't want him blaming you for not having kept a better eye on me.'

'Blame me!' She was indignant. 'I'm not the one to blame. He was too soft with you from the start. Letting you go to the village dances and round on the milk cart with young Michael. And then giving way to your ridiculous scheme to grow flowers.' She almost spat the next question. 'Whose brat is it, anyway?'

Maddie gasped aloud. 'It's Michael's.'

'Huh! I don't believe that for a minute. It's some village lad's, I don't doubt.'

'It is Michael's. It is.' Maddie was almost in tears at the injustice of the woman. How could she believe that it could possibly be anyone else's?

'I love Michael. I wouldn't let anyone else . . .' she hesitated and then added, 'touch me.'

Harriet's lips were a thin, unforgiving line. 'You dirty, foul-mouthed little trollop. Well, if it is his, you've led him on. I don't blame him. I blame you. You're out on your ear now, that's for certain. Because I'll not stand by and see you pull a fine young man like Master Michael down into the gutter alongside you, saddling him with your little bastard.'

She pulled her arm from Maddie's grasp and turned to leave the room. The girl sank down onto the bed and groaned. She knew what Harriet had said was true. She had no reason to doubt the older woman's knowledge and during the past week she had wondered why what she had first thought was a bilious attack was going on so long. It had struck her as very odd. Now she knew why.

That the housekeeper would take great delight in telling the rest of the household, Maddie had no doubt, so she dragged herself up again and dressed.

Better face the music, she told herself.

Halfway down the stairs, she heard the raised voices. Frank's and then Michael's.

'How could you? A young girl in our care, Michael. And she's still under age. You could go to prison for this, never mind the trouble you've brought on her and shame upon this house.'

As Maddie opened the door leading from the stairs into the living room, she saw that Michael and his father were standing on the hearth rug in front of the fire, staring at each other. His face white, Michael said, 'What do you mean, under age?'

'She's only fifteen, for God's sake.'

'No. Oh no. She can't be. She's sixteen. Surely, she's sixteen?' He was casting about frantically. 'She had a birthday. She told us so. We had a party. She's got to be sixteen.'

'She was fourteen when she came here,' Harriet put in. 'So now she's fifteen.'

'Fourteen?' Michael's voice was a strangled whisper of disbelief. 'How could she have left school at fourteen? I was fifteen when I left. So was Nick.'

Frank ran his hand through his hair. 'You stayed on a little longer because you were at a Grammar School and Harriet wanted Nick to stay on a little longer too. The statutory school-leaving age has only gone up to fifteen this last year.'

'I didn't know, Dad. I swear I didn't. I thought she was sixteen. I never touched her until after that party. And I wouldn't have done so yet, if – if . . .'

His voice trailed away and he looked so desperate and almost afraid that Maddie longed to run to him, put her arms about him and tell him that she would take all the blame. She wouldn't let anything dreadful happen to him. But she remained quite still just inside the door, watching and listening.

Then she heard Michael pull in a deep, shuddering breath. 'I'll take care of her, Dad. I'll . . .'

'And how are you going to do that? The farm is barely supporting us now. With another mouth to feed and without Maddie able to work, how do you think we're going to manage? And changing to growing blasted flowers. I wish I'd never listened to her now. In fact, I wish to God . . .'

Frank became aware of Maddie standing, ashen-faced, in the doorway. He glanced at her and then looked away, running his hand distractedly through his thinning hair yet again. Harriet, standing at the end of the table, her arms folded beneath her bosom, watched the scene unfolding before her, a gleam of satisfaction in her eyes.

Nick was sitting at the table, his eyes downcast on his cereal bowl, though he was not eating. Only Michael came to her. He put his arms about her and his voice was gentle now as he said, 'Oh Maddie. I'm sorry. Why didn't you tell me?'

'I . . .' At his kindness, Maddie felt the tears spill over as she laid her cheek against his chest. 'I didn't know.'

Now he held her at arm's length and looked down at her. 'What do you mean, you didn't know?'

Blinking through her tears, she stammered, 'I didn't understand why I was being sick in the morning.'

'You mean you haven't seen a doctor?'

Maddie shook her head.

'Oh well, then . . .' Instantly there was relief in his voice. 'Maybe you aren't.'

'But Mrs Trowbridge . . .' she began.

Now his tone was bitter. 'Oh aye, we all know that our dear housekeeper would do almost anything to get you sent away.' He looked over his shoulder, his eyes narrowing as he looked towards Harriet and speaking directly to her now. 'But what I can't understand is why you brought Maddie here in the first place.'

'Her sort should be punished. They bring misery to good folk around them with their devious, scheming ways. And I was right, wasn't I? She's brought trouble on this house, just like I said she would.'

'So why?' Michael persisted. He had let go of Maddie and was moving back towards Harriet now. 'Why did you bring her here?'

'That's my business,' she snapped.

'Let's not go into all that now,' Frank said wearily. 'We've got to think what's the best thing to do.'

Harriet rounded on him. 'Whatever do you mean? There's only one thing to do. Throw her out. Out on the streets where the little slut belongs.'

'Harriet, no one is going to be thrown out. My son is as much to blame as Maddie.'

'Oh no. No, no, no,' Harriet screamed at him. 'I won't have you blaming Michael. He's not to blame. It's her. She led him on. It could be anybody's. Any one of the village lads. She's always running to the village to see that Jenny. How do we know what she gets up to when she's away from here?'

Very slowly and deliberately, Frank said, 'Maddie stays here.' There was a moment's silence in the room before he added with a heavy sadness, 'It is Michael who must go away.'

Now it was Maddie who cried, 'No, oh no.'

Frank came towards her and though he didn't touch

her and his eyes were shadowed with sorrow, there was understanding in his tone. 'Look, it'd be better if he went away. At least, for a while.'

'See how you've broken up this family.' Harriet's spiteful tone would not be silenced.

For the first time in her life, Maddie's resolve crumbled. Tears poured down her cheeks and she flung herself against Frank, begging, pleading hysterically. 'Please, oh please, Mr Frank, don't send him away. I'd sooner you sent me away. Not Michael.'

'Let her live in the woods,' Harriet said. 'That's where her sort belong.'

Frank turned and glared at her. 'If you don't shut up, Harriet, it will be you leaving this house.' The woman stared back, but, for the moment, she said no more.

Frank stroked Maddie's hair. 'There, there, love. Don't get so upset. It's not good for the child. You must think of the bairn, now, you know. After all . . .' Gently he released her limpet hold on him and looked down into her face. 'It is my grandchild.'

Fresh tears welled and she buried her face against him. 'Oh Mr Frank, I'm sorry. I'm so sorry.'

The argument wrangled on for several days. Michael did not want to go.

'I don't want to leave you, Maddie. Dad's right. It is my fault just as much as yours. You'll be sixteen very soon. In March. I can't understand why we can't get married then.'

Bending over the tray of budding tulips, she asked in a small voice, 'Do you really want to marry me, Michael, or are you just saying it now because – because of . . .?'

Standing beside her in the warm greenhouse, he

answered quickly, 'Of course I want to marry you. It's just a bit sooner than we'd thought, isn't it? That's all.'

They'd never talked of marriage before, so even though she wanted to believe him with all her heart, Maddie couldn't quite believe, deep inside her, that he wasn't just saying it now because of the coming child. What was the phrase – a shotgun wedding? Well, no one was holding a shotgun to Michael's head. He had no need to marry her.

They worked on in silence. 'I think,' Maddie said. 'Your dad's worried that with me having no family, the authorities might start asking too many questions, about my age and that.'

'I just don't know how you're going to manage all the work, if I do go away like Dad suggests, that's all.'

'I know.'

The silence between them grew longer. There was nothing left to say – it had all been said – and there seemed no way round the problem.

Michael straightened up and eased his back. 'You go into the house, Maddie. You look so tired and there are dark shadows under your eyes. I don't like to see you looking like that.'

'But . . .'

'No "buts",' he said firmly. He stepped in front of her and put his hands on her shoulders. He looked down into her upturned face. 'Oh Tulip, I wouldn't have hurt you for the world, but I think it would be best if I did go.'

'No, please, Michael. Please don't leave me.' She clung to him again, desperately, not caring now who saw them.

Gently he disentangled himself from her clinging arms, but held her hands between his own. 'I must. But I will come back. I promise you faithfully, I will come back.'

Tears blurred her vision as she pulled away from him and stumbled blindly out of the greenhouse, quite forgetting in her misery to open and close the door carefully so that she did not cause a sudden rush of cold air, uncaring, for once, about her precious flowers.

She did not go into the house. She could not face Frank's worried expression nor the glee in Harriet's eyes. Instead she went out of the gate, into the lane and turned towards the village, but halfway along she took the fork in the road that led to the woods belonging to Mayfield Park. She met no one and was thankful. Sobbing, she ran on and on until she came to the edge of the trees. Gasping for breath she leant against a trunk for a moment but then plunged into the leafy shadows. Mindless of the briars scratching her legs and tearing at her clothes, she crashed her way through the undergrowth until she came to the clearing.

The bed of tulips that grew year after year without, so far as Maddie knew, any tending showed nothing now of the colourful display that would be there in three months' time. Now the ground was cold and hard and bare.

Maddie flung herself down where the golden flowers would bloom, digging her fingers into the ground. She rested her head on her arm and cried until exhaustion overtook her.

She didn't see a figure amongst the trees, who stood uncertainly, watching her weep.

Twenty-Eight

'But where can she be?'

'I thought she'd come into the house. She was looking so tired,' Michael, facing his father, spread his hands. 'I told her to come in and I'd finish off in the greenhouse.'

'What time was that?'

'Just after two.'

Frank turned to Harriet. 'Did she come in?'

The woman shrugged. 'Not that I saw.'

'Nick? Have you seen her?'

'No, Mr Frank. And I've looked all round the out-houses. Even . . .' He cast a sly look towards Michael. 'Even the hay shed.'

'She might have gone to see Jenny, Dad,' Michael suggested.

'That's a thought. I'll go . . .'

'No, I'll go. I can be there in five minutes on my bike.'

Half an hour later Michael returned with a breathless Jenny, who had run all the way alongside him.

'What's wrong?' Her eyes were wide and fearful.

'Hasn't she told you?' Harriet feigned surprise. 'I thought you'd have been the first to know. I thought you were like sisters.'

'Told me what?' Poor Jenny's glance was going from one to the other, her voice frantic now. 'Tell me? What's happened to her?'

Harriet bent and thrust her face close to the girl's. 'She's got herself pregnant, that's what.'

The words were said harshly, without a vestige of feeling or understanding and the woman smiled maliciously as Jenny's open mouth formed a horrified, 'Oh no.' But at least Jenny didn't need to ask who was the father of Maddie's child, for her glance went straight to Michael.

Frank's deep voice intervened. 'Do you know where she might have gone, love?'

'She was very upset when she left me,' Michael said. 'I – I'd just told her that I thought it best if I did go away for a while . . .' His voice trailed away.

'We thought she might have come to you?' Frank went on, but as Jenny shook her head, he asked, 'Do you think she would go back to the Home?'

Now the shake of her head was vehement. 'She rather die than go back there . . .' And then realizing what she'd said, the girl clapped her hand over her mouth with a little squeak and tears filled her eyes.

Frank put his arm around her shoulders. 'Don't worry, love. We'll find her.'

Maddie roused to the sound of soft and gentle singing, like the crooning of a lullaby. She blinked, rubbed her eyes and sat up and then she blinked again, this time in surprise. Sitting on the opposite side of the tulip bed was a woman. A pretty woman with long, curling fair hair. She wasn't looking at Maddie but at the ground, her fingers gently pull out a stray dead weed and then patting the earth as if she were willing the blooms to sprout up under her touch. Maddie held her breath, not wanting to break the spell of the pale winter sunlight shining through the trees on to the woman's hair, casting a golden halo around her head. She looked up and Maddie stared straight into her blue eyes. Slowly, Maddie let out her breath, yet, still, she dare not speak even though the singing had now faded away. The woman's eyes were looking at her and yet they didn't really seem to be seeing her. There was a vacant look in them. No, Maddie decided, that wasn't quite fair. It was more a dreamy expression, as if the woman were lost in a world of her own; an imaginary world that, to her, was far more real than life around her.

Softly, hesitantly, for she had the feeling that the stranger would shy away like a frightened doe if alarmed, Maddie said, 'Hello.'

The woman stared at her and now her eyes seemed to focus properly on Maddie's face. She smiled but did not answer and then she bent her head again, her gaze once more upon the ground.

Suddenly, Maddie realized who this woman was. She had seen her once before. Only the once, peering out the rear window of a motor car as it passed them by in the market place. This was Amelia Mayfield.

'They are beautiful, aren't they, in the spring?' Maddie said gently. 'Did you plant them?'

The vacant look was back as Amelia's shoulders lifted fractionally. A light breeze rustled through the trees and the sunlight faded. Maddie shivered, but the woman seemed impervious to the sudden change. Softly, deep in her throat the crooning began again.

Maddie was fascinated by her and although she knew she ought to be getting back to the farm, somehow she could not bring herself to rise and walk away from Amelia.

She looked, Maddie thought, to be in her mid-thirties and yet her manner and actions were those of a child. An innocent, lost child. Poor Amelia. So it was true what they said about her, that her tragic love affair had affected her mind and that she was kept hidden away in Mayfield Park for her own protection.

Should she be out here, then, Maddie wondered, alone in the woods? Was she allowed out this far alone? She was still debating what she should do when she heard a voice calling and the sound of someone crashing their way through the undergrowth.

'Amelia? Are you there, dear? Amelia? It's Theo. Don't be afraid. It's only Theo.'

Maddie watched as Amelia took not a scrap of notice. It was as if she didn't even hear her brother calling. She just carried on singing and smiling to herself.

Without making a sudden movement that might startle her, Maddie stood up and tiptoed to the edge of the clearing.

'Mr Theo,' she called. 'We're here.'

For a moment the sounds of movement through the trees ceased and then, beginning again, came towards her.

'Miss March!' He said, catching sight of her but immediately his concerned glance went beyond her to his sister sitting on the ground. At the sight of her, Maddie saw him relax visibly. Then his glance came back to her and she saw him frown as he took in her dishevelled appearance and her tear-stained face.

'Miss March, are you all right? Is there – anything I can do?'

Maddie summoned a brave smile. 'Thank you, Mr Theo, but I'll be fine now. I – I must be going, but . . .' She glanced back over her shoulder towards Amelia. 'I didn't like to leave her here alone.'

'Thank you.' So briefly, that later she was to wonder if she had imagined it, he reached out and touched her hand.

'I – must go.' She turned away from him but at the edge

of the clearing she paused and looked back towards the woman still sitting on the grass. Then her glance took in the tree where the desperate young man had taken his own life. Love made you weak and vulnerable, Maddie thought. She had never shed so many tears in her life as she had during these past few days. Strangely, though she could not have explained why, she felt stronger now. Perhaps it was seeing the poor, lost creature, still mourning her beloved, that made Maddie, in that moment, determined to face whatever blows life inflicted upon her. Never, never, she vowed, would she allow anyone to have such power over her that she ended up like Amelia Mayfield.

'They're all out looking for you,' was Harriet's greeting. 'Running around like headless chickens over a little trollop like you that don't deserve it. But there, that's men's stupidity for you.'

With a quiet dignity, Maddie said, 'I'm sorry if I've caused anyone concern.'

'Oh, you've caused concern, all right. You'd have done us all a favour if you had taken yourself off and never come back.'

Maddie returned the woman's look. 'Perhaps you're right, Mrs Trowbridge. Perhaps that's exactly what I should do, because if Michael does go – as he says he will – life's not going to be worth living in this house. Not for me. Is it? You'll see to that, I've no doubt.'

She turned and went out of the back door again and walked to the gate. She saw Frank and Michael walking down the lane towards her and she waved. As they neared her she said, 'I'm sorry to have worried you, Mr Frank.'

He gave her a curt nod and said, 'Well, as long as you're all right. But don't do it again.' Without another word he went through the gate, across the yard and into the house.

Maddie's troubled eyes followed him. 'He's angry with me, isn't he?'

Michael put his arm about her shoulders and sighed. 'You had us worried, Maddie. Where were you?'

'I . . .' She hesitated, not wanting to tell him where she had been. He might read more into her actions than even she had meant. 'I went for a walk that's all. I needed to be on my own. To think. Michael . . .' She twisted to face him. 'It would be better if I went away. Right away. There's places for people like me.'

He touched her cheek with the tip of his finger, trying to brush away the dried salt of her tears. 'You've spent all your life in an institution. I won't let you go back into one. It's my fault as much as yours. More, really.' He put his arms around her and held her close. 'We'll work it out, Maddie. But you must be brave if the best thing is for me to go away . . .' His hold tightened, hugging her to him. 'Just for a while. Just until after your birthday. Then I'll come back and we can be married.'

'Are you really sure you want to? You're not just saying it?'

''Course I'm not. I love you, Maddie.' He laid his cheek against her hair. 'Don't ever think otherwise. Promise.'

Muffled against him, she said, 'Promise.'

The day Michael left, Maddie thought her heart would finally break.

They had not made love again since the discovery of her pregnancy, but now Maddie longed to be in his arms, to be loved just one more time before he went away but he had seemed distant, awkward with her.

'Come on,' he said now, taking her hand. 'Let's go for a walk. There's time before the train goes. I want to talk to you away from the house.'

They walked to the field and leant over the gate. 'In a couple of months or so, this will be your very own rainbow field framed in gold, Maddie.'

They had planted the bulbs in blocks of different colours, pink, red and purple. But more than any other colour, they had planted Maddie's favourite yellow.

'Hey,' he turned to look at her, grinning. It was the first time he had really smiled in ages. 'Remember what the gypsy said that day? Maybe that's what she meant. Everything you touch will turn to gold.'

Maddie picked the green mould from the top bar of the wooden gate with her fingernail. 'She also said, I'd have joy and sadness in equal measure. She was right about that, wasn't she?'

Tears threatened again.

'Don't cry, Tulip,' he said, putting his arm about her shoulders. 'I'll come back, I promise you. Then we'll get married and be a real family.' He turned to face her, tenderly cupped her face in his hands and gently kissed her mouth. 'Whatever happens, Maddie, always remember that I love you and that I will come back.'

They turned and walked back to the house, their arms wrapped around each other, not caring, for once, who saw them.

The moment of Michael's leaving was strained and awkward.

'I'll come with you to the station, son,' Frank said, but Michael shook his head.

'No, Dad. I'd sooner you didn't.' He nodded stiffly

towards Harriet. His easy, teasing manner towards her had disappeared completely now, but to Nick he said, 'I'm sorry the work is going to fall on you now.'

To Maddie's surprise, Nick smiled. 'S'all right. We'll manage.' And the two young men shook hands.

Michael stood a moment looking round at them all, as if committing their faces to memory, but his glance came back to rest on Maddie. 'I'll write,' was his last promise as he raised his hand and walked away across the yard and out of the gate.

Twenty-Nine

'Well, I hope you're satisfied with yourself. You've broken up this family good and proper. I suppose next you'll lose Mr Frank his farm all together with your fancy notions. Flowers, indeed. Whoever heard of a farmer growing flowers?'

'Shut up, shut up,' Maddie rounded on the woman. 'The fields are doing well. We've a lot of work ahead with the weeding and then the picking and you'd do better to support your beloved Mr Frank than finding fault.' Boldly, she moved closer to the housekeeper. 'Why don't you give him a bit of credit? If he hadn't wanted to do it, then he wouldn't have done, would he?'

Harriet's mouth was a sneer. 'Oh, you've a lot to learn about men, girl. They're weak, the lot of 'em. They always make a mess of things and leave us women to pick up the pieces. And then blame us for it happening in the first place. You caught him when he was down and not know-ing which way to turn. And up you come with a fancy notion and he grasps at it, like a drowning man. And Michael, too. If he is the father of your child, and I for one don't believe he is, but if he is, then I expect you caught him when he wanted a bit of comfort.'

Maddie gasped as the tirade went on.

'And what's he done now but run away, leaving us to face all the gossip? Aye, and maybe a visit from the police an' all. And what'll they do to Mr Frank? They'll likely

221

Margaret Dickinson

think he's the father of your bastard and throw him in jail. Oh, I know about you. You've bad blood in you and bad blood will always out.'

'You know nothing about me. How can you?'

'Oh, I know what I know,' Harriet said smugly and began to turn away. Maddie caught hold of her arm.

'What do you mean, you know about me?'

'Let go of me this instant . . .' Before Maddie had time to loosen her hold, the woman raised her right hand and dealt the girl a vicious slap on her left cheek, then she gripped Maddie's shoulder so fiercely that her fingers dug into the girl's flesh. She bent forward, pushing her face close to Maddie's. 'Why don't you do us all a favour,' she hissed. 'And hang yourself from that tree in the woods?'

Shocked by the woman's venom, Maddie pulled herself away and ran out of the back door, across the yard and into the lane. She was shaking and her cheek stung. She couldn't go back to the field to help with the hoeing. Mr Frank would want to know what had happened and she didn't want to tell him. He probably wouldn't believe her anyway. He would never believe that the woman he had taken into his home when she had been destitute could say such a thing. Even Maddie could hardly believe it herself now. She knew Harriet hated her, but even she had not realized quite how malicious the woman was.

She found herself walking towards the village. She quickened her step. Jenny. I must see Jenny.

As she opened the shop door, Mrs Grange behind the counter and her one customer turned see who had come in.

Maddie's heart sank as she saw who the customer was.

222

'Well, well, look who it is?' Mrs Potter's voice was thick with sarcastic glee. 'I've just been hearing about you. Got yourself into trouble even quicker than I thought.'

Maddie, her jaw hardening, glanced at Mrs Grange, whose face turned pink. She lowered her head, hiding beneath the brim of the blue hat she always wore.

'I've come to see Jenny.' Maddie held her head high and returned Mrs Potter's stare.

'Well, now,' Mrs Potter folded her arms under her ample bosom. 'I don't know if we ought to let her see the likes of you. You might lead her into your bad ways. What do you say, Mrs Grange? I'm only thankful I got rid of you afore you brought shame on my orphanage.'

' 'T'isn't your orphanage. If it's anyone's, it's Sir Peter's.'

'He's ill now and Mr Theo might have been voted on to the Board, but he hasn't the say-so that his father had. Besides, I can twist that young man round my finger any time I want.' Mrs Potter turned to Mrs Grange, 'I shouldn't let her see young Jenny, if I were you.'

Anger flooded through Maddie. She was back on familiar ground, facing the woman she had never been afraid of because she didn't care a jot what Mrs Potter thought about her or what she could do to her.

'I will see Jenny. Just try and stop me . . .' And before either Mrs Grange or Mrs Potter could even move, Maddie was around the counter and through the brown curtain into the rear of the shop.

'Jen? You here, Jenny?'

There was the sound of footsteps on the stairs and a door opened and she was there.

'Maddie! Oh Maddie!' Jenny's excited squeak left Maddie in no doubt as to the girl's pleasure at seeing her. They hugged each other and both began to speak at once and then laughed together. Then Maddie's face sobered as she held the girl at arm's length and said quietly so that the two women in the shop could not hear, 'I wish you hadn't told Mrs Grange about me. The whole village will know now.'

Jenny's eyes widened. 'I didn't, Maddie. I haven't said a word to anyone. Really, I haven't.'

Maddie stared into her eyes and saw the truth there. 'I'm sorry, I couldn't think . . .' Then she stopped. Of course. Harriet Trowbridge. Although the woman rarely left the farm, the only place she did visit occasionally was the village shop. In fact, she was quite friendly with Mrs Grange who often did shopping in Wellandon for the housekeeper from Few Farm. Hadn't it been she who had bought those dreadful second-hand clothes from the market stall? Maddie reminded herself. No doubt, she thought wryly, she had been instructed by Harriet to buy the dreariest, most shapeless clothes she could find.

'Oh well,' she sighed. 'It was bound to get out eventually, but, you see, because I'm not sixteen 'til next month, Michael could get into dreadful trouble. He could be arrested.'

'But he's gone away now, hasn't he?'

Was there nothing the village shop didn't know? Maddie wondered. She nodded.

'Well, then, that's all right. Isn't it?'

'I don't know,' Maddie said heavily. 'If everyone knows now, then sooner or later the local bobby's going to hear of it, isn't he?' She almost added, And I know someone who'll probably make sure he does.

'Oh Maddie, don't worry. It'll be all right,' Jenny smiled. 'Just think how lucky you are. You're going to have a little baby to love. A baby all of your very own.' Then, as other thoughts crowded in, her first delight faded.

'You are all right? I mean, they're not throwing you out at the farm?'

Maddie shook her head. 'No, but now Michael's gone, it's awful. Mr Frank hardly speaks and Mrs Trowbridge only opens her mouth to be nasty. She's vicious, that woman.' Maddie wrinkled her brow thoughtfully. 'I know she doesn't like me, but I can't understand what I've done to deserve such hatred.'

'What about Nick?' Jenny blushed even as she said his name. 'He's not nasty to you, is he?'

'No. Funnily enough he's been nicer ever since Michael went. But he's under his mother's thumb. What she says, goes, as far as he's concerned.'

Jenny was thoughtful. 'I don't see quite why everyone's so worried. You'll be sixteen by the time the baby's born, won't you?'

'Yes, but I wasn't when – when it happened. You know?'

They all knew the facts of life. It had been explained to them by Mrs Potter who had left the girls in her charge feeling that the whole business was not only distasteful, but sinful too, even within marriage, let alone outside it.

Jenny hugged her again. 'Don't worry, Maddie. As long as you can stay at the farm, it'll be all right.'

'If only I knew where he's gone. What he's doing. If he's all right. I can't sleep at night for thinking about him.' Maddie gulped back the tears that threatened.

'He'll write soon. When he's got settled somewhere,' Jenny comforted. 'And then, when you've had the baby, Michael can come home and you'll be so happy.'

As Maddie rested her cheek against her little friend's hair and closed her eyes, she sent up a silent prayer that Jenny might be right.

But somewhere, deep inside her, she dared not even hope that she would be. The words of the gypsy came back to her: 'joy and sorrow in equal measure'. Well, she had known the joy, had touched the heights of ecstasy with Michael. Even through the days and weeks of the foot and mouth disaster and struggling against the harsh winter, even through all that, his love had given her faith in the future. Their future. Together.

Maddie's very soul shuddered as she realized that though the hell of the last few weeks had been dreadful, it did not equal the heaven she had known. If the prophecy were true, then Maddie March would have to face a great deal more anguish yet.

No letter came from Michael in the first week.

'He'll be busy getting settled in,' Frank said and added, unable to keep the anxiety out of his tone. 'Wherever he is.'

Nor during the second week and by the third week the disappointment was showing in Frank's eyes too.

Maddie plunged herself into work, trying to stave off the sickness that still gripped her each morning and the ache in her heart.

'Don't worry,' Nick said as they worked side by side. 'He'll get in touch as soon as he can.'

Maddie tried to smile. 'You've been awfully good since Michael went.'

It was true. Nick went out earlier than normal every morning, returning at breakfast with the mail in his hand, his grey eyes sympathetic when, each day, there was still no word.

'You know,' Maddie said slowly, 'I could understand

it, in a way, him not writing to me. But I would have thought he'd've written to his dad.'

She saw Nick glance at her and then away again.

'What? What is it?'

He gave an exaggerated sigh. 'Maddie, I know you're – well – in love with him, I s'pose . . .'

'Of course I am.' She was hot with indignation. 'How can you even think I'd have – that I'd have . . .' she pointed to her own stomach, 'done anything with him if I hadn't been?'

Nick was shaking his head sadly. 'Oh Maddie, I tried to tell you, but you wouldn't listen.'

'What?' There was a sudden icy feeling creeping round her heart.

'You're not the first, you know.'

She was silent a moment, remembering the girl at the dance. Flatly, she said, 'I didn't think for one moment that I was.'

'I mean – you're not the first he's got pregnant.'

'*What!*' Now she was shocked and hurt. She felt as if Nick had thrust a knife into her heart. Instinctively protective, she crossed her arms over her stomach. 'Who? When?' she demanded.

Nick shrugged. 'Brenda somebody. She had a babby last year and the gossip in the village said it was Michael's.'

'Oh, gossip. Is that all? I mean, did the girl come here? Did her parents tell his dad?'

Nick shrugged. 'How should I know?'

'You seem to know plenty,' she said tartly.

'Maddie . . .' His tone was reproachful. 'I'm only telling you for your own good. I don't like to see you getting hurt.'

She frowned. She hated it when anyone said something

227

was for her own good. It had been one of Mrs Potter's favourite phrases.

'Tell you what,' Nick was smiling now, 'soon as we hear where he is, I'll go and see him for you. Put your mind at rest, like.'

Maddie was thoughtful. 'Well, I could go.'

'No, no,' Nick said swiftly. 'That wouldn't be a good idea. If anyone guessed, it could get him into trouble. A lot of trouble. No, it'd be better if I went.'

'Or his dad. His dad could go.'

'I think Mr Frank is too upset with him at the moment.'

Maddie sighed. 'I suppose you're right. But there doesn't seem to be much chance of anyone being able to go to see him if we're not even going to hear where he is.'

Before Nick should see the tears welling in her eyes, Maddie turned and walked away. I won't cry, she told herself fiercely. Whatever happens, I'm not going to cry ever again.

Thirty

The following morning at breakfast they heard Nick's boots pounding across the yard even before he flung open the back door and almost fell into the kitchen.

'There's a letter.' He held out a torn and muddy envelope, the writing all smudged where the ink had run. 'I found it in the lane. The postman must have dropped it.' He held it out to Frank who took it and carefully unfolded the sheets of paper inside.

'Is it from Michael?' Maddie could no longer hold back her excitement.

Frank nodded. 'It's dated two weeks ago.'

Maddie's face was a picture of joy. 'There, I told you. He did write. That stupid postman. Just wait 'til I see him.'

Frank was reading the letter. 'It's very short,' he murmured. 'But he does give us an address. He's joined the Army.'

'He must be wondering why we've not written back.' She paused before she asked, unable to keep the longing from her tone, 'Is there a note for me?'

Frank looked up at her. 'Sorry, love. Not this time, but he says he'll write to you very soon.'

Maddie swallowed the lump in her throat and smiled bravely. 'Well, I just hope the postman doesn't drop that one in a puddle.' She looked at Nick. 'Thanks,' she said simply and rose from the table, leaving her breakfast untouched.

Later in the day Nick found her in the fields.

'Mr Frank ses I can go to see Michael.'

'What about your mother? Has she given her divine permission?'

'I wish you wouldn't be so hard on my mother. It's just her way, you know.'

Maddie said nothing.

'She's had a hard life.'

'Really?' She could not keep the sarcasm from her tone. Harriet Trowbridge's life didn't seem all that hard to Maddie.

'Yes. After my father died, she had nowhere to go. No other family. Mr Frank took her in as his housekeeper.'

Maddie nodded. 'What happened to your father?'

'I'm not sure. He died. She never talks about him and I never ask. It always upsets her.'

'Well, I'd want to know, if I was you. I'd ask her.'

There was a pause before he asked quietly, 'Do you ever wonder about your own parents?'

''Course I do. But there's not a lot of point in trying to find out anything. I was dumped outside the orphanage, that's all I know. Obviously, they didn't want me then and since no one's ever come looking for me, they still don't want me, even if they are out there somewhere.'

'We've got a lot in common, really, haven't we?'

'Have we? I don't see how. At least you've got a mother, even if she won't tell you much about your father.'

'And you're going to be a mother soon. But do you really think that your baby will ever have a father either?'

Angry tears smarted her eyes, but she would not allow them to fall. 'Of course it's got a father. Michael.'

Very softly, Nick said, 'But he's not here. Is he?'

They worked on in silence, until Maddie could hold back the question no longer. 'When are you going to see him, then?'

'Day after tomorrow.'

'Will you take a letter for me?'

'Of course, Maddie.' His tone was gentle now as she felt him touch her arm and turned to see that he was smiling. A wide, generous smile that lit his whole face. 'I only want you to be happy, Maddie. I wish you'd believe that.'

There was a sudden lump in her throat at his kindness. 'I do,' she said and bent her head over the growing bulbs.

'Is he all right? Where is he? Can I go and see him?'

The questions tumbled from Maddie's lips on Nick's return. He glanced at her and then quickly away again, almost as if he could not meet her eyes.

'What is it? What's wrong?'

'He – he thinks it best if you don't meet up. At least, not yet.'

'Did you give him my letter?'

''Course I did.'

'What did he say?'

'That he'll write to you soon.'

'Did you tell him about his letter to us getting lost? And that was why none of us had written to him?'

Nick nodded.

'And?'

'And what?'

'What did he say?' Maddie insisted. 'Tell me everything he said. Please, Nick.'

'He's doing his basic training. He says it's very hard and exhausting. After that, he'll get posted somewhere. Maybe abroad, even.'

'Abroad?' Maddie was horrified. 'But he'll get leave, won't he? He could come home on a visit, couldn't he?'

'Yes, he'll get leave, but he thinks it's best if he doesn't come home.'

'But he said, when I was sixteen, he'd marry me. Did he mention that?'

'He doesn't want the Army finding out about you being pregnant and underage. If he starts asking for leave to come home to get married when he's only just gone in, they might start asking awkward questions.'

Maddie turned away back to her work with mixed feelings. Michael was all right. Nick had seen him, but he had not brought back the loving messages Maddie longed to hear. No promise of marriage now, not even a suggested meeting nor a letter for her.

Maddie bit down hard on her lower lip. I won't cry, she told herself fiercely. I won't.

'He's not coming home, Mr Frank.'

'I know, love, I know.' His face was sorrowful, too, and Maddie again regretted the trouble she had brought to this kindly man's door. Yet she would never say she was sorry about the coming child. Michael's child. Her child. Their child. And one day they would be married. She knew they would.

'Maddie,' Frank was saying slowly. 'I've been thinking.'

She held her breath as fear flooded through her. He was going to send her away. He'd changed his mind about standing by her. It would be Mrs Trowbridge's fault. She'd gone on and on about it. About the shame and the trouble that Michael might be in. And Maddie was sure that it was she who had spread the gossip around the village. So now, Mr Frank wanted her gone.

'I . . .' Frank removed his cap, ran his fingers through his hair and then replaced the cap. 'I don't know how much Nick has told you about his visit to Michael.'

Maddie repeated, word for word, what Nick had said. When she had finished, Frank, much as Nick had done, glanced at her and then lowered his gaze.

'Maddie, love. Nick says that Michael isn't sure he should marry you now.'

'What? But he said he loves me.'

Frank reached out and touched her shoulder. 'I'm sure he does, but he's so young. You both are . . .'

Despite her promise to herself, her lower lip trembled and tears welled in her eyes. 'You're turning me out?'

'No, no,' Frank's denial was swift and obviously genuine. 'No, never think that, Maddie. Please.' He sighed deeply. 'Michael doesn't want to be tied down. Not yet. He has a chance to see a bit of the world now he's in the Army.'

'I don't believe you. Nick's said all this, hasn't he? I don't believe him.'

'It's what Michael told him. What Michael asked him to tell us.'

Maddie was silently fighting the tears.

Now Frank put his arm about her shoulders. 'We must think of you and the child and what is best for both of you.'

Michael marrying me would be the best thing for both of us, she wanted to shout, but still she could say nothing.

'Look, Maddie, there's something I want you to think

233

about. Very carefully. I . . .' He paused as if searching for the right words. Maddie looked up into his face and saw the concern for her in his eyes as he went on, 'I – I want you to think about marrying me.'

Maddie was speechless with shock. Marry Mr Frank? The thought appalled her. She liked him, loved him in the way she might love a father-figure, but marry him? When she loved Michael?

His arm about her tightened. 'We could be married as soon as you're sixteen and then, if the gossips want to say it's my child, well, all the better. Michael will be safe then. It'd be the best thing for everyone. So what do you say, love?'

Maddie tore herself away from him. 'No, no. Oh, I couldn't.' She turned and ran.

Thirty-One

'You scheming little hussy.'

For a moment Maddie thought Harriet was going to strike her again but then the housekeeper turned her attention to Frank. 'Have you taken leave of your senses? 'Course I know you're only doing it to save your son. And I can't blame you for that, I suppose. But I can't see why you think you have to go as far as marrying this little slut.'

Quietly, Frank said, 'She's carrying my grandchild.'

'Huh! And how sure of *that* can you be, eh?'

Frank glared at her. 'I'm sure.'

'Well, that's it then. We're leaving. Nicholas and I won't stay another minute in this house if she's to be mistress of it.' Her face twisted into a sneer. 'I hope you'll be very happy together, a cosy little twosome to manage all the work.' She jabbed her forefinger towards Maddie's stomach as she said, 'And how much longer do you think she's going to be any help?'

Frank ran his hands through his hair. Wearily, he said, 'Harriet, there's no need for you to go anywhere. Nothing's going to change around here.'

'Not change? Not change?' Harriet screamed at him. 'When she becomes Mrs Brackenbury and sleeps in your bed?'

'I want to protect Maddie and the child – and my son.' He glanced sympathetically at Maddie before adding, 'You've got to believe it, Maddie. Michael's not coming back. And in a way, I can't find it in mesen to blame him. Oh, I know he ought to stand by his responsibilities, but he's too young to be saddled with a wife and child. I'm only sorry, Maddie, that he's landed you with it all. That's why I want to try to help.'

Maddie's eyes blazed. 'Don't you say you're sorry about the bairn. Don't anyone say they're sorry. I'm not. I'm glad I'm having Michael's baby. And if he doesn't want me or his child, that's up to him. But I'll never be sorry. Never!'

The two looked at her in astonishment and then a small smile twitched at Frank's lips. 'I wish my son had your courage, lass. Really, I do.'

'Courage, me foot,' Harriet snarled. 'She's a scheming little hussy who's wormed her way in here and reckons she can end up running all this.' She swept her arm in a wide arc to encompass not just the house, but all the land around it. She leant closer to Maddie, 'Well, let me tell you, you little madam, Sir Peter'll not let a bastard orphan without a name be one of his tenants. And especially not *you*.'

'Harriet! That's enough.'

'Aye, it's enough all right. I've had enough, an' all.' She turned as if to leave there and then, but was stopped when Maddie said clearly, 'I'm certainly not trying to take Mr Frank's farm away from him. Although,' she couldn't help adding wickedly, 'I think Mr Theo might well grant me the tenancy.' She paused and then went on quietly, 'Besides, I haven't said I'll marry Mr Frank.'

The woman turned and, her eyes narrowing, said, 'Ah, but you will. It's all part of your plan, isn't it, girl? By heck, I rue the day I brought you here. Well, I've only mesen to blame. I know that. Not for the first time, do I wish you'd never been born. Aye, and I'm not the only one who wishes it an' all.'

'What do you mean?'

'Nothing. Nothing at all.' She turned away and went into the kitchen from where they heard the clattering of pans being banged about in temper.

Maddie looked at Frank, who shrugged helplessly.

'Will she go, d'you think?' she asked.

'I doubt it. Where would she go? No, Harriet'll not leave.' For a moment Maddie thought he sounded wistful, almost as if he were wishing she would. He sighed heavily and then looking at her steadily, he said quietly, 'Think about what I said, love. It'd be for the best. I'm sure of it.'

Maddie's sixteenth birthday came and went and still she would not agree to marry Frank. In April, she was able to stand at the end of the field and see that her dream had come true. Stretching before her was her 'rainbow' field. Pink and yellow, red and purple. She should have been elated, bursting with pride and joy. Yet her sweet success tasted like dust in her mouth, her dreams were in ashes for there was no Michael standing beside her, sharing what should have been the most wonderful moment of her whole life. Instead, the beautiful blooms, bright in the sunlight, mocked her unhappiness.

Surely, he had loved her as she had loved him and, deep in her heart, she knew she always would. Surely, his sweet words could not have been all lies and yet, as day after day went by and there was no word, no letter – nothing – even Maddie's faith in him faltered.

As she stood with her hands protectively over her stomach, looking out across the fields, she felt a tiny flutter beneath her ribs and knew it was the moment that her child had first moved. It lived and moved within her. It was a little piece of Michael that she would cherish for ever. He could never leave her completely because she had borne his child and those bonds could never quite be severed, not by anyone. Not even by Michael himself.

For the first time since his departure, Maddie smiled and lifted her head to the bright blue sky, feeling the breeze on her face. She had a home, she still had the support and gentle kindness of Frank and soon she would have a child to love and care for. For the first time in her life, she would have someone who truly belonged to her. She would have a family. But, a little voice told her, your child needs a father.

'Mr Frank, what do you say to the idea that this year – our first year – we sell as many of the flowers as we can? If we pick them at the moment they're just coming into flower, we should get the best of both worlds, shouldn't we?'

'How do you mean, love?'

'Well, we can sell the flowers and still get a fair amount of nourishment back into the bulb to build up our own store of bulbs for next year.'

'Not sell to the dry bulb market, you mean?'

'Not this year.'

'I thought you had to leave as much stem as possible,' Nick put in. 'Just take the head off. We can't do that if we're going to sell them as cut flowers, can we?'

'No, I know. But I thought we'd try to hit the middle of the road, just this year. What do you both think?'

Now she included them both and glanced from one to the other.

Frank and Nick exchanged a look and then Nick said, 'Well, I think it's a good idea.' He smiled across at Maddie, 'But then your ideas always are.'

Maddie laughed. 'Flatterer.' Then she turned to Frank, who nodded and said, 'I don't see why it shouldn't work. It might not be what Bill Randall would tell us we ought to do, but I'm willing to give it a try. We've got a good outlet for the blooms already in place that . . .' He stopped abruptly and glanced, embarrassed, at Maddie.

'It's all right,' she said quietly and reached out to touch his hand where it lay on the white table cloth. 'You can say his name, you know. The outlet that Michael set up.'

She saw sadness in his dark eyes, a sadness that reflected her own and once more she was filled with guilt at the sorrow she had brought upon this good man.

'Yes, yes,' he was saying swiftly now. 'And I was thinking that I ought to sell the car and buy a truck. It would be much more useful to take the boxes of flowers to the railway station,' Frank said. 'Besides, when do we have time to go out in a car now?'

'That is a good idea. And Mr Randall says we ought to think about turning the old cowshed into a cold store,' Maddie said. 'We can't keep asking him to store our bulbs for forcing in his cold store, can we?'

Theo had been as good as his promise. The crewyard had been covered over, though the smaller buildings – the cow-house, pigsties and Rajah's stable – had stayed as they always had been but were now enclosed within the huge, asbestos-covered barn. The area that had once been the walled yard was now a level concrete floor – a vast space for sorting and packing cut flowers and for grading bulbs. The original small buildings were ideal for storage.

'More expense,' Harriet muttered as she set mugs of cocoa on the supper table. 'You and your grand ideas.'

Frank ignored her grumbling and carried on the conversation as he carved the meat and handed out the plates. 'You find out all about it, love,' he said to Maddie, 'and we'll see.'

When the time came for the picking, Maddie found that when she bent to pick the blooms, the growing mound of her stomach got in the way. She tried squatting, rather that stooping, and found it was easier.

'You all right, Maddie?' Nick asked with concern.

'I'm fine,' she answered, trying to raise a bright smile.

He sighed. 'I wish I could take all the workload off you,' he said worriedly. 'But there just aren't enough hours in the day . . .'

'Nick, you're being wonderful the way you've helped since – since . . . Well, just lately. I am grateful.'

'I wish you'd see a doctor,' he blurted out, reddening a little at having to touch on a delicate matter. 'You haven't seen one at all, have you?'

Maddie shook her head. 'I daren't, Nick. A doctor would ask awkward questions. Besides, there's no doubt now that I am expecting, so I don't need it confirmed. And I'm healthy enough. I don't need any medical attention. So, why bother?'

'Well, I just thought . . .' His voice trailed away uncertainly.

She smiled at him. 'It's nice of you to be concerned. No, really, I mean it. And I would go – despite the embarrassing questions – if I thought there was anything wrong with me that might harm the baby.' Softly she added, 'I meant what I said. I am sorry for the trouble it's caused. More sorry that you will ever know that Michael has had to go away, but I will never, ever, be sorry about the baby.'

Nick was staring at her. Then, his face scarlet, he mumbled awkwardly, 'We'll look after you, Maddie. You and the baby.'

He turned away abruptly then and went to the far end of the field to start picking a fresh batch of dark red tulips.

Maddie watched him go, shaking her head. He was a strange boy, she thought, but he really did have a much nicer side to him. And these days she was seeing much more of it.

Thirty-Two

'Do you know what happened this afternoon?' Maddie told them as she served steaming potatoes at supper time. 'Some woman stopped her car in the lane and came to the gate to ask if we sold cut flowers. You know, by the bunch, straight out of the field.'

'Did you sell her some?' Nick asked.

'Well, no, because we've got an outlet, haven't we?'

'But only for our best blooms. They don't take the rubbish ones that have opened too far, now do they?'

'No, but it wouldn't be fair to sell her that sort either, would it?'

'Depends,' Nick said, cutting the slice of boiled ham and dipping it into the mustard on the side of his plate before popping it into his mouth. 'There's a big difference between the top-grade flowers we send to London and the absolute rubbish that is only fit to be thrown away. I mean, we can't physically get to every flower just at the perfect moment to pick it, can we? If you'd picked her the sort of flowers that we wouldn't send to the markets, but that still look pretty good and if you hadn't charged too much, I reckon she'd've been happy enough.'

'You know,' Frank said, entering the conversation for the first time. 'Nick might have a very good point there. I know some of the growers have buckets of flowers stood at their farm gates and sell to passers-by and I'll tell you something else that Bill Randall was telling me this morn-

ing. There's a local growers' association been formed . . .
Oh and by the way he reckons we should join, but what I
was going to say was that the members of this association
have set out a route all round the fields this year for
sightseers to follow. He says there's more and more folks
coming to the area every year to see the tulip fields.'

'I can believe that,' Maddie said. 'I saw a bus down our
lane this afternoon. I thought it must be a day trip gone
down the wrong road, but I wonder, now you've said
that.'

'There you are, then,' Nick smiled. 'It'd be a bus trip all
right, but it'd've come to see the tulips.'

They looked at each other around the table and then,
for some reason she couldn't quite explain the three of
them all looked in Harriet's direction.

'What? What are you looking at me for?'

'I was just thinking, Harriet, that you could have some
flowers here, outside the back door and sell to callers,
couldn't you?'

'Oho, not me, Mr Frank. I've enough to do with all the
cooking and the housework. Besides, I don't want
strangers traipsing up to the back door.'

'Well, it's true you do have enough work, Harriet,
because none of us have time to give you a helping hand.
I'm sorry, I shouldn't have suggested it.'

'I tell you what we could do,' Maddie said, feeling
excited and enthusiastic for the first time since the dreadful day that Michael had gone away. 'In fact, there's two
things we could do. One, we could have a trestle table
and flowers in buckets at the gateway into the field and
also,' she grinned triumphantly around the table, 'we
could sell them to Mrs Grange in the corner shop for her
to sell on.'

There was a silence before Nick, frowning slightly,

asked, 'Why should she want to sell them? Not many of the locals would buy flowers. Most of them grow them, if not in their fields, then at least in their own gardens.'

'Not for the locals,' Maddie said, 'for the sightseers. If they're coming here in their cars and even by the bus load, you can't tell me that a good few of them won't drop in at the corner shop to buy drinks or a snack. In fact, we ought to suggest it to Jen that she gets Mrs Grange to sell sandwiches and cups of tea. She might even open up a little tea shop.'

'Do you know,' Harriet said softly, surprising them all, 'that's something I would love to have done. Run a little tea shop.'

There was a silence before Frank said, 'Well, why don't you? You could do it here, if you like. We could . . .'

'No, oh no!' Harriet held up her hands, palms outwards as if fending him off. 'I didn't mean it. I couldn't do it. I couldn't mix with folk, now could I? Not now. Not after . . .' She broke off and stood up, beginning to pile the dirty plates together. 'I wasn't serious. I only meant that if things had been different, it's the sort of thing I could have done. But not now, as things turned out . . .' Maddie saw her look down the length of the table straight into Frank's eyes. 'I couldn't. Besides,' she added with definite finality, 'like I've just said, I haven't the time.'

'It's a shame,' Maddie said softly, her gaze on the woman's face. 'You're such a wonderful cook, it couldn't help but succeed.'

Harriet's eyes swivelled to look at Maddie, who met her gaze steadily. For a fleeting moment there was a genuine rapport between them. Harriet recognized that Maddie's words were sincere and briefly, oh so briefly, she was touched. But then she picked up the plates and turned away towards the kitchen and the moment was lost.

'Where are you going, all dressed up?'

Nick stood before her, smiling and playfully barring her way across the yard.

'I'm going to find Michael and talk to him myself.'

Anxiety crossed his features. 'Oh Maddie, don't do that. You'll only get hurt. Let me go again. Let me find him and talk to him. Tell him what Mr Frank has suggested.'

'I want to see him. I need to hear it from him myself. If it's really true that he no longer . . .' she swallowed painfully before struggling on, 'cares for me, then I must accept it and move on with my life. I'm ready to do that now, but first, I must find out if it's true.'

'Don't you believe me?' he asked, suddenly offended that she should doubt his word.

She hesitated a second before she made herself say, ''Course I do, but – but I thought if I could see him, talk to him again, he . . .' Her voice trailed away. The truth was, she didn't quite believe Nick. But she wouldn't have believed anyone who had told her the same news. She needed to hear it from Michael himself.

'Look, he'll have moved on from where he was. And we haven't heard any more from him, have we? We don't even know where he is now. Tell you what,' Nick went on swiftly as he saw Maddie's dejected look, 'as soon as we hear, I'll go and talk to him again and tell him what his dad's suggested. I don't reckon he'll like that. Not one bit. No more than I do. I don't think you should marry Mr Frank, tying yourself to an old man like him.' He reached out and touched her hand. 'I mean, even if Michael doesn't want to marry you, later on you might meet a young feller who wouldn't mind you having a babby already. Someone who – who really cares about you. Someone who just wants to look after you and make you happy.'

Maddie glanced at him doubtfully but said nothing, her mind returning to Michael. She sighed. 'If you think he'll not be there any more, then I suppose there isn't any use in me going. At least, not today.'

Now Nick took hold of her hand and said, with more authority in his tone than she had ever heard in his voice, 'Leave it to me, Maddie.'

It was two weeks before another letter arrived.

'He's written to me,' Nick told them waving an envelope, but not offering for any of them to read the letter. 'I was right. He's finished his basic training.' Nick pulled a face. 'Ses it's been hell. I'm going up to see him tomorrow. But it's miles away. Somewhere up in Yorkshire. I'll have to be away overnight.'

'That's all right, lad,' Frank said. 'I'll give you the money for the train fare. It's good of you to go. I'd go mesen, but him and me'd only fall out and it wouldn't look good. And Maddie certainly can't go.'

'I don't see why not,' Maddie muttered.

As ever, Harriet defended Michael. 'You stay away from the lad. You've caused enough trouble for him already. Fancy him having to leave his home and family all because of the likes of you.'

'He'd have been gone by now, anyway,' Frank said patiently. 'He'd have been called up for National Service.'

'Mebbe so. But he won't be able to come home on leave, will he? Not while she's still here.'

'If Maddie would only agree to marry me like I suggested, he could come home. The gossip will be turned on me then.'

'Aye, and have you thought what might happen to you? You're so wrapped up in helping everybody else, your son and even this little trollop here, that you haven't stopped to think what they might do to you. You'd never stand prison.'

'If that's going to happen, then I shall go away,' Maddie said determinedly.

The housekeeper rounded on her. 'You'd have done better to have packed your bags and gone long since, if you'd really thought anything about this family. And when your bastard's born, stick it in an orphanage. It's what they did to you, isn't it?'

Maddie stared at her for a moment. 'What do you mean "what they did"? Who do you mean by "they"?'

For a brief moment, Harriet was flustered. 'Well, somebody dumped you outside that orphanage, didn't they?'

'Yes,' Maddie said slowly, still staring at the woman. 'Yes, they did.'

For a fleeting moment it had sounded to Maddie as if Harriet Trowbridge knew just who had left her on the doorstep of the Mayfield Home.

Thirty-Three

When Nick left the following morning, his mother loaded him with food parcels for Michael. 'They'll not be feeding him like he's used to.'

And Maddie loaded him with messages. 'Tell him I need to see him. Tell him – tell him . . .' She hesitated. It was difficult to give this young man, who was still only little more than a boy, intimate messages to pass on. 'Tell him I love him. It doesn't matter if he doesn't want to marry me. I understand that. I'm not bothered, just so long as – so long as . . .' She faltered unable to ask directly if Michael still loved her.

Nick touched her hand. Gently, he said, 'Don't worry, Maddie. I'll talk to him and when I come back I'll tell you everything he said. Word for word.'

'Promise?'

'I promise.'

She watched him go, questioning why it was not she who was going. She despised what she considered weakness in herself. Once, she would have gone, whatever anyone said, yet now it was as if she dare not go, dare not face the truth she feared to hear.

Her hands covered her belly protectively. 'Love is making you weak,' she murmured to herself, wondering if the old fearless, Madeleine March who hadn't cared a fig for anyone – except Jenny – was gone for ever.

As Nick rounded the corner in the lane and disappeared

from view, she turned away but for the rest of the day her mind was not on her work. It was on a train heading north to see Michael.

The following day Nick returned late at night looking pale with tiredness.

'What did he say? Is he all right?'

'Let him get inside the door, girl.' Harriet took the overnight bag from her son's hand and led him to the table. 'Sit down, lad, and get something inside you. You look worn out.'

'It's them trains, Mam, great noisy things, pothering smoke. And then I had to walk two miles from the station to the camp and wait in a cold guard room for an hour 'til they'd let me see him.'

Maddie stood at the end of the table, watching him eat, biting back the tumult of questions.

Nick glanced up at her once or twice but then quickly down again at his plate as he wolfed his meal.

'Eat slowly, Nicholas,' his mother scolded. 'You'll get indigestion. You look as if you haven't eaten for two days.'

'I haven't,' he mumbled, his mouth full.

'What?'

'Only what you gave me, Mam.'

'But didn't you get breakfast this morning where you stayed?'

'No, they don't serve it in the railway station waiting room.'

Harriet gasped. 'You mean, that's where you slept? In the waiting room on the station?'

Nick nodded.

The housekeeper cast a resentful glance at Maddie as if to say, There, look what my son has had to suffer because

249

of you. But Maddie was not concerned about Nick's few hours of discomfort, even if they had been on her behalf.

'What did he say?'

Frank came to her and put his arm about her shoulders. 'Come and sit by the fire, love, and when he's finished eating, Nick can bring his tea and sit with us and tell us what happened. Come along,' he urged finally as Maddie stiffened herself against his arm.

A few minutes later, they were all seated around the fire but Nick still avoided looking at Maddie. He cleared his throat and glanced uncomfortably at Frank.

'Michael said to tell you, Mr Frank, that he won't be coming back to the farm, not even when he's finished his National Service. He – he said to tell you that he's taken to the Army life. He intends to sign on as a regular.'

'What?' Frank was staggered, his mouth agape.

'He can't. He must come home,' Maddie cried.

'How can he possibly know if he likes the life yet? That's ridiculous. Are you sure that's what he meant, lad?'

The young man nodded. 'I pleaded with him, Mr Frank. I said just what you've said, but he was set on it.'

'I don't believe you,' Maddie whispered.

'Did you tell him what I had proposed?' Frank asked. 'About Maddie, I mean?'

Nick nodded.

'And?'

'He agrees it's the best idea for everyone.'

Maddie gasped and her insides trembled. 'No, no. I don't believe you,' she cried as her eyes stung with tears she would not allow to fall. 'He wouldn't agree to that. He couldn't . . .' Her voice fell away and there was silence in the room, the only sounds the flames crackling and hissing in the grate. But even before the warmth of the fire, Maddie shivered. She felt as if her heart were turning into ice.

'I'll have to go and have a chat with the vicar,' Frank said. 'I need to know what we have to do.'

Maddie glanced at him but said nothing. She didn't want this marriage. She really didn't. And yet since Michael's final rejection of her, it seemed the only way. At least in the eyes of the world her child would be legitimate. It would not carry the stigma of 'bastard' all its life. It was for this reason alone that Maddie had finally been persuaded to agree to the marriage.

'Although you're sixteen now,' Frank was saying, 'I think we still need parental consent, but because you haven't any parents . . .' His voice petered away as he frowned, thinking. 'I suppose Sir Peter is your guardian, in loco parentis, I think they call it.'

'What does that mean, when it's at home?' Harriet asked sarcastically.

'In place of her parents and I'm just assuming it's him because she lived at his orphanage.'

'I don't know,' Maddie said now. 'Mrs Potter always said that once we were school-leaving age, we were out and couldn't go back, so I don't see . . .'

'Don't argue with Mr Frank,' Harriet snapped. 'You want to think yourself lucky. Now he's having to go round telling folks, we can expect a visit from the police any day now, I shouldn't wonder. Want to see him carted off in handcuffs, do you?'

Maddie swallowed. For the sake of her child, she would marry its grandfather, though the lie she was being forced to live out went against her instinctive honesty.

'No one must ever know the child is Michael's,' Frank pleaded with the whole household. 'Beyond these four walls, the child is mine. I'm counting on you, Harriet, just as I'm counting on you both to stay here. You and Nick.'

Maddie watched the conflict visible on the woman's face. She was sure now that Harriet Trowbridge had harboured hopes of marrying Frank herself, but now these hopes were dashed for ever. Maddie held her breath, half-hoping that the woman would keep to her threat, pack her bags and leave.

But now Harriet and Frank were staring at one another, their gaze held by the past in which neither Maddie nor even Nick had any part.

'More secrets, eh Frank?' Harriet said softly.

'Aye, more secrets, my dear.'

Slowly, Harriet nodded.

'And Nick?' Frank persisted. 'He'll not say anything? Because I don't think he's in favour of this plan. I think, maybe, he thinks that when he's older . . .' Frank gestured towards Maddie.

Harriet's eyes widened in horror. 'What? You mean – he . . . With her? Oh no. Never.'

Frank put his head a little on one side and smiled as if he had just played his trump card.

Harriet was still struggling with the conflict raging within her. At last she said, 'Well, in that case, Mr Frank, there's nothing more I can say.' And both Frank and Maddie knew that to save her son from even thinking of marrying Madeleine March, Harriet Trowbridge would finally sacrifice her own hopes.

They were married in July after the main work of lifting the bulbs for storage through the summer had been done.

'You'd do better to make out you're older than you are. Put seventeen when you sign the register.'

'More lies, Mrs Trowbridge,' Maddie muttered.

'What's a lie, if it saves him from prison, eh?'

Maddie shuddered, but for the first time in her life she had to agree. Perhaps in such dire circumstances, a lie was justifiable.

'Besides,' Harriet went on. 'It's not really as if you are certain about your age, is it?'

'Mrs Potter said . . .'

'And what does Alice Potter know?'

Maddie stared at her. 'You know her?'

'What? Oh . . .' For a moment Harriet was flustered as if realizing she had said too much. 'Of course I know her. I met her when I brought you here. And . . .' she wagged her finger in Maddie's face, regaining her control now, 'I rue the day I did.'

'But you referred to her as Alice just now.'

'I did no such thing. I said Mrs Potter. Your hearing must be defective.'

'There's nothing wrong with my hearing. You said, "And what does Alice Potter know?"'

'I did no such thing. Don't argue with your elders and betters, girl.'

'Elder, maybe,' Maddie muttered. 'Better, certainly not.'

'What did you say?'

Maddie grinned at her. 'Nothing, Mrs Trowbridge,' she said innocently, thankful that if anyone had defective hearing, it was the housekeeper.

'Have you told the vicar my age?' Maddie asked Frank as they drove towards the church in his motor car. 'Because Mrs Trowbridge thinks I ought to say I'm seventeen.'

253

Frank glanced sideways at her. 'I wouldn't want you to lie. Not for me, Maddie, and not in church especially.'

'I've always been truthful,' Maddie said slowly, 'even if it got me into trouble. Somehow, I can't tell lies.' She paused and looked sideways at him. 'I wasn't lying that time about the hen-house, you know.'

Frank sighed. 'No, I know you weren't, love.' He paused and then haltingly said, 'There's things about Harriet you don't understand. Maybe one day, you will. But just trust me, Maddie, will you?'

She looked at him again, this time long and hard. His face was in profile to her as he kept his gaze firmly fixed on the road ahead. It was a good, honest face, she thought. A little troubled. In fact, a lot troubled. There were dark shadows beneath his brown eyes and he didn't seem to smile as much as he had when she had first come to the farm. Maddie felt a stab of guilt. She had been the cause of some of his anxiety, though she could hardly be blamed for the difficulties with the farm.

They did not speak again until he drew the car to a halt outside the church, switched off the engine and turned to face her.

'Before we go in, Maddie love, there's just something I want to say to you.' He licked his lips that were suddenly dry. 'We both know why we're doing this.'

Maddie nodded and determinedly swallowed the lump that rose in her throat as she thought of Michael.

It should be Michael standing beside me today. I should be about to become Mrs Michael Brackenbury, not Mrs Frank. But she said nothing. Michael didn't love her, or at least he didn't love her enough. She was on her own now. And she'd do whatever it took to protect her child. With a deep sigh for what might have been, Maddie knew she must face the future without Michael. In that moment, she locked away all memories of him, all thoughts of him and looked to the man at her side. The man who was willing to give her child a name. When it was born, it would bear the legitimate name of Brackenbury and even though there would perhaps be another lie to be told when she registered the child, at least it would have every right to that surname and Frank, legally, would be its father.

Frank was speaking again, haltingly with embarrassment. 'I want you to know that I don't expect you to be a wife to me. What I mean is, I shall make no demands upon you. The marriage will be in name only.'

Maddie looked at him then, full in the face. That good, kind and caring face that she was already very fond of. Suddenly, she smiled at him, 'Oh no, Frank,' she said, calling him by his Christian name for the first time without the title Mister in front of it. 'Oh no. If we are to be married, I shall be your wife in every way.'

For a moment he looked startled and then he too, smiled. He reached for her hand and raised it to his lips. His voice slightly husky, he said, 'Well, if you're sure, my dear.'

'I am,' Maddie said firmly and then added, 'Can I ask you something now?'

'Of course, love.'

'I – I don't want to pry . . .' Suddenly, she felt hesitant, but before she married Frank she wanted to know the answer to something that had been puzzling her ever since she had come to Few Farm. 'Or – or to bring up painful memories for you, but would you tell me what happened to your first wife and why you never talk about her?'

As Frank leaned back against the car seat and sighed heavily, Maddie said swiftly, 'Oh I'm sorry, I shouldn't have asked . . .'

'No, no, love. I can understand that it must seem a bit

odd to you.' He glanced at her and smiled gently. 'Specially for someone who probably longs to know about her own family.'

Maddie found it difficult to speak as the long buried yearning rushed to the surface. More than ever before, as she waited for the birth of her own child and now as she was about to enter into marriage, she missed the comfort of a mother, father and even of brothers and sisters.

'It must seem to you as if we don't want to talk about her,' Frank was saying softly, 'but nothing could be further from the truth. I loved Michael's mother dearly but she died at his birth. She's – she's buried here in this church-yard. In fact, if you like, when we've seen the vicar, I'll take you to see her grave.'

Maddie nodded and whispered, 'I'd like that.' There was a pause and then she asked, 'But why do you never talk about her? Why are there no photographs of her around the house?'

'There were at first. In every room and for the first year or so after her death I never stopped talking about her. My sister came to look after the baby and me at first. I think I must have driven her mad going on and on about Elizabeth and how happy we'd been. But she was very good. She never complained. I think she realized it was my way of coping.' He sighed. 'But my sister couldn't stay for ever. She had her own life. And it was when Harriet moved in as my housekeeper that things had to change. She'd had a very unhappy experience. I can't tell you about it, Maddie, because I gave my word to her years ago never to talk about it, but because she wanted the past buried, it was difficult for me to talk about mine. Gradually, I noticed she removed all the photographs of Elizabeth and the only one I have left is in my bedroom.' He turned to her. 'But I'll put that away now, if you . . .'

'No, no,' Maddie reassured him. 'Not on my account, please.'

'So,' Frank went on, 'the only time I could ever talk about Elizabeth was to Michael as he grew older.'

There was silence and although he said no more, the unspoken words hung in the air. *And now he's gone, there's no one I can share my memories with.*

Maddie leaned across and gently kissed Frank's weather-beaten cheek as she whispered, 'Well, you can talk to me about her, any time you like. In fact, I'd like you to.'

Again he raised her fingers to his lips as he murmured simply, 'Thank you, my dear.'

Thirty-Four

'I suppose I ought to go and see Michael again and tell him he has a son.'

Nick was standing at the end of the big double bed in the main bedroom that Maddie now shared with her husband and had done since the day of their marriage.

She smiled to herself when she remembered the look on Harriet Trowbridge's face when she had moved all her belongings, such as they were, from the tiny room along the landing into the master's bedroom. The woman had said nothing but the high colour on her cheeks, her tight mouth and eyes that sparkled suspiciously with tears of either disappointment or rage – Maddie could not have said which – spoke loudly her feelings.

'You needn't bother on my account,' Maddie said tartly now and brushed the downy head of her tiny infant with her lips. 'I don't care if he knows or not. John has a father.'

Nick jumped visibly and his eyes widened. 'You're – you're not calling him that, are you?'

Maddie blinked. 'Yes. Why shouldn't I?'

'Does – does me Mam know?'

'Nobody knows yet. I've only just decided. We said we'd leave the naming until we knew whether it was a boy or a girl. Well, now we know. And his name's John.'

'So – so Mr Frank doesn't know?'

'No.'

'Oh. Er – well, I think you'd better see what he ses.'

'Why. What's wrong with the name?'

'Nothing. But . . .'

'But what?'

Nick waved his hand and said, 'Oh nothing. See what Mr Frank ses.' He turned as if to leave when Maddie said, 'Nick, there is someone I'd be ever so grateful if you would tell.'

He turned back to look at her.

'Jenny. Would you go and see her for me, please? And ask her to visit?'

He pulled a face. 'All right. Just so long as she doesn't start following me about all over the place again.'

As Nick left the room, Maddie lay back against the pillows and closed her eyes. She felt elated, triumphant. She had her baby. A fine, healthy son. The birth had been surprisingly easy. All those old wives' tales about being in agony for days had not happened for Maddie. She hadn't even had time to wait for the midwife to arrive and Frank had delivered his own grandson.

The baby snuffled in his sleep and Maddie laid her cheek against his head. 'Oh John, part of me longs for your real daddy to see you. I'd love to see you in his arms and see the pride and joy in his eyes, just like it was in your grandad's when he handed you to me for the first time. But you're never going to know your real daddy, my darling boy. He – he doesn't want to know us any more. Either of us.'

In the privacy of the bedroom, Maddie allowed the tears to fall. Just this once, she told herself.

'You never miss a trick, do you, you little hussy, to humiliate me?'

Maddie was startled from a light sleep to find Harriet

259

bending over her. 'What – what on earth are you talking about?'

'It's not enough that you've taken the only man who's ever shown me any real kindness, but you have to stick the knife in and twist it, don't you? Wanting to call your little brat, John. Oh, but you're clever, I'll grant you that. Cleverer than even I'd given you credit for.'

Maddie blinked, feeling vulnerable and helpless under the woman's verbal attack that felt as if at any minute it might turn physical. Weak from the labour of her child's birth, relatively quick and easy though it had been, for the first time in her life, Maddie felt threatened.

'What are you talking about?' she asked in a voice that sounded far firmer than she felt.

'You know very well what I'm talking about.' She leaned closer and Maddie could feel the angry woman's spittle raining on her face. 'Oh I under-estimated you. That was my mistake. I thought I could get my revenge on you, but I was wrong. But . . .' the face came even closer so that their noses were almost touching, 'I aren't finished yet, girl.'

Suddenly, she straightened up, turned and left the room.

Maddie sank back against the pillows. 'Well,' she said aloud and glanced down at the cradle beside her where her son slept on, serenely undisturbed. 'What on earth was all that about?'

She heard Jenny's excited chatter on the landing even before the door opened and she was rushing headlong into the room. 'I came as soon as I could. Nick came to the shop to tell me. How are you? Where is he? Can I hold him? Ooh . . .' The last was a long-drawn-out sigh when she bent over the cradle. 'Isn't he just perfect?'

Maddie laughed. 'Well, I don't know about that. You might not think so if he woke you every three hours, even all through the night, demanding to be fed.'

'I wouldn't mind,' Jenny murmured, never once taking her gaze from the baby. 'When will he wake up? Can I hold him if he does?'

'Of course you can, but come and sit by me.' She patted the bed beside her and Jenny came reluctantly and perched on the edge, but still her glance was on the child.

'I'm sorry I missed your wedding,' Jenny said.

'Me too, but – well – in the circumstances it all had to be done very quietly.' She paused a moment before she said hesitantly, 'Jen, there's something I've got to ask you. A big favour.'

''Course. What is it?' Jenny was still only half listening. She was leaning away again, watching the baby and his every tiny movement.

'Jen, listen to me a minute. This is important.'

Jenny giggled. 'Sorry, Maddie, but I love babies. You know I do.'

Maddie remembered now how the only time she had ever seen Jenny really happy at the Home was when a baby had arrived. Sometimes she had been allowed to help in the nursery. Maddie had thought, at the time, that it was because it took her away from the other girls' teasing, but now she realized it was because Jenny had genuinely loved the little mites.

'What is it, Maddie?'

Maddie took a deep breath. This was very difficult for her. 'You know I never tell lies, that I always try to be truthful?'

Jenny nodded.

'Well, I have to ask you to help in a little – well – not exactly a lie but not quite telling the truth. Mr Frank wants

261

people to think that the baby's his. That way, if there's any trouble because I was underage when I conceived, it'll be him they'll come after not – not Michael.'

'Well, I can try,' Jenny's tone was doubtful, 'but I think everyone in the village knows it's Michael's and that's why he's gone away. Mrs Trowbridge saw to that. It was her that told Mrs Grange, 'cos I asked her and she said it was. I know Mrs Grange's a bit of a gossip, Maddie, but she's not malicious. Not like Mrs Trowbridge.'

So, Maddie thought, she had been right. She sighed. 'Oh,' she said flatly, 'so it's too late to kill the gossip then?'

''Fraid so, but I shouldn't worry about anyone coming after Mr Frank. If they'd been going to do that, they'd have done it by now. By the time the rumour did get round the village and probably PC Parsons got to hear of it, Michael was long gone.' She leant forward. 'Have you ever stopped to think that Mrs T might have deliberately spread the rumour once Michael was safely out the way so that Mr Frank wouldn't be blamed?'

Maddie stared at her. No, she hadn't thought of that. 'She wouldn't . . .' She began and then stopped. She had been going to say, 'She wouldn't do that to help me', but now that she thought about it, such an action was not to help her but to save Frank and that Harriet Trowbridge would most certainly have done.

Maddie closed her eyes and shook her head and lay back against the pillows. 'Oh, it's all too much. Maybe you're right. Maybe we should just let well alone.'

'What did you put on the birth certificate?'

Maddie pulled a face. 'Frank wanted me to put his name but when it came to it I couldn't. I explained it all to the Registrar and he said that in the circumstances it would be best left blank. If the real father isn't there to say he's the father, then I couldn't put Michael's name on anyway.'

'Oh well,' Jenny patted her hand. 'At least he's got his mum's name on the certificate and the name Brackenbury that's really his. That's a lot more than you and me have got, Maddie.' She paused and then asked, very softly, 'Do you ever wish you did know who your real family are? Why – why they left you like they did?'

Realistically, Maddie said, 'Not really,' and added wryly, 'I might not like what I find out. Why, does it bother you?'

Jenny glanced down at the patchwork quilt covering the bed and traced her finger around the hexagon-shaped patterns. 'Yes,' she whispered. 'It does bother me. I have the strangest feeling sometimes that I ought to know, I mean, that I ought to be able to find out.' She looked up then, straight into Maddie's eyes. 'For both of us really. We're so alike. And it was funny how we were both left outside the same orphanage in the same way and only a few months apart. We might be related. We might even be sisters. Oh Maddie, I'd love to be your real sister.'

'Your head's full of romantic notions, Jenny Wren. Real life's not like that.' Her voice hardened. 'Look what's happened to me. I fell in love with Michael and I really thought he loved me in return. And what happens? Off he goes leaving me with a bairn. If it hadn't been for the goodness of his father, I'd be living in Mayfield Wood by now. No, Jen, don't get any romantic dreams of someone turning up to claim you as their long-lost daughter. We're the bastards of some trollop, just like Mrs Potter always said we were.' She paused and looked at the crestfallen face of her friend. She reached out and took her hands. Then she smiled, 'But I grant you, it is just possible we

could be sisters. You were newborn when you were abandoned, but I wasn't. I was at least a month old, they
thought, if not more. So shall we settle for that, eh?'

'Oh yes, Maddie. Yes.' Jenny wrapped her arms about
Maddie and hugged her close almost squeezing the breath
from her.

'How are you feeling, love?'

Frank came and sat on the side of the bed and took her
hand in his.

Maddie had been asleep and now she roused herself,
yawned and stretched and glanced immediately to the
cradle at the side of the bed.

'You were both sound asleep. I didn't want to wake
you, but I have to talk to you,' Frank whispered, his voice
so low that she could hardly hear him.

'Don't tell me. The name.'

Frank nodded.

'Mrs T was up here a while ago, but I really couldn't
understand what she was on about. She was talking in
mysteries.'

There was such a look of deep distress in his eyes that
Maddie said at once, 'Oh I'm sorry if the name means
something to you I didn't know about.' Her mind was
running riot. Perhaps it was the name of someone in his
family he'd lost, perhaps . . .

'It's not me it upsets, but Harriet. Like I told you before,
I'm not at liberty to explain everything to you. All I can
tell you is that it was her husband's name. Nick's father's
name.'

'I see,' Maddie said slowly, though even now she did
not fully understand.

'It brings back tragic memories for her. She thought

you'd done it on purpose, but I've told her that's nonsense. How could you possibly have known her husband's name?' He paused. 'What did make you think of that name, Maddie?'

'I honestly don't know. I just like it, I suppose.'

'Well, it would be kinder if you could think of another name you like.'

'Of course,' she agreed readily.

Frank raised her hand to his lips in an old-fashioned courtly gesture. 'Thank you, my dear.'

'Is there a name you like, Frank?'

He smiled sadly, 'Well, the obvious one is Michael, isn't it?' Her face tightened and seeing it, he hurried on, 'But of course that's not a good idea for several reasons.' He thought for a moment and then said, 'What about Adam?'

'Adam.' Maddie repeated the name once or twice savouring the sound of it. 'Yes, I like it.' Her eyes clouded for a brief moment, feeling for a moment the acute loneliness of one without any blood relatives to call her own. 'I wonder what my own father's name was?' she murmured wistfully.

Moved, Frank took her into his arms. 'Don't, love. We're your family now.'

Maddie returned his hug, comforted by his kindness and yet her heart still ached for Michael.

Her face buried against Frank's shoulder, she screwed her eyes tightly shut as if trying to blot out the memory of his face. I won't think of him, she vowed. He's gone for ever. I won't even think of him again.

But she knew it was a vow she could not keep.

Thirty-Five

The first day that Maddie ventured downstairs, she was greeted with an ecstatic welcome from Ben. She made a huge fuss of the dog and then carefully introduced him to the wriggling, gurgling little baby in the pram.

'How do you think he's going to be with him, Frank?' Maddie asked quietly, as Ben stood looking into the pram, his nose resting on the side, his tongue lolling, his tail wagging.

'I think he'll be all right, but we should watch him at first.'

But it seemed that Ben, robbed of his four-legged charges, undertook to stand guard near the pram every time it was set outside in the front garden or the yard.

Fondling the animal often, Maddie would bury her face in his rough coat and whisper, 'He's little Michael, Ben. And you miss his daddy, as much as me, don't you?'

The dog, seeming to understand, would whine and try to lick her face in comfort.

Once Maddie was really up and about again, the household slipped into a routine, though it was an uneasy one. Harriet rarely spoke to Maddie, except when she was obliged to do so, but her manner towards Frank, instead of being resentful, seemed to Maddie to be even more fawning than before.

Though it irritated her, it did not really bother Maddie, but there was something that did worry her far more. She was anxious for the safety of her child. Soon she would have to return to the fields for, in another few weeks, it would be planting time again and it would not always be practical for her to take the baby with her. There was no alternative but to leave the child in the care of the housekeeper. I'd sooner leave him with Ben, Maddie thought to herself.

The first morning she returned to outdoor work, Maddie worked in the glasshouses, close to home and went into the house every hour to check on the child.

'I thought he might be hungry,' she made the excuse, which she hoped was a plausible one since she was still breast-feeding him.

'I can always give him a bottle,' Harriet said and sniffed. 'I haven't quite forgotten how to do it, you know.'

Maddie said nothing, but bent over the cradle, her anxious eyes examining him. But he was sleeping peacefully, his tiny fingers curled in repose.

As if sensing her unease, Harriet came to stand on the other side of the cradle. 'I do know how to look after a baby, you know. He'll be quite safe with me.'

Maddie raised her eyes slowly and the long look she gave the woman said it all. Not a word passed her lips, but she knew Harriet Trowbridge would be left in no doubt as to her suspicions.

As she left the house again, Maddie realized that the housekeeper now had a weapon more powerful than ever before; she could hurt Maddie through her child. The only thing – or rather person – who protected Maddie and her baby was Frank.

But the woman was so devious, Maddie thought. If there was a way to do something that would not point the finger of blame at her, then Harriet would do it.

Maddie sighed. Once more, her overwhelming love, this time for her child, had made her vulnerable.

Over the next few months, Maddie had to admit that her fears seemed groundless. Far from carrying on her resentment towards the child, Harriet was captivated by the little chap. It was not until Maddie overheard Harriet talking to Frank one evening that she began to understand a little perhaps why, even though her antagonism towards Maddie herself was still evident, Harriet was charmed by Maddie's son. Harriet obviously thought that Maddie was upstairs when in fact she was in the kitchen heating the baby's bottle that had now become necessary since her own milk was not so plentiful. So Harriet made no attempt to keep her voice low and her words carried clearly through the half-open door.

'Do you know, Frank, I can't bring myself to dislike the little fellow.'

'Why on earth should you, Harriet?'

'Because he's *hers*.'

Frank's heavy sigh was clearly audible. 'Oh Harriet, I don't understand why you're so against poor Maddie. After all, you brought her here from the orphanage. If you remember, it was you who was adamant we should have a girl from the Home. I wasn't so sure myself at the time.'

'I had my reasons.'

'What, exactly?'

'Well . . .' There was a brief pause and Maddie sensed that Harriet was floundering for a reply. 'Well, with an orphan you've no parents demanding this, that and the other. No one coming to see if they're working a few more hours than they should. Checking up. All this Welfare

State – huh! Hard work never hurt anyone. I don't hold with it, all this namby-pambying children today.'

'And was that the only reason?'

There was a pause before Maddie heard Harriet say sharply, 'You're too sharp by half, Frank Brackenbury.' Then her voice softened as she deliberately changed the subject. 'It's like having Nicholas little again and this time I can enjoy looking after the little man without all the worry I had then.'

Maddie heard the low murmur of Frank's voice but as the milk boiled up and threatened to spill over, she made a dash for the saucepan and could hear no more.

So Maddie returned to her work in the fields with a lighter heart and though she still did not entirely believe that Harriet would never bring her pain through her child, she did now think that the woman would not harm the baby boy.

'It's nice to have you back,' Nick said, as they planted row after row of bulbs alongside each other.

'It's nice to be back.'

'You have recovered quickly, haven't you? And you've got your slim figure back, except . . .' His voice faded away but Maddie had seen that his glance lingered on the fuller shape of her breasts.

Nick was only a few months older than herself and it was natural that he should start to be interested in girls. And since she was the nearest . . .

'Have you got a girlfriend, Nick?' she asked, keeping her tone light, teasing, but not unkind.

'Huh, who'd look at me? Besides, they wouldn't get further than the gate, now would they?'

'What about Jenny? She really likes you, you know?'

'Does she?' His tone was non-committal.

'Why don't you ask her out sometime? You could take her to the village dance or to the pictures.'

'I don't think . . .' he began and then he glanced up and stopped whatever he had been going to say. 'What's he doing here?' Now his tone was full of belligerence.

Maddie straightened up. 'Who?' she began and then, as she saw the rider on horseback picking his way carefully down the edge of the field, she said, 'Come to see what we're doing with his land, I expect.'

The rider had dismounted and was standing beside his horse holding the bridle and watching her as Maddie stepped carefully towards him along the single row left empty between the bulbs.

'Good afternoon, Mr Theo. Have you come to see how we're getting on?'

He smiled as he touched his riding hat with his whip. 'Good day to you. I trust I find you well?'

Closer now, Maddie looked into his eyes and saw that his enquiry held genuine concern. She wondered if he knew. At his next words, she was left in no doubt.

'I understand congratulations are in order.' His voice was soft and its tone still kindly, yet the smile was gone from his mouth and there was a strange look in the depths of his eyes. 'Both on your marriage and the recent birth of your son.'

'Thank you,' she said quietly.

'And the child? All is well with you both?'

'Thank you, yes.'

'Ah. Good, good.' He paused, shifting uneasily from one foot to the other. Then turning to other matters he became more at ease. 'I've brought you some good news.'

'Really?' Her heart lurched. Was it Michael? Had he

somehow got news of Michael? It was the first thing that sprang to her mind.

'Yes. I've just had word from the authorities that you can plant another two acres of bulbs this year and I'm sure it won't be long now before restrictions are lifted altogether.'

Despite the plummeting of her heart in disappointment, Maddie smiled, 'That is good news. Thank you.'

There was a pause as for a moment he held her gaze. Then he glanced over her shoulder and said, 'By the look on Nick's face, I'm keeping you from your work. I must go. Be sure to give my regards to – er – your husband.'

He gathered the reins in his hands and mounted. 'Good day to you . . .' There was the tiniest pause before he added, 'Mrs Brackenbury.' Then, once more, he guided his horse carefully along the side of the field towards the gate.

She stood watching him until she heard Nick's truculent voice behind her say, 'Are you going to help me plant the rest of these bulbs today or not?'

Thirty-Six

It was a bright warm autumn day when Maddie tucked baby Adam into the deep-bottomed black pram and wheeled him down the lane towards the village. She had promised to visit Jenny and Mrs Grange at the corner shop and today she had allowed herself the afternoon off to do just that.

She parked the pram outside and climbed the steps to push open the door. The loud clang of the doorbell made the two people standing behind the counter and their one customer look up.

'Oh Maddie.' She heard Jenny's cry at once as she came darting around the counter from her place and saw Mrs Grange nodding a welcome.

After the first greeting, Maddie glanced towards the young man standing near the counter, holding his hand out for his change from the old-fashioned till.

'Well, if it isn't Stinky Smith. Fancy seeing you.' Almost before the words were out of her mouth, she felt Jenny's sharp nudge in her ribs.

'Don't call him that any more, Maddie. He's got a nice job in town now, in an office, haven't you Sti . . . I mean, Steven?'

Maddie looked him up and down and had to admit at once that the name no longer suited him. Standing before her was a well-dressed young man in a suit, white shirt and tie with his once unruly hair slicked neatly back.

But the grin he gave her was as cheeky as ever. 'And I hear the name the Mad March Hare doesn't fit you now.' The grin widened. 'The mad bit might, of course, but I hear you've changed your name.'

Maddie was suddenly on the defensive, wondering what was coming next, but Stinky – or Steven – as she told herself she must now call him, seemed quite at ease. 'Where is the little fellow then? Outside is he? Come on, Ma, let's have a look-see.'

'Cheeky young imp, you are,' Mrs Grange laughed but came round the counter and passed through the door Steven held open for her. Puffing, she descended the three steep steps and bent over the pram.

'He's a lovely little chap. Hasn't he got a shock of dark hair? Get a lot of indigestion when you was carrying him, did you, love?'

'Not particularly,' Maddie laughed.

'Ah well,' Mrs Grange nodded sagely, 'they always say if you have it bad when you're carrying, the babby'll have a lot of hair.'

At that moment the child whimpered and wriggled.

'Bring him inside. I should like to have a hold of him.'

'Well, I'd best be on me way,' Steven said. 'See you, Jen. Don't forget. Sat'day night?'

Jenny turned a little pink. 'All right.'

Minutes later, they were sitting in Mrs Grange's back room and she had taken the child from Maddie. Cuddling him against her ample bosom, she rocked him gently to and fro.

'Now then, now then,' she crooned, 'let's have a proper look at you. Why, you are just like your daddy was when he was a babby. He was a handsome little chap an' all.'

Maddie frowned and then forced herself to laugh and

say, 'Oh Mrs Grange, you don't look old enough to remember Frank as a baby.'

The huge bosom heaved with laughter. 'I aren't, lovey. But I do remember Michael as a bairn.' Now she stared straight at Maddie as if defying her to deny the truth.

Maddie felt herself colouring and dropped her gaze. So what Jenny had told her had been true. It was too late to stem the gossip and, for once, the gossip had been the truth.

She heard Mrs Grange chuckle softly and say, 'Don't worry, lass. All the village know the truth and they know that Mr Frank has married you to save that young scally-wag's skin.' She laughed even louder as she added, 'Even the village bobby knows all about it, but he's not going to do owt when you and the bairn are being well cared for and that young scamp safely out of the way, now is he? He knows as well as the rest of us, that Mr Frank's not to blame.'

'I . . .' Maddie felt herself growing hotter by the minute.

'Mind you,' Mrs Grange went on. 'I must say I was surprised at young Michael going off like that. I had him made of sterner stuff than that. Oh, I know he flirted a bit with the village lasses and I don't doubt there's more than one around here fancied her chance with him, but I wouldn't have thought he would have deserted you the way he did. And I have to say it . . .'

And who would be able to stop you, Maddie thought, but she held her tongue between her teeth to stop the words from slipping out.

'We'd have thought better of him if he stayed and faced the music and stood by you.'

'I – it's not as simple as that,' Maddie blurted out, forced to speak about something she had vowed she never would again.

'No, lass, I don't suppose it is. Life ain't simple. It never was.' The woman was still rocking the baby in her arms, but now she was glancing from Maddie to Jenny and back again, a thoughtful look on her face. 'Are you sisters?' she asked bluntly.

Maddie and Jenny exchanged a glance and then, with a similar gesture, they both shrugged. 'We don't know who we are, really,' Maddie explained and added wryly, 'only that we were both not wanted 'cos we were dumped on the steps of the orphanage only a few months apart.'

'Were you really?' Mrs Grange said. 'Now, I'd call that more than a coincidence, wouldn't you?'

'Wh-what do you mean?' Jenny stammered.

The woman opened her mouth, but at that moment the shop door bell clanged loudly and Mrs Grange held out the child towards Maddie and levered herself up from her chair. 'No rest for the wicked,' she laughed as she waddled through into the shop.

They heard voices and were surprised when only seconds later Mrs Grange poked her head back around the curtain. 'It's Nick Trowbridge looking for you, lass. He ses can you go home. There's been an accident.'

Maddie's eyes widened. 'An accident? Who?'

Clasping the baby to her, Maddie hurried into the shop and around the counter. 'What's happened?' she demanded.

Nick was white-faced. 'It's Mr Frank. A fork's gone through his foot. He needs to go to the hospital.'

'Have you called a doctor or an ambulance?'

Nick ran his hand through his hair ruffling it and making it stand up on end so that he looked wild. 'No, no. I came to find you. I didn't know what to do.'

'Where is he?'

'In the field – where it happened.'

'What? You've just left him there? Alone?'

'I didn't know what to do.'

'Leave the bairn with us, lass, and you go,' Mrs Grange offered. 'He'll be all right.'

Maddie did not hesitate, but passed the child back into the woman's arms.

'There, there, my pretty,' Maddie heard her crooning to the gurgling child as she hurried out of the shop. 'You'll be all right with me and young Jenny here . . .'

'Come on,' Maddie urged Nick. 'We'd better run.'

By the time they reached the field, Maddie's legs were trembling and her breathing laboured. She hadn't realized, until put to the test, just how much the birth of her child had sapped her strength.

'Down here.' Nick led the way along the side of the field and then Maddie could see Frank lying on the ground.

Maddie took one look at the blood oozing out of the man's boot and seeping into the earth. 'Go back to the village phone box and phone the doctor,' she said swiftly to Nick. 'On second thoughts, you'd be quicker going to his house. It's only across the road from the phone box.'

Nick was off again at a run but Maddie called after him. 'Get Michael's bike from the barn. You'll be quicker.'

Then she knelt on the wet earth and gently touched the man's arm. 'Frank?'

He opened his eyes and groaned. 'Oh Maddie. Thank goodness you've come.' He reached up and gripped her hand. 'Can you – get me boot off, lass?'

'Do you think I should?'

Frank, biting his lower lip, nodded.

Carefully, Maddie loosened the laces and eased the boot from his foot. As she did so the blood flow seemed to increase until to Maddie's horror it was pumping from the wound.

'I don't think I should have done that. It's – it's made it worse. It's bleeding more.'

'No, no, it'll be all right. It'll wash the dirt out. Take the sock off an' all.'

The blood was vivid against his white skin and now she could see that there were two wounds where the fork had pierced his foot.

'I've been meaning to throw those old boots away. It serves me right for being such a penny-pincher. The fork wouldn't have gone through a decent pair of boots.'

Frank now levered himself up on to his elbow and looked down at his foot. 'I've a clean handkerchief in my pocket, lass. Get it out and bind it tightly round the foot now.'

Maddie did as he asked, but the thin cotton was soon soaked with blood.

'Press your fingers on top of the hanky over the worst wound, lass. That'll stem the flow a bit.' Again she did as he bid.

Frank tried to smile. 'You'd make a good nurse, lass.'

It seemed an age before Maddie lifted her head and saw Nick hurrying down the field, with the doctor, complete with medical bag, close behind him. But Maddie had the sense to keep the pressure on the wound until the doctor knelt beside her and took charge.

Only then, did Maddie stand up and stumble a little way down the field to retch into the hedge bottom.

'It's all your fault.' Harriet's tirade was scathing. 'I 'spect he was worrying over you and all the trouble you've brought. I wish I'd never brought you here. I shouldn't have let my own . . .' The woman stopped abruptly and contented herself with a malicious glare at Maddie.

'It was my fault,' Nick said agitatedly pacing the kitchen. 'I didn't look what I was doing. I was digging away along the row and then I stuck me fork to one side to bend down to pull some weeds out by the roots and I – I didn't realize . . . I mean I hadn't heard him come up beside me. I stuck the fork straight through his boot.'

Maddie stared at him. '*You* stuck the fork through his foot?'

Nick nodded miserably.

'I didn't see him, Maddie.'

'But – but . . .' She began and then fell silent. She couldn't understand how anyone could be that close and yet Nick had not seen, heard or even felt his presence.

'I didn't look round and it was windy and I'd got me scarf tied tight round me ears. I didn't hear him.'

Maddie sighed. 'Oh well, it can't be helped. Accidents happen.'

'And what if Mr Frank's wound goes septic? What if he gets lockjaw and dies? What then?' Harriet rounded on her son.

Maddie felt the colour drain from her face whilst Nick looked stricken with guilt.

'He – he won't,' she tried to declare stoutly, but even to her own ears, her tone lacked conviction. 'He won't,' she said again and then added uncertainly, 'will he?'

But Harriet only smiled nastily as if to say, 'We'll see. We'll see.'

Maddie turned away. Frank was safely in the local hospital and receiving the very best attention, but she must go back to fetch Adam from the shop. She could imagine that Mrs Grange and Jenny would be hard pressed to pacify a very hungry child by this time.

As she passed by the coat pegs in the wash-house, from the nearest one she caught sight of Nick's yellow scarf dangling there. She stopped and for a moment stood very still, thinking hard.

There was something wrong. Something about that scarf but, in her agitation, for the life of her she could not think what it was.

Thirty-Seven

Frank did not stay in hospital, although the doctor called regularly at Few Farm to check on the wound.

'We ought to tell Michael,' Maddie, though reluctant now ever to let his name pass her lips, felt obliged to make the suggestion.

'I'll go.' Nick's offer was swift.

Three pairs of eyes looked at him.

'There's no need for that,' Frank said quietly. 'I'm hardly at death's door.' He turned his head away and stared into the fire. Maddie felt the familiar pang of guilt for she could hear the regret in Frank's voice. He was missing his son.

'We could write to him,' she suggested.

Sharply, Nick said, 'We haven't an address.'

'So how do you propose to go to see him, if you don't know where he is?'

'I'll just go back to the camp he was at and they'll tell me where he is now.'

There was silence before Maddie, frowning, said, 'Well, can't we write to the Commanding Officer of the camp and ask him to forward a letter on? Surely they do that sort of thing?'

'It'd be easier if I went in person,' Nick insisted stubbornly. 'Then we'd know he'd got the message.'

'It really doesn't matter,' Frank murmured, but his tone denied his words. In his voice, Maddie could hear the longing to see his son. She bit down hard upon her lower lip. It was a longing that was echoed deep within her own heart, if only she allowed herself to admit it.

This time when Nick left to visit Michael, Maddie sent no letter, or messages. She could not even bring herself to wish Nick a 'safe journey' and for the next two days she threw herself into work, caring for her baby and planting in the fields.

She was not unhappy, she told herself over and over. How could she be? She had a beautiful baby boy, who was a delight and a joy to her. Through the kindness of Frank Brackenbury, she had his name, a home and she knew he was very fond of her. It was far more than she might have expected with her background. And yet, though she strove not to let her thoughts dwell on him, she could never forget Michael and what might have been, what could have been, she thought sadly.

But Maddie was not a girl to allow bitterness to fester and warp her nature, like Harriet had done. She had never held any resentment against her parents for abandoning her even though she had often been curious to know why. During her time in the Home, she had never been unduly worried about knowing what her roots were – not like it seemed to bother Jenny. Yet now that she had a child of her own, Maddie found that the urge to find out about her blood family was growing stronger. Out in the fields where the work, even though she loved it, was repetitive and monotonous, she had time to think. To keep her mind from wandering to what Nick might be doing and what Michael was saying to him, she focused her thoughts on all the clues – few though they were – about her birth. And Jenny. She could not disregard Jenny. Although, at first, their game of being sisters had been a pretence, merely a way of believing that they each belonged to someone, Maddie now had the strange and insistent feeling that they were, somehow, connected to each other.

Maddie went over all that she knew. She had been left at the Home in March 1932 and had been some weeks old, though no one had been prepared to state a definite number. Then in the September of the same year, a new-born baby had been abandoned outside the Home in a very similar way. Jenny had been very tiny, Maddie remembered one of the nurses at the Home once saying so. Perhaps she had even been born prematurely. That thought had not occurred to Maddie before now. Then, she had not known so much about giving birth.

They certainly looked alike. Their hair colour was the same, although Jenny's was curly. They both had blue eyes.

Then there had been the gypsy. Maddie wasn't quite sure whether she believed in anyone being able to foretell the future, but the dark-eyed Romany had been uncannily near the truth in some of the things she had said. And she had refused to read Jenny's hand. Was it really possible that she had seen something she knew she could not reveal?

Maddie shook her head. Mentally she was going round in circles. She was no nearer finding out the truth of her parentage, or Jenny's, than she ever had been.

She sighed, stood up and eased her back. Time to go and feed her son. At least he'll always know who his mother is, she vowed. If only . . .

Maddie clenched her jaw and marched along the furrow to the end of the field, firmly dismissing any thoughts of Michael from her mind.

*

'He says he won't ever come home again.'

Despite her determination to put him out of her mind, at Nick's words Maddie's legs threatened to give way beneath her. 'Not – not ever?'

Nick shook his head.

'But why? I mean – surely he wants to see his father, if – if not me and his son?'

Nick shrugged. 'What's the point? Now Mr Frank's married you and taken on Adam as his own son, what's the point in him coming back at all? Only cause more trouble. That's what he said.'

'I – see.' Maddie said slowly. But she didn't see at all. Not really. She could scarcely believe all that Nick was telling her. Surely Michael, the Michael she knew and loved, could not be so heartless towards his own father, even if his feelings towards her had changed.

'Did . . .' she licked her lips, 'did he mention me or – or Adam?'

Nick shook his head.

'But you told him he had a son? You told him his name?' Despite her resolve, she could not stop herself asking the questions.

'Of course I did,' Nick was defensive. 'That's partly what I went for, isn't it?'

'And he said – nothing?'

Again Nick shook his head and avoided her direct gaze.

'He didn't want to come home to see his father?' When Nick still did not reply, Maddie said again flatly, her last vestige of hope gone, 'I see.' And now she did. Michael wanted to sever all ties with her, his son and even with his father. The huge lump that rose in her throat threatened to choke her, but Maddie lifted her chin and said, 'Well then, if that's the way he wants it, we all know where we stand now, don't we?'

She turned away from Nick before he should see the tears in her eyes. She would never again allow anyone to see her shedding tears over Michael. Not ever, she vowed.

But Harriet would not let the matter rest. 'I would never have believed it of him,' she declared at the dinner table. 'I'd never have thought that he could be so callous and towards you of all people, Mr Frank. You did tell him about the accident, Nicholas, didn't you?'

'Yes, Mam.'

Maddie watched as Frank pushed the food around his plate, totally uninterested in eating. She sighed, but said nothing, feeling once more the heavy weight of guilt pressing upon her.

Thirty-Eight

'Why don't you ask Mrs Grange, Jen?'

The next time she and Jenny were alone together, Maddie brought up the subject of their births.

'I didn't know you were so interested. When I used to say I wished I knew who my mam and dad were, you always used to shut me up.'

Maddie looked down at the sleeping infant in her arms and stroked his blond hair gently. 'Did I? I'm sorry, Jen.'

The girl shrugged. ''S all right. I'd got you.'

They glanced at each other and smiled. They'd certainly shared all their lives together, just like real sisters.

Jenny nodded towards Adam and said shrewdly, 'I suppose having him has made you wonder more about your real family, has it?'

Maddie nodded.

'Well, I'll ask her.' She laughed. 'There's one thing certain.'

'What's that?'

'Mrs Grange will tell me everything she does know.'

The two girls laughed together.

'There's someone else you could ask, an' all. Stinky. Do you remember that day in the woods when we were kids? The day he took us to see the tree?'

'Will you please stop calling him Stinky?' Jenny said, with a firmness Maddie had never before heard in her tone. 'His name's Steven.'

285

'Oh-ho,' Maddie teased. 'This is getting serious. Jenny Wren, you're blushing.'

Accused of it, Jenny's face grew pinker.

'Are you going out together, then?'

'Well . . .' Jenny glanced at her coyly. 'We went to the pictures again last week.'

'So, is Nick out of favour now, then?'

Jenny shrugged. 'I like him. In fact, just between the two of us, I like him best, but he doesn't seem interested in me. I – I think it's you he likes.'

'Me? Don't be daft, Jen. His mother detests me.'

'Maybe so. But Nick doesn't.'

'Oh, I think you're wrong there,' but even as she spoke, her denial lacked conviction. 'Anyway,' she went on, 'why don't you bring Steven, to the farm? Maybe that way you could make Nick jealous.'

'I couldn't do that,' Jenny said primly. 'It wouldn't be fair on Steven.'

'Well, bring him anyway. I quite like old Stinky. He's certainly turned out a lot better than I thought he would.'

'Only if you promise to call him *Steven*.'

'All right, all right. I'll try. Really I will.'

'I won't have strangers coming here. Especially not from the village. Poking and prying into everybody else's business.'

'They're my friends, Mrs Trowbridge,' Maddie said quietly, but firmly. 'And they're coming for tea on Sunday.'

'Well, don't expect me to get it ready.'

'I won't.'

'I shall stay in my room. You can bring me my tea on a tray.'

'Yes, I'll do that. It'd be a pleasure.'

Harriet eyed Maddie suspiciously, not sure whether she had imagined the sarcasm.

'Have you asked your husband?'

'Yes, I have, and he's quite happy about it.'

Harriet sniffed but could say no more.

It was a merry little party that sat around the tea table the following Sunday. Steven, as Maddie kept reminding herself to call him, was excellent company. He laughed and joked with Nick, who, obviously relieved that Jenny had transferred her affections elsewhere, was kinder to the girl herself. Once or twice, Maddie saw Jenny glancing between the two young men, a slight frown creasing her smooth forehead, almost as if she were comparing the two.

I wonder who will win? Maddie thought to herself.

'Where do you work, Steven?' Frank asked. 'With your father?'

'No. Me elder brother's going to take on the smith.'

Frank smiled. 'Another Smith as our smith, then?'

It had always been a village joke that the blacksmith should be called Smith. Steven smiled. 'That's right, but there isn't enough business now for more than me Dad and our Ron. So I got mesen a stall on the market.'

'I thought you'd got a posh job in an office?' Maddie said.

Steven pulled a face. 'I had. But I left. I couldn't stand being cooped up inside all day and shuffling bits of paper about. It didn't seem like real work to me.'

'What do you sell?' Maddie asked.

'Anything and everything that'll make me a bob or two.'

Maddie laughed. 'Bunches of tulips for Christmas?' It

287

was the thing that was uppermost in her mind at the moment. The work in the greenhouses was progressing well and they were promised a bumper crop. She had already brought in the first trays to be ready in time for Christmas. But Maddie's worry was selling them at the right time and at a good price.

Last year Michael had dealt with all that and she wished now that she had learnt more about how he had made his contacts in the first place. They still had the ones he had found, but now, with their increased production, she needed more outlets.

'You're on,' Steven was saying. 'But I shan't be able to take all those two greenhouses will produce. But I presume you've got other outlets.'

'Just a couple, but we need more now.'

'Oh well, then, I'll see what I can find out for you.'

Later, washing up together in the kitchen, Maddie said, 'Well, Jen, did you ask him?'

'Ask who, what?'

'Did you ask Steven if he knew any more village gossip that might help us find out who we are?'

'Oh that. Oh yes, but he doesn't know anything about us.'

'What about Mrs Grange?'

Jenny frowned. 'Yes, I asked her, but do you know, it was most odd. She clammed up when I started asking her. Reckoned she knew nothing about any babies being left outside the Home.'

'But you didn't believe her?'

Jen shook her head. 'Knowing the village grapevine like I do now, no, I don't.'

'And you couldn't get her to tell you anything?'

'Not a word.'

There was silence, before Maddie said, 'So, we're no nearer finding out who we are, are we?'

'We could ask Mrs Potter.'

'I wouldn't ask her if she was the last person on this earth to ask,' Maddie said vehemently.

To this, Jenny made no answer.

Steven was as good as his word and by the time the blooms were ready, there were more buyers from London clamouring for their flowers than they could supply.

'I know we can't get rid of the little barn because we need that for storage and parking the truck under cover, but you know we could knock the hen-house down and put another greenhouse there for next year,' Nick suggested. 'We've only got a dozen hens or so now for eggs for ourselves and they could easily live in a much smaller shed. What do you say, Maddie?'

'I'll talk to Frank.'

Nick looked mutinous. 'Why do you always have to ask him? You know he's so soft with you that he'll go along with anything you say. Besides, I don't think he's very well. He's slowed up a lot lately. Haven't you noticed?'

To her dismay, Maddie realized that she had not. She had been so wrapped up in the care of her child and the work with the tulips. But now she thought about it, since autumn had turned into winter, he had spent more and more time huddled near the range in the living room.

Now, she would certainly talk to him.

Later that night in the darkness of their bedroom as they lay together, the child asleep in his cot at the end of their bed, Maddie put her hand out and touched Frank's shoulder.

'Mm?' He stirred at once. 'What is it, love? What's the matter?'

'I'm sorry. Were you asleep?'

'Not really.'

'Frank, are you feeling quite well? You've been looking a bit tired lately.'

'I'm fine, Maddie. I do get a bit of an ache still in my foot, but I don't say anything about it. I don't want to upset Nick. It was an accident.'

'But are you sure the work's not too much for you? We have been dreadfully busy.'

He turned towards her and she moved into his embrace. He kissed her gently. 'My darling girl, I'm touched that you should be so thoughtful. But I'm fine, honestly, although . . .'

'Yes,' Maddie prompted.

'Well, I must admit I've been feeling a bit under the weather. I've been having a bit of stomach trouble lately.' He chuckled, 'But I daren't say anything in case Harriet thinks I'm blaming her cooking.'

'Then you must go to the doctor. It can't be anything you've eaten, because Harriet is a good cook. I will say that for her.'

Softly, close to her ear, he said, 'Even though you can't find it in your heart to say anything else good about her?'

'It's hard to.'

She felt his breath sigh against her face. 'Oh Maddie, if only you knew. She deserves your pity more than your censure. She's had a very difficult and unhappy life. I wish I could tell you all about it, but it's not my secret and years ago, when she first came here, I promised her faithfully I would never tell another living soul. I can't break that promise, Maddie, not even to you.'

'I know, I know,' she said gently. 'Don't worry about it. Go to sleep, but in the morning, you, Frank Brackenbury, are going to the doctor.'

Thirty-Nine

'If I'm not better after Christmas, I'll see the doctor then. But I can't let him tell me I've to stop work all together. Not just now, can I?'

'If you think that is what he would say, Frank, then you certainly ought to see him.' Maddie smiled, trying to make light of it, but the anxiety never left her eyes. 'If you don't go, I'll call him here.'

Frank smiled. 'Aye, I know you would. But I promise you I'll go if I feel worse, all right?'

'We-ell,' she said slowly, watching his face, trying to decide just how much he was holding back from her. 'Just so long as you promise that you'll go after Christmas if you still don't feel really well by then.'

'All right,' he agreed and they left it at that.

In December they were all busy in the glasshouses and, to Maddie's relief, Frank did seem much better. He did not put in as many hours' work as she and Nick, but they could not have managed without his help.

'Have you spoken to Frank about another greenhouse?'

'Not yet, but I will after Christmas. Can you fetch another tray in, Nick? I'll clear this corner out . . .'

'See, we are getting short of space. We could do with another one,' he said, as he went out of the door, closing it carefully behind him.

I know, I know we could, Maddie answered him silently in her head. But where is the money to come from?

They were doing well, there was no doubt about that, but most of their bulb stock went back into the ground the following year and cut flowers alone would not support them.

Frank saw to all the financial side but, now and then, he did discuss it with her.

'We must start to pay Sir Peter rent again from January, you know,' he had told her only the week before. 'We've had our one year's grace.'

As she swept the corner clear of scattered earth, the figures ran through her mind. Then suddenly, she was motionless, staring down at the concrete floor. There, in the far corner, she saw the imprint of their hands – hers and Michael's – joined together for ever and surrounding them, his drawing of a tulip. She squatted down and, trembling a little, she laid her hand over Michael's imprint. His hand had touched this spot. She closed her eyes and felt the tears well behind her eyelids and sting her throat.

Then, with a swift, angry movement, she stood up and brushed the earth into the corner, covering the cruel reminder. How happy they had been that night. How . . .

I won't think about it, she told herself firmly. I won't even remember it's there.

But for the rest of the day the image of the two hands, their fingers entwined, was in her mind and disturbed her sleep that night.

On Boxing Day, Jenny came to visit, this year bringing Steven with her. She had delivered her presents to Few Farm on Christmas Eve, but Steven brought the biggest ever seen.

'Come in, come in,' Maddie said as she opened the
door, trying to smile. At once Jenny said, 'What is it?
There's something wrong. I can see it in your face.'

Maddie gave a quick, rueful smile. 'Can't hide anything
from you, Jenny Wren, can I?'

'No,' the girl said solemnly. 'But then we're sisters,
aren't we?'

'Are you?' This was the first time Steven had heard
them say it and now he glanced from one to the other.
'You are a bit alike, but I didn't know you really were . . .'

'We're not,' Maddie said at once. 'At least we don't
know what we are, because we don't know anything about
our backgrounds, do we?'

As Steven opened his mouth, Jenny forestalled him.
'Never mind about that now. Tell me what's wrong,
Maddie. Is it Adam?'

'No, no,' Maddie said swiftly. 'It's Frank. He was very
sick in the middle of the night. He says he must have
overeaten and drunk too much.' She made a helpless
gesture with her hand. 'And, yes, we did overdo it a bit
yesterday. Mrs Trowbridge put on such a marvellous
Christmas dinner it was hard to resist, but . . .'

'But,' Jenny took the words from her, 'you think it's
more than that?'

'He's not been really fit for a few weeks, although he
had seemed a little better just before Christmas.'

'It could be a stomach ulcer, you know,' Steven volun-
teered. 'My dad's got one and every so often he's as sick
as a dog and then, when it settles down, he's all right for
a bit. You should get him to see Dr Hanson, Maddie.'

'Oh, I will now, don't you worry. First thing tomorrow
morning, he's down to that surgery. But come on in. He's

294

downstairs, even though he's still feeling a bit fragile and he won't stop apologizing to us all.'

'Are you sure you want us to stay?' Jenny asked worriedly.

'Of course. He'd only be upset to think he'd spoilt the day.'

Jenny beamed. 'Right then. Now where's my little man? Where's Adam?'

'He can't find anything wrong,' Frank said on his return from the surgery the following morning. He sat down in the chair by the fire, exhausted even by the short trip to the village.

'I thought as much,' Harriet said. 'I suppose you . . .' she jabbed a finger towards Maddie, 'are trying to make out I'm poisoning him with my cooking.'

Maddie gasped. 'The thought never entered my head, Mrs Trowbridge. You're a wonderful cook.'

The woman glanced at Maddie but the words had been said so genuinely that even she could not doubt Maddie's sincerity. Not this time.

'You've been working too hard, Mr Frank,' Nick said, smiling down at the man and putting his hand on his shoulder. 'Now, don't you worry about a thing. Me and Maddie can cope with the work for the next few weeks. You just rest and get yourself better.'

Frank smiled and patted Nick's hand. 'You're a good lad, Nick. I don't know what we'd do without you both.' His glance took in the housekeeper, too, but then his worried eyes came back to Nick. 'Are you sure you can manage the battery house? You must be very careful in there, you know.'

'I'll be careful,' he promised and Maddie marvelled yet

again at Nick's confidence, which seemed to be growing daily. She went to the cradle placed by the window and picked up the child. She planted a swift kiss on his round cheek and then carried him to Frank. 'So the only thing you've got to do for a while is play with your . . .' she hesitated fractionally before adding, 'little boy.' She didn't want to say 'grandson' and she could never bring herself to call him Frank's son.

'Oh well, I can do that all right,' Frank said, smiling happily as he took the child onto his knee.

Adam, now almost five months old, gurgled up at the man Maddie knew he must be brought up to believe was his father.

Frank's condition worsened. Within two weeks he was too weak to get out of his bed. His skin looked yellow and was cold and clammy to Maddie's touch.

'I feel so weak and dizzy,' Frank moaned. 'I've never felt like this before in the whole of my life.'

Between them they nursed him and Maddie was grateful for Nick being there. He sat up with Frank through the night sometimes whilst Maddie moved back into the tiny bedroom she had once occupied, taking the cumbersome wooden cot with her, squeezing it in to stand between the narrow bed and the wall.

'You need your rest,' Nick told her. 'You've the baby to think of. I can snatch a couple of hours in the day if I need it. You can't.'

He carried tray after tray up the stairs with anything that his mother could think of to tempt Frank's appetite. But Harriet was distraught. 'I don't know what to do. Everything I give him seems to make him sick. Nicholas, has he eaten that soup you took up?'

'Yes, Mam, most of it. But I had to spoonfeed him. He hadn't the strength to sit up and take it himself.'

For the first time ever, Maddie felt sorry for Harriet. The woman was beside herself with anxiety and it showed not only in the way she fretted about Frank, but also her manner towards Maddie had, for the moment, changed dramatically.

'Maddie, send for the doctor. Please. He ought to take him to the hospital.'

'I don't think that's a good idea, Mam,' Nick said before Maddie could even reply. 'How can they look after him any better than us?'

'I think your mother's right. He needs medical and nursing care that we can't give him.' She turned to Harriet. 'I'll go to the village and ask the doctor to call as soon as he can.'

'Let me go,' Nick said at once. 'You've the child to care for.'

'No. I'll go, Nick. I can take Adam in his pram.'

'But I can be quicker on my bike.'

Quietly, Maddie said, 'No, Nick. I'm going myself.'

'Don't you trust me?' he blurted out, his face turning red.

She stared at him for several moments, before she asked slowly, 'Now why on earth should you think that?'

Nick gave an angry snort and blundered from the kitchen, slamming the back door behind him.

The doctor was just hurrying down the steps of his house towards his car when Maddie arrived.

'Doctor, Frank's much worse. He's so weak. Please, would you come and see him?'

The doctor glanced at his watch. 'I'm on my way to a

difficult confinement, a breech birth. I'll look in to see
Frank on my way back.'

'Thank you, doctor. We'd be very grateful.'

As the doctor moved away in his car and she turned the
pram towards home once more, a voice hailed her.

'Maddie, Maddie. Wait a minute.'

She glanced over her shoulder to see Steven Smith
running towards her. 'How's things?' he said as he drew
level and fell into step beside her. 'How's Mr Frank?'

'Not good, Stink – Steven.' She glanced at him, but he
only grinned. Even in her anxiety the nickname she had
always used came naturally. 'I've just seen Dr Hanson and
asked him to call again.'

Steven nodded. 'Good.' There was a brief pause before
he said, 'Is there anything you need a hand with? I don't
have a market anywhere on a Monday. I know you must
be missing Mr Frank's help.'

'Well, there is something. Could you take the boxes of
flowers to the station tonight on your lorry? We've a
couple of trays ready in the greenhouse and I'm going back
home now to pick and pack them.'

'Of course I can. What time do you want me to come?'

'They've got to be there in time for the six o'clock
train.'

'Right. I'll be there in good time, Maddie.'

There was a pause, but he still walked alongside her
making no effort to leave her. Suddenly, he said, 'You
calling to see Jen?'

'Yes, but I can't stay long. I must get back to pick those
flowers.'

'I'll come along with you then.'

Again there was silence between them as they walked
along until Maddie asked slyly, 'Are you and Jen going
out together, then?'

Steven pulled a face. 'I wish we were. Oh, she'll come out with me. To the pictures and that, but, well . . .' He hesitated and Maddie noticed that his face had reddened slightly, so she finished his sentence for him.

'She doesn't seem as keen on you as you are on her?'

'That's about it.'

She wondered whether to tell him about Jenny's infatuation with Nick, but decided it would be kinder to say nothing. Instead she advised, 'You just carry on asking her out and being nice to her. I think you'll win her over in the end.'

'You think so?' He sounded so unsure, so unlike the Stinky Smith she thought she knew. He'd been a little imp at school, but she'd always been a match for his devilment and had never felt intimidated by him. Nor by anyone else, she thought with an inward smile, if it came to that. Yet now, obviously in love with Jenny Wren, Steven was diffident, almost shy.

How love changed people, Maddie thought wryly, thinking back to her own weaknesses where Michael, and now little Adam, were concerned.

She smiled up at Steven and, mentally crossing her fingers, said, 'I'm sure of it.'

As soon as Dr Hanson saw Frank, he said, 'He'll have to go to the hospital. I'll arrange it. Pack whatever he'll need and I'll send an ambulance.'

'No, I'll be fine,' Frank said weakly from the bed. 'I just need to rest. That's all.' They watched him as he tried to raise himself, but he could hardly lift his arm up, let alone push himself up to a sitting position.

The doctor's face was grim as he went downstairs and

faced the three of them in the living room. 'I think you would be wise to contact his son.'

Harriet's eyes widened and she let out a little cry and staggered, reaching out blindly for a chair to support her. At once Maddie was at her side and easing her down into Frank's chair by the fireside, where she lay back moaning, 'Oh no, no.'

Maddie said haltingly, 'We don't hear from Michael now. Only Nick has seen him since he left home. And the last news we had of him was that he would never . . .' She pulled in a deep breath. 'Come home again.'

The doctor's voice was gentle as he turned to Nick and said, 'Well, I think you should try to see Michael again and tell him that if he does not come home soon . . .' His voice deepened. 'He may never see his father again.'

Behind them, Harriet began to sob.

Forty

At just gone half past four, Steven's lorry drew into the yard. He climbed down, slammed the door and was calling out as he came across the yard, 'Maddie? Where are you?'

She poked her head out of the door of the big barn and shouted, 'Here. I'm in here. I haven't got the packing finished yet. Frank's had to go to the hospital.'

Steven nodded. 'I guessed as much. I've just passed the ambulance on its way to Wellandon. Here . . .' He picked up a bundle of raffia and moved to stand beside her. 'Let me help. A dozen to a bunch, is it?'

Maddie grinned at him. 'Baker's dozen.'

'Tut-tut.' Steven shook his head. 'And there I was thinking what a clever business woman you were. Just think how many you're giving away. For every twelve bunches, you're giving a whole bunch away.'

'Ah,' Maddie tapped the side of her nose. 'But they can't come back at me then and tell me one of the blooms was too far out or a stalk damaged. We did talk about it, me and Frank,' her voice shook a little, thinking about the man who had become so dear to her and who at this moment was being admitted to hospital. She should have gone with him. She should be at his side, but the flowers would not wait and they were their livelihood. She knew he would understand. 'But we decided,' she went on more strongly, 'that if we gave a little, we might not get any complaints.'

'And have you had any?'

'Complaints?' Despite her anxiety, she smiled at him. 'Not one.'

A shadow fell across the open doorway of the barn.

'Oh! Hello, I didn't know you were here.' Nick's tone was flat, devoid of any note of welcome.

'Come to lend a helping hand,' Steven grinned at him. 'Maddie asked me if I could take the boxes to the station.'

'There was no need. I take them.'

'You'll have enough to deal with here,' Maddie put in quickly. 'Now Frank's so ill.'

'How do you think I've been managing these last weeks and helping look after him?' There was a barely concealed sneer in Nick's tone now. 'It'll be easier now he is out of the way.'

'Nick . . .!' Maddie began but swiftly he added, 'You know what I mean. Now that he'll be well looked after, we can concentrate on the work. That's all I meant.'

Steven had his head down now, concentrating on tying the bunches and laying them carefully in the wooden boxes, but Maddie could see that there was a tightness to his mouth that had not been there before Nick's appearance.

'These boxes are returnable, aren't they?' Steven said, changing the subject.

'Yes. But sometimes we have a job to get them back.'

For a moment, he appeared to be deep in thought, then he said, 'I might be able to help you out a bit there . . .'

'I thought you might,' Nick said, sarcastically. 'Well, if you're taking over, I'll get on with the work in the battery house. Or do you want to have a go at that an' all?'

'Nick!' Maddie was suddenly angry, but before she could say more, Steven touched her wrist and said softly, 'Leave it, Maddie.'

'Steven, I'm so sorry,' she said, as Nick disappeared across the yard towards the battery house.

Steven shrugged. 'Funny lad, isn't he?'

Maddie sighed and said softly, 'Moody, I suppose you'd call it. But with a mother like he's got and the life she's made him lead, well . . .' She said no more, but knew that Steven understood her meaning.

Frank was in hospital for a week during which time they did all sorts of tests, yet still they could not put a name to the cause of his debilitating illness.

'I'm coming home tomorrow,' Frank told Maddie on the following Sunday afternoon.

'Have they said you can?'

'No,' he smiled at her and held up his hand as she began to protest. 'But I feel so much better and I hate being here. I'll be better at home.'

'Will they let you come?'

'How are they going to stop me?'

'Oh, Frank, you mustn't go against the doctor.'

'I won't, Maddie. But Dr Hanson will be in tomorrow morning. I'll have a word with him then. Just you bring my clothes tomorrow afternoon.'

'I heard Mr Brackenbury was ill. I came to see if you needed any help?'

Maddie gave a little gasp of surprise at the sound of his voice. Behind her, she had heard the greenhouse door open and gently close, but she had not looked up from picking the tulips.

'Oh, Mr Theo. I'm sorry, I thought it was Nick coming in.' She stepped towards him down the narrow aisle between the rows of trays on either side of the glasshouse, brushing the earth away from her fingers.

'No, please, don't let me stop you. I know how important it must be to crop the blooms at just the right time. We can talk as you work. That is . . .' he hesitated, 'if I won't be in your way?'

'Of course you won't. But I would like to get on. I've these to pack for Nick to take to the station and . . .' she smiled, 'time's already running out on me.'

'Then, please, do carry on, Maddie. I'm sorry – Mrs Brackenbury.'

Maddie laughed as she turned back to her task. 'Call me Maddie. Everyone does.'

'Thank you. Then you must call me Theo, without the Mister.'

She glanced briefly over her shoulder at him. 'I couldn't do that. It wouldn't be right.'

'Why ever not?' Then softly, he added, 'I'd really like you to.'

'Oh – well . . .' Maddie was unaccountably flustered. To consider calling Sir Peter's son by his Christian name in such a familiar manner was against all Mrs Potter's strict rules. And even though she was no longer under the woman's thumb, the upbringing was hard to leave behind. 'I'll try.'

Whilst Maddie worked, they talked. Theo wanted to know all about Frank's illness and what was being done. Then Maddie asked, 'How's your father?'

'Better, but not better, if you know what I mean. He's recovered from the stroke as far as he's going to.'

Maddie said nothing, but glanced at him enquiringly. She heard him sigh as he said, 'He's paralysed and there's little hope of further improvement.'

'I'm sorry,' she said with sincerity, although her pity

was more for the young man standing beside her than for Sir Peter.

'Yes,' Theo said quietly. 'He's not the . . .' He hesitated and Maddie had the feeling that he altered what he had been going to say. 'The man he was.'

There was a long silence now whilst he watched her work. It was not an uncomfortable silence between them yet Maddie felt obliged to break it. 'I'm sorry that Mr Frank hasn't sent you any rent yet. He means to start paying you again this month, with the New Year, but . . .'

Theo held up his hand. 'Please, Maddie, don't even mention it.' He smiled at her. 'To tell you the truth, I had forgotten all about it. Our estate bailiff sees to all that and it really hadn't crossed my mind again.'

'Well, we hadn't forgotten.'

'No, I know that. But don't worry about it just now. You've enough to cope with.' He stood idly slapping his riding crop against his legs as he watched her work. 'These flowers are lovely. You really have done well, Maddie.'

Maddie gathered together a dozen or so golden blooms and, turning, gave him a wide smile. 'Please, would you take these for your sister?'

Embarrassed, he held up his hand, 'No, no, really, I didn't mean . . .'

'I know you didn't,' she said softly. 'But please take them to her. I – I know how much she loves them.'

Their glances met and held and he gave a tiny nod, acknowledging that she understood far more than was being said between them.

'Thank you,' he said quietly, reaching out for them. There was no need for him to say more except, 'I'd better be getting along and not hinder you any longer. Give my regards to Mr Brackenbury.'

'He's hoping to come home tomorrow.'

'Then I'll call to see him next week. Goodbye for now, Maddie.'

'Goodbye, Mr Theo, and thank you.' Somehow she just couldn't bring herself to drop the 'Mr'.

'As I said,' he murmured softly. 'Don't mention it.'

As the sound of his horse's hooves down the lane died away, Nick came into the greenhouse. 'What did he want? Come to demand his rent?'

'Exactly the opposite,' Maddie said tightly. 'He'd forgotten all about it.'

'Oho, I bet!' Nick countered sarcastically and went out again, slamming the door so that the glass rattled.

'Mind the . . .' Maddie shouted after him, but already he was striding across the yard, too far away to hear, so that her voice fell away on the final word, '. . . plants.'

'Oh, it's good to be home.' Frank gave a deep sigh of satisfaction as he lowered himself into his chair.

'Well, I must say you look better, Mr Frank,' Harriet fluttered around him, bringing a rug for his knees and prodding the fire into blazing warmth.

'I feel it, Harriet, I'm thankful to say.'

'Have they said what it is?'

Frank shook his head. 'No. Some sort of gastroenteritis, they think.'

'Have they given you a special diet . . .?'

'Oh Mam,' came Nick's voice. 'Let the poor man get settled before you start firing questions at him.' He came and laid his hand on Frank's shoulder. 'It is good to have you back, but I'm sorry, I must go and start the generator or we'll have problems.'

Frank looked up, suddenly worried. 'Are you managing all right, Nick?'

Maddie saw the fleeting flash of resentment in Nick's eyes, but it was gone in an instant and she hoped that Frank had not noticed it.

'Of course I am,' he said and smiled so genuinely that Maddie had to admire his self-control. 'I had a good teacher.'

Maddie went out to the greenhouse, leaving Harriet to fuss around Frank. There were three more trays ready for cropping and packing.

'Will you be able to take these to the station this evening?' she asked Nick when he joined her in the greenhouse.

'Sure you don't want to ask Steven?'

She glanced at him but he was grinning at her and she smiled back. 'He was only trying to help and we were a bit pushed that day, Nick.'

'I know. And you're right.' He came and stood close to her and, to her surprise, he put his arm around her shoulders. For a moment, she stiffened under his touch. It was what Michael used to do and the memory hurt. Then she relaxed, relieved that Nick seemed prepared to accept outside help now and again.

Softly, so that Frank would not hear, for they were in the greenhouse attached to the house wall and both Frank and Harriet were only on the other side of the living-room window, Maddie said, 'We'll have to have some help come April. This year there'll be more to cope with than even the three of us can manage. And that's if Frank's fully recovered.'

'Oh, he'll be fine by then,' Nick said airily. 'But you're right. And to be honest, I'd sooner it was Jenny and Steven than complete strangers.'

There was silence between them for a moment, but still Nick did not remove his arm. 'Maddie,' he said slowly. 'I've been thinking that perhaps I should still go to see Michael. Like the doctor said.'

She looked at him, their faces close together. 'Why? He's so much better now. I – I don't think his life's in danger now.' When Nick made no reply, she added, 'Do you?'

He sighed before answering. 'I really don't know what to think. I just wondered if – if the hospital have found something that they're not telling us about.'

'They'd tell me, wouldn't they? As his wife?'

'You're very young, Maddie. Maybe they wouldn't tell you. Or me.'

'What about your mother then?'

She felt him shrug. 'She's not his next of kin. Besides, she didn't even go to visit him in hospital, did she? Actually, that did surprise me, you know. I thought she would have made the effort for Mr Frank.'

'But you think . . .' Maddie said slowly, beginning to see the reason behind his suggestion. 'That they would tell his son? They would tell Michael?'

'Yes, I do.'

She was thoughtful for some moments, though her hands were still busy picking the flowers. As she moved to reach over, Nick's arm fell away from her shoulders. His action had surprised her and although his touch had not really bothered her, when his arm was removed, she felt relieved.

'Maybe you're right,' she said at last. 'Maybe you should see him again and at least tell him everything that's happened. I suppose . . .' The words were difficult to say. 'It's only fair.'

'It's more than he deserves,' Nick muttered. 'But I'm thinking of Mr Frank more than – him.'

'Me too,' Maddie murmured, but in her heart she knew that was not strictly the truth.

There was no way that they could keep the reason for Nick's absence for two days a secret from Frank and although he objected at first, Maddie could see that his protests were only half-hearted.

'Now don't you go sleeping in station waiting rooms again. It's too cold this time of year,' his mother insisted, ladening him up with food parcels, not only for Michael this time but enough to sustain Nick for two days, too.

'No, I won't. I'll find somewhere I promise. No more, Mam,' he held up his hand as she tried to stuff yet another parcel into his rucksack. 'I'm biking to the station. I really can't carry another thing.'

Maddie walked with him to the gate. 'Tell him everything, Nick, won't you?'

'Don't worry, Maddie. I'll sort it out.'

And he was gone, wobbling down the road on his bicycle and whistling cheerfully.

Forty-One

That evening as Maddie was undressing Adam in front of the warm glow from the range, without warning the lights went.

Harriet, in the kitchen making cocoa, gave a cry of alarm. 'Oh, the milk! I can't see – wait a minute, there's a torch in the table drawer.'

Maddie sitting perfectly still until her eyes became accustomed to the dim light cast by the fire, heard Harriet scrabbling about. 'It's all right,' came her voice again. 'I've found the torch.'

Maddie finished undressing Adam and waited until Harriet came into the room, the light from the torch wavering in front of her.

'Will you be all right if I take the torch? I must go and see what's happened.'

'Don't you go out there. Mr Frank wouldn't want you anywhere near his battery house.'

'Mrs Trowbridge, I can't leave it. The pump will stop and the greenhouses will go cold. I'll go up and see Frank.'

Carrying Adam against her left hip, Maddie took the torch and climbed the stairs. Frank was in bed and, because he had already put out the light, he was unaware of any problem.

'Frank, I'm sorry to wake you . . .'

'Mm . . .?' came his sleepy voice. 'What is it, love?'

310

'The lights have all gone out. What do I do? Isn't there a lever in the battery house that I just put up a notch?'

'Don't you go in there, Maddie. Let me go.' He pushed back the bedclothes and began to get out of the bed.

'I can manage it, if you just tell me what to do.'

'No, no. I don't want you going in the battery house and besides,' he smiled at the child in her arms, 'that little chap is dropping to sleep in your arms. You put him to bed. I'll go and see to things out there. I can't understand it, though,' he added as he pulled on his trousers over his pyjamas and tapped his pocket to make sure he had his keys. He slipped his arms into his dressing gown and thrust his feet into his slippers. 'Nick had the engine running only yesterday. I can't think what's happened.'

He paused only to light the candle in its pink holder that always stood on the bedroom mantelpiece and then he took the torch from her hands. 'Can you manage with that light to put him to bed?'

'Yes, but . . .' He was moving quite strongly out of the bedroom. Maddie, torn between going with Frank, and seeing to her child, said, 'Are you sure you're all right, Frank?'

'Yes, yes, love. You see to Adam, bless him.' He came back and planted a kiss on the sleepy little boy's head. Then he looked at Maddie, his brown eyes twinkling, his cheeks, though a little thinner just lately, creasing into such a loving, caring smile, that she smiled back at him. Their glance held for a long moment before Frank turned away and headed for the stairs.

'The lights have come back on,' Harriet greeted Maddie a little time later when at last she came downstairs. Adam, though tired, had taken a long time to settle. 'But Mr Frank's not come back in.'

311

Maddie stared at her. 'Not come back in,' she repeated stupidly. 'But I thought when the lights came on again, he'd be back in. I just thought he'd stayed down here to have a hot drink . . .' Her voice faded away.

'He shouldn't have gone out there in the cold. Couldn't you have done it?'

'He wouldn't let me. But I'd better go out and see what's happening. Listen out for Adam if he starts to cry, won't you?'

Harriet's face positively beamed. 'Of course I will.' And though Maddie knew that Harriet would probably find an excuse to climb the stairs and bend over the cot, crooning softly to 'her little man', she had no choice but to go out to Frank.

Whatever could be wrong that was keeping him out in the cold battery house so long?

Maddie ran to the barn at the side of the house and pulled open the door. Thankfully, he had not closed it behind him, locking her out, for Maddie had no other key. Only Frank, and now Nick, had keys to the battery house. 'Frank, Frank, where are you?'

His torch lay on the floor casting an eerie beam of light . . .

Maddie's scream echoed around the rafters and a bird, perching in the eaves, flew off in fright. Frank was lying on the floor directly beneath the control panel, his mouth agape, his eyes wide and staring and she knew without even touching him that he was dead.

'Well, it looks like accidental death to me,' Dr Hanson said. 'It looks as if he's reached up to the panel and then fallen backwards and hit his head on this.' He pointed to the sharp corner of the concrete plinth on which stood the engine and the generator. 'Of course, he might even have had a heart attack. There'll have to be a post-mortem and an inquest, Maddie, but it should be quite straightforward.' He looked up at the police constable standing solemnly in the doorway, notebook in hand. 'You agree?'

'Well, yes, but I was just looking at his hand, doctor. Looks odd to me. Do you think there could be a fault on that there thing?' Constable Parsons nodded towards the brown knob on the control panel.

'Well, get it checked, if you're not happy.'

The constable made a note in his book. 'Sad though, ain't it? I always thought what a clever chap Frank was to generate his own electricity.' Sorrowfully, he looked down at the twisted form lying on the ground. 'Shame if it turns out that's what's killed him.'

Maddie turned away and saw Harriet standing in the doorway. Woodenly, the housekeeper moved towards them, staring straight ahead, past Maddie, past the policeman. She stepped into the battery house and knelt down beside Frank. She leaned over him and stroked his forehead, a low, keening sound coming from her throat.

From her apron pocket, she took a pair of scissors and, reverently, she cut a lock of his hair and held it in the palm of her hand. Then she straightened up and walked out of the barn without speaking to, or even glancing at, anyone.

PC Parsons closed the door and checked that it was locked. 'I'll get Frank moved for you, love. We don't want to think of him lying there all night, but after that, you mustn't come back in here and you mustn't let anyone else come in here either until I've had an expert check that there control panel. I just want to be sure what's happened here.'

'Of course,' Maddie nodded. 'Nick's away and neither me nor Mrs Trowbridge want to go back in there.' A sob caught at her throat and she stumbled away.

The following afternoon, as darkness closed in around the farm, Maddie stood at the gate, huddled in her warmest coat, yet still shivering, though more from the shock and the dreadful night and day she had just lived through than from the cold.

She heard him whistling first even before she saw the dim, wavering light of his bicycle lamp coming towards her. She wanted to run towards him, but her legs would not move and she was still standing there, like a statue, when he spotted her almost at the last minute. He wrenched on his brakes and the wheels slithered on the loose gravel as Nick brought the bike to a standstill.

Before she could speak, he said, 'Michael won't come. I told him how – how serious it is, but . . .' His glance at Maddie was apologetic. 'I did try, Maddie. Honestly, I did.'

'It's too late,' she said bluntly. 'Frank's dead.'

She was sorry she had broken the news so abruptly when she saw, even through the dark, Nick's face turn white and his lips part in a horrified gasp. He gulped before he stuttered, 'B – but he seemed so much better. He . . .'

'It wasn't the sickness. He's been killed. There was an accident. In the battery house. We don't quite know what happened . . .' Her voice trailed away and unshed tears filled her throat.

'Me Mam?' Nick asked hoarsely. 'How is she? Is she all right?'

'She's taking it very badly. She's sat at the kitchen table all day just staring into space.'

'Why aren't you with her, then? What are you doing out here?'

'I – I had to come out. Adam's in bed asleep and I came out to the greenhouse . . .'

'Oh aye. You'd still have to carry on working, wouldn't you, Maddie? Nothing's as important as your blasted tulips, is it? They still have to be picked, even on the day poor Mr Frank's died.'

He pushed hard down on the pedals and rode into the yard, leaving Maddie standing by the gate, staring after him.

'I'm sorry,' she said to Nick the following morning. 'I didn't mean to sound unfeeling. It's my way of dealing with it. To work hard. Keep busy. It's the only way I can cope. I'm going to miss him dreadfully. I owe him a lot.'

'You owe him everything,' Nick was not about to let her off lightly. 'Where would you be without him, eh? Out on the streets. You and the kid, both. That's where.'

For once, Maddie stifled the sharp retort that sprang to her lips. She did not say the words 'And by the sound of it, but for him, that's where you and your mam would have been an' all.' Instead, she said gently, 'You're right. But we all say things when we're upset.' She waited for him to apologize for what he had said, but Nick was silent.

Maddie sighed. 'I must get changed and go into town. To the hospital to – to collect his things. That's where they took him,' she added, explaining. She waited again, this time for him to say 'Do you want me to come with you?' But once more, Nick said nothing, only nodded.

Maddie squared her shoulders. Very well, she thought. I'll go on my own. In fact, I won't even ask them to look after the baby. I'll take Adam to Jenny and Mrs Grange.

A little later, as she was manoeuvring the pram out of the back door, Nick came to the kitchen door. 'You haven't talked the funeral arrangements over with me Mam. Don't you think you should?'

As the pram bounced over the threshold, Maddie looked back at him briefly. 'Of course I shall, but I can't do anything yet.'

'Why not?'

'Because there'll be a post-mortem and an inquest.'

The horrified look on his face startled her. His voice was a strangulated whisper as he asked, 'A post-mortem? What on earth for?'

Maddie shrugged. 'It's usual in sudden deaths.'

'But – but they know what killed him. You said the doctor said so himself.' There was a strange desperation in his tone. 'Why can't the doctor just sign the death certificate?'

Maddie shrugged. 'Maybe he will. I don't know.'

'They shouldn't be cutting poor old Frank about now. Why can't they let him rest in peace?'

The vivid picture of her husband's body being mutilated, however sensitively it was done, disturbed her, but to cover it she said brusquely, 'It'll hardly hurt him now, will it?'

He hesitated before saying, 'No, but it will destroy me Mam.'

'Actually, I think your mother would rather like to know what his mystery illness was. After all, that was what killed him, in a way.'

'I don't understand what you mean.'

'Like you say, perhaps he was careless because he

wasn't feeling well and, because of that, your mother seems to be blaming herself.'

'How can she?'

Again Maddie shrugged. 'Her cooking, I suppose.'

'What? You mean, she thinks her cooking made him sick? That's stupid.'

'Of course it is. I know that. But again, it's because she's so upset. She's not thinking clearly.'

Suddenly, she felt sorry for the distressed young man. He must have looked upon Frank as his father. She reached out and patted his arm. 'Don't worry. It'll be all right. I must go. You just look after your mam.'

After his harsh words earlier, she dared not ask him to do any work in the greenhouses.

'Of course we'll look after him,' Mrs Grange bustled round the counter, her hands outstretched already to pluck the child from his pram. 'I'm so sorry for your trouble, lass. Mr Frank was a good man. A kind man. Look how he took you into his home and looked after you.'

Maddie felt a lump in her throat and could only nod.

'And you're not the first, neither. There, there, my little man. My word, you grow every time I see you. He'll be walking afore you know it, Maddie.' She raised her voice. 'Jenny. You there, love? Adam's here.'

Maddie smiled faintly to find herself ignored.

Jenny appeared and hugged her. 'Oh Maddie, isn't it dreadful? Have – have you sent word to Michael?'

In her embrace, Maddie stiffened. 'There's not much point. Nick's just been to see him to tell him how desperately ill his father is – was. But he didn't want to know.'

'Oh, so that's why Steven saw Nick on his bike the other night, riding through the village?'

317

Maddie nodded. 'Yes, he only got back last night.'

'No, this was the night before last. Late, it was. Gone midnight.'

Maddie shook her head. 'No, it couldn't have been Nick. That was the night he was away, seeing Michael.'

'Steven must have got it wrong then,' Jenny shrugged and went on, 'and you say Michael didn't want to come home to see his father even though he was so ill.'

Maddie bit her lip to stop it trembling.

Jenny was appalled. 'That's terrible. But even so, I think Michael has a right to know what's happened now. After all, he's Mr Frank's heir, isn't he?'

'No,' Maddie shook her head. 'I am. And after me, Adam. He told me that he'd made a new Will and – and cut Michael out of it entirely.'

'Oh no,' Jenny breathed. 'I never realized he was so bitter.'

'I didn't, until he told me that. It was after Nick had been to see Michael several times and then the last time he went, I mean before this time, he came back with the message that Michael had no intention of ever coming home again. So . . .' She sighed heavily. 'He made a new Will.'

Jenny bit her lip. 'But I still think you should send word to Michael. Somehow. It's his *father*.'

The two girls stared at each other, both thinking the same thing. If we had only known our father, then we wouldn't treat him this way whatever family quarrel there had been.

'I must go,' Maddie said flatly. She raised her voice as she added, 'Thanks for looking after Adam, Mrs Grange.'

'It's a pleasure, love. Any time.' And she knew the woman meant it.

It was not until she was on the bus to Wellandon that

she remembered Mrs Grange's words. 'And you're not the first he's taken in, neither.'

'The doctor has signed the death certificate. The blow on the head when he fell killed him.'

'So,' Nick said slowly. 'It wasn't anything to do with the electricity then?'

Maddie shook her head. 'No, the expert they sent out said he couldn't find anything wrong on the control panel, or anywhere else for that matter.' She frowned as she murmured, 'So we still don't know what caused the lights to go out in the first place.'

To this, Nick said nothing. Instead he asked, 'So, what have they put as the cause of death?'

Maddie dropped the piece of paper onto the table. 'Read it for yourself. It's all in long medical words that I don't understand.' Still, she could not erase the dreadful picture from her mind of how she had found Frank. 'Where's your mother, Nick? I'd better talk to her.'

'You do what you like. You're his wife.'

Well, it wasn't taking very long for Harriet Trowbridge to get back to her normal, resentful self, Maddie thought wryly. 'But what would he have wanted? To be buried in the village churchyard?'

'Where else? He's lived here all his life. His wife's buried there.' There was a malicious gleam in her eyes as she said, 'I'm sure he'd want to be put next to her.'

Maddie ignored the intended slight. 'And the service? What sort of service would he want?'

'Well, he wouldn't have wanted a fuss, if that's what you mean.'

319

In a low voice, Maddie said, 'But he'd have wanted his son here, wouldn't he?'

To this, Harriet made no reply.

'I'm not going traipsing after him again,' Nick declared. 'It's a waste of time. He won't come. I'll write to the camp. At least I know where he is at the moment and the letter won't get passed from one camp to the next like I did when I went looking for him.'

'Is that what happened?'

'Oh, you don't know the half of it. You haven't asked, have you?'

'Nick, I'm sorry. I . . .'

Suddenly, he smiled the smile that lit up his whole face and he put his arm about her shoulders. 'No, I'm sorry, Maddie.'

Before she could stop herself, she felt herself stiffen under his touch, but she managed to smile at him and say, 'It's all right, Nick. We're all upset by what's happened. But we've got to stick together and help each other.'

'Oh Maddie,' he whispered close to her ear. 'You don't know how glad I am to hear you say that.'

Forty-Two

'I can't face it. I can't go.'

Harriet sat at the kitchen table in a flood of tears. 'I can't face all those prying eyes, all the gossip going on around me.'

Maddie looked down at the woman with a mixture of sympathy and exasperation. Why on earth couldn't she pull herself together and attend Frank's funeral?

She tried to keep her voice level as she said, 'If anyone's going to be gossiped about, I should think it'll be me, not you.'

'Oho, you don't know the village folk like I do. They've long memories and long knives.'

'We'll be with you. Nick and me. We won't leave you.'

'What about the baby? I'll stay here and look after the baby.'

'Mrs Grange is going to have Adam. She'll bring him to the church, but if he cries then she'll take him straight out.'

'See . . .' Fresh tears flowed. 'You don't even trust me to look after him now.'

Maddie sighed, but managed to hold on to her patience. 'I never thought for a moment that you wouldn't want to come to Frank's funeral. He'd want you there. You know he would.'

She sniffled miserably. 'Well, if you put it like that.'

'I do put it like that. Never mind the nosy parkers from

the village. What do they matter? Think what Frank would have wanted.'

It seemed the whole village was there when Frank was laid beside his first wife. Maddie read the headstone. 'In Loving Memory of Elizabeth, beloved wife of Frank Brackenbury, who died 1st October 1929, aged 23'. She would see that Frank had a similar headstone, Maddie promised silently. For she had loved him, she realized now. Oh, not in the same way as she had loved Michael. Never in the same way. She doubted she would ever love anyone else with that same overwhelming passion. But Frank had been a kind and gentle husband. She wished now that they could have spent many more years together.

As she turned away from the yawning hole, she saw Theo Mayfield standing amongst the throng of people. As the villagers began to move away, Maddie noticed that he did not move. He stood very still and, knowing he was watching her, she felt drawn to move towards him.

Nearing him, she held out her hand. 'It was kind of you to come today. Frank would have been very touched.'

She felt his warm grasp. 'Your hands are cold, Maddie. It's been an ordeal for you. Please allow me to take you home in my car.'

Swiftly, she shook her head. 'Oh no, no. It wouldn't do.'

He was smiling gently at her. 'You surprise me. I always thought you didn't mind flouting convention.'

She knew his words were not offensive so she smiled in return. 'No, I don't. I've done a bit of it already, haven't I?'

He nodded. 'Yes, and I admire you for it. And I'm

about to do a little "flouting" of my own, Maddie. I'm going to grant you the tenancy of Few Farm in your own name. How does that sound?'

Maddie gave a long sigh of relief and tears sprang to her eyes. 'Oh Mr Theo, I can't tell you how grateful I am.'

She felt the slight pressure on her hand, which he was still holding. 'It's not your gratitude I want, Maddie.' The words were so softly spoken that later she was not sure whether she had heard him correctly, for now he released her hand and gave a little bow. 'I must have a word with Mrs Trowbridge and her son. She seems very distressed.'

Maddie nodded and glanced back to where Harriet was having to be almost bodily supported by Nick. 'She is. But then, she's been his housekeeper for a long time and I think ... Well, best just to say I think she had a high regard for him.'

Theo murmured, 'So they say,' before he added, with genuine sympathy, 'Poor Mrs Trowbridge.'

As he left her, Jenny, with Mrs Grange carrying Adam, came to her. Hovering just behind them was Steven. The girl, as always, flung her arms about her. 'Oh Maddie, Maddie. It's so awful.'

'I know, I know, love.' She hugged Jenny quickly and then reached out for her son, who was fretful and holding out his arms towards her.

'Poor little lamb,' Mrs Grange crooned as she handed him over. 'It's as if he knows something's wrong.'

'I'm sure he does,' Maddie said, holding him close to her and taking comfort from the warm little body next to her own. 'Now he's lost two daddies.'

The faces before her were solemn and their glances fell away as if they were embarrassed to meet her eyes.

'We must get home. Poor Mrs Trowbridge seems about

on the point of collapse. Thank you for coming . . .' Her glance included Steven. With more murmured words of condolence from them, Maddie moved away.

It was as she walked down the pathway, through the churchyard towards the gate that to her left in the farthest corner of the churchyard, she saw a tall, fair-haired figure standing with a bunch of flowers in her hands. The woman was looking down at just a patch of ground. There was no headstone, no visible grave, for the ground was overgrown with long grass and nettles.

Maddie stopped and though Adam wriggled in her arms and now kept up a constant grizzle of discomfort, for a moment she ignored him.

'Amelia Mayfield?' she murmured and screwed up her eyes to try to make out the figure more clearly. 'What on earth . . .?'

And then, without being told, Maddie knew. That must be where Amelia's lover was buried. In that far corner of the churchyard, most probably in unconsecrated ground, which was the usual resting place for suicides. Then she saw Theo walking towards his sister, saw him gently take the flowers from her hands and lay them on the ground at her feet. Then he put his arm about her shoulders and led her away to his car.

Tears blurred Maddie's vision and though she would not allow them to fall, her heart went out to the lonely, distressed figure of the woman who had mourned her lost love for so long.

As long as, deep in her heart, Maddie would mourn for hers.

'Making up to him, smiling at him and before poor Mr Frank was cold in his grave. I saw you.'

It hadn't taken Harriet long to resume her goading.

'Mam, give it a rest,' Nick frowned at his mother, standing up to her more boldly than Maddie could remember.

'Trying to get round him to give her the tenancy to this place, I shouldn't wonder. Oh, but you've another think coming, girl, if you think that's ever going to happen. My Nick has more right than you ever did—'

Bluntly, Maddie interrupted. 'It already has.'

'What? What do you mean?'

'It's already happened. Mr Theo told me at the funeral. He's going to draw up a new document, all legal, with me as the sole tenant.'

With that Maddie turned and left the house, but not before she had seen the look of pure hatred in Harriet's eyes.

But what disturbed her the most was to see that same look mirrored for a fleeting, unguarded moment, in Nick's eyes, too.

Forty-Three

'I suppose,' Harriet said, sitting down at the supper table, 'it would be too much to ask that you and Nicholas should have joint tenancy of the farm?'

'Oh, Mam,' he said at once. 'Don't spoil it for Maddie. It's a wonderful opportunity for her, especially with her background.'

Maddie glanced at him, stung to retort, but the words died on her lips as he added hastily, 'Well, you know what I mean. But you deserve it, Maddie. It was your idea and you've worked as hard as any of us. You have to admit, Mam, that her idea has worked.'

Maddie saw Harriet's glance and heard her sniff of disapproval, but now, she said nothing.

Nick was smiling broadly, his whole face alight, his eyes crinkling behind his glasses. There was not a trace of the bitter resentment Maddie thought she had seen earlier.

'No, you have the tenancy, Maddie,' he said and added, jokingly touching his forelock, 'but I would like to continue working for you, ma'am.'

Thankful for his change of heart, Maddie laughed. 'I couldn't manage without you, Nick.' Then, summoning up all her reserves of forgiveness and understanding, Maddie turned to Harriet and added, 'Nor you, Mrs Trowbridge.'

*

Theo Mayfield was as good as his word and he brought all the official papers to Few Farm himself for Maddie to sign. When everything was settled, he smiled at her and said, 'Now, you shall be the first to know my bit of news.'

Maddie's eyes widened. He must be getting married. And the thought came unbidden, Oh what a lucky girl whoever she was, to have Theo as her husband. So sure was she that this was what he was about to tell her, that it took a few moments for her to take in what he was actually saying.

'Although I've taken over the running of the estate since my father's illness, there is so little for me to do. The estate bailiff has been with us for years . . .' He pulled a comical face. 'To tell you the truth, Maddie, he knows more about running things than I do. So . . .' he was smiling so happily, his eyes dancing, 'I'm setting up my own solicitor's practice in Wellandon. You probably didn't know that I went to university to study law. I'd got my law degree and had even done the necessary practice with a law firm in Peterborough, but then my father fell ill and . . .' He spread his hands. 'Well, you know the rest. But this . . .' he indicated the papers she had just signed, 'is the first legal tenancy agreement I've drawn up as a fully-fledged solicitor. You, Maddie, are my first client.'

She rose from the table. 'Then I think we should drink to that, Mr Theo, even if it is only with Mrs Trowbridge's elderflower wine.'

She fetched glasses and the decanter from the sideboard. Pouring a little of the clear liquid into each glass she held hers up and looked at him. 'A toast to – to . . .' Then she laughed. 'Oh, I don't know the name of your firm.'

'It's to be a partnership. Mayfield and Crouch. Tom Crouch was with me at the firm in Peterborough. He's a great character and couldn't wait to come in with me.'

'Then here's to your success, Mr Theo. To Mayfield and Crouch.'

He echoed her words and then added, 'And to you, Maddie, as the new and legal tenant of Few Farm. Here's to you.'

They settled to a new routine, uneasily at first, but as the years passed and Maddie made no move to oust Harriet Trowbridge or her son from Few Farm, their lives together continued. Adam grew sturdy and strong and became the apple of Harriet's eye. It seemed as if, robbed of Frank to fuss over, the woman needed an outlet for her strange, doting affection. Maddie herself never expected – nor got – any kindness or even friendliness from the woman. What puzzled her, though, was why Harriet never lavished love on her own son. She was possessive towards Nick and still tried to rule his life, yet Maddie had never once seen her even touch him. She never kissed him, never hugged him nor even patted his shoulder. But now, she positively drooled over little Adam, until the growing child himself began to squirm away from her clinging hands and wet kisses. Maybe it was because, Maddie thought pensively, with each day Adam grew, heart-achingly, more and more like Michael.

Funny woman, Maddie would shake her head sometimes. But at least she had no fear now that the housekeeper would ever harm the child out of spite against his mother.

Towards the end of 1949, Nick was called up to do his National Service but arrived home after only the first week. 'I've failed me medical.'

'What?' Harriet's eyes, for once, had been wide with fear.

Nick had laughed and put his arm about her shoulders. 'It's all right, Mam. I'm not going to drop dead. But the doctor just said I wasn't A1 and it's enough to exempt me.'

'So, you mean you haven't got to go away at all?'

Nick's grin widened. 'That's about the size of it, Mam.'

'Well, thank goodness for that,' Harriet had said. But even then, Maddie remembered, she had not hugged her son, nor even made any further enquiries as to the details of his health problem. And Nick, she noticed, did not volunteer the information either.

Only she, Maddie, had said later, 'It's nothing serious, is it, Nick?'

'Oh no,' he had smiled, but for the moment no longer flicked back his hair. That had been cut to Army regulation shortness. 'No, I'm still fit enough to work, if that's what you're worried about.'

'Well, of course it is.' But she said the words playfully so that Nick would know that she was genuinely concerned about him.

Steven did go to do his National Service, but every leave he rushed home to be with Jenny.

'Why on earth don't you put that poor lad out of his misery and marry him?' Maddie said, exasperated. 'He absolutely adores you. Who'd have thought it? Stinky Smith in love.'

'Oh Maddie,' Jenny had smiled and, for once, had not reprimanded her friend for the use of the nickname. 'I do like him a lot. In a way, I love him, but . . .'

'But you're still hankering after Nick.'

Easy tears filling her eyes, Jenny nodded as she whispered, 'I've loved Nick from that first time I came to the farm. Can you remember?'

'Oh yes,' Maddie murmured, feeling guilty at the memory. 'And I thought you were after Michael.'

'Michael!' Jenny's eyes were large. 'Whatever made you think that?'

'He was kind to you. Bought you some shampoo. Just like he had for me. I – I thought he liked you. I was jealous.'

'You? Jealous of me? Oh Maddie, how could you even think he'd look at me when you were around? I could see even then how it was between you.' Her face sobered. 'How I wish it could have been different for you.'

They stared at each other. Softly, Maddie said, 'Me too.'

'For God's sake stop going on about *her*.'

They were working side by side in the field. Nick stood up suddenly, towering over Maddie who was bending down, carefully placing the bulbs in rows in the ground. 'I don't like her,' he said harshly. 'I never have. You can tell her so. Tell her to marry Steven Smith.'

Slowly, Maddie stood up and faced him, staring openmouthed at his outburst. She had broached the subject, trying to sound him out once and for all so that she could help Jenny make up her mind. But she had not expected such a vehement, passionate denial. But at his next words, she began to understand.

'There's only one girl I've ever wanted. You. But you had to go and fall for Michael and all his smooth talk, didn't you? What chance did I have against him? And then, to make it worse, when he left you, you had to go and marry his dad. You couldn't wait, could you, for me to grow up? I'd have married you, Maddie, whatever me Mam said. I'd have loved you and looked after you. Aye, and Michael's bastard too. I'd have put up with him, too, if I could have had you.'

He flung the basket of bulbs on the ground so that they spilled out and rolled in all directions and stamped off, his boots leaving deep footprints in the soft earth.

Perplexed, Maddie stared after him.

For the rest of the day, Nick avoided her and Maddie was grateful. She needed to think. His outburst had shocked her. She had never thought, never dreamt for one moment, that Nick felt like that about her. But then, she reminded herself, she had been so wrapped up in Michael from the first moment she had set eyes on him that she had never given a thought to Nick. And after Michael had left, she was so devastated that she had allowed herself to be talked into marriage with Frank. Not that she regretted that, she told herself hastily. Frank had been a good man, a caring husband and father to Adam. But now Frank's protection was gone. And she must face the fact that Nick might believe she would turn to him now. Surely, she reasoned, he was only imagining his feelings for her. He hardly met any other girls, thanks to his mother. So it was only natural that the adolescent boy – who was now a man, she reminded herself sharply – had imagined himself fond of her. There was Jenny, of course, who had worn her heart so openly on her sleeve, but whom he had rejected. She sighed. Oh, why did life have to be so complicated?

Later, she told Jenny what had happened. 'I'm sorry if it hurts you, love, but you've got to know. Don't waste your life pining for him.'

Jenny sighed heavily. 'I suppose part of me knows that

already. But I didn't want to be unfair to Steven, sort of treating him as second best. You know?'

Maddie nodded, feeling a lump in her throat. For her, anyone and everyone would always be second best to Michael.

Jenny smiled tremulously and pulled in a deep breath. 'Well, I've a lot of thinking to do. Besides, we may be jumping the gun. Steven hasn't actually asked me yet.'

Now Maddie laughed. 'He will, oh he will, Jen. As sure as the sun will rise in the east tomorrow morning.'

The next time they met – over the supper table – Nick did not refer to his earlier outburst at all. Maddie was surprised, but relieved. Instead, he chattered on about the day's work and planned the following day's jobs with Maddie nodding approval. Mentally, she crossed her fingers that his earlier outpouring would not be repeated.

As the seasons came and went, the whole district around Wellandon flourished and became renowned for its bulb growing. From the first tentative idea, 'Tulip Week' grew just like the flowers themselves and stretched over three weekends. Every year more and more sightseers followed the planned route around the fields. A Tulip Queen, chosen from the young girls who worked in the industry, toured the fields on the three Sundays, dressed in a long gown with a velvet cape and a crown upon her head.

Six years after Few Farm had, in desperation, turned to horticulture, Nick was able to say, 'I've counted at least twenty buses down our lane today and as for the number of cars, well, I just lost count of those. And we've sold all the flowers that were on the stall at the field gate.'

'Really? That's brilliant. But they were the last of what we've got available to sell as cut flowers this year. We must knob the rest.'

Nick nodded agreement. 'I know and we ought to start that tomorrow.'

'We must,' Maddie said firmly. 'And this year, Adam is old enough to help.'

Suddenly, for no reason that she could think of, Nick said, 'Time that lad had a proper father again. When are you going to marry me, Maddie?'

His words startled her. From the day he had first told her of his feelings, he had never again mentioned them and as the months and years had passed, she had begun to believe that the boyish infatuation had withered.

Now, standing before her, was the man he had become. He still wore spectacles and his hair still flopped forward, to be flicked back every now and again with a quick toss of his head. But he had filled out. His shoulders were broader, his body lithe and strong and although he would never have the striking good looks of Michael, or even of Theo Mayfield, nevertheless, when he smiled, his face had a cheeky, boyish charm.

Maddie pulled in a deep breath and tried to make light of his question. Even she wasn't sure if it was even intended to be serious. 'Well, not this week, Nick. We're too busy.'

'Yes,' Nick said slowly, but now he was no longer smiling. 'That's what I thought you'd say.'

'I don't know how we'd have done it without you.' Maddie put her arms around Adam's shoulders, but her words included not only her son, but Jenny and Steven too. 'We've had a bumper crop this year and without you all

333

helping to head and now lift them, I think we'd have lost some.'

It was a warm evening in June and the five of them were walking back towards the farmhouse, all hoping that Harriet had prepared what would for them amount to a harvest supper.

'The only thing that upsets me,' Steven said, 'is when we headed them back in April there was nothing we could do with the discarded heads. Just a huge mound of glorious colour dumped in the corner of the field. Such a waste.'

Maddie laughed. 'Can't you think of a way to make a bob or two out of them?'

'We-ell, I have got something in mind.'

'What?'

'Ah,' he tapped the side of his nose. 'Now you just wait and see. The Mad March Hare's not the only one who can come up with brilliant ideas, you know.'

'Go on then, Stinky,' she nudged him playfully. 'Prove it.'

'I will,' he promised, a serious note now beneath the banter. 'Oh, I will.'

Forty-Four

'Over my dead body.'

As Maddie came in the back door and took off her boots in the wash-house, she could hear Harriet's voice raised hysterically.

'You'll not marry that slut while there's breath in my body, Nicholas. It's bad enough that we have to live here under her sufferance . . .'

Maddie slipped her shoes on and opened the door into the kitchen. They were facing each other across the kitchen table and Harriet, in the midst of rolling out pastry, was shaking her rolling pin at Nick.

'What on earth's going on?' Maddie demanded and they both turned to look at her. Harriet lunged towards her, arm raised, and Maddie flinched beneath the expected blow and raised her arm to protect her head. But Nick moved quicker than either of them and grasped his mother to pull her away.

'No!' he shouted. 'You'll not lay a finger on Maddie. You hear me?'

Maddie was shocked by the stricken look on the woman's face and, despite the threat, she was moved to feel sorry for her. Now Harriet sagged against Nick in defeat and would have fallen to the floor if he had not held her upright, his arm about her waist. Her arms hung down limply now and the rolling pin clattered to the floor.

Nick almost dragged her into the living room and

pushed her roughly into a chair. Then he stood over her. He opened his mouth but at that moment they heard Adam's footsteps clattering down the stairs, his merry voice calling as he opened the door into the room. 'Mrs T, Mrs T, are you going to make gingerbread men for tea?'

Then he stopped abruptly when he saw that all was not as normal.

'What is it? Are you poorly, Mrs T?' He came to her and put his hand on her arm and smiled that same engaging smile that had once been Michael's. His brown eyes were full of a concern that was strangely adult in the eight – almost nine – year old. Harriet drew him to her and held him fiercely. For once, sensing her distress, he submitted to her embrace without protest. Above his head, Harriet regarded her own son with bitterness.

'At least,' she said, 'this little chap loves me.'

'There's no call to talk like that, Mam,' Nick was more composed now, but his tone was still tight with anger. 'Just calm yourself down and forget all about what I said. Besides . . .' he gave a quick, sideways glance at Maddie. 'Nothing's been settled yet.'

'And it'd better not be,' Harriet said and her resentful gaze was now turned upon Maddie.

'What's been happening?'

'Nothing. Nothing, Maddie. Leave it. It's best left.' And then, in a voice so low that his mother could not hear, he said, 'For now, at least.'

He turned and slammed his way out of the house before Maddie could make her feelings known. For once, she was in full agreement with Harriet. If what she thought had been said was true, then she too would have said, 'Over my dead body.'

*

'Maddie, Maddie. Where are you? I've got something to tell you.'

Jenny was calling out as soon as she stepped into the house and then the door into the kitchen was flung open. 'You'll never guess . . .' she began and then stopped short as she saw Maddie carefully placing a tiny candle on the cake she had been decorating.

'Oh Maddie, that's lovely,' Jenny said, closing the door and coming to stand beside the table. 'You know, I really can't believe that Adam is ten years old already. Don't the years fly by.'

Maddie stood back to admire her handiwork. 'There, what do you think to that?'

'He'll love it. However have you managed to make it in the shape of a train, even with wheels and a funnel? And then the carriages behind with three candles on each.'

'Oho, I can't take the credit for making it. That was Mrs Trowbridge.'

'I'd have thought she'd have wanted to put the finishing touches to it herself then. Where is she? Out?'

'Out? You've got to be joking. She never goes out. You know that.'

'Where is she, then?'

'Lying down.'

'Lying down? Mrs Trowbridge. Now you've got to be joking, Maddie.'

Maddie shook her head, a worried frown creasing her forehead. 'No, I wish I were. She's not been feeling too good lately. You know . . .' She looked up at Jenny and kept her voice low. 'It worries me a bit. It's just like poor Frank when he started to be ill.'

'Do you think you should have the water in the well checked?'

Maddie nodded. 'I'd thought about that, too. Yes, I will if it goes on.'

'What does Nick say?'

'Tells me not to fuss. Says she's getting on and she's bound to get ill now and again.'

'Getting on? How old is she?'

'Don't know exactly, but she must be getting on for fifty.'

'Fifty! That's not old, Maddie. Mrs Grange is sixty-five and won't even think of giving up the shop.' She giggled mischievously. 'I reckon she'll still be trying to serve her customers when they carry her out feet first.'

'Jenny!' Maddie laughed, pretending to be shocked, but secretly she was happy to see that 'poor, little Jenny Wren' had blossomed into a pretty young woman with a saucy sense of humour. No doubt Stinky Smith's influence had a lot to do with that.

'Talking of Nick,' Jenny was saying, carefully now. 'How does he treat Adam? I mean, would he make a good father to him?'

Maddie glared at her. 'Now, don't you start, Jen. I've no intention of marrying Nick, or anyone else for that matter.'

Jenny sighed. 'I don't want to see you spending the rest of your life alone.'

Jenny was the one person to whom she could say anything, confide the innermost secrets of her heart. Maddie sat down and faced her. 'Look, Jen,' she said quietly now and with more than a trace of sadness in her tone. 'I've only ever really loved one person in my life, apart from you and that's very different. I was fond of Frank, very fond. He was a lovely man and I miss him, but if I hadn't been so young and alone with no family of my own, then – then I probably wouldn't have married him.

But I'm not going to marry again unless I fall in love –
really in love – with someone. And I don't feel that way
about Nick. And I don't think I ever will.'

Jenny nodded and had a confidence of her own to
share. 'Poor Nick. And do you know something, Maddie?
That's how I do think of him now. As "poor Nick". I
think when I first thought I loved him, it was because I
felt so sorry for him. He seemed like me. So shy and lost.
No friends. But now, with Steven, it's so different. He's
always so cheerful and happy-go-lucky. Always full of
ideas and plans.' She shook her head. 'Now, Nick just
seems so moody and – to be honest, Maddie – a right
misery.'

'Yes,' Maddie agreed quietly. 'But who can wonder at
it?' She pointed to the ceiling and Jenny knew she was
referring to Harriet, resting in her room above them. She
echoed Jenny's words. 'Poor Nick.'

There was silence between them until Jenny said, 'And
we're still no nearer finding out who we are, are we,
Maddie? Maybe we have got family somewhere. Does it
bother you?'

'Not really.' Maddie laughed wryly. 'I'm too busy to
think about it much. But maybe . . .' Her tone sobered. 'I'd
like to know if only for Adam's sake.'

'I know. I've been thinking more about it too, just
lately. And the reason I have is all tied up with my news.'

'Oh Jen, I'm sorry. What is it you want to tell me?'

'Steven's asked me to marry him now he's "on his feet"
as he puts it. And now I've realized who it is I really love,'
her cheeks grew faintly pink, 'I've said "yes".'

'Oh darling,' Maddie jumped up and flung herself
around the table to hug Jen. 'That's wonderful. When?'

'We're going to get engaged at Christmas and married
next summer.'

'This is marvellous news. Do tell Steven how glad I am, won't you?'

'You can tell him yourself tonight. He's coming to Adam's birthday party this afternoon.'

'Double celebration then.'

Over the years Steven's gift as a salesman had made him one of the most popular market traders in the district. He now employed others to run his stalls on the various local markets whilst he delved into other areas where he could 'make a bob or two'.

That evening when at last an over-excited ten-year-old had finally been persuaded to go to bed, Maddie, Nick, Jenny and Steven toasted the news of their engagement. Even though she had made the effort to join in the party for her 'little man' who was now growing so fast that he would soon no longer fit the endearment, Harriet was still feeling unwell and had gone to bed too.

'There's something else to celebrate an' all,' Steven said, his grin wide. 'It's all settled. Next year there's to be a proper Tulip Parade with decorated floats and everything. We tried it this year, you know, with one lorry from a local firm to carry Miss Tulipland 1958 and a couple of decorated cars to follow, but next May we're hoping that more locals will take part and make a proper do of it. There's a chap coming over from Holland to help design the floats and show everyone how to build them. You'll have to send one in from Few Farm, you know, Maddie.'

'We wouldn't have time to be taking part in such nonsense,' Nick said sourly, before Maddie could speak. 'We've enough to do.'

'Oh, I don't know, Nick. It would be good publicity for us and fun too.' She turned to Steven. 'Do you know how to build a float?'

'Roughly. Ideally it ought to be designed around a

340

vehicle of some kind, so that it can be self-propelled and take part in a parade through the town centre. You make a metal frame – my brother can do that for you if you like – in the shape you want and then cover it with straw that's been stitched together to make a sort of straw matting. Then that's cut to shape too and last of all – and that can only be done at the very last minute – you pin on the tulip heads.'

'What, each one? Individually?' Jenny asked.

Steven nodded. 'Yes. With wire shaped like a huge hairpin. It's a lot of work but the result is worth all the effort.' He beamed with satisfaction as he added, 'And all those lovely flower heads being used instead of thrown away.'

They laughed together – all, Maddie noticed, except Nick.

Forty-Five

'Jen, do you think you could give us a hand with the flowers?'

April was upon them again and the workload facing Maddie was daunting. For once, even she felt unable to cope. 'Of all the times for it to happen, Mrs Trowbridge has to go and be ill again. I've the house to see to now and looking after her.' As the words came out of her mouth, they sounded unfeeling even to Maddie's own ears. 'Adam can help after school and at weekends and in the holidays, but Nick'll never manage everything on his own.'

Jenny raised her eyebrows, but seeing how harassed Maddie was, she made no comment and merely said, 'Of course I can. Do you want me to ask Steven too?'

'Would you? Oh thanks.'

'I'll have a word with Mrs Grange. I've some holiday due.'

'Some holiday that'll be,' Maddie said, apologetically.

Jenny smiled and murmured, 'Oh I don't mind.'

Smiling for the first time in days, Maddie hugged her. 'Oh, it's good to have a sister, even if we have only adopted each other.'

'I'm getting the doctor to your mother, Nick. She's getting worse instead of better. And what worries me is that she has all the same symptoms that Frank had. I'm going to

342

talk to the doctor and ask him if he thinks it could be the water in the well. Maybe we ought to get it tested.'

Nick wrinkled his forehead. 'If it was the water, then we'd all be ill, wouldn't we?'

Maddie spread her hands helplessly. 'I don't know. I just don't know. Oh, I feel so ignorant about things like this.'

'You can't know everything, Maddie.'

'But I can find out. I'll ask the doctor how to go about it.'

Dr Battison gave her all the help she needed, but when the report on the well water came back, there was no problem.

'Crystal clear and a lot healthier than some of the water our townsfolk have to drink,' Dr Battison told her.

'So that's not it.'

'No,' Dr Battison agreed, but the way he said the word implied that he thought there was more they could do.

Maddie looked at him. 'What? What is it?'

The doctor was frowning and shaking his head. 'Her symptoms puzzle me. Of course they're similar to gastro-enteritis, but . . .' He sighed. 'There's something niggling me. Something's not quite right and I'm damned if I know . . .' He cut his own sentence short and appeared to be lost deep in thought.

'That's what Dr Hanson said about Frank,' Maddie murmured.

'What?' His tone was suddenly sharp with interest.

Dr Battison was new to the area. He had arrived the previous year to take over the country practice when Dr Hanson had retired. He was young, dynamic and go-ahead and whilst many in the village had yet to trust him completely – such had been their faith in the old doctor – Maddie had liked him at once. This was only the second time she had had cause to meet him, the first being when she had taken Adam to the surgery to be told the boy had chicken pox.

'I said, that was what the doctor said about my husband when he was ill just before he died.'

The young man was frowning. 'But I understood that your husband was killed by an accidental fall in the barn where you have your electrical equipment?'

'He was. But he was very ill just before it happened. He'd been in hospital and they'd got him a lot better and sent him home. He had no more of the sickness but he was still very weak and – and . . .' She faltered a little, remembering once more her nightmarish discovery. 'He shouldn't really have gone out there. He should have left it all to Nick. But Nick was away for the night and the lights went out . . .' Her voice trailed away. It sounded, even to her own ears, such a pathetic reason for a man to lose his life.

But Dr Battison was not sitting in judgement. 'Tell me more about the illness he had before that happened.'

Without invitation, he sat down at the table and, following his lead, Maddie sat down opposite him.

'Well,' she began, wrinkling her brow, trying to remember exactly how it had been. 'His illness started just like Mrs Trowbridge's has done. Very slowly so that at first no one, not even the one who's ill, takes a lot of notice. She's been getting stomach trouble on and off for almost a year now and I remember the first time she had a bad attack because it was on Adam's tenth birthday last August. I remember thinking then that it was like Frank had been. I even said so to Jenny.'

'Jenny?'

'Jenny Wren at the corner shop. She lives with Mrs Grange.'

'Oh yes, I know. Go on.'

'Well, I can't tell you any more really.'

'Was the well water tested then?'

Maddie shook her head. 'No. Dr Hanson admitted Frank to hospital and they did some tests, but before the results were through, Frank came home. He'd been much better in the hospital, you see. The accident happened the next day and I suppose . . .' Again her voice faded away, but the doctor nodded understandingly and finished the sentence for her. 'It was no longer necessary to know the results, especially if none of the rest of the household were affected.' He looked at her sharply. 'You weren't, were you?'

Maddie shook her head. 'Not until now.'

Dr Battison was thoughtful, idly tracing a figure eight on the tablecloth with the tip of his forefinger. 'And now there's still only one member of the household ill?'

'You say the symptoms are like gastroenteritis?'

'Mm.'

She stared across the table at him. 'But you're not completely satisfied that it is that, are you?'

'No,' he said shortly and was silent for a moment, still thinking, before he said, 'I'm going to take her into hospital for observation and run some tests.'

'What sort of tests?'

Suddenly, he seemed evasive. 'Oh, the usual.' He stood up but now he was avoiding looking at her directly. 'Pack a few things for her and I'll arrange the ambulance for this afternoon.'

Maddie held the back door open for him. 'Goodbye, Doctor. Thank you for coming.'

He nodded briefly and she watched him as he crossed the yard. She had begun to close the door when she saw him stop and glance towards the huge barn. She saw him look back towards the house, but because the back door was now almost closed and she was watching him through a tiny slit, she knew he could not see her. To him, it would seem as if she had shut the door and gone back into the house.

Dr Battison walked towards the door to the barn and disappeared inside it.

'Now, just what are you up to?' Maddie said aloud and then she realized. He was probably looking for Nick to talk to him about his mother. After all, Nick was her relative, not Maddie. She was about to pull the door open again and step out into the yard to tell him that his searching the barn was fruitless, that Nick was in the fields, when she heard Harriet's cries from upstairs. 'Maddie, oh Maddie. Come quickly.'

Clicking her tongue against her teeth in exasperation, Maddie closed the door and ran lightly up the stairs, 'I'm coming, Mrs Trowbridge, I'm coming.'

Harriet was hanging over the edge of the bed, retching into the chamber pot. Maddie put the palm of her hand against the woman's forehead, smoothing the grey hair out of the way. The skin felt clammy to her touch and when the exhausted woman lay back against the pillows once more, Maddie could see the perspiration glistening on her face, now drained of all its natural colour that had been replaced by a strange tinge of yellow.

'What – what did he say?' Harriet asked weakly.

Touching her hand, Maddie said gently, 'You're to go into hospital. I'm to pack a few things for you . . .'

'No, no, I don't want to go. I want to stay here. Nick can look after me, if I'm too much trouble to you.'

'Oh Mrs T,' Maddie said. Feeling guilty now because she had, at first, been irritated by the woman's illness, she used the pet name that Michael had always used. 'You're no trouble to me. But it's for the best. They'll find out what's wrong with you and . . .'

'I don't want to go.' Her voice was rising hysterically. 'I won't go. You just want to get rid of me so you can have this place to yourself.'

'That's not true. You know we can't manage without you. Any of us.'

Harriet was sobbing now. 'Oh little Adam. I shan't see him again.'

'Don't upset yourself, Mrs Trowbridge. We'll come to visit you and I'll bring Adam.'

She was reaching out, clasping Maddie's hand. 'You will? You promise?'

'Of course I do.'

She seemed to relax a little and later, as she and Nick watched the ambulance drive away down the lane carrying Harriet to the cottage hospital in the town, Maddie thought how sad it was that her thoughts in that moment of crisis had been not for her own son, but for Adam.

Not for the first time, did Maddie feel a stab of pity for Nick Trowbridge.

Forty-Six

'How is she?'

They were standing in the hospital corridor, the three of them, Maddie, Nick and Adam, too, looking, for once, solemn faced.

The sister shook her head. 'No change, I'm afraid,' then added with an encouraging smile, 'but it's early days yet.'

'Can we see her?' Nick asked.

'Of course. But only two at a time and I would ask you to stay no longer than half an hour. She is very weak.'

'Thank you,' Maddie began to move towards the ward at the end of the corridor.

'Excuse me asking . . .' Maddie turned back to look at her as the sister nodded towards the brown bag Maddie was carrying. 'Is that a change of clothing for her?'

'Well, yes, partly. A clean nightdress and hankies, but I've brought a few eggs and some pasties . . .'

The sister's mouth pursed and she shook her head again. 'I'll take the clothes, but I must ask you to take any food back home. Mrs Trowbridge is to have only the diet the doctor has prescribed for her. He gave strict instructions that she was to be allowed no food at all to be brought in to her.'

Nick tried a weak smile. 'Not even grapes?'

But the sister was unsmiling. 'Nothing. The doctor was most specific about it.'

'Well, I can understand that,' Maddie said at once.

'Obviously, it's all part of trying to find out what's causing her sickness.' She smiled. 'But you're welcome to the eggs, Sister, and the pasties, if you can make good use of them.'

She saw the woman hesitate and smooth the palms of her hands down her white apron. She ran her tongue around her lips before she said, almost reluctantly, 'Thank you, Mrs – er . . .'

'Brackenbury,' Maddie supplied.

'Mrs Brackenbury, but I'd better not.'

Adam was moving away down the corridor, anxious to find the woman who had always looked after him whilst Maddie was working. She was like a grandmother to him.

'You go,' Maddie said to Nick. 'You and Adam go in first and then send him out after ten minutes or so and I'll come in. You stay with your mother all the time we're allowed.'

Nick smiled ruefully. 'I'm sure she'd rather have Adam all the time than either of us.'

'Go on,' Maddie pushed his shoulder gently. 'Go on with you.'

When they arrived back at Few Farm after that first visit, they found Jenny pacing the yard.

'There you are. I was just about to give up and go home. Have you seen her? How is she?' Though she asked the usual question, Maddie could see at once that there was more than just her concern for Harriet troubling Jenny.

'Come on inside and I'll make us all a pot of tea.'

'Don't bother for me, I must start the generator up else we'll have no electricity by morning,' Nick said.

'Can I go to the village on me bike, Mam?' Adam asked. 'To see Donald?'

'Who's Donald?'

'Donald Fisher. He's just come to live in the village and started our school.'

'All right but be home by six o'clock. You hear?'

'Yes, Mam.'

'And change into your old trousers first. I don't want you ruining your best pair.'

'Yes, Mam,' they heard him shout as his feet pounded up the stairs.

Maddie smiled at Jenny. 'Looks like it's just you and me for tea, then.'

Jenny nodded and Maddie couldn't help noticing that the girl looked relieved.

The reason became obvious as soon as they sat down on either side of the kitchen table with cups of tea in front of them.

'I'm glad I've got you on your own,' Jenny began when Adam had gone hurtling out of the yard gate on his bicycle. 'There – there's something I've got to tell you.'

'Oh dear,' Maddie said lightly, trying to take some of the worried look from Jenny's face. 'Not expecting, are you?'

Jenny gasped and her mouth dropped open. 'No, I'm not,' she retorted indignantly.

'Well, don't make it sound as if it's the worst crime in the world,' Maddie said and could not keep the trace of bitterness from her tone as she added, 'I'm sure Steven wouldn't desert you.'

'No, I don't think he would,' Jenny replied quietly. 'But it's not that. It's – it's about you.'

'Me?'

'Yes. There's gossip in the village about – about Mrs Trowbridge's illness.'

Maddie shook her head, baffled. 'What about it?'

'That – that it's like Mr Frank had.'

'We know that.'

'They're saying that it could be that – I mean . . .'

'Oh for Heaven's sake, Jen, spit it out. Just what are the old busybodies saying?'

Now the words came out in a rush. 'That you're poisoning her. That you poisoned Mr Frank to get the farm and now you're trying to get rid of Mrs Trowbridge. Everybody knows the two of you have never got on.'

'I – am – *what*?' Maddie was horrified that anyone could even think such a thing, let alone voice it aloud.

'Maddie, I'm sorry. But I thought you ought to know . . .' Her voice trailed away into a whisper.

'Oh I ought to know, all right.' Maddie stood up as if she would confront the gossipmongers there and then. 'Who's saying these things, who's . . .?'

'Maddie, just sit down and listen, will you?'

Frowning, her mouth pouting, Maddie reluctantly lowered herself into the chair again. 'How do the village folk know we don't get on, unless someone's told them? Mrs Trowbridge doesn't mix with any of them and I've certainly never said anything.' She glared at Jenny, who said defensively, 'Well, it wasn't me. But there's several people who know. They've long memories, village folk, and it was common knowledge when you first came to the farm. Folk used to get their milk and eggs and butter from here then, don't forget.'

'Mrs Trowbridge has always said that.'

'What?'

'That the villagers have got long memories. Seems she was right.'

Jenny was frowning now. 'There's a lot more to it than

you and me know, Maddie. Even Mrs Grange keeps hinting at secrets and scandals from long ago, but she'll never really tell me what she's on about.'

'Have you asked her?'

'Not – not really.'

Grimly, Maddie said, 'Then maybe it's time you did.'

Forty-Seven

Because of Jenny's warning, it was not such a shock to Maddie when PC Parsons wobbled up the yard on his bicycle, dismounted and leant it against the wall of the house.

'You there, young Maddie?' He opened the back door and walked into the wash-house without waiting for an invitation.

He'd always called her that from her days at the Home. He wasn't the sort of man to alter his ways just because she was now twenty-seven and he close to retiring age.

'At the moment, I am,' she said, opening the kitchen door. 'Come away in. Cup of tea?'

He eyed her over the spectacles he wore, as he removed his helmet and tucked it under his arm. 'I don't think I will just now. Thank you.'

He manoeuvred his bulk around the kitchen table and followed her into the living room where he placed his helmet on the table and sat down.

Coming straight to the point, as was his way, he said, 'There's nasty rumours going around the village, lass, that you've not been as careful as you might have been with washing your hands after dealing with weedkiller and rat poison and such-like on the farm before you serve up the dinner.'

Maddie stared at him. A cheeky retort sprang to her lips, but although he had broached the subject in a half-comical way, his expression was very serious. This was not a laughing matter and she would serve herself no purpose by treating his visit in a jocular manner.

Holding his gaze, Maddie said calmly, 'I'm always very careful, Mr Parsons, about such things. And I very rarely touch the weedkiller or the rat poison. That's Nick's job.'

'You suggesting that it's Nicholas who is poisoning his mother?'

Now Maddie was getting angry, but she managed to keep her voice level as she said, 'I'm suggesting that neither of us is doing any such thing.'

'Well, someone is. The doctor's tests show that she has a high level of arsenic in her system.'

Maddie gasped and knew that the colour fled from her face. She was helpless to stop it as the policeman continued relentlessly. 'But you do have arsenic on the farm, don't you? Dr Battison saw it for himself in the barn.'

Speechless with shock now, Maddie's thoughts were reeling. This was a nightmare. An horrific dream. She would wake up any minute to hear Harriet banging on her bedroom door to wake her up. It had to be. It couldn't really be happening.

She was suddenly cold and shivering. It was all too terribly real.

'Mam, Mam . . .' Adam was bursting in through the back door. 'Donald's dad won't let him play with me any more. He ses . . .' The boy stopped short as he saw the policeman sitting at the table, then, his gaze still on PC Parsons, he sidled to his mother to stand beside her.

Maddie put her arms about him. She forced herself to speak, but her voice was a hoarse whisper as she said, 'Adam, go and find Nick for me, will you?'

The boy sped away, pleased, she guessed, to escape.

PC Parsons was nodding sagely. 'I expect that Donald's father's heard the rumours an' all.'

Maddie stared at him. 'Are you arresting me?' she asked bluntly.

'No,' he said, but before she could breathe a sigh of relief, he added, 'Not at the moment. But I would like you to come down to the station with me and make a full statement.'

'What on earth about? I've told you, I . . .'

'Well, to answer questions then. We want some answers, Mrs Brackenbury.'

Now Maddie knew real fear. It was the first time ever that the friendly PC Parsons had ever called her by her surname.

But PC Parsons was no longer being friendly.

In her wildest nightmares, Maddie had never thought to find herself in a prison cell. The tiny square room brought back the claustrophobia of the cupboard beneath the stairs that Mrs Potter had used as her own particular prison cell for wrongdoers. But in there Maddie had been able to hear the sounds of the other girls, of the household going about its routine. Everyone took their turn in the cupboard and everyone knew that soon they would be released.

But now, Maddie had no such reassurance. Here she could hear nothing of the world beyond the heavy door and the thick walls and had no idea what was to happen to her.

They had questioned her for four hours in the police station in Wellandon. Even PC Parson's police house in Eastmere had not been official enough. She had been arrested, cautioned and brought to the town in a police car, driven through the village for all to see. And when the questioning got them nowhere, they locked her in a cell where she spent a cold and sleepless night.

A cold-eyed detective sergeant interviewed her, walking around her whilst she sat at the table and a young detective constable, sitting opposite her, took notes.

'Why did you do it, Brackenbury?' Gone was any pretence at politeness. Now she was a suspected criminal.

'I didn't.'

'Thought you would inherit all his money and the tenancy of his farm?' He thrust his face close to hers. 'And you did, didn't you?'

Helpless against his reasoning, which, even to her ears, sounded plausible, Maddie was silent.

'And now you want to rid yourself of his housekeeper. You've never got on, the two of you, have you?'

'I haven't done anything,' she protested. 'Not to Frank nor to Mrs Trowbridge.'

He strolled around behind her, his closeness making every nerve in her body tingle. Slowly he came around to stand facing her, then he leant on his hands on the table, towering over her. 'How did you do it, eh? So that you didn't poison everyone in the household.'

'I didn't have anything to do with the meals before Mrs Trowbridge was taken ill.'

'But you have since, eh?'

'Well – yes.'

'So, it would have been quite easy for you to administer a first, small dose of arsenic, just enough to make her ill and then, when you took over the food preparation, you began to increase the dosage, eh? It would be easy then to put it into just her food, wouldn't it?'

'I didn't. I swear I didn't do anything to harm anyone.'

He ignored her protestations as if she had not spoken.

'Who's next, eh? Her son, Nicholas, or . . .' He leant menacingly closer and his voice dropped to a shocked whisper, acting as if he couldn't believe even her capable of such wickedness. '. . . .Your own son?'

Maddie gasped, staring at him. Now she began to tremble. What hope had she of proving her innocence if this man could believe she could do such a thing?

He straightened up now and resumed his pacing around her. Maddie wasn't sure which was the most unnerving.

'You say you didn't have anything to do with the preparation of food?'

'No. Mrs Trowbridge did all that.'

'Nothing at all?'

'No.'

Again he was in front of her and now he thumped both fists down onto the table so suddenly that Maddie almost leapt from her chair. 'You're lying! Do you mean to tell me that you never prepared anything that the people in that household ate or drank? You never so much as made a sandwich, or a pot of tea, or . . .' The menace in his tone was back. '. . . The cocoa at night?'

She opened her mouth to ask 'How did you know?' but without uttering a word she clamped her lips tightly together.

'Ah, *now* we've nothing to say, have we?' He jabbed his forefinger towards her. 'You put arsenic in the house-keeper's cocoa that you used to make every night for the whole family. And I dare bet that was the way you did it with Frank Brackenbury, too. And when we've exhumed his body, we'll prove it.'

He turned on his heel and left the interview room, leaving Maddie staring after him, open-mouthed and very afraid.

She was taken back to the cell and left alone for the

next two hours before being taken back to the interview room again. Here, there was always one constable or another in the room with her, but they never spoke to her. Even when someone brought her a cup of tea, they did not speak, even though she said, automatically, 'Thank you.'

Eventually, the door opened and Maddie stiffened, expecting the return of her ruthless inquisitor. Instead, it was another stranger to Maddie who now entered the room and sat down in front of her. He was dressed in plain clothes, like the previous one, but whereas the first detective had been thin and wiry, this one was very overweight. His jacket was undone and his shirt buttons strained as he moved, looking as if they would pop off at any moment. He had a round, florid face and he breathed noisily, but to Maddie's surprise he was smiling at her as he sat down on the opposite side of the table.

'My name's Detective Inspector Johnson and you're Maddie, aren't you?' As she nodded, he went on. 'Yes. Now let's see if we can clear this little matter up and we can all go home, eh?' He leant back in the chair and linked his fingers across his belly. 'My colleague a bit rough on you, was he? Well, he's only doing his job. But let's you and me see if we can sort this out, all nice and friendly like, shall we?'

Maddie felt herself begin to relax a little. At least she felt that she could talk to this one, that he would listen.

'Let's say you didn't do it deliberately. Let's say it's all been a terrible accident. Did you ever mix up weedkiller, Maddie?'

She shook her head. 'No. Nick always did that.'

'Nick?'

'Nicholas Trowbridge.'

'Ah yes, Nicholas. Mm.' DS Johnson regarded her steadily. 'We have a statement from Mr Trowbridge that says although it was normally his job, he had shown you how to do it. That true?'

'Well, yes. On a farm like ours, we have to be able to do each other's jobs, just in case one of us is ill . . .' Her voice trailed away. Every time she spoke it seemed as if she dug a deeper hole for herself. She felt as if, at any moment, the sides were going to cave in and she was going to be buried alive.

'So . . .' his tone was still deceptively mild, but she saw the sudden spark in his eyes. He had her now, he knew he had her trapped. 'You admit you know how to mix up weedkiller or maybe rat poison with a base of arsenic, which you keep on the farm? And you also admit that it was the custom for you to make the cocoa at night?'

In a small voice, Maddie could say nothing other than, 'Yes.'

Now he leant forward and rested his arms on the table. 'So, how do you think it looks to us, Maddie?'

A spark of resilience ignited inside her. Maddie faced him with surprising calm. 'It must look to you,' she said slowly, 'as if I'm guilty. I see that. But I'm not. I swear to you I have done nothing to harm anyone.'

Her gaze held his steadily and for a brief moment she saw the flicker of doubt in his eyes. Then slowly he stood up. 'You're a cool one, I'll say that for you.'

They were the last words she exchanged with anyone for twenty-four hours.

Forty-Eight

'Am I allowed to send a message to a friend?'

When a constable brought a meal into the cell, Maddie asked the question. During the time she had been left alone, she had been doing a lot of thinking. Though fear still clawed at her belly and the food they brought every few hours stuck in her throat, nevertheless, she was calmer now and able to think more rationally.

'What friend might that be?'

'Jenny Wren who works at the corner shop in Eastmere.'

The constable glanced over his shoulder as if unsure whether he should be even speaking to the prisoner, let alone doing favours for her. In a low voice, he said, 'She's already been in to the station three times, asking about you.'

Maddie gave a tremulous smile and relief and gratitude flooded through her. Jenny would never let her down.

'Please, when she comes again . . .' Maddie said, for she was sure she would. 'Could you ask her to look after Adam? That's my son. He's only ten. It's not fair on Nick that he should have to look after the boy. He'll have enough to do trying to keep things going on the farm.'

There was relief on the constable's face. 'Oh, that's all right. One of the things she said to tell you was that the lad was staying with her and Mrs – er – Grange, is it?'

Maddie nodded and breathed a sigh of thankfulness. 'Yes, Mrs Grange.'

As he turned to go, he even smiled at her. 'That's all right, then.'

'Yes, yes, it is. Thank you.'

It was not until the heavy door had clanged behind him and she was alone once more that Maddie realized she had not asked him what else it was that Jenny had said.

Maddie passed another night in the small, dark room, though this time she did sleep a little. The following morning shortly after breakfast, she was taken once more to the interview room and mentally she steeled herself for yet more questioning.

As she waited, with only the silent constable sitting in the far corner for company, she wondered which of her two interrogators it would be this time.

The door opened and the desk sergeant announced, 'A visitor for you. Your solicitor.'

Maddie looked up and began to say, 'But I haven't got a solicitor . . .' but the words remained unspoken as she gave a start of surprise as the man walked into the room.

'Mr Theo.'

He was smiling as he came and sat down opposite her, placing a folder of papers on the table beside him. But she could see the concern for her in his blue eyes. For the first time in a very long time, tears threatened to overwhelm her.

'Maddie.' His voice was gentle. 'How are you? Are they treating you well?'

She could not speak for the lump in her throat, so she nodded. The lump grew bigger as he reached across the space between them and took both her hands into his. The warmth of his touch filled her with a new hope. He had come to help her. She knew he could see the unshed tears welling in her eyes, as he patted her hands and said, 'There, there, we'll soon have you out of here. They can't hold you longer than another few hours without charging you and they haven't done that, have they?'

Maddie shook her head and her voice was husky with emotion as she said, 'I don't know what they've done, except ask me lots of questions and then not believe my answers.' She bit her lip and, unable to prevent the quaver in her voice, added, 'Mr Theo, do you believe me? You don't think I – I could poison anyone, do you?'

His reply was swift and genuine. 'Of course I don't. Why else do you think I'm here?'

For a moment she clung to his hands like a drowning person. 'I don't know, but I'm so glad you are. Thank you, Mr Theo.'

'For a start, Maddie, let's drop the Mister, shall we? From now on it's Theo. You did promise once before,' he added softly. 'Remember?' Without waiting for her agreement or otherwise he gently released her hold on him and opened the file lying on the table. 'Now, let's start at the beginning. Since they are involving Frank Brackenbury's death in their enquiries, we shall have to do so as well. When exactly did he fall ill and can you remember his symptoms?'

Maddie frowned, trying to dredge back in her memory. 'Adam was about five or six months' old because I remember asking him to look after him whilst I worked. That was before he got really bad, whilst he was still able to sit by the fire in the living room, you know.'

'No, go further back than that. The very first time you saw that there was something wrong.'

Now she remembered. 'It was Nick who remarked on

it first. He asked me if I'd noticed that Frank seemed to be slowing up in his work.'

'And had you?'

'No, not until Nick mentioned it. But then, I was always so busy what with Adam and trying to build up the new business . . .' And, she added privately, trying not to think about·Michael.

'Mm. And then what happened?'

'Well, I asked Frank if he was feeling all right and he admitted that he had been feeling "a bit under the weather" as he called it. He said he still had a bit of pain in his leg.'

'His leg?'

'Yes, there'd been a bit of a mishap. Nick had accidentally speared Frank's foot with a fork.'

'And was that all that was wrong?'

'No, Frank said he'd been having a bit of stomach trouble . . .' She broke off as she met his steady gaze. Theo nodded and said quietly, 'Go on.'

'He made a – a joke and said he hadn't wanted to make a fuss in case Harriet – that's Mrs Trowbridge – thought that he was blaming her cooking.'

'And was he?'

Maddie shook her head, 'No, of course not. It was only said in fun. I know it was.'

'So then what happened?'

'Well, I made him go to the doctor, but he came back and said the doctor – Dr Hanson it was then – couldn't find anything wrong.'

'But he got worse?'

'Yes. Every day we could see him getting weaker although it was very gradual over quite a long time, but in the end he couldn't get up out of his bed. I called the doctor to the house then to see him. He . . .'

'Wait a minute, don't go so fast, Maddie. I want you to think back very carefully. Who prepared Frank's food or drink during that time? Who nursed him when he took to his bed?'

'Well, we all did. Of course Mrs Trowbridge cooked all the meals, just as she always did. But I made drinks and even Nick carried his meals up and sat with him throughout the night sometimes to let me get a bit of rest. He was ever so good . . .'

'Nick?'

'Yes, but . . .' Her eyes widened as she stared at him. 'Oh no, you don't think – you can't think . . .?'

Theo held up his hand, palm towards her, 'Maddie, I'm not thinking anything at the moment. I am just trying to establish what actually happened and the order of events to get things clear in my own mind. Now, go on.' He reached across the table again and gave her hand a quick squeeze. 'You're doing very well. You've got a wonderful memory.'

So Maddie went on with her story, remembering in detail all that had occurred leading up to Frank's death. She didn't consider herself to be clever or to have a particularly good memory. It was just that everything was so clear because it was not possible to forget that dreadful time. Sometimes, she wished she could have blotted out the whole thing. And now she was being asked to relive it again and, all the time, Theo made notes on a large, lined notepad. She told him everything right up to the time she had found Frank in the battery house and they had all believed that in his weakened state, he had been careless.

When she fell silent at last, Theo shuffled his papers together. 'Have the police asked you to sign anything?'

Maddie shook her head.

'Well, they might want you to make a formal statement

before they let you go. If they do, don't sign anything until I'm here. You understand.'

'Yes, Mr . . . Yes, Theo.'

As he stood up, she asked, 'Will they really let me go?'

Theo glanced at his watch. 'They'll have to, unless they're going to charge you, and I don't see how they can.' Her hopes soared only to be dashed at his next words. 'At least, not yet.'

'You mean – you think they will?'

Theo's face was sober. 'It depends what evidence they find. They'll no doubt be interviewing Dr Battison and, I'm afraid, they'll be searching the farm and taking away any kind of poisonous substances they find on the premises.' He glanced at her sympathetically. 'And then, of course, there's what the forensic team find in Frank's body.'

Maddie shuddered, seeing horrific pictures of poor Frank being disturbed from his resting place. It wasn't right and yet she'd have to let it happen if it was all that would prove her innocence. 'It's so awful,' she said aloud. 'Them digging him up.'

Theo sighed. 'It's the only course open to them – and us, I'm afraid. I've already asked at the hospital if by any chance the blood samples that were taken to do those tests on him when he was ill might have been kept. But, of course, they weren't, because at the time there were no suspicious circumstances surrounding his death. That was quite obviously an accident.'

'I suppose they'll be saying next that I tampered with something in there so that he got a shock and . . .' Maddie muttered.

'Don't worry about that. I can easily prove you know nothing about the workings of the electricity supply. You don't, do you?'

Maddie shook her head. There was a pause and then she asked, 'What do they need to test for poison in his body then? Blood samples?'

'Yes, or tissue or hair or . . .'

'Hair?' Maddie was staring at him.

'Yes, why?'

Excitedly, Maddie said, 'Mrs Trowbridge cut a lock of hair from poor Frank before they took him away. I saw her do it.'

'Did she, by Jove?' Theo too was looking excited and hopeful. 'Where is it?'

'It'll be in her bedroom. Nick could find it.'

He stood up. 'I'll go to the farm now and see him, Maddie. This just might save them the trouble of exhuming Frank's body.'

'And when they test the hair and there's nothing there, they'll let me go?'

'Oh, you won't have to wait as long as that. I'll have you out of here in the morning. What they'll probably do is release you on police bail to return to the police station in two or maybe three weeks. That depends on how long it takes them to make their enquiries. But, you must be prepared, my dear, that if they do find traces of arsenic, then . . .' Theo said no more and when he had left, Maddie felt even more lonely than she had before he had come.

Forty-Nine

Theo arrived again next morning and demanded her release and Maddie found herself outside the police station, blinking in the sunlight and pulling in great gulps of fresh air. But before she had time to savour her freedom, Theo was hustling her towards his car.

'Come on, Maddie, I don't want us to attract attention.' He almost pushed her into the back seat and got in beside her, slamming the door and ordering his chauffeur to drive off immediately.

'What do you mean?' she asked as the car reached the outskirts of the town and gathered speed.

Theo leant back against the plush upholstery and sighed. 'I'm sorry, Maddie, but the locals have you charged, tried and convicted already. They think you're guilty.'

'Everyone? Even – even Jenny?'

Theo managed to laugh. 'Oh not Jenny. Dear, loyal little Jenny. You'd be amazed what she's been up to on your behalf. It was she who came up to the Hall with the ever-faithful Steven in tow, to ask me to help you.'

'She did?'

'She most certainly did. Quite the little tigress in defence of her own, isn't she?'

Maddie stared at him. Jenny? A tigress? Loyal, yes, she'd known that. But a tigress? Now this was something new.

'You know, she intrigues me. In fact, you both do. But – er . . .' He hesitated before murmuring, 'But you for quite a different reason.' Then more briskly, he asked, 'Do you know anything at all about her background?'

Maddie shook her head. 'No. No more than I do about my own. But we've a lot in common. We were both abandoned outside the Mayfield Children's Home. Me at a month or so old – they were never quite sure just how old I was – but Jen was newborn.'

'Really? And when was this?'

'1932.'

She saw his eyebrows rise as, again, he said, 'Really?'

'Why?'

But now he seemed disinterested as he turned his gaze away from her. 'Oh nothing. I just wondered. Anyway . . .' He reached out and took her hand, 'I'm sorry, my dear, but I have to tell you that Nick couldn't find the lock of Frank's hair you mentioned, so they are still going to exhume the body. And besides, to be honest, I don't think they would have taken just that lock of hair as sufficient evidence, even if we had been able to find it.'

The brief hope that had sustained her through the past night, died.

They were passing through Eastmere now and Maddie became uncomfortably aware of the curious glances of the villagers. Some even took a step towards the car, bending to peer in through the windows as the vehicle slowed to a halt outside the village shop.

'You wait here in the car,' Theo said. 'I'll fetch Adam.'

'Isn't he at school?'

'No. We thought it best to keep him at home for a

while. He was getting taunted. Children can be very cruel to each other, can't they?'

Oh indeed they could, Maddie thought grimly, remembering the times when she had championed poor Jenny. And now, ironically, it was Jenny defending Maddie's son. Life had a peculiar way of coming full circle, Maddie thought.

Maddie jumped suddenly as an egg splattered against the car window beside her and she heard the jeering of three youths.

'Lock the car door, miss,' the chauffeur advised, 'until you see Mr Theo coming back.'

'Oi, you!' Startled again, Maddie glanced round but then she saw that the shout had come from Steven who had appeared in the shop doorway. She saw him jump down the three steps and run after the youths.

Maddie sat huddled miserably in the back seat feeling more of a prisoner now than she had in the cold, dark cell at the police station. Through the rear window she watched as Steven caught up with one of the lads, grabbed hold of him and shook him, shouting and shaking his fist into the lad's face. The boy – little older than Adam, she saw now – looked frightened out of his wits. His two mates had disappeared round a corner, leaving him to face the man's wrath alone.

At least someone's on my side, Maddie thought. And Stinky Smith of all people.

'Maddie, oh Maddie.' Jenny's smiling face was suddenly outside the car window and as Maddie released the lock on the door, she climbed in and sat close beside her, putting her arms around her and holding her close. 'Thank goodness, Mr Theo got you out of that dreadful place. How are you? Are you all right?'

Maddie avoided answering her question by asking another. 'How's Adam? Is he all right?'

'Sort of. He's upset that his so-called friends have all turned against him.'

'Oh Jen. Thank God for friends like you and – and Steven. What would I do without you?'

'Silly thing,' Jenny laughed. 'We're sisters. Remember?'

She looked over Jenny's shoulder and saw that Theo and Adam had appeared now at the top of the steps. With his hand resting protectively on the boy's shoulder, Theo seemed to be looking up and down the street before they emerged from the doorway. At the sight of her son, Maddie's heart turned over. She had been away for only a short time and yet it had seemed an eternity. As she looked into his eyes, she could see that it had left its mark on Adam too. The boy had grown up overnight, it seemed. And there was something else, too. More than ever, he was like his father.

She was never going to be allowed to try to forget Michael, she thought, for with her every day was a living, breathing reminder.

'Won't you stay here with us?' Jenny was urging her, bringing her thoughts back to the present.

'What? Oh no – no, thanks. I must get back to the farm. There's work to do.'

Jenny's eyes were still troubled. 'Do you really think you should go back there? I mean – Nick's still there.'

'Nick? Why shouldn't he be there?' Maddie searched her friend's face. 'You don't mean – oh you can't mean – that Nick thinks I'm guilty.'

'No, no, he doesn't, but . . .' Jenny turned away, ducked her head and got out of the car. 'Mr Theo, she wants to go back to the farm.'

Then Theo came to the car and, though he made no

effort to get in, he bent down and looked in at her. 'Don't you think it might be better for you to stay here? Mrs Grange is agreeable, if that's what's worrying you. Or you can come to the Hall if you prefer.'

'No, no, I must get home.'

'I don't like you being out there on your own. The feeling in the village is far worse than I had imagined. Jenny and Steven – and young Adam – have just been telling me.'

'Then it would be far worse to stay here,' Maddie argued reasonably. 'And I'd be putting innocent people – Mrs Grange and Jen – at risk too.'

Theo seemed to be struggling with some inner conflict.

'What?' Maddie asked. 'What is it?'

'Nothing,' he said swiftly, a little too swiftly to be convincing. It was as if he wanted to say something but didn't know whether he should do so. Eventually, he said, 'Well, at least let Adam stay here. Please, Maddie. We'll bring him to the farm to see you. Every day. I promise. But just let him stay here with them. At least – for the time being.'

Much as she wanted to be with her son, Maddie nodded. 'All right then, but just let him get into the car for a minute. Let me talk to him.'

Theo straightened up and beckoned to the boy.

'Oh darling,' Maddie put out her arms as he climbed in beside her. 'This is all a horrible mistake. You don't believe I did anything wrong, do you?'

'Oh Mam . . .' Suddenly he was grinning at her. 'Of course I don't. None of us do. Only the stupid villagers who don't know you.'

She hugged him to her. 'That's all right then. I can stand anything if only you believe in me.'

He put his arms around her waist and buried his face

against her shoulder. His voice was muffled as he asked, 'Are you sure you're going to be all right at the farm?'

'Of course, I am. Nick's there.'

Adam raised his head and as she looked down into his upturned face, Maddie shivered suddenly at the strange expression in the young boy's eyes.

Fifty

Nick came towards her with his arms outstretched as the car drew into the farmyard.

'Maddie! Thank goodness you're all right.' He was smiling happily, his face alight with relief. He hugged her to him and then held out his hand towards Theo. 'Mr Theo. How can we thank you enough for your help?'

To Maddie's surprise, Theo ignored Nick's outstretched hand and instead said curtly, 'It's not over yet. I should wait for the outcome of the post-mortem before you begin to celebrate.'

But Nick's smile stayed in place. 'What can they hope to find from that?' His tone was derisory. 'They'll find arsenic in his body, I don't doubt.'

Maddie felt a shiver of alarm as she glanced at the frown on Theo's face. 'Why do you say that?' he asked Nick sharply.

Nick shrugged. 'Stands to reason. It's in the ground all around here, isn't it? It's used in weedkillers, isn't it? More than likely the ground is sodden with it.'

Theo said nothing but his steely gaze never left Nick's face.

'May we you offer you a drink, sir?' Nick said.

'No, thank you. I must be on my way.' Now his glance lingered on Maddie. 'If you need anything, you know where to find me.'

With that, he gave a curt nod towards Nick and climbed

back into the car. Nick put his arm around her shoulders as they stood and watched the driver reverse down the track and into the lane.

'Phew. Thank goodness he's gone. Poking his nose in where it's not wanted.'

'Oh Nick, don't say that. He got me out of that awful place.'

'He got there first, I'll grant you. And with his position around here, they would listen to him. But don't think the rest of us weren't trying.' For a moment there was belligerence in his tone. 'We don't need his sort. I'll look after you, Maddie. It's just you and me now. We'll be all right together.'

Deliberately, she asked, 'How's your mother?'

'Much better. They're talking about her coming home the day after tomorrow.'

'What? Here?' With bitter sarcasm, she added, 'You mean they're actually going to let her come back here where I might try to poison her again?'

'Oh, I've explained all that to them at the hospital. I told them it was all a dreadful accident. Mam must have somehow been mixing up the weedkiller and then gone back to her baking. They seemed to believe me. Now, come on in. I've got a lovely meal ready for you to welcome you home. See, I knew they'd have to let you go. They can't prove a thing.'

They were walking towards the house as Maddie said thoughtfully, 'But your mother never touches the outside work. She never has anything to do with the weedkiller.' She stopped and stared at him. He had moved ahead of her a little before he turned to glance over his shoulder at her and said, 'I know that and you know that. But they don't.'

'That's not the point. How did your mother come to get arsenic in her system, then?'

Nick shrugged and spread his hands. 'Your guess is as good as mine.'

'You mean, you think I did it?'

''Course not.'

'Then how . . .?'

He came towards her again and put his arm about her shoulders and tried to draw her towards the house. 'I've told you. Somehow, it was a dreadful accident. Do stop worrying about it, Maddie. I've got you home and all to myself. I'll look after you. I won't ever let anyone take you away from me again.'

For the moment, Maddie allowed him to usher her into the house, through the wash-house and the kitchen and into the living room where, she had to admit, a wonderful spread awaited her.

'Oh Nick,' she was moved to say. 'You've done all this? For me?'

For the rest of the evening, Nick laughed and joked and kept the conversation away from what must have been at the back of both their minds. Maddie tried to respond, was grateful for his efforts in trying to take her mind off things, but she was worried for Adam and anxious about the impending post-mortem. As Theo had said, it wasn't over yet.

As he locked up for the night, Maddie was surprised to see Nick take the shotgun from its usual corner behind the door in the living room and place it on the kitchen table. 'Just in case we get any unwelcome visitors from the village,' he said, winking at her.

'Nick, you can't do that. Oh, don't let's cause any more trouble.'

'It's all right. It isn't loaded. It's only just to frighten them off. You go up to bed, Maddie. I think I'll stay down here and keep watch.'

'You're making it sound like a siege.'

'It may well be. You've never been on the receiving end of these folks' viciousness. But me and my mam have.'

'Whatever do you mean?'

'It's a long time ago now, but I tell you, you don't know 'em and what they can do. Not like I do.'

'But, Nick, you need your sleep. We've a lot of work to catch up on tomorrow.'

'I've kept up with it pretty well. And I can doze in the armchair. I'll be all right, honestly. You go up and get a nice bath. There's plenty of hot water. I've made sure of that for you.'

She knew she ought to thank him for all his efforts to welcome her home, to pamper her, but somehow the words stuck in her throat. There was something unsettling about his attitude. Something she could not quite put her finger on.

Maddie was thoughtful as she went up the steep stairs, wishing for once that there was a door to the bathroom with a good, sturdy lock.

She need not have worried. Nick remained downstairs whilst Maddie bathed and washed the smell of the police station cell from her hair, but once in the bedroom she had shared with Frank, she heard Nick's footsteps coming up the stairs and along the passageway, nearer and nearer.

She knew a sudden irrational fear as he tapped on the door and said in a soft voice, 'You all right, Maddie?'

Her voice sounded high-pitched even to her own ears as she said, 'Of course. Thank you, Nick. Good night.'

'Good night, Maddie. Sleep tight.'

As the sound of his footsteps moved away again, she let

out the breath she had been holding. She was imagining it all. The events of the previous two days had shattered her nerves and left her unable to think straight.

Nevertheless, for some reason she could not have explained, before she put out the light and climbed into her bed, she took the ladder-backed chair from beneath the window and lodged it beneath the door knob.

Fifty-One

The following morning – Saturday – Jenny and Steven brought Adam to the farm as they had promised. The boy rushed into his mother's arms, hugging her tightly around the waist. 'We've come to help you in the fields. Me and Jen, that is. Steven's got to go to Peterborough this afternoon to meet someone, but we can stay, Mam.'

'There's no need,' Nick interrupted, coming up behind her. 'Everything's under control.' He nodded towards Jenny and Steven. 'Me and Maddie can manage.'

Steven gave a hearty laugh that to Maddie's ears sounded forced. 'You mean you're going to pick that lot on your own? Just the three of you?' He nodded in the direction of the field where this year's crop was planted. Row upon row of tulip heads waved and danced in the breeze. Maddie's rainbow field of vibrant colour. Steven shrugged. 'Oh well, if you're sure.'

'We'll manage,' Nick said again.

'Are you staying to lunch?' Maddie asked Jenny and Steven.

'No, no,' Steven said, a little too quickly. 'I must get going if I'm to get to Peterborough for one.' He glanced at Jenny and Maddie saw them exchange a secretive smile.

'I'm staying all day,' Jenny said brightly. 'Until Steven gets back.' Then she looked at Nick as if daring him to defy her.

Maddie was astonished. She would never have believed

it of her little Jenny Wren. But what was it Theo had called her? A tigress. That was it. A tigress in defence of her own.

But Nick was not to be defeated easily. 'I really think you'd be helping Maddie most if you took Adam back to Mrs Grange's and kept him there. Out of harm's way.'

'Out of harm's way? What on earth are you talking about, Nick?' Jenny retorted. She put her head on one side and stared at him. Levelly, she asked, 'How can Adam possibly come to any harm here?'

'We might very well get a visit from some of the villagers. The ones,' Nick said pointedly, 'who think Maddie is guilty. Mr Frank was very popular around here. They might take it upon themselves to form a lynching mob.'

'Don't be silly, Nick. We're not living in the Wild West.'

'Huh, you don't know these folk like I do,' he muttered.

Quietly, but with a sureness Maddie had never heard before, Jenny said, 'Oh but I think I do, Nick. Yes, I think I know the village folk very well now. Probably a lot better than you, stuck out here at Few Farm.'

Churlishly, he said, 'Stay if you must, but I have to go into town this afternoon to see my mother and while I'm gone, I want Maddie to stay in the house and lock the doors.'

Suddenly, Maddie realized how she was allowing everyone else around her to make decisions for her. Of course, she had needed Theo's help – still did – but she was not going to allow Nick or anyone else to dictate to her what she could or could not do.

'I'll come with you to the hospital. I'm not going to barricade myself away here. I've nothing to feel guilty about.'

Jenny gave her another quick hug. 'That's the Maddie I know.'

She saw Adam glance quickly at Jenny and Maddie had the strange feeling that there was a kind of conspiracy between them, between the three of them, if it came to that: Jenny Steven – and Adam. 'Can't we all go, Mam? I'd like to see Mrs T.'

Without any further reference to Nick, Jenny said, 'Right, that's settled then. Off you go now, Steven, or you'll be late.' Again, a special look passed between them and for a foolish moment, Maddie felt excluded and so alone.

Then Jenny was tucking her arm through Maddie's and glancing over her shoulder, but Nick had moved away. 'It'll be all right,' she said in a low voice as they waved Steven off. 'I promise you, Maddie. Everything's going to be all right.' And then, obviously deliberately changing the subject, she said in her normal voice, 'Steven's brother has finished the metal frame for your float for the Parade. It's not long now, is it?'

Maddie sighed. 'Oh Jen, I really wanted to be a part of the first real Parade, but now . . .' She left the words hanging in the air. It was a question she could not – dare not – even try to answer.

Harriet was sitting up in the end bed when they entered the ward. It seemed to Maddie that there was a lot of whispering as they passed between the row of beds on either side, but she kept the smile fixed on her mouth and her eyes on Harriet.

'How are you feeling?' she asked at once as they drew near the end bed.

'Better, but it's no thanks to you, is it?'

Maddie's heart sank. So, they had told her. But her next words seemed to belie this. 'Sat here day after day with

not a visit from either of you. Not even young Adam's
been to see me. And me own son . . .' Her reproachful gaze
rested on Nick now. 'You haven't been near me for three
days.'

'We've – er – been a little busy, Mam.'

'Ah well, yes, of course work comes before anything or
anyone else, doesn't it?' She sniffed. 'Always has done.
Even when poor Frank was alive.'

Nick fetched a chair and placed it beside the bed for
Maddie. As she sat down, he rested his hand briefly on her
shoulder and Maddie saw at once the startled look in
Harriet's eyes as her glance went from one to the other.

'We've had a spot of bother, Mam, but everything's
going to be all right now.'

'What sort of bother?' Harriet's tone was sharp with fear.
'Not – not Adam? Nothing's happened to Adam, has it?'

'No, no. He's waiting outside with Jenny. They'll come
in to see you in a few minutes.'

'What's she here for?'

The explanation came haltingly from Maddie's lips.
'Adam's been staying with her. At the shop. Just for a
night or two.'

'Maybe that's just as well until I get home.' Harriet
sniffed again. 'You two can't look after him properly,
you're always too busy. What that lad would do without
me, I don't know.'

Nick sat on the edge of the bed and took his mother's
hands in his. 'Well, when you come home, we'll just be
one happy family again, won't we?' He turned and winked
at Maddie, who managed a weak smile. For once she was
lost for words. Anything she might say to Harriet, even
though the woman seemed ignorant of recent events,
would have a hollow ring even to Maddie's own ears. She
almost wished now that Harriet had been told the truth.

To deal with her anger would have been far easier. But to sit here, trying to make polite conversation and, worse, plans for an uncertain future was impossible.

Behind her the whispering went on. Well, the rest of the ward seemed to know something even if Harriet didn't, Maddie thought wryly. No doubt one of their visitors had come in with the choice bit of gossip but no one had had the nerve to tell Harriet Trowbridge.

'So, when are they letting you out?' Nick asked and Maddie shuddered at his choice of words.

'Monday morning. I thought it would be tomorrow, but the sister says the doctor must see me before they can discharge me.'

'Right-o,' Nick said cheerfully. 'I'll come and fetch you home in the truck. I'll ask the sister on the way out what time you're likely to be ready.'

They chatted spasmodically for another half an hour, but when the silences became longer than the periods of talk, Nick stood up. 'We'd better be going. Come along, Maddie . . .'

'You go, Nicholas,' Harriet said, 'I want a word with her. And then you can send Adam in for a minute.'

Nick frowned. 'What do you want to talk to Maddie about?'

'Never mind, just run along.'

Still, Maddie thought, she speaks to him like a little boy and she could sympathize with the scowl on Nick's face as he left the ward without another word to his mother.

'Now then, you,' Harriet began and Maddie's heart sank. So she did know after all. For a brief moment she closed her eyes and steeled herself against the expected onslaught. But in the next instance, her eyes flew open as Harriet said, 'Is there something going on between you and Nicholas, because there'd better not be?'

'What – what do you mean?' Now she was more than ever puzzled.

Harriet reached out and grasped Maddie's arm. Her grip, in view of her recent debilitating illness, was surprisingly strong. 'There can't ever be anything between you and Nicholas. You hear me, girl?'

'There isn't . . .' Maddie began, but she was shocked into silence at Harriet's next words.

'Because you're his half-sister.'

Fifty-Two

Maddie felt as if she had been punched just below the ribs. Her legs threatened to give way beneath her and her head began to swim.

'What – what did you say?'

'I said – you're half-brother and sister. You, girl, are the bastard of my husband and that little trollop at the Hall, Amelia Mayfield. But you're not to say a word to Nicholas. I don't want him knowing what bad blood he's got in his veins. You hear me, girl, not a word to him.'

Maddie's mind was in turmoil. It couldn't be true. The woman had gone mad. Her illness had turned her brain. She pulled herself free from Harriet's grasp and staggered the length of the ward, reeling like a drunkard, unheeding now that the eyes of all the other patients were watching her.

They were waiting for her in the corridor. His hands thrust deep into the pockets of his trousers, his forehead creased in a petulant frown, Nick asked, 'What was it she wanted?'

'I – er – oh – nothing, just – just, you know . . .' Maddie floundered.

'No, I don't know. That's just it. What's the matter? You've gone white. What's she been saying?'

Jenny was at her side in an instant. 'Sit down, Maddie. I'll get a nurse to get you a glass of water.'

Maddie swallowed and leant against Jenny. 'I'm all right.'

'What's she said?' Nick demanded again. 'Tell me or I'll go back and . . .'

'No, no,' Maddie said swiftly. 'Leave it, Nick. Please. It's nothing – nothing. Just . . .' She latched on to the first thing that came into her fuddled mind. 'She wants me to do some shopping for her. Women's things, you know?'

'Is that all?' His face cleared. 'Why didn't she say so then instead of making a big mystery out of it. I thought for a moment someone had told her about what's been going on.'

He tried to take hold of her arm, almost as if trying to prise her away from Jenny. Maddie flinched at his touch. 'Don't,' she said, before she thought to stop herself. As she saw the frown on his face once more, she made herself say, 'I'm fine, really. Come on. Let's get home.'

'Can't I see Mrs T?' Adam asked, casting a forlorn glance at the door leading into the ward.

'Just run in and have a quick word with her then,' Jenny said, taking the lead. 'But only a minute, mind.'

The boy sped away but by the time they had walked out of the hospital and towards where the truck was parked, he had caught them up. 'She ses the first thing she's going to do when she gets home is bake gingerbread men for tea.'

'You sure you're all right in there, Adam?' Jenny asked as she helped him climb into the open back of the truck. 'It must be a bit draughty.'

The boy grinned. 'I'm fine. I'm just glad it's not raining.' He looked towards Nick. 'Just don't go fast round the corners, Uncle Nick. I might get thrown out.'

Nick laughed, his face creasing into lines of laughter. 'Well, that's one way of getting rid of you.'

Despite the recent shock, Maddie thought, why can't Nick be like that all the time? Laughing and joking, he was so much nicer. But now, suddenly, she was seeing him through very different eyes.

Was he really her half-brother?

As they got out of the battered old truck in the yard of Few Farm, Jenny held out a hand to help Adam climb out. 'You're still with us then?'

He grinned cheekily at her. 'You don't get rid of me as easily as that.'

'Well, I hope not,' Maddie thought she heard Jenny murmur.

That night, after Jenny had gone back to the shop taking Adam with her, Nick locked all the doors and double-checked the windows.

'I think if the villagers had been going to do anything, they'd have done it by now,' Maddie remarked.

'Can't be too careful,' Nick said, laying the shot gun on the kitchen table again.

The following day, they laboured side by side in the fields. Maddie worked automatically for her mind was still reeling from Harriet's revelation. She had hardly slept, going over and over Harriet's bitter words.

Was she really Amelia Mayfield's daughter? Perhaps that explained why she had felt so drawn to the poor woman. Maddie drew her hand across her forehead with a sigh as another thought struck her. And if she was, then Theo was her uncle.

She stood quite still for a moment wondering why the realization did not bring her the expected pleasure. She admired and liked Theo. Very much. So why did the thought that she was related to him bring a strange stab of disappointment?

As dusk fell and they packed up for the day, Maddie turned back and stood gazing at the field of tulips, glowing bronze in the setting sun.

'Isn't that the most beautiful sight you've ever seen?' she murmured, a catch in her voice, but Nick was already too far away to hear. Tears blurred her vision. 'I don't want to lose it all,' she whispered, suddenly filled with dread at what the coming week might bring.

'You going to stand there all night?' came Nick's truculent voice from down the lane as he trudged towards the farm, carrying a hoe in one hand and in the other, the shotgun that, since the day of Maddie's release from police custody, he had carried everywhere with him. He had even, she had discovered afterwards, taken it in the back of the truck hidden beneath a pile of sacks when they had visited the hospital in Wellandon.

Maddie dragged her gaze away from the lovely view and turned to follow him, wondering how, on the one hand, there could be such peace and tranquillity and beauty whilst on the other, such tragedy and menace and ugliness were hanging over her

'Nick? Nick, where are you?'

Maddie stood in the middle of the yard. It was halfway through the Monday morning and still he had not left for the hospital. She had never thought that she would be anxious to see Harriet Trowbridge back home, but now she had a whole list of questions she needed to ask her. Whether she would be able to wheedle any answers out of the woman, was another matter, but Maddie was determined to try.

She heard a movement in the big barn. Nick was there, sweeping the floor. 'There you are. What time have you to go to the hospital to fetch your mother?'

'This afternoon,' Nick said, setting the brush against the wall and coming to stand in front of her. 'And you're to stay in the house while I'm gone. You hear?'

'Look, Nick, I'm very grateful for all that you've done. All that you're still doing, but stop ordering me about. There's a lot of work to do and I mean to get on with it. If any of the lads from the village do come here – and I don't think they will now – they're hardly likely to harm me, are they?'

'Oho, you don't know what they're capable of . . .'

'Just what are they capable of, Nick? Tell me, because I'd really like to know.'

They stood glaring at each other, but then the anger died in Nick's face. He put his hands on her shoulders.

'Oh Maddie, we were meant to be together, you and me. I've always known it.' His grip tightened and he pulled her towards him into his embrace. She put her palms flat against his chest and tried to push him away.

'Nick, don't . . .'

'It ought to be just the two of us here, Maddie. Just you and me working side by side, with no one else to interfere.'

'Don't be silly, Nick. Your mother's coming home this afternoon. And Adam . . .'

'She'll have to come here for a while. I know that, but we can get rid of her – somehow. We can get rid of them both and then it will be just the two of us.'

'No! What on earth are you saying?' Maddie wrenched herself free and, standing back from him, stared into his face.

There was a wild look in his eyes, a look of desperate longing for her. But it was not the look of love, but of obsession; a jealous, self-centred obsession that sought to oust everyone else from Maddie's life.

'Nick,' she tried to keep her tone calm and placating, tried, desperately, to be understanding and kind. 'There can't be anything between us. You must know that . . .'

Nick laughed, but there was no humour in the sound. Now, to Maddie's ears there was only menace. He stepped towards her, his arms outstretched again, but she backed away.

'Maddie, Maddie, don't. I love you. I want to be with you always. Just the two of us. Don't you realize how I feel about you? How I've always felt about you?'

Maddie shook her head. 'No, no, Nick. I'm very fond of you. But I don't love you. And besides . . .'

Nick's features were contorted with rage. 'It's him, isn't it? I'll kill him if you . . .'

'Who? Who are you talking about?'

'Theo Mayfield.'

Now Maddie gave a nervous laugh. The idea was so preposterous that even amidst the drama of the moment, she could see the funny side. 'Don't be stupid, Nick. Mr Theo would never look at me.'

'Oh, but he does. He does look at you – *that way*.'

She stared at him, suddenly remembering all the occasions when Theo had smiled at her, touched her hand, paid her compliments and, yes, she had to admit it now, there had been more in his eyes that ordinary friendliness.

She swallowed and tried to laugh it off, but even to her own ears her laughter sounded hollow. 'Don't be silly. There's only one person I've ever really loved and he left me, didn't he?'

Nick's eyes narrowed and there was a devious look in them. 'You think so, eh?'

'What – what do you mean?'

'Nothing. He's gone and good riddance. And Theo Mayfield? Well, you're not the sort of girl he'd marry, are you? Oh, a quick tumble in the hay. Get you pregnant, yes. But his sort wouldn't marry you.'

How could he profess to love her and yet say such cruel things? Maddie thought. He doesn't even know what love is.

That's it, she thought with sudden, blinding clarity. That's it. Nick has never known what it is to be truly loved. Not by anyone. Not even by his own mother.

He was speaking again, dragging her back to the moment. 'But I'll marry you, Maddie. I've always wanted you . . .'

'Nick, please, you must listen. We can't – your mother . . .'

'Forget my mother, I've told you . . .'

'No, no, listen to me. You don't understand. The other day in the hospital, when she called me back. It – it wasn't what I told you.'

'What do you mean?'

'She – she told me something. Something about us. You and me.'

'Oh, I know she doesn't want us to . . .'

'It's not just that,' Maddie interrupted him. 'She has a reason. A very good reason, if what she said is true.'

There was silence in the huge barn now, only the sound of the rafters creaking and the breeze straying in through the open door to rustle a stray piece of raffia on the concrete floor.

Slowly Nick said, 'What did she say?'

'That I am the daughter of your father and – and Amelia Mayfield. That you and I are half-brother and sister.'

The silence in the barn lengthened and deepened as they stared at each other.

'I don't believe it,' Nick said hoarsely at last. 'It's another of her lies to stop us . . .'

At that moment there was the sound of a car pulling into the yard. Thankfully, Maddie turned and, before he could put out a hand to restrain her, she ran to the doorway.

Relief was in her voice as she said, 'It's Steven's car.'

She could see him behind the wheel and beside him, Jenny. Already, Adam was clambering out of the back and running towards her. 'Mam, Mam. This gentleman's come to see you. He says he knows you.'

Then Maddie saw the tall, dark-haired man unfolding himself from the back seat of the car.

The whole earth seemed to spin around her. Her vision blurred and her legs were suddenly weak. As if from a great distance, she heard a voice speak his name and realized it was her own. She stood staring at him, drinking in the sight of him. He had changed little in the eleven years since she had seen him. If anything, he was even more good-looking. His shoulders were broader, his skin tanned and healthy. There were a few lines around his eyes and tiny flecks of white at his temples, but there was a change. She could see it now as he came closer. It was in his eyes, those dark brown eyes that once had been full of laughter. Now, there was a sadness in their depths.

She wanted to run to him, to pummel his chest and cry out to him, 'Why? Why, did you leave me? Why did you never come back?' and then to clutch him to her, winding her arms around him and holding him so close that he could never go away again. But she could not move a muscle. She stood rooted to the spot staring at him and saying again just the one word.

'Michael!'

Fifty-Three

He was standing before her now, looking down into her upturned face, taking her hands into his. And his touch still had the long-forgotten magic. She wanted, oh how she wanted to hate him, to scream at him and call him all the vile names she could think of and yet here she was trembling at the sight of him, the love surging through her once more at the feel of him. She was aware of no one else in the world at this moment, not her son standing beside her looking up from one to the other, watching them, a broad smile on his face. Not Steven and Jenny standing beside the car, their arms around each other. She had even forgotten Nick, behind them somewhere in the barn. At this moment there was only Michael and Maddie in the whole world.

'Michael, oh Michael.' She said his name over and over again, breathing it, savouring it, revelling in the sound and shape of the word that she had refused for so long to let pass her lips.

'Maddie.' He whispered and the word was a loving caress. She looked into his eyes and still, even after all this time, she could see the love in them for her shining out.

And now she said it, voiced the question that had been a searing wound in her heart for almost eleven years. 'Why, Michael? Why?'

'I could ask you the same question, Maddie?'

'Me? Why me? I wasn't the one who went away and never came back. I wasn't the one who deserted you.'

'Deserted you?' The shock on his face was genuine. 'I never deserted you. It was you who said you never wanted to see me again, that you were marrying someone else.'

'Who told you that? Who . . .?' And then she stopped short and whispered the name at the same instant that Michael said, 'Nick.'

As realization began to trickle through her mind, she said flatly, 'Nick came back from visiting you to say that you no longer loved me. That you were joining the Army and never coming home again.'

Michael's face was grim. 'I think Nicholas Trowbridge has some explaining to do. Where is he?'

'Right here.' His voice came out of the shadows at the back of the barn.

They moved towards him, Maddie, already with the anger growing inside her, and Michael, still holding her hand. Adam, puzzlement in his face, followed them.

The three of them were already in the middle of the barn when Nick emerged from the shadows and they saw that he was holding the shotgun levelled towards them.

Maddie gasped and at once grasped Adam's shoulder and pushed him behind her. At the same moment she felt Michael's hand tighten on hers and he, too, gave a brief glance behind him to make sure that the boy was protected by them both.

'Take it easy, love,' he murmured to Maddie. 'Leave it to me.'

'Get away from her,' Nick said and when Michael made no move to leave Maddie's side, they both heard the click as the hammer was pulled back and the gun cocked. 'I said, get away from her.'

Still pointing the gun at them, Nick moved around them

393

so that he was a little nearer the door, cutting off any escape route.

'Move!'

Maddie gave Michael's hand a quick squeeze. 'You'd better do as he says. I don't think the gun's loaded, but . . .'

'Oh, it's loaded, Maddie. It has been all the time. I was ready for anything. The police or the villagers. Anybody. No one is going to take you away from me again. You hear? No one.'

'Nick,' she tried to keep her voice calm and level. 'Put the gun down. Let's talk about this. Please.'

'Get away from her.'

Michael sighed and, reluctantly, moved a short distance from Maddie and Adam.

'Over there, right away from her.'

Michael backed towards the side of the barn, his gaze fixed upon Nick as the barrel of the shotgun followed him, pointing at his chest.

'You shouldn't have come back, Michael. You've spoilt everything. Now I'm going to have to kill you.'

'No, please. Don't shoot.' Trembling, Maddie stretched out her hand towards Nick. The barrel swung and pointed at her now. 'Please,' she whispered, begging as she had never begged in her life. 'Please, at least let Adam go?'

'Why should I?' His tone was harsh and cruel, so different from the voice she knew so well. Or thought she had known. 'If it weren't for him and . . .' The barrel of the shotgun wavered slightly and then swung sharply away from pointing at Maddie and the boy towards Michael, standing so still and silent in the shadows. 'You!'

There was such venom in his voice, a bitter hatred that had been festering for eleven long years.

Behind him, a shadow appeared in the barn doorway. A woman's shadow.

'Maddie?' came Jenny's voice. 'What's going on? Are you all right?' Maddie's eyes widened and she gave a little gasp of fear. Then she touched Adam on his shoulder, giving him a tiny push. 'Go,' she breathed. 'Go to her.'

She saw him glance at the two men, who seemed, now, only aware of each other.

'Go on,' she urged.

Adam took a step, his gaze still on the men. Then he ran. The barrel swung again, following the small figure hurtling towards the open door and Jenny.

As she saw Nick's finger move towards the trigger, Maddie lunged forward, her hand outstretched to push the barrel aside and spoil his aim.

'No!' Maddie cried but the deafening blast drowned her scream. Lead shot splattered against the wall of the barn and in the doorway Jenny fell, sprawling in the dirt.

Heedless of the danger now, Maddie flung herself forwards. 'Jen, oh no. Jenny!'

She was only vaguely aware of Nick running past her out of the barn, of Steven running towards them and, as Nick passed him, Steven lunging at him, trying to grab him. But Nick pushed him away. She heard Michael's voice, close by her, shout, 'Let him go. He's dropped the gun.'

Then Steven was running forwards. 'Is she hurt? What about Adam?'

'I'm okay,' the boy said quickly and then the four of them were now bending over Jenny, afraid to touch her and yet . . . Gently, Steven cradled her in his arms. They saw the blood oozing through her dress near her thigh. Her face was deathly pale and her eyes closed.

*

'Where do you think Nick's gone?'

Maddie was the first to ask the question two hours later when the four of them, Michael, Adam, Steven and herself had returned to the farm. Adam had escaped unscathed and Jenny's injuries were far less than they might have been.

'You saved Adam's life,' Michael told her huskily, 'and probably Jenny's too. If they'd caught the full blast of that shotgun . . .'

They had taken Jenny to the casualty department and had been reassured that she would recover quickly once the pellets had been removed from her leg and her hand.

'I really don't know,' Michael said now in answer to her question. 'And at this moment I don't care where he is. You and me, Maddie . . .' He took her hands. 'Have got a lot of talking to do. But first . . .' he turned and smiled at Adam and his voice was hoarse as he added, 'I want you to introduce me to my son.'

Maddie saw Adam's eyes widen and his mouth dropped open as he glanced from Michael to her and then back again.

'My dad. You're – you're my dad?' There was no mistaking the excitement and the joy in the boy's voice and all Michael and Maddie could do was to nod in unison for neither, at that moment, could speak.

Adam was grinning as he turned to Steven and said, 'Hey, Uncle Steve. This is my dad.'

'Yes, old son, I know.'

Maddie cleared her throat and said, 'I thought perhaps you'd told him.'

Steven shook his head. 'I daren't,' he said, comically 'Jen threatened me with all sorts of dire punishments if spoiled the moment for the three of you. And,' he added glancing at each of them in turn, 'I see that she was right

But now,' he added as he put his hand on Adam's shoulder, 'let's leave your mam and your dad to themselves for a bit, eh? And we know Jen's in good hands, so – what shall we do? Go fishing?'

Adam glanced at both Maddie and Michael, reluctant for a moment to leave, but then he smiled as he looked up at Steven and shook his head. 'I'd like to, but there's a lot of tulips need knobbing if we're to get a good crop of bulbs this year and build a float in time for the Parade.'

The adults glanced at one another and Steven winked at the other two as he said, 'Right you are, then. Lead the way . . .'

Michael watched them go, the man and the boy crossing the yard side by side. There was a catch in his voice as he said, 'Oh Maddie. My son. After all this time, I've found my son.'

He turned then and opened his arms to her and she went into them as if the years between had never happened.

Fifty-Four

Much later, Michael said, 'Now, we must talk.' They sat together, squeezed into the armchair at the side of the fire that had always been Frank's. 'Incidentally . . .' He patted the arm of the battered old chair fondly. 'Where's Dad?'

Stricken, Maddie stared at him. 'You mean, you don't know?'

'Know what?'

'Oh Michael.' Tears sprang to her eyes. Tears for Frank, tears for Michael and even for herself. 'He – he was taken ill ten years ago. Adam was about five months old . . .'

Realization was clouding Michael's face. 'You mean, he's dead?'

Haltingly, she told him about his father and they sat together in silence for several moments. She laid her cheek against Michael's hair, feeling his inner struggle to come to terms with the dreadful news. His father had been dead for ten years and he had not even known.

'Didn't you get Nick's letter?' she asked gently at last.

Michael shook his head.

'But Nick came to see you when he was very ill. To ask you to come home to see him.'

Michael's voice was hoarse as he said, 'No, he didn't He only ever came to see me once. To tell me . . .' He reached up and traced the line of her face with a gentl finger. 'To tell me that you never wanted to see me agai and that you were going to marry someone else for th

398

sake of the baby. Until this morning, I didn't even know I had a son and I still don't know who – who your husband is. Is it Nick? Are you married to him?'

'Oh Michael,' she buried her face against his neck. 'This is awful. Awful.'

He put his arms tightly around her and held her close, burying his head against her hair. After a few moments, he raised his head. 'Tell me everything from the beginning, Maddie. Tell me your side from the day I went away. And then, I'll tell you mine.'

'Jenny and Steven didn't tell you anything then?'

Michael shook his head. 'No, apart from introducing me to Adam when I arrived this morning, they hustled me straight out here.'

'So they haven't even told you about – about the trouble I'm in?'

Again Michael shook his head.

'So why did you come back now?'

'Steven met me in Peterborough last Saturday. He told me you needed me, that you wanted to see me, but he wouldn't say why. But I didn't need to be told any more, Maddie. I've waited years to hear that you wanted to see me again. I couldn't get here fast enough, but I couldn't come back with him then. I had to go back to camp and explain to my Commanding Officer that I needed compassionate leave – urgently. '

'How did Steven find you? We've had no word from you for years.'

There was a strange look on his face as he said, 'I'm beginning to understand that, but all Steven did say was that he'd been to Mr Theo for advice and he was able to find out where I was stationed. I stayed in the Army after my National Service. I didn't know what else to do, since – since it seemed I was no longer welcome at home.'

Maddie groaned and closed her eyes at the eleven wasted years, but whispered, 'Oh thank God for Theo.'

Michael blinked and then asked, 'Theo, is it now?'

'He's been very kind to me. He – he's my solicitor. But for him, I'd still be in the cells at the police station.'

'The what!'

Sitting so close, she felt his muscles tighten.

Maddie sighed. 'Oh Michael. There's so much you don't know . . .' she looked at him sadly, 'and so much I don't know either.' Her face was filled with sorrow as she said, 'And when you've heard the whole story, you might want to get on the first train out of here again.'

'Never, my darling,' he reassured her huskily. 'Whatever it is, we're going to face it together.'

So she told him all that had happened since the day he had walked out of her life. She told him of her love for him, her hurt at his desertion and how she had buried all feelings for him so deep that she would hardly ever allow his name to pass her lips.

'So Adam knows nothing about me? And yet he seemed to take the news quite calmly just now.' There was a note of pleasure in Michael's tone as he added, 'He even seemed pleased.'

Now came the most difficult part of all. 'Well, I've never actually told him that Frank was his father. He was only little when he died, but he's been led to believe . . . Oh Michael, this is awfully hard . . .'

'Go on, Maddie.'

'It – it was your father I married.'

'Dad? You're joking?'

'No. He – he was very kind to me. He persuaded me that it was the best thing for the baby. And when Nick after one of his supposed visits to you, said you neve wanted to come home again and that you were signing on . . .'

Michael was silent trying to take in the enormity of the news he was hearing.

Maddie swallowed painfully but went on with her story, bringing him right up to date with the frightening events that were taking place now.

'You mean, they're digging poor Dad up?'

She nodded, unable to speak.

'My God! This is a nightmare.'

'I know. That's just how I feel. But it isn't, Michael. It's happening and there's nothing anyone can do to stop it.'

His face was grim. 'There must be. There must be something we can do . . .' His voice died away helplessly.

There was a silence between them before Michael took a deep breath and began to speak.

'Nick's deceived us both. He's played the go-between and yet lied to both sides. As I said, he only ever came to see me once, but I've written countless letters, sent cards at Christmas and on everyone's birthday. I even sent gifts at Christmas to the child I knew I must have, even though I didn't know whether it was a boy or a girl.'

'We never got any of them. We only ever knew about two letters. No wonder Nick always met the postman or went to the post office to collect the mail.'

'He's been very, very clever.'

Bitterly, Maddie said, 'Twisted, I'd say.'

'He must be in love with you himself, Maddie. That's the only explanation for all this, for everything he's done. He wants you for himself and he's tried to get rid of everyone else and . . .'

They were staring at each other now and then simultaneously they both cried, 'Nick.'

'It was him,' Michael said. 'He must have given Dad the arsenic and then, when they took him into hospital and started to do tests, he must have got scared and tried something else.'

'You – you mean, you think you caused the accident in the battery house?' Maddie was horrified to think that Nick could want to kill the man who had been like a father to him. 'But how could he have done it?'

Michael shook his head thoughtfully. 'I think he might somehow have caused a problem with the batteries.'

'But that wasn't what killed him. He fell backwards and hit his head. If Nick did plan it, he couldn't have been sure of that happening, could he?'

'No,' Michael agreed. 'But we've always been told how dangerous the battery house is. Dad instilled it into all of us. Maybe – maybe Nick *thought* it would kill him. It was just chance that, in a way, it did. But I still can't work out how he did it.'

Maddie bit her lip, frowning. 'There's something else I ought to remember, and I can't. It's – it's something about that night but I can't . . .'

Michael kissed her forehead and murmured, 'Don't worry, darling. Maybe it'll come back to you.' He sighed heavily. 'There's nothing going to make it come right, and yet . . .' His voice fell away as he murmured, 'I would like to know exactly what he did do.'

'And – and now? Do you really think he's been trying to poison his own mother?'

'I wouldn't put anything past him, not after what you've told me and what he tried to do today,' Michael said grimly. 'He could have killed Adam and Jenny, you know. By the way, where is Mrs T? Is she still in hospital?'

Maddie's eyes were wide as she gaped at him. Then despite the sadness of the last hour or so and all th trauma they both knew they still had to face, she clapped her hand over mouth to silence the laughter that bubbled up inside her. 'Oh heck. I forgot all about her. She'll still be sitting there in her hat and coat waiting to be brought home.'

Fifty-Five

'There's something else,' Maddie said as they walked hand in hand out to the field where Steven and Adam were picking the heads from the tulips.

'Oh no,' Michael said. 'I really don't think I can handle any more.' He gave her a rueful smile as he said, 'Go on, then. My shoulders are broad enough.'

Indeed they were, Maddie thought, for a brief moment revelling in the strength of him that she needed so desperately at this moment, more than ever before.

'I think we ought to leave Mrs Trowbridge where she is for the moment, if the hospital can keep her. At least for another day, if we can.'

''Til we find Nick, you mean?'

'Well, that, yes,' Maddie agreed. 'But she said something very odd to me the last time I visited her. Nick put his arm round me when we were with her and she looked absolutely furious. I thought, like we've always known that she doesn't want him to have a girlfriend or even friends of any sort, but it was more than that.'

'Go on.'

'She sent him out of the ward, said she wanted to speak to me alone. And do you know what she said?' They both stopped and turned to face each other, standing in the lane leading to the field. 'She said – she said that Nick is my half-brother.'

'Your what? How on earth does she make that out?'

404

'She said I was the bastard of her husband and Amelia Mayfield.'

Michael actually laughed aloud. 'Oh Maddie, this is getting dafter by the minute.'

But Maddie was not laughing. She said nothing and Michael's face sobered. He put his arm around her shoulders at the sight of her stricken face.

'Don't worry, darling. I'm back now and we'll sort everything out. I'm here to take care of you now. I'll look after you.'

They were the same words that Nick had used, but oh what a world of difference there was between the two people who uttered that same promise.

With Michael's arm around her, they walked on and came to stand at the end of the field, watching Adam and Steven moving steadily down the rows, carefully deheading the tulips. Field after field of blooms stretched far into the distance.

'You did it, my darling Tulip,' Michael said softly and at the sound of his loving nickname for her, Maddie's eyes filled with tears. The rainbow danced and blurred before her eyes, but now she allowed the tears to fall unashamedly and unchecked for they were tears of happiness. Michael was home, beside her once more, this time for ever.

They were all squeezed into Mrs Grange's tiny living room behind the shop, sitting around the table or in the two fireside chairs. Adam perched on the arm of one of them, leaning against his mother's shoulder. Even Theo was with them. He had arrived at Few Farm to tell Maddie the bad news, that the result of the post-mortem had revealed extensive amounts of arsenic in Frank's remains.

'It's no more than we expected, Mr Theo,' Michael had

said and went on to tell him swiftly of the day's cata-
strophic events, finishing by saying, 'We're just on our way
to Mrs Grange's – all of us . . .' he gestured not only
towards Maddie, but to Steven and Adam too. 'To see if
she can throw any light on the mystery for us. It might
help us to understand Nick a little better.'

'May I come along?' Theo had said. 'I think, with what
I've found out too, we may be able to piece things together.'

And so now they were sitting in the small room whilst
Mrs Grange bustled around with cups of tea and fancy
cakes. 'I'll just close the shop and then we won't be
disturbed,' she said. 'You are sure my little Jenny's going
to be all right, though? She's like a daughter to me, you
know.'

'She'll be fine, Mrs Grange. Honest,' Michael reassured
her.

'Oh Michael, it's so good to see you again. And I can't
think what Mrs Trowbridge will say when she knows
you've come home.'

'No,' Michael said quietly and glanced at Maddie.
'Neither can I.'

They waited, sipping their tea, whilst the woman scur-
ried around her shop, locking the door and turning the
notice on the door to 'Closed', switching off the light and
emptying the till of its money. Returning to the room, she
dumped the cloth bag of notes and coins into a drawer in
the sideboard and took her place at the table, patting the
ever-present blue felt hat into place. 'Now then . . .' She
was smiling and seemed, Maddie thought, excited at the
prospect of being the centre of attention for the next few
minutes. 'How can I help you?'

Maddie saw Theo and Michael exchange a glance
before Michael took the lead and said, 'Mrs Grange, we

should be very grateful if you would tell us all you know about Mrs Trowbridge and Nick. About their past.'

The woman glanced at Theo, but when he smiled and nodded encouragement she took a deep breath and began. 'Well, it's all a long time ago now. Early Thirties it would be, Thirty-one or -two, something like that.'

They waited patiently, without interrupting her, whilst Mrs Grange dredged through her memory, reviving the old gossip of years ago.

'Harriet's name wasn't Trowbridge then, it was Cuppleditch.' She looked around the gathering triumphantly and was obviously disappointed when everyone stared at her blankly. 'She was Harriet Cuppleditch, married to John Cuppleditch?' Again there was silence whilst they waited for her explanation. But then as she opened her mouth to speak, Theo muttered, 'My God, you don't mean . . .?'

'I do,' Mrs Grange beamed. 'Him that hanged 'issen in your woods, Mr Theo.'

A ripple of movement went around the room as everyone shifted uneasily.

''Course it weren't your fault, Mr Theo,' Mrs Grange added hastily. 'You was only a bairn. The Cuppleditch family, John's parents that is,' she went on, 'all lived in one of Sir Peter's cottages. John's father, Matt, was Sir Peter's head groom and John, as soon as he left school, went to work with his dad in the stables. Harriet was a kitchen maid in the house. That's how they met. She lived in, of course, at the Hall. They did in them days. John married Harriet . . .' She paused and wrinkled her forehead. 'Come to think of it, I reckon Trowbridge was her maiden name. Yes, I'm sure it was. Anyway, they got married. They were too young, only eighteen or so and things didn't go right from the start. They moved in with

John's parents and there was already a big family of them. John was the eldest of five children, so at that time in their little cottage there'd have been mam, dad and four kids and then John and Harriet and their babby, Nick, when he was born . . .' she wagged her finger and smiled, 'only six months after they was wed, an' all. So it was a shotgun wedding.'

Maddie shuddered at the reference to a gun and put her arm around Adam. 'Well, about this time, Mr Theo, your sister, Miss Amelia, started to learn to ride and as young John was so good with the horses, they asked him to teach her.' She nodded at Theo. 'I bet your dad rued the day he'd had that bright idea.'

Theo said nothing but glanced down at his hand resting on the table, lines of sadness etched into his kind face.

'She was such a pretty little thing in those days, Miss Amelia. Always laughing and chattering. So friendly to everyone she met. She always made you feel you were her equal, you know what I mean?'

She did, Maddie thought, for Theo was just the same. He never played the lord and master like his father had done. He never tried to rule other people's lives. He just tried to help them. She felt a flush of embarrassment creep up her neck. The tale had to be told, Maddie knew, but she wished that Mrs Grange was not telling it with such glee.

'Well, as I say. She was so pretty, so lively, such fun and poor John's wife, Harriet, had turned into a real misery since she'd had the babby. Maybe if they'd had their own home, things would have been different. But who knows? Anyway, John and Amelia fell in love and when Sir Peter found out, he locked her away at the Hall. But it was too late. She was already expecting John's child.'

408

Maddie gasped aloud and knew now that the colour drained completely out of her face. Mrs Grange was looking at her now and nodding. 'That's what Harriet means. She thinks you're that child.'

Now Theo was leaning forward, his arms resting on the table. 'I never knew my sister had a child.'

Mrs Grange turned to look at him. 'You'd be too young to be told, Mr Theo. You were only about eight, if I remember rightly. Your father did everything he could to keep it secret. But in a village like this, there's not much that escapes us.' She tapped the side of her nose. 'But we know how to keep quiet when need be.'

Oh they'd have kept quiet all right, Maddie thought, with a sudden spurt of bitterness. They'd have gossiped and revelled in the juicy bit of scandal amongst themselves but the livelihood of most of the villagers depended on Sir Peter Mayfield. They'd have kept their counsel, all right. They'd have kept Sir Peter's family secret for him. Right until this very moment.

'And you mean to tell me that Amelia had a baby and she just dumped her outside the Orphanage?' Theo was quite defensive now. 'My sister would never have done such a thing.'

'Of course she wouldn't. But your father would and by the time the child was born, she was, well, a bit turned in her head, like. You see, John had hanged himself by then. She was grief-stricken and I expect they hustled the baby away and told her it was stillborn or summat.'

There was a murmur around the room.

Theo asked harshly, 'Why on earth did John hang himself?'

'When your father found out about them, he sacked both John's father, Matt, and John and turned the whole family, aye, Matt, his wife and all the bairns and John and his wife and child, out of the cottage. They lived rough in the woods for weeks and it was winter. February time, I reckon. Matt's wife was expecting another bairn . . .'

'Matt's wife?' Theo said. 'Don't you mean John's?'

But Mrs Grange was adamant. 'No, it were Matt's wife. I tell you there was a big family of them and you often get that, you know. A child can sometimes be older than its own aunt or uncle.'

Theo pulled a disbelieving face but said no more.

'Well, poor Matt's wife – Mary, I think they called her – gave birth there in the woods, in the freezing cold and she died. After that, John went haywire. Out of his mind with guilt. He was absolutely beside himself that not only had he been the cause of his whole family getting turned out of their home, but, indirectly, he'd caused his own mother's death. And, of course, he'd lost Amelia too. He just couldn't live with the burden of guilt, poor feller.'

There was silence before Maddie asked, 'What happened to the baby that was born in the woods?'

'Everyone thought it must have died, too, and been buried with the mother, because soon after, Matt left the district taking the older bairns with him, but there was no young babby with them when they left. Even I know that, because I saw them the day they went. He came into the shop, Matt did, to buy a bit of food, you know. I made him up a hamper, at me own expense, I did, 'cos I felt so sorry for the poor man.'

If she was expecting congratulations for her generosity, Mrs Grange was disappointed. Everyone in the room was far too shocked by what they were hearing to even think of it.

'But Mrs Trowbridge – I mean, Harriet Cuppleditch – stayed here?' Michael asked.

'Your dad took her in. A wonderful man was your

410

father, Michael. He'd lost your mam and he needed a housekeeper to look after him, and you, so he took Harriet and young Nick into his home and treated them like his own family.'

'So that's why Harriet would never mix with the village folk. She would only ever come as far as your shop.'

'Aye well, she knew I knew everything, but I'm no gossip.' She preened herself. 'I'm only telling you all this now because you asked me to.'

That was true, Maddie thought. The woman had made a few remarks over the years, hinted at the mystery, but she had never been guilty of rattling the skeletons in other people's cupboards.

But now she had her moment of glory and she was relishing it.

Theo glanced across the room towards Maddie, a thoughtful frown on his face. 'You say, Mrs Grange,' he said slowly, 'that Mrs Cuppleditch gave birth in February?'

'About then. I'm sure that's right. I know it wasn't long after Christmas.'

'And what year?'

'Like I said, Thirty-one or -two. Somewhere there.'

'I want you to be more precise than that, Mrs Grange, if you can. Please think back very carefully.'

There was silence as Mrs Grange tutted and huffed and puffed as if racking her brains. 'I know,' she said suddenly. 'It was about the same time as that little baby got kidnapped in America, 'cos I remember thinking . . .'

'You mean the Lindbergh baby?' Theo interrupted.

'Yes, that's it, because . . .'

'That was 1932. March 1932.' He gave a weak smile as if to apologize for seeming so clever. 'I had to swot up the case as part of my studies for my law exams,' he explained.

Maddie was staring at him. 'That's when I was left

outside the Home. That's why they called me Madeleine
March. Because I was found in March and because –
because the name Madeleine was written on a piece of
paper and pinned to the blanket I was wrapped in. I heard
Mrs Potter telling Mrs Trowbridge the day she came
to . . .'

Suddenly it was all falling into place. There had always
seemed something strange about the way Harriet, who
never went out anywhere, had visited the orphanage to
pick out a girl to work at Few Farm. Not *a* girl, Maddie
realized now, but *the* girl. Again she remembered Harriet's
words. 'Are you sure this is the one?' Harriet had, for
some twisted reason of her own, sought out the child she
believed had been born to her own husband's lover.

'But why?' Maddie asked and only realized she had
voiced the question aloud when Michael said gently, 'Why
what, love?'

'Oh, nothing. Go on, Theo. You were going to say
something.'

'Well,' Theo said slowly, as if he too were thinking
aloud. 'I've always been puzzled by you and Jenny.'

'Jenny?' Maddie was surprised.

'Mm. You see, there's a resemblance between you.
People remark on it, don't they?'

Maddie nodded. 'We – we even called ourselves sisters
at the Home and – and it was more than just because we
had no family and wanted to belong to someone.'

'But you see,' Theo went on. 'Although you are a bit
like each other, it's Jenny who always reminds me of my
own sister.'

Now he stared straight at Maddie. 'I didn't know about
my sister having a baby, but I do remember – very vividly
– being told that she was very ill with an infectious disease
and that I could not see her for several weeks. That was in

the summer of 1932. And the reason I can remember it so clearly is because in the September I was hustled away to boarding school at eight years old and wasn't even allowed to say goodbye to Amelia. Now,' he added bitterly, 'I know why.'

'So you think,' Michael was leaning forward, 'that Jenny is your sister's child.'

'Yes. I do.'

'So. What about Maddie? Who is she?'

Now everyone's eyes turned to look at Maddie and she felt herself reddening under their scrutiny.

'I think she's the baby that everyone believed had died in the woods. I think she's Matt Cuppleditch's child.'

There was silence whilst everyone digested Theo's reasoning. They must all have found it plausible for not one of them raised any argument.

Michael reached out and took her hand in his. 'So somewhere, Maddie, my darling, you do have a family.'

'You're my family, you and Adam,' she said and began to say, 'I don't need . . .' But she stopped mid-sentence. She did need them. She wanted desperately to know the rest of her family. The realization surprised her. She had thought herself a loner, able to cope with life on her own, but suddenly she found herself longing to know the truth.

As if reading what was in her mind, Theo said gently, 'If we can find Matt Cuppleditch or his older children, they could confirm whether the baby did die or whether he left the child at the Home. But Maddie,' there was compassion in his eyes as he looked across the room at her, 'just remember how very difficult it must have been for him . . .'

She was shaking her head. 'Oh I don't blame him, don't think that. If anyone's to blame then it's . . .' She stopped, appalled at what she had been about to say.

'I know,' Theo said softly, his deep voice suddenly shaky with emotion. 'Don't think I condone the part my father must have played in all this.'

'You were only a bairn, Mr Theo,' Mrs Grange reached across the table and patted his arm. 'Only eight years old. No one can possibly blame you.'

'I know, Mrs Grange. But at least now I can try to put things right a little. With your agreement, Maddie, I'll try to find the Cuppleditch family and then we'll see, eh?'

She nodded, but then added in a whisper, 'But what about the other business, Theo? What about the forensic evidence they've just found?'

'I don't think you have anything to worry about that any more, Maddie, my dear. It's obvious now who did try to poison Frank and his own mother.'

'Nick?'

Soberly, Theo nodded. 'He was obviously in love with you, but that love became an obsession. A dangerous obsession.'

'What do you think he'll do? I mean after he ran away from the farm and we haven't seen him since? Where do you think he's gone?'

Theo sighed. 'There's no knowing what he might do. He knows now that he can never have you. Michael's return has shown him that.'

'Oh no! No!' Maddie's eyes were wide and her hand fluttered nervously to her mouth. 'Oh, he wouldn't, would he?'

'What? What are you thinking, Maddie?' Michael asked urgently as she turned tear-filled eyes towards him.

Her voice was a hoarse, terrified whisper as she said, 'His father, John Cuppleditch, couldn't have the girl he loved and look what he did.'

Fifty-Six

They found him hanging from the very same tree where, twenty-seven years earlier, his father had died.

The police took charge. It was they who cut his body down and gently carried him out of the wood to the waiting ambulance that took him away to the mortuary.

'How are we to tell his mother?' Maddie said, as she and Michael stood with their arms around each other watching the vehicle bounce away over the uneven ground until it reached the road.

'I think I had better do that, don't you?'

'I think you're the only one who can. You or Adam, but he's far too young to have to do that.'

'Are you going to tell Jenny?'

'Yes, yes. That'll be a mixture of sadness and joy, won't it? Poor Nick is dead and yet, we are pretty sure now that we are related. Not sisters, but aunt and niece.'

'You must tell her what Theo said, that once she knows the truth, he wants to take her to meet her mother, Amelia.'

'He's such a kind man, Michael. I don't know what I'd have done without him these past few weeks. Even over the years, if it comes to that.'

'Should I be jealous?'

Maddie had no such pretensions. She had not believed Nick's ravings. 'No. He's just a really kind person. I'm glad . . .' She stopped and only went on again, haltingly,

415

when Michael prompted her. 'I was going to say, I'm glad he's running things now, but that sounds as if I'm glad Sir Peter is the way he is. Paralysed and unable to speak. But I wouldn't wish that on anyone.'

'I know. But Fate has a peculiar way of sorting things out sometimes. Maybe it's all for the best, eh?'

Jenny was ecstatic to think she was really related to Maddie.

'Now don't get your hopes up too much,' Maddie tried to warn her. 'Theo's got to trace the Cuppleditch family first and even then . . .'

'Oh we are, Maddie, I just know we are.' Sitting up in the hospital bed, her hand and leg swathed in bandages, nevertheless Jenny looked the happiest she had ever looked. 'I'll have to start calling you "Auntie Maddie".'

'There are two people waiting outside to see you,' Maddie teased her. 'Each with the biggest bouquet of flowers I have ever seen in my life. I reckon they're trying to vie with each other to outdo the other.'

Jenny's eyes widened. 'I suppose – I hope . . .' she said firmly, her eyes sparkling with love, 'that one is Stinky Smith.'

They giggled together like two schoolgirls. 'But,' Jenny went on. 'Who's the other one?'

'Your "Uncle Theo"!'

'How did she take it?'

Maddie, her task the easier one of the two, was anxious to know how Michael had fared having to tell Harriet about Nick.

'Surprisingly well, but I had a long talk with the sister

before I told her, just to make sure it was all right to do so, you know, and they're going to keep her in for another few days to make sure she doesn't have a bad reaction to such awful news.'

Michael's face was grey with sadness. Maddie put her arms around him. 'It must have been awful for you to have to tell her that, especially the first time you saw her after all this time.'

'That's what's worrying me, really. I'm just wondering whether she really took it in about Nick. I mean, she was so pleased to see me and then she was asking about Adam and telling me all about him and what I'd missed by staying away. As if it was my fault,' he added bitterly.

Horrified, Maddie said, 'You didn't tell her everything Nick's done?'

''Course I didn't. It was bad enough what I did have to tell her. Mind you, maybe she ought to be told some day.'

'We'll see,' Maddie said.

He glanced at her and then looked away again, an anxious look in his dark eyes. 'Maddie, what are we going to do about her?'

'Do about her? What do you mean, do about her?'

'Well, what's going to happen to her when she's fit enough to come out of hospital?'

Maddie blinked at him, not understanding. 'Am I being particularly thick or something? I thought she'd come back here. This is her home, isn't it? You don't mean you don't want her here, Michael?'

'No, no,' he said swiftly as relief flooded his face. 'But I thought you might not. After all, she's never been very nice to you, has she?'

Maddie smiled. ' "Born and bred in a briar patch, Brer Fox, born and bred in a briar patch." '

'Eh?'

She laughed. 'Oh never mind. You ask Jen sometime. She'll tell you what it means, to her and me anyway. But to get back to Mrs T. You're right. She's never liked me, but now I know why, I can understand. But she loves Adam. Don't ask me why, when he's my son, but she does. She's always loved him more than she loved her own flesh and blood. Maybe because he was *your* son. Even when I first came here, I could see that you were her favourite.'

'Poor Nick,' Michael murmured and shook his head sorrowfully.

Yes, it was poor Nick, she thought for even though he had robbed her of eleven years of her life and put her family through a frightening ordeal, she felt no bitterness towards him, no hatred or resentment. What she felt for the unhappy young man was an overwhelming pity.

'It's very sad when no one in the world loves you, not even your own mother.' There was such a wistful sadness in Maddie's voice that Michael put his arms around her and held her close.

'I love you, Maddie. I always have, from the first moment you came to the farm.'

She nestled against him, feeling safe and really loved now. For the first time in the whole of her life she knew she was loved and wanted by the man she had given her heart to. 'But I know what it feels like. Both Jen and me know just what it feels like.'

He stroked her hair. 'I know, I know. And I'm going to do my damnedest to find your family for you.'

She put her arms around him. 'You're my family. You and Adam. We're a real family now.'

He chuckled and she heard the sound deep in his chest. 'Well, we will be once I can drag you to the church and get a ring firmly on your finger, Mrs Brackenbury. Oh hell!'

He stopped and she lifted her head and looked into his eyes. 'What is it?'

He looked down at her. 'I've just thought. I hope there's no bar to me marrying my step-mother.'

They stared at each other and then simultaneously, they both burst into fits of laughter, leaning against each other.

'It's – it's not funny,' Maddie gasped.

'I know,' Michael spluttered. 'It's – it's deadly serious.' He fell back on the bed, his chest heaving as he fought to control his mirth – and failed.

Maddie flopped down beside him and soon the laughter subsided as they lay in each other's arms and found again the joy they had known so long ago.

Fifty-Seven

They brought Harriet home from the hospital three days later.

'Sit down by the fire, Mrs T,' Michael said, 'and . . .'

'Now stop fussing me, Michael. I'm quite fit again now. Just let me get back into my kitchen. Maddie's no time to be running about after me. The work's all fallen on her shoulders now.' For a moment the lines on her face drooped with sadness and, despite her protestations, she sat down heavily in the chair.

'You take it easy, Mrs Trowbridge. We can manage,' Maddie tried to keep her voice cheerful.

The woman looked at Michael and no one could have missed the hope and joy in her tone as she asked, 'You're staying? You've come home?'

Michael smiled and nodded. 'You're not going to get rid of me again, Mrs T, I'm afraid.'

She reached up and touched his face and said huskily, 'I never wanted it in the first place, lad.'

He held her hands and bent over her. 'I know, I know. But I'm back now – at least I will be once I've got myself out of the Army – and we're going to take care of you.' He glanced at Maddie to include her, to make sure that Harriet understood just how it was going to be. 'We're all going to take care of each other.'

'Where's my boy?' Harriet asked suddenly, giving both Maddie and Michael a shock. They exchanged a worried glance but then at Harriet's next words they both breathed a sigh of relief. 'Where's Adam?'

'He'll be in later.'

Harriet nodded and, with a sigh of contentment lay back in the chair, and closed her eyes.

Michael gestured to Maddie and they were about to creep away, when she said, 'I'm sorry for what Nicholas did. I'm sorry he hurt the two of you the way he did.'

They turned and looked down at her, exchanged another glance and with mutual silent agreement sat down.

'Who told you?' Michael asked gently.

'I worked a lot of it out for myself. I've had a lot of time to think laid there in that hospital bed.' She sniffed. 'Uncomfortable beds they are. I'll be pleased to get back into me own tonight.'

Maddie hid her smile.

'And then,' Harriet went on, 'there was a lot of whispering in the ward. I heard snatches when they thought I was asleep. What's happened to Jenny? Something's happened to Jenny, hasn't it?'

'She's going to be fine. She was hurt, but she's going to be all right.'

'How? What did he do?'

'The gun went off. I don't think he meant . . .' Michael was trying to be kind, but Harriet said sharply, 'Gun? He had the gun?'

'He was trying to protect Maddie. He – he wanted Maddie himself.'

Harriet nodded. 'I guessed as much.' She looked at Maddie now. 'Did you want him?'

Maddie shook her head. 'No. I've never wanted anyone in my life except Michael.'

Harriet nodded. 'You shouldn't have married Mr Frank, you know.'

'No, I know that now. I'm sorry if . . .'

Harriet flapped her hand. 'Oh, I don't mean because of me. He'd have never married me.' She smiled sadly. 'I loved him, of course, but if he'd felt anything for me except pity, he'd have married me long before that, now wouldn't he?'

Michael and Maddie were silent for there was no answer they could give without wounding the woman further.

'I was as bad as you,' Harriet nodded towards Maddie. 'I should never have married John. Oh, I thought I was in love with him. He was me first boyfriend, but we were so young. And silly. When I found I was expecting, we got married. It was the only thing to do in them days or end up in a home for unmarried mothers.' She shuddered. 'I tried to be a good wife to him. I cooked, washed and cleaned for him. Bore him a son. All men want sons, don't they? So they say. And then how did he repay me? Seduced the daughter of his employer and got us all thrown out of our home. I didn't deserve that. None of us did.'

No, Maddie wanted to cry, but did you ever show him affection? Did you make him feel loved? Did you let him know that you needed him? Aloud, all she could say was, 'No, of course you didn't deserve that. I'm sorry.'

'But living with his folks, we never had a chance and the love died. Then, of course, when he fell for Miss Amelia . . .' She broke off and looked at Maddie again. 'I did come to the Home to pick you out, you know. I knew their baby had been abandoned outside the Home. One of the maids who worked at the Hall knew about it. I reckon the whole village knew, but nobody ever said a word. I was curious to see what his child was like. I wanted – wanted . . .' For a moment she dropped her head down a she whispered, 'I wanted to take revenge on you. And then I even used you like a weapon over Sir Peter.'

'Sir Peter?' Now Maddie was mystified.

Harriet nodded. 'That time you and Mr Frank went to the Hall and he wouldn't give his permission to change the use of his land. I went to see him the next morning.'

So, Maddie thought, remembering now, Theo had been right.

'I – I threatened to tell all I knew about him leaving Amelia's child – his own grandchild – outside the orphanage.' She put her hand across her face now in shame. 'And the next day he had that stroke. I must have caused it.'

Now it was Maddie who reached out and took the wrinkled hand between her own. 'Don't, Mrs Trowbridge. Don't upset yourself. It's over now. All in the past.'

'No, no,' Harriet's voice was stronger. 'I must tell you. I want to talk about it. It's been like a weight all these years. Maybe if I'd told Nicholas the truth, talked to him about his father, been honest and open, then maybe all this would never have happened. I've got to take a share of the blame.'

'No, no . . .' Michael began, but she shook her head, denying him the right to excuse her.

'Poor Nicholas,' she said. 'I never wanted him in the first place and then I resented him because of what his father had done and I shouldn't have done that. It was cruel.' She sighed. 'And crueller still of me to love you, Michael, more than my own flesh and blood. But I couldn't help it. You were such a sunny-natured little boy and Nicholas was always so difficult. It was so easy to love you.'

And then Adam, too, because he had been Michael's son, Maddie thought, but she said nothing.

'Maybe if I'd shown Nicholas more affection . . .' Harriet sighed heavily and added, 'I can't turn the clock back, can I?' She patted Maddie's hand. 'But I can try to make it up to you.'

'Mrs Trowbridge, there's something you ought to know. We've – er – found out a bit more in the last few days. We've talked to Theo and, well . . .' Maddie faltered, not knowing if she could carry on. She looked to Michael for help.

Responding, he took over, saying gently, 'We believe that Maddie is not your husband's child, but his sister.'

'His sister?'

Michael nodded. 'There was a baby born in the woods, wasn't there, to John's mother?'

Harriet nodded. 'Yes. There was. I was there. I was there when poor Mary gave birth.' Harriet shuddered. 'You could hear her screams echoing through the trees. It was awful.'

'And she died, didn't she?' Michael prompted. 'Mary, did you say her name was?'

Harriet nodded. 'Yes, she died that same night. There in the woods, in the freezing cold.' She paused and then went on. 'After that, the villagers took pity on us all. Your father took me and Nicholas in and folk in the village looked after the rest of the family. I think they all felt guilty when they heard what had happened. All except Sir Peter, that is. He hadn't an ounce of pity in him, that man.'

'And the baby? Mary's baby?' Maddie asked softly.

Harriet glanced at her. 'She stayed with her father and later, I heard she had died, though I was surprised 'cos when she was born she was a lusty little thing, a real fighter, you know.' Harriet was staring at Maddie now as the realization crept into her mind and she murmured, 'A real little fighter, just like you.'

424

There was silence in the room, the only sound the singing of the kettle on the hob.

'We think,' Michael went on, 'that when the family left the village, they left the baby at the Home.'

Harriet nodded, though her gaze was still fastened on Maddie. 'To think that I helped deliver you, there in the darkness and the cold. I held you and tried to keep you warm against me. I even fed you from my own breast because I still had milk . . . And all this time I thought you'd died.'

Gently, Michael said, 'There's something else we must tell you.' He hesitated, unsure how Harriet would take the news. 'We believe that the other child, Amelia's baby, is – is Jenny.'

Harriet's gaze swivelled and fastened on Michael. 'Jenny?'

'Yes. Mr Theo says she resembles his sister, although there is a likeness between Maddie and Jenny. But there would be, wouldn't there? After all, they are aunt and niece.'

Harriet nodded slowly. 'Yes, yes, they would be. And you and me,' she turned again to look at Maddie. 'We're sisters-in-law, then, aren't we?'

Maddie nodded.

A smile twitched at the corner of Harriet's mouth. 'So, I picked the wrong one from the Home, then, did I?'

'Seems like it.'

'Serves me right,' and added with some of her familiar spirit, 'I shouldn't have been such a bitter, twisted old bat.'

'How – how shall you feel about Jenny now?' Maddie had to ask, had to know, for Jenny was a very important part of her life and always would be.

Harriet sighed and leant her head back against the chair. 'It's over now, all over. I don't feel that awful hatred any more. Just a terrible sadness. I shan't take it out on Jenny, I promise you.'

Impulsively, Maddie leant forward and kissed Harriet's pale cheek. 'Thank you, Mrs Trowbridge. Now, Michael and I must get some work done. We've a float to build for the Parade on Saturday. You sit and rest.'

'No, no.' Harriet heaved herself up. 'I've some ginger-bread men to make for Adam when he comes home. I promised. Besides, I can't wait to get back into me kitchen. I 'spect it's in a right mess.'

Maddie chuckled. She had never thought that she would be thankful to hear that the housekeeper had not lost all her grumbling ways.

'Right, we'll be off.'

'Dinner will be ready at twelve thirty and don't be late in.'

'No, Mrs Trowbridge.'

'I suppose,' Harriet said, 'now that we're sisters-in-law, you'd better call me "Harriet".'

Maddie grinned at her. 'I'd prefer "Mrs T".'

Harriet smiled, tremulously at first, but with a growing sureness. 'Mrs T, it is, then.'

They left her to return to her kitchen and her work of caring for the household. 'We must fetch Adam home,' Maddie said softly, closing the door between the kitchen and the wash-house, behind her. 'It'll help her to have him back here.'

Reaching up to lift a coat down from the pegs and searching for his Wellingtons, Michael said, 'The sooner the better. I can't wait to start getting to know my son.'

But Maddie was hardly listening, she was staring at the yellow scarf that Michael had just uncovered as he removed the coat from the peg. Nick's scarf.

'What is it, love? You look as if you've just seen a ghost.'

Maddie leant against the wall, her gaze still on the scarf. 'I – I feel as if I have. I've just remembered something else.'

'Oh, what you were trying to remember about the night Dad died?'

Maddie shook her head. 'No, no, not that. Something else. When he got injured with a fork.'

'Injured? You didn't tell me about that. What happened?'

Swiftly, Maddie recounted the events, ending up by saying, 'I remember Nick saying that he didn't hear Frank coming so close to him because he had his scarf tied tightly round his ears against the wind.' She stared at Michael now, her eyes wide. 'I was so upset at the time, it didn't register properly, but I do remember later looking at that scarf here on the peg, so he couldn't have been wearing it. Oh Michael, do you think he did that on purpose, too?'

'Wouldn't be at all surprised,' Michael said drily. 'And when I get time, I'm going to have a snoop around the battery house, just to see if I can piece together how he did that. Because I'm sure now that he did. What I can't understand is *how* he did it, if you say he was away for the night. He could have easily done something if he'd been here, but he had to be away, didn't he, to make it so that Frank had to be the one to go out?'

'Oh!' Maddie clapped her hand over her mouth. 'Now I've remembered. It was Jenny.'

'Jenny?'

'Yes, she said that Steven thought he'd seen Nick on his bicycle in the village that night and I said no, he must have been mistaken and it must have been the following night, the night Nick came back, that he'd seen him. But now . . .'

Grimly, Michael nodded. 'It's all starting to fit together now, Maddie. Come on, we're going to look around that barn right now.'

Fifty-Eight

It took them two hours of searching every nook and cranny in the battery house and then in the big barn; of feeling along dusty shelves, of sweeping cobwebs from every corner and scrabbling through rusty, neglected tools.

'What exactly am I looking for?' Maddie stood back, smudges of grime on her face.

'I'm not really sure, I . . .' Michael glanced at her and then came towards her, 'Oh Maddie, you look just like the day I first saw you.' Gently, he wiped away the smudge from her forehead and then kissed her.

Playfully, she smacked his arm. 'Now don't start that, else I'll take you into the hay shed again . . .'

Michael chuckled. 'I'm game if you are.'

They fell against each other, kissing and laughing until Maddie said breathlessly, 'Oh do stop. We must find whatever it is we're supposed to be looking for.'

'Yes. Right,' Michael said, firmly setting her away from him. 'Remind me later to carry on where I left off, though.'

'Oh I will. I certainly will,' she whispered and they smiled at each other.

It was when Michael tipped out the bin that held the corn for Harriet's hens that they both heard the chink of metal on the concrete floor. Squatting down, they delved beneath the pile of corn and unearthed a round brown knob, very similar to the knob on the control panel in the battery house. Michael picked it out and wiped away the

429

dust. He stood up slowly, holding it in the centre of his outstretched palm. 'So, that's how he did it?'

'How? What is it?'

'A metal knob instead of a bakelite one. The minute Dad touched this, he would have got a nasty shock.'

'Would that account for the marks on his hand?'

'Probably. I think Nick hid somewhere . . .' He glanced about him towards the buildings on two sides of the big barn. 'In here somewhere, maybe. He'd've had to move the spring pointer off the studs to change the knob,' Michael murmured, thinking aloud. 'So then the lights would go out and he'd leave them off so that someone would come out. But how did he know it wouldn't be you?'

Maddie shook her head. 'Frank never taught me anything about the battery house.' She shuddered. 'But I nearly did come out that night. I didn't want Frank to come out in the cold and I wanted him to tell me what to do.'

'But Dad did come out,' Michael said softly, 'just as Nick hoped.'

'Then what?'

'Well, I think after the accident had happened, he switched the knobs back somehow, hiding this one deep in this bin. Mrs T would never have guessed what it was, even if she'd ever found it. Then I think he did leave and that's when Steven saw him cycling through the village.'

'You're – you're not going to tell Mrs T all this are you?'

Michael shook his head. 'No. There's no need. The poor woman's got enough to come to terms with. No, Maddie we'll keep this just between ourselves.'

For a moment he gripped the metal knob tightly in his hand and Maddie saw tears sparkle in his eyes. 'Poor Dad,' he said, brokenly.

Maddie went to him and they put their arms around one another, each remembering Frank Brackenbury in their own special way.

It was the day of the Tulip Parade and everyone at Few Farm was trying to put the recent nightmare behind them.

Nick had been buried quietly in the lonely corner of the churchyard near his father. Only his mother, Michael and Maddie were there to mourn him. Although Harriet had shed no tears, she had clung to Michael's arm and leant heavily against him throughout the short service conducted at the graveside. Maddie could understand the tumult of emotions the woman must be feeling. Her own feelings were chaotic; sadness for poor Nick and for Frank, who should still have been with them. Yet there was joy, too, in having Michael home and knowing he loved her. And then, there was Jenny. Her darling little Jenny Wren. They really were related after all. If only, Maddie had thought as the vicar's voice droned on, if only I could know the rest of my family . . .

Now, today, they all wanted the Tulip Parade to signify a new beginning. Maddie and Michael had worked through the night to finish their float for the Parade. Adam had been sent to bed, still protesting, at midnight but they had stayed in the big barn all night, pinning the tulip heads on to the straw matting.

'Who made the frame? It's very clever,' Michael asked, standing back to admire the shape of the huge tulip sitting on the open back of the farm truck. Even the cab was decorated with an archway of flowers above it in rows of different colours, like a rainbow of tulips in the sky.

'Steven's brother, Ron. He works as the blacksmith now. He's very clever with his hands. Must get it from his dad.' She paused a moment, the head of a golden tulip resting in the palm of her hand. 'I wonder what I get from my family?'

'A way with animals, I shouldn't wonder. I'll never forget the way you handled Ben and waded in amongst the cows without batting an eyelid.' They smiled at each other, remembering. 'By the way what happened to poor old Ben?'

'He was so miserable after your dad died and with no real work to do since the cows had gone, we let him go to a farmer near Holbeach. It – it . . .' She hesitated again. 'It was Nick's idea.'

'Even wanted the poor old dog out of the way, eh?' There was silence before Michael went on, 'Yes, I reckon that's what you've got from your family. Their way with animals . . .' He grinned at her. 'To say nothing of a way with people, too. Your dad was head groom for Sir Peter and didn't Mrs Grange say that your brother was very good with them, too? That was how he came to teach Miss Amelia to ride?'

'Mm,' Maddie said absently, now scarcely listening. She had latched on to the words 'your brother' and now she said them aloud, savouring the sound of them. 'My brother.'

'What? What did you say, love?'

She smiled self-consciously, but there was no need to be shy with Michael. Never again would there be secrets or awkwardness between them. 'I was just trying out how it sounded. My brother. I've never been able to say it before.'

'Or dad. You've never said that either.'

'No,' she said wistfully. 'Do you think I'll ever get the chance?'

''Course you will. Trust Mr Theo. He'll find them. He said he would.'

Maddie smiled at the almost childlike faith Michael now had in Theo. Any charges against Maddie had been dropped as soon as Theo had explained to the police all that had happened. They were satisfied that the tragic young man who had taken his own life had also been guilty of administering arsenic to Frank, to his own mother and even allowing Maddie to stand accused of his crimes.

'Mr Theo's put adverts in this week's local papers already, hasn't he?'

'Yes, but they could be anywhere. My father could be dead. He'll be quite old by now, won't he?'

'Well, getting on a bit, yes. But that doesn't mean to say he's not still alive. How many other brothers and sisters did Mrs Grange say there were, apart from poor John?'

Maddie remembered exactly. 'Four besides me and John. But I don't know whether they were girls or boys. Maybe somewhere I really have got a sister.'

'Harriet would know.'

'Yes, I've thought about that. But I don't like to keep bringing the subject up. I don't want to upset her.'

'I shouldn't worry too much about that. She seems her old self again.' He grinned at Maddie. 'Ordering us all about, just like she always used to. I even heard her call you "girl" the other day.'

Maddie laughed. 'Yes, she did. But somehow, it doesn't have the same sting to it now. And,' she added pulling a comical face, 'at my advanced age, it's quite a compliment.'

'There,' Michael said as he popped the last tulip head into place. 'I think that's finished. What do you think?'

Maddie felt the lump in her throat. 'It's beautiful.'

'And all our own work,' Michael said proudly.

'With a bit of help from Stinky Smith and his brother,' Maddie reminded him.

'Oh yes. Who's going to be the Tulip Queen?'

'A young lass from the town.'

'It ought to be you,' Michael put his arm around her.

'I'm too old,' Maddie laughed and kissed him. 'But thanks for the compliment.' They stood admiring their handiwork. 'Who's going to drive it in the Parade? You?'

'No, I think we'll let Ron Smith drive it for us. He's earned it, don't you think? Besides,' he gave her waist a squeeze, 'I want to watch the Parade with you and Adam. I can't bear to be parted from you for as long as an hour,' he teased.

'Now you can stop all that canoodling,' came Harriet's voice behind them at that moment. 'Your breakfast's ready.'

They turned to find her standing in the doorway of the barn and went towards her, their arms still around each other. Michael put his free arm about the older woman and together they went into the house.

'Maddie! Maddie!'

They were standing watching the Parade, the four of them, when Maddie heard Jenny's voice calling her name and turned to see her pushing her way through the crowd.

Her hand was still bandaged and she was limping slightly, but Jenny was smiling happily.

'Are you all right?' Maddie said as she hugged her. 'Should you be out of hospital so soon?'

Jenny giggled. 'They couldn't keep me. They took all the bits of shot out and I badgered the doctor to let me out. But Steven and – and Theo . . .' she glanced back over her shoulder, 'have been so kind. They scarcely let me out of their sight. If Steven's not with me bullying me to take care, then Theo is. Oh Maddie, it's so wonderful to have a real family and what's even better is to know that we – you and me – are really related. Every morning when I wake up and remember, I still can't quite believe it.'

Maddie felt a swift stab of envy, but immediately felt guilty. She had her family. Michael and Adam, and even Harriet now, and still she had Jenny. She would have to be satisfied with that.

Jenny was interrupting her wandering thoughts. 'When the Parade's over, Theo wants us all to meet him at the White Hart for tea. Mrs Trowbridge as well.' Jenny leant closer to Maddie and whispered, 'Does she know about me?' When Maddie nodded, Jenny added, 'And how did she take it?'

'All right. She's changed.' Maddie grinned, 'Well, not *that* much, but she's coming to terms with the past. No more grudges.'

Jenny gave a sigh of relief. 'Thank goodness. Anyway, you'll come to the tea party then?'

There was an air of excitement about Jenny and Maddie wondered briefly if there was an announcement to be made about Steven and herself. Maybe, Maddie thought, they've finally set a date for their wedding.

'We'll be there,' Maddie promised. 'All of us.'

'Good. I must go. See you later . . .' And she disappeared into the crowd as quickly as she had come.

'It's going to grow and grow, this Parade, Maddie. Whoever thought it up, it's a brilliant idea.'

'Well, Steven was in on it from the first, but several people have all worked together to make it happen.'

'Only a few floats this year but, you watch, every year there'll be more and more.'

'Look, Mam. Here it comes. The first one's the Tulip

Queen.' Adam was pointing excitedly to the first float in the procession. The pretty girl in a long white dress and a tiara upon her head, sat at the centre of a huge flower with red petals, waving to the crowd as the float passed by. The following decorated lorry had a large crown fashioned out of metal and adorned with flower heads. After that came a car with a circle of flowers around it at bumper level, so wide that it doubled the width of the car.

'How on earth is he going to get that round corners?' Michael laughed.

Then came a tractor almost completely covered with red flowers and the lettering 'Join the YFC' picked out in golden tulip heads. The next float was their own from Few Farm, proudly driven by Ron Smith almost hidden beneath the profusion of flowers.

'Oh Mam, just look at that one.' The last float in the procession was perhaps the biggest of all; an enormous butterfly, the details of its wing markings picked out with different coloured tulips.

'Isn't that beautiful?' Maddie breathed. 'Steven was right, when he said there ought to be a better way than just dumping the discarded heads. What a lovely way to make use of them.'

'Now, next year,' Michael was laughing beside her, 'we'll build the biggest and the best float ever.'

Despite all the recent tragedy that had touched them all, a warm glow of happiness spread through Maddie's soul. Michael would be here, with her and Adam, next year and all the years to come.

Even if she never found out the truth about her family, she could be happy with that.

Fifty-Nine

As the last marching band passed them by, Michael said, 'Come along, we'd better go and find Jenny and Steven – and Mr Theo.'

He was waiting for them in the bar at the White Hart and came forward to greet them.

'I've hired a private room,' he told them. 'But before we go in . . .' He took Maddie's hand and looked down at her. 'I have a surprise for you, Maddie, but I thought I should, in fairness, warn you.' His glance went beyond her now to Harriet. 'And you, Mrs Trowbridge. I didn't want it to be a shock for you. For either of you.'

Puzzled, Harriet glanced at Michael, who put his face close to hers and whispered in her ear. For a moment the woman looked startled, but then she nodded. 'I'll be all right, Mr Theo. Maddie has a right to . . .'

Before she could say any more, Theo smiled and put his finger to his lips. 'Not another word, Mrs Trowbridge, or you'll spoil my fun.' He held out his arm to Maddie and said softly, 'Are you ready?'

Maddie gave a laugh that sounded strangely nervous. 'Well, I'm not quite sure what for, but yes.'

Michael, with Harriet on his arm and Adam bringing up the rear, followed behind them.

As he opened the door, she saw Steven first and then Jenny sitting beside Amelia Mayfield and holding her hand.

'Oh Theo. I'm so glad. How lovely to see them

together.' In a low voice she asked, 'Does your sister understand?'

Quietly, Theo said, 'I'm not sure, but we're hoping in time . . .'

'Oh thank you, thank you for doing this for Jenny . . .' Maddie began to say, but Theo was shaking his head. 'That's not the surprise, Maddie.'

She became aware then that there were three other people standing at the far side of the room. An old man, leaning on a stick, and a younger man and woman standing one on either side of him.

Maddie looked at them and when her glance came to rest on the woman, her mouth opened in a shocked gasp. She was older than Maddie, possibly by as much as ten years, but she had the same fair hair, the same blue eyes, and even the same saucy smile that lit up her eyes until they sparkled.

It could be me in a few years time, Maddie thought. And then she knew. This was her sister. It had to be.

Theo was leading her towards them and she was clinging to his arm, suddenly afraid that her legs were going to let her down.

The old man was staring at her and as she drew closer she could see that tears were coursing down his wrinkled cheeks, but still he never took his gaze away from her. And as she stood before him, she heard his whisper. 'Madeleine.'

The stick fell out of his grasp and clattered to the floor. The old man tottered and swiftly the two on either side of him caught hold of him and steadied him. But he seemed oblivious to his own frailty, for he was stretching out both his arms to Maddie.

She went into them, putting her own arms around his neck and murmuring, 'Dad, oh my daddy.'

'My baby, my baby!' He was weeping openly now against her neck and clutching her to him. 'I'm sorry. Forgive me. It broke my heart to leave you, but I couldn't take care of you. You might have died like my poor Mary. I didn't know what else to do. Forgive me. Forgive me.'

There was scarcely a dry eye in the room. Even Harriet was fishing in her handbag for her handkerchief.

And then as Maddie drew back and looked into Matt Cuppleditch's face, she held his hands between her own and said, 'It's all right. It's all right, really. There's nothing to forgive. I'm just so happy to have found you.' She looked to the two standing beside him. 'All of you.'

Then they were all laughing and crying together. Theo brought a chair for Matt and they clustered around him, all speaking at once.

'We saw the piece in the paper and showed it to Dad,' the woman began to explain. 'Then Roland . . .' she nodded towards the man, 'rang Mr Theo.'

'I wanted to come back for you, so many times,' the old man was murmuring, 'but I felt so ashamed of just leaving you there . . .'

'We're living near King's Lynn now. It's not far away . . .'

'He's talked so often about you. I'm Alison, by the way. Aren't we alike . . .?'

Her brother, Roland, was interrupting. 'There's two more of us, but they live in London. They're coming to see you as soon as they can. But they've families. You've more nephews and nieces, besides Jenny.' He smiled across at Jenny, anxious to include her.

'You know about Jenny?' Maddie asked and her new-found brother nodded. 'Mr Mayfield . . .'

'Theo, please,' Theo put in.

Roland smiled, 'Theo has explained everything.'

There was no bitterness, no recriminations, they were just so happy, all of them, to be reunited. The only difficult moment was when Maddie turned and drew Harriet forward. 'You remember Harriet, don't you?'

There was a silence in the room now as everyone watched and waited.

Matt looked up at her and then held out his hand. 'Of course we do. How are you, my dear?'

Harriet was overcome and unable to speak but she took the old man's outstretched hand and nodded vigorously. Relieved, everyone began to talk at once again.

It was all right. Everything was going to be all right.

To one side of the room, unseen by Maddie, Michael held out his hand to Theo. 'Thank you, Mr Theo, for all you've done for Maddie. Thank you for making her happiness complete.'

Theo took his hand and placed his other hand on Michael's shoulder. His voice was husky as he said, 'You're a lucky man, Michael Brackenbury. Take care of her, won't you?'

'Oh I will, Mr Theo. I will.'